It was like the fly chasing the spider

Kitt recognized the name on the business card, and she recognized the firm he represented. Mel Belyle, Corporate Attorney, Castle Enterprises, New York.

Castle Enterprises was the corporation created expressly to handle the housing project in Crystal Creek. And this was the man her boss had predicted would never speak to her.

Yet here, in all his glory, was Mr. Belyle himself, trying to pick her up. She began to sound him out. "So," she said with a demure smile. "wh⸺ ⸺⸺ to Austin?"

"Business," h⸺

"I'm going ⸺⸺ ⸺'t a lie. "I haven't see⸺ ⸺t of touch with family,

For a split s⸺ ⸺ wavered. He didn't answer her question. ⸺o what do you do?"

She shrugged as if her job was of small interest. "I work for the Gilroy Group." This was misleading, she knew. The Gilroy Group owned six magazines, but was far more famous for its other holdings, especially its television network.

His eyes kindled with mischief. "Gilroy? Are you connected with that *Uptown Girls* show?"

You lecher, Kitt thought. "That would be telling. I'm not going to discuss it until I know you much, much better."

He leaned closer. "That can be arranged. What do you want to know?"

"Everything," she said. "Tell me simply everything."

Dear Reader,

Things are changing in Crystal Creek, Texas. The question is, who will decide the future of this fabled land? Will it be the McKinneys, its fiery leading family, determined to defend the heritage of the Hill Country?

Or will it be the mysterious outsider, Brian Fabian? He commands a greater fortune than anyone else in Crystal Creek—and he has a secret weapon. That weapon is negotiator Mel Belyle, brilliant, charming, handsome— and ruthless.

Mel comes to Crystal Creek with a score to settle and a fight he intends to win. But he hasn't counted on a certain redheaded reporter. Kitt Mitchell is a spitfire with an attitude as big as Texas itself.

This is the twenty-ninth book in the series about Crystal Creek. I'm proud to be taking part in its ongoing story and hope you enjoy visiting A *Little Town in Texas*.

With warmest regards,

Bethany Campbell

Books by Bethany Campbell

HARLEQUIN SUPERROMANCE

837—THE GUARDIAN
931—P.S. LOVE YOU MADLY
1052—THE BABY GIFT

A Little Town in Texas

Bethany Campbell

HARLEQUIN®

TORONTO • NEW YORK • LONDON
AMSTERDAM • PARIS • SYDNEY • HAMBURG
STOCKHOLM • ATHENS • TOKYO • MILAN • MADRID
PRAGUE • WARSAW • BUDAPEST • AUCKLAND

ISBN 0-373-71129-8

A LITTLE TOWN IN TEXAS

Copyright © 2003 by Bethany Campbell.

This edition published by arrangement with Harlequin Books S.A.

Visit us at www.eHarlequin.com

Printed in U.S.A.

To Linda Bitcon, a friend for all seasons.

CHAPTER ONE

"SEND IN THE SPITFIRE," Heywood Cronin said to his secretary. "The whirlwind. You know which one—from staff writing. The little redhead."

"Kitt Mitchell? Yes, sir," said Miss Lundeen.

"Writes like an angel," muttered Cronin. "Dresses like a bag lady."

"Oh, no, sir," Miss Lundeen said mildly. "She just likes to be casual."

"Casual," Cronin said with a snort. "She'd be a pretty girl if she'd dress up. *O tempora O mores.* That's Latin, Miss Lundeen. Do you know what it means?"

"Yes, sir. O, the times, O, the manners."

"Anyway," Cronin said, "send her in."

Miss Lundeen exited with such speed and silence it was as if she evaporated. Cronin looked at the picture of his wife, framed in platinum, on his desk. She was in her wedding gown, and a damn fine gown it was. He missed the 1950s when women had waists and wore pearls and full skirts and exciting shoes with pointed toes and high heels.

He chased the thought from his mind. That was looking backward. It was thinking like an old geezer. He was a man who looked forward, and that's why journalism awards half-covered his office. He intended to collect a few dozen more before he cashed in his chips. It was one of the reasons he cultivated young writers like the spitfire.

In a few moments, Miss Lundeen announced her. "Kitt Mitchell, sir."

And in she walked. Cronin fought against wincing. The

woman wore cargo pants and a pale blue camp shirt. Her shoes made her look like she was going to climb the Alps.

She was a petite woman, barely over five feet tall, and she was slight rather than shapely. Still, Cronin thought, she was a fetching little thing. Maybe she dressed like Indiana Jones to fend off unwanted male attention. She could attract men like a magnet—if she wanted.

Her most startling feature was her long, flame-red hair. Her skin was fair, her eyes were blue, and her eyebrows and lashes auburn. She was pretty enough, but Cronin always found himself noticing the vivacity in her face before her actual features. In motion she was swift as a hummingbird.

She had a reputation for being sassy, of not being afraid of the devil himself. This did not mean that Cronin did not make her nervous. He made everyone on his staff exceedingly nervous; he considered it part of his job.

"Sit down, Mitchell." He ordered, he did not invite.

Kitt Mitchell gave him a measuring look and sat down in the leather chair before his desk. His desk was mounted on a dais so he could stare down, lordlike, upon whomever sat in that chair.

She returned his gaze with wary coolness. "Miss Lundeen said you wanted to see me."

He laced his fingers together and peered harder at her. She didn't squirm, not one whit. Was he losing his touch? He'd wipe that calm off her face.

"Yes," he said, hitting her with it immediately. "I'm going to give you the assignment of your life."

Her fair skin went paler. Her blue eyes got wider.

"This story won't just *change* your career. It will *make* your career."

She seemed speechless. Good. Inwardly he smirked.

"This is big stuff, Mitchell," Heywood Cronin told her. "It's got everything—money, mystery, power struggles.

Sex. Revenge. But most of all, human interest. Your specialty.''

He sat back with satisfaction and watched his words sink in.

DELIGHT FLOODED KITT. Suddenly Heywood Cronin, elderly, grizzled, balding and bent, looked as radiant as a spirit guide to her.

Then he squinted through his thick glasses and smiled his thin smile. ''Go home and pack. Monday you leave. For Crystal Creek, Texas.''

Crystal Creek? Kitt felt as if the office ceiling had crashed down on her. Dismay swept away her delight. Crystal Creek was the *last* place in the universe she wanted to go. Heywood Cronin no longer seemed luminously benevolent. He seemed like a capricious troll playing games with her life.

''Well?'' he demanded, leaning toward her over his vast desk.

Say something! Kitt commanded herself. She cleared her throat. ''Well, Mr. Cronin, you see...I—I'm *from* Crystal Creek. It could cause a conflict. It would be hard for me to write objectively about it.''

Cronin hunched lower, as if crouching for attack. ''I want objectivity—up to a point. I also want feeling. Passion. A town ripped in twain, blah, blah, and so on.''

''But—but, you see—there could be a problem—''

''No,'' Cronin said, shaking a bony forefinger. ''*You* see. What you call a problem, I call opportunity. You can write about this place because you're *of* this place. You tap into its deepest psyche. It's your old hometown. The site of your fondest childhood memories. And so forth.''

Kitt blinked hard. ''You mean you *knew* I grew up there?''

He laughed the laugh that was famous at *Exclusive* magazine. It was described as the gurgle of ice water pouring over a grave. ''Of course. That's why I picked you.''

''Oh,'' Kitt said tonelessly. She'd hoped he'd chosen her for her ability.

''That,'' he said with a dismissive wave, ''and the fact

you can write. I assume you've lots of connections in this one-horse town? Relatives? Old friends and neighbors? People who'll pour out their hearts to you?''

Kitt drew a deep breath, mind whirling. She didn't think of Crystal Creek as her hometown; she tried not to think of it at all. When she'd left, she'd meant to leave forever. People opening their hearts to her? Hardly.

But—there was Nora.

Ah, yes, thank God there was Nora. A lifeline back then. And possibly a lifeline now. "I know people, yes," Kitt said vaguely.

"Then you know what this story's about? Eh? Do you?"

Kitt's mind spun more swiftly. "It has to be about Brian Fabian," she guessed. "About his buying land there. To build some megahousing development."

Cronin sank back into his chair and folded his hands over his vest. "Ha. You do have sources. Yes, Brian Fabian. He's *always* news. He sells magazines, by God."

So that was Cronin's angle, Kitt thought. If Brian Fabian was interested in Crystal Creek, so was *Exclusive* magazine. Cronin knew what fascinated the public, and he played that fascination like a magic flute.

Cronin's eyes stayed fixed on her, gauging her. "Tell me what you know about Fabian."

Kitt told him what she knew, what everybody knew—next to nothing. Fabian was a billionaire and almost total recluse. No known photo existed of him. Information about his private life usually proved to be false or misleading or both.

Facts about his business ventures were just as elusive. They were hidden in a maze of mergers, partnerships, shell corporations and deals of dizzying complexity.

"I'd guess he's the mystery in the story," Kitt mused. "And the money and power." Then she added, "And probably the sex."

One thing certain about Brian Fabian was his appetite for beautiful women. But none of these women ever talked about him. Never a one said so much as a word. His affairs remained as secret as everything else.

Cronin gave her a crooked, tight-lipped smile. "The sex? Not Fabian—this time. Sex came into the story with the lawyer he sent there to buy land. Nick Belyle. He fell for some local Venus and did the unthinkable. He violated Fabian's confidence. He told about the plans for the development."

Kitt said, "I heard."

Nora had sent a long, excited letter about it. At the time, Kitt had given it little thought. So Fabian wanted a few thousand acres in Texas for some harebrained housing development—so what? For him such a project would be no more important than a mere whim, an expensive toy.

"That lawyer," Cronin said, tapping his mahogany desktop, "let the cat out of the bag. And it was a rabid wild cat. Fabian wants to start a 'planned' community. The folks in your old neighborhood want to stop it."

It's not my old neighborhood, she wanted to retort. But she said, "I heard that, too."

"A clan named McKinney's leading the battle. Know 'em?"

Kitt's body stiffened. J. T. McKinney owned the biggest ranch near Crystal Creek, and the McKinneys were the most important family in the county. Kitt knew more about them than she cared to remember, more than she *dared* to remember.

But she let her face betray nothing. "Yes. I know—most of them."

"They're stubborn, and they're full of fight," Cronin said, watching her expression closely. "They've got money and power. One of them's out of the country—Cal—but the rumor is he's coming back for this. Of course, next to Fabian, they're small potatoes. Nothing, really."

Cal's name hit her like a physical blow, but Kitt didn't flinch. She was too proud. The McKinneys were part of her distant past, thank God. Especially Cal. But to go back to

Crystal Creek and write about them? About *him?* Her nerves jangled in protest.

She shook her head. "If you want a story on the Mc-Kinneys—"

Cronin waved his hand negatively. "No, no. They're only one part. It's the whole town—the whole county. It's split. Some want the development. Some don't. A house divided against itself. That's the drama."

Kitt allowed herself a skeptical smile. "But to fight Brian Fabian—"

"Yes," Cronin said with pleasure. "A classic David and Goliath story. Except, of course, David gets his brains bashed out. Creamed. Murdered."

Kitt kept her face carefully blank.

"Hopeless cause," Cronin mused. "Idiotic actually. But valiant. I want both sides of the story, of course. Part of your job is to give the reader the point of view of the underdogs. Those kindly folks who live and love in your hometown. Their way of life ending forever. Heartrending."

Inwardly Kitt squirmed. Did Cronin just want sob sister stuff from her? She was a better writer than that. Furthermore, even if the McKinneys weren't the sole players, they *were* involved. She couldn't help it—the fact made her profoundly uneasy. "I see," she said without enthusiasm.

"*Do* you?" he challenged. "There's something you haven't asked. I expected more from you, Mitchell. Why haven't you asked about the revenge part?"

Kitt squared her shoulders and tried to fake him. "I was about to. My sources—" she meant Nora, of course "—never mentioned such a thing."

He steepled his fingers and peered over them, eyes glittering. "That's because your sources don't know yet. And *you're* not to tell them. You're going there to gather information—not leak it."

Her chin jerked up defiantly. She'd never leaked a story, never purposely influenced one, and she never would.

Cronin smiled at her reaction. "Here's the nitty-gritty.

Brian Fabian wants more land. And he's so incensed at his turncoat lawyer—''

"Nick Belyle," furnished Kitt.

"—that he's sending down the man's own brother to finish the job."

Kitt's interest shot up several notches. "His own flesh and blood?"

"Yes. His younger brother. Mel. Ruthless man, I'm told. I've had research prepare a folder of information for you on each of them."

Kitt narrowed her eyes. "Brian Fabian's setting brother against brother? Like…the Civil War?"

"Yes. It's quite nasty. I like it," said Mr. Cronin.

Kitt didn't. "What kind of a man would go gunning after his own brother? There must be more to this feud than just company loyalty. When I talk to him—''

"You won't. He won't," Cronin said. "If Mel Belyle opens his mouth, it'll only be to bite your head off. Fabian hates the press."

"I could try—" Kitt began.

"Forget it," ordered Cronin. "I repeat. Mel Belyle will *not* talk. Neither will his brother. They've both signed confidentiality agreements. You'll have to rely on those good country people, your neighbors."

Again Kitt ached to object. These people were not her neighbors, and she'd turned her back on them long ago— with good reason. And there was the very real question of how objective she could be. This worried her. She should shock Cronin and tell him she didn't want this story.

But then Cronin said the magic words. "Do a good job of this," he said silkily, "and you'll be promoted from staff writer to contributing editor."

Her misgivings vanished as if a lightning bolt had sizzled them out of her brain. Contributing editor? For a promotion like that, she would cover a story in the hottest part of hell.

EVERY DAY AFTER WORK when the weather was decent, Kitt went for a run in Central Park. Then she showered, nuked a frozen dinner and settled down to read.

She unplugged the phone because men sometimes called, and recently she wasn't in a mood to bother with them. She was currently between boyfriends, a state she didn't mind a bit. It was restful.

Now, wearing her ratty bathrobe, she flopped onto her sofa and opened the folder on the Belyle brothers. True to Fabian form, the information about them was scant.

There were actually three brothers, and their widowed mother had moved with them from Texas to New York. She'd worked for Brian Fabian as a cleaning lady or maid. Accounts differed, but he'd befriended her.

All three sons had gone to law school, and all three had taken jobs with Fabian's firm. Rumor said that Fabian had been a patron to them.

Nick Belyle, the brother who'd defected, had gone to Harvard. Mel, the one being sent to fight him, had gone to Yale. Research had provided copies of their transcripts. Both had A averages. Kitt gave a grudging whistle of approval—these two should be able to wage a hell of a battle.

Mel made the gossip columns from time to time, dating models. Fabianesque, that appetite for beautiful women. Otherwise, the brothers kept their private lives private. That, too, was in Fabian's mode.

Until Nick settled in Texas, he'd kept on the move for the corporation, living in a dozen different places. Mel stayed based in New York. His address was fancy. Very fancy.

And that was it. There were a few boyhood and teenage snapshots of Nick. None of Mel. Also missing was any mention of either brother's hobbies, clubs, political affiliations—nothing. Kitt closed the folder, wishing the research department had dug more deeply.

She was going to have to do her own detective work and find the details herself—starting now. She would call Nora in Crystal Creek.

Nora was her aunt, but the word *aunt* always sounded august and elderly to Kitt. Nora was neither. Nora was thirty-three, just five years older than Kitt. She was bright, funny, down-to-earth, and generous.

Nora had made only one mistake in her life, and it had been disastrous. As a sixteen-year-old girl, she'd got pregnant and married a man who'd thrown all her dreams off-track.

Nora had grown up wanting one thing: to be a teacher. After her divorce, she'd sweated blood to finish college. She'd married again, a good man. She'd even taught for a while, but circumstances had seemed to conspire against her.

Now, instead of teaching, Nora had a dead-end job. She worked fifty weeks a year, six days a week in a cow town café and managed a tatty little motel, too. Kitt shook her head at the waste.

She dialed Nora's home number. She listened to the phone ring and thought of Crystal Creek. It still seemed ironic to be going back, but perhaps, at last, it was time. A feeble ghost or two might still haunt her, but this would be her chance to lay them to rest.

When Nora answered, she hooted with surprise to hear Kitt. "Kitt-Kat!" she cried. "Can you read minds? I was just thinking of you. I loved that piece you wrote about the little girl who plays chess."

Kitt thanked her, feeling the pinch of guilt. Nora followed Kitt's career proudly and read every issue of *Exclusive*. She sent notes of praise and funny cards and newsy letters, but Kitt was usually too busy to answer at length. Now and then she dashed off a postcard or an e-mail. It was not that she didn't love Nora, but…

She paused, picturing Nora's pretty face and blue-gray eyes. How often in the past had she turned to her, a girl barely older than herself, for comfort? Now she was turning to her again—but for reasons of ambition.

Kitt took a deep breath. "Listen, Nora, I'm coming down

there next week. On Monday. I hope it's not too short a notice.''

''Here?'' Nora sounded delighted. ''That's great! I can't wait to see you. Good grief, how long has it been?''

''Twelve years,'' Kitt said. Another guilty twinge stung her, and she tried not to think of her long absence.

''Twelve years,'' Nora said in wonder. ''It's not possible. It can't be.''

''The prodigal returns,'' Kitt said, trying to make a joke of it.

''It's about time,'' laughed Nora. ''I was starting to think you got too citified. You wouldn't claim us any more.''

''I've got an assignment,'' said Kitt, trying to sound casual. ''To write about Crystal Creek. The current troubles. You know, that whole land grab thing with Brian Fabian.''

For a moment, Nora went strangely silent. At last she said, ''Write about it? I don't know. Folks around here might not like it....''

Kitt made her voice conciliatory. ''We'll talk about it when I get there, okay? The main thing is I get a chance to see you. It's been so long...I mean, I can still come, can't I? Even if I'm on assignment?''

This time Nora didn't hesitate. ''You're *always* welcome,'' she said with warmth. ''And I want you to stay with us. At Chez Slattery. I insist.''

It was Kitt's turn to pause. For the first time since that afternoon she had a strong rush of apprehension about the McKinneys.

Nora was married to the McKinneys' foreman. She lived within sight of the main house. For Kitt, it was uncomfortably close, too close.

''That's good of you, but I shouldn't. I mean, if the people in town *don't* like what I write, they could hold it against you.''

''I know you're always fair,'' Nora said loyally. ''That's one of the best things about your articles. You put emotion into them, but they're fair. Really, stay with us—please.''

"No," Kitt insisted. "It wouldn't be in my best interest, either. If I stay with you, it'll look as if I've taken sides before I've even started."

Kitt drew in her breath and held it. What she was saying was sound in journalistic principle. But she also could not bear spending a week or more living on the McKinneys' land. Suddenly the ghosts of her past did not seem so few or so feeble.

Nora sighed. "I can understand that. I'd certainly never want to compromise the integrity of your story. But you can spend time with us—can't you? You can't work all the time."

"You'll be the first person I'll come see," promised Kitt. "I'll drive straight to your house. Won't even check into the hotel first. The old hotel—you said they remodeled it?"

"You won't recognize it. You know that you could stay for free at the motel, instead," Nora said ruefully. "But it'd hardly be doing you a favor. We're putting in a new heating and air-conditioning system. It's a mess."

"No, it's better I stay on neutral ground," Kitt replied.

Nora laughed. "Oh, Kitt—these days there is no neutral ground in Crystal Creek. But it'll be a kick to have you home."

Home. The word almost froze Kitt. She tried to shake off the cold, empty feeling. New York was where she lived now, and she wanted and needed no other place to call home.

She pushed the emotion away and got back to her job. "The McKinneys," she said with seeming casualness, "they're leading the fight against Fabian?"

"J.T.'s the president of a citizens' group. It's running him ragged. I wish Cal could get home, but he's tied up in business in Australia."

He's not there yet. Good, Kitt thought with a wave of relief. But he would soon be back—Cronin had said he would.

Kitt made herself press on. "Is there any word of Fabian

making another move down there?'' She knew, of course, that he was about to.

"We hope not," Nora said. "J.T.'s got about all he can handle. He's got Fabian tied up in lawsuits for the moment. And all the major ranchers have refused to sell any more land. But anything *might* happen. J.T. doesn't need any nasty surprises."

"I see," Kitt said noncommittally. She couldn't warn Nora that just such a nasty surprise was on the way, and it would come in the form of a man named Mel Belyle.

In CRYSTAL CREEK the next day, Nora realized that Kitt's phone call had sent a strange restlessness tingling through her.

The Longhorn Coffee Shop was languid, enjoying a rare Saturday morning lull. Nora savored the quiet and looked out the front window at the blue sky and sunshine and the strolling people.

This was the first time in two long weeks that the sky had been bright and clear. Every day had brought clouds that sprinkled, rained, or poured down storms. Suddenly, she yearned with all her heart to join those people out in the beautiful sunlight and be free, like them.

What would she do if she had a Saturday all to herself? A whole day to do anything she wanted? She leaned her elbows on the windowsill, giving herself up to this sinful fantasy. For starters, there were books to be read, tempting stacks of them, seductive heaps of them...

The crash of shattering glass hurtled her back to reality. Nora straightened, squaring her shoulders. She was training a new waitress, LaVonda Pollack. "Vonnie?" she called apprehensively.

The girl's voice, nervous, came from the kitchen. "It was only an empty bottle. I'm cleaning it up. Sorry."

"It's all right. Don't worry." Nora sighed and pushed a hand through her ash-brown hair. Then she busied herself readying for the lunch hour rush. She had tables to wipe, fresh place mats to put down, condiments to restock.

Nora's regular assistant, Kasey, was on vacation. Her other waitress, Shelby, had just gotten married, and Nora had been lucky to get a replacement—even if it was Vonnie.

Finding good, steady help for the café was hard. The hours were long, the pay only adequate, and the waitresses had to count on tips to make a decent living. Nora missed Shelby, and she envied her. Shelby had gone back to college for her master's degree.

Sometimes in her heart of hearts, Nora still wished for life without the Longhorn. But the place was hers, and she was lucky to have it. Once the café had almost sold, but the deal had gone sour at the last moment, and Nora took that as a sign. It belonged to her and she belonged to it. There was no escaping and no use complaining.

The door opened, its bell jingling, and her vague discontent fled. When she saw who entered, her heart flew up in happiness.

Three tall men stood in the entryway. All wore Stetsons, western-cut shirts, jeans and expensive boots. Each was handsome, but in a different way. It was J. T. McKinney with *both* his sons, not only Tyler—but Cal.

The sight of Cal dizzied her with happiness. He and his family had been gone for months. She threw herself into Cal's arms, half-laughing, half-crying, hugging and being hugged. Cal laughed out loud, Tyler gave a tight smile, and J.T. sighed as if in resignation.

"Cal," she said in disbelief. "When did you get back?"

"This mornin'," he said and whirled her around. Then he stopped and beamed the smile that showed his killer dimples. "Lord, is it possible? You're prettier than ever. Got a kiss for me, sweet thing?"

Then he was bending, his lips firm and affectionate against her cheek. "Mmmwha!" he said, drawing back slightly.

She drank him in. Next to her husband and son, she loved Cal McKinney more than anyone else in the world.

He was as irresistible as ever, his hazel eyes just as full of high spirits. He had his hat brim tipped at a cocky angle, and though he was in his thirties now, he still had his boyish, sexy, carefree air.

He grinned again. "That worthless husband of yours has gone off and left you alone today, the fool?"

Nora hooked her arms around his neck. Her husband, Ken, was J.T.'s foreman and Cal's best friend. "Ken's in Medina. He should be back by tonight. Oh, Cal—it's so good to have you home."

"Good to be home. Mighty good."

"And the rest of the family?" she asked. "They're here?"

"Serena and the twins? Couldn't go nowhere without 'em, could I? They're sleeping at Daddy's. It was a long trip. I hope those twins sleep a week. Ever been on a plane thirty-six hours with twins? Close to hell as I ever want to get."

She laughed and led him to the nearest booth. "Let me get you some coffee. Or are you too wired?"

"Never too wired for your coffee, darlin'. Or your cheesecake. I've been thinkin' of your cheesecake for the last three thousand miles. It was all that kept my spirits up. You got pumpkin?"

"I do. The first of the season. You want it with whipped cream?"

Cal closed his eyes in mock ecstasy. "Yes. Say it again. It's like you're talkin' dirty."

She gave him a playful swat. She turned to Cal's father. "And what can I get you, J.T.?"

"I wondered if you were ever going to notice me," J.T. drawled.

Nora laughed. "I always notice you. You're not an easy man to ignore."

"Except when he's around," J.T. said with a rueful nod at Cal.

Cal looked amused, but his brother, Tyler, didn't smile.

J.T. said, "Give me black coffee with no caffeine and a piece of gingerbread. But no whipped cream."

Cal patted his father's chest over the heart. "Gotta take good care of that ticker, Daddy."

"I learned that the hard way," J.T. said, pushing the sugar bowl farther away. Almost ten years ago he'd had a major heart attack.

"And you," Nora said to Tyler, "you'll have black coffee, skim milk on the side and a plain donut."

Tyler nodded.

"You *still* have that same thing?" Cal asked in disbelief.

"Yep," said Tyler.

"You don't *ever* change it?"

"Nope," said Tyler.

"God," Cal said, shaking his head. "You're so predictable."

Tyler gave him a level look. "So in your way," he said, "are you."

"Ah," said J.T. "The sound of quibbling. How I've missed it. Family's a wonderful thing. Isn't it, Nora?"

"The best," she said. She looked at the three of them fondly.

J. T. McKinney owned the biggest ranch in the county. He was in his early sixties now, but still straight and tall. His thick hair was silver, and although time had carved lines in his face, women said he was as handsome as ever—and some said he was even more so.

Tyler, the black-haired elder son, resembled his father, with the same dark eyes and stubborn jaw. Nora knew that he was a good man, but his feelings often ran too deep and silently for his own good.

And Cal—unlikely as it was, Cal was now a golden boy. Tyler had graduated from college with honors. Cal had been kicked out with multiple dishonors. Like a dutiful son, Tyler went back to the Double C to work with his father. Cal hit the rodeo circuit and spent the next ten years raising merry hell without wasting a thought on responsibility.

Then Tyler had a brainchild. He studied hard and toiled even harder to turn almost a thousand acres of Double C land into a vineyard and establish a winery. He did everything by the book, with science and forethought.

Cal fell into business only because he fell in love. He was surprised to find he had a knack for making deals. He'd turned Serena's small boot-making business into a big one, then diversified. He invested, and his investments multiplied.

Now Tyler was still struggling to make his winery one of the best in the state. His wife had left him once, and he'd almost let her get away. The last ten years had often been rocky for him. In contrast, Cal was rich, with a marriage smooth as silk. Who could have predicted such a thing?

There were tensions among the three men. Nora could see it even now, when they should be happy in their reunion. Still, for all the undercurrents that ran among the men, they were bound together by ties of blood. If anyone was foolish enough to take on one McKinney man, he took on all three.

They had their differences. They always would. But to Nora, these three men weren't simply *from* Crystal Creek. They *were* Crystal Creek, its generous and complex heart and soul.

CHAPTER TWO

MEL BELYLE RACED like hell through the Dallas airport. He dodged, he wove, he sprinted. The crowd in the concourse formed a slow-moving human maze, but he negotiated it with a keen eye and his fanciest footwork.

It didn't matter. He still missed his flight to Austin.

He turned around in disgust and bumped—hard—into the little redhead. She'd been on the same flight as he had from New York. How in blazes had *she* got there so fast? Did she have wings on her heels?

He blinked in surprise. She didn't. "Excuse you," she said, her voice full of irony.

Hmm, he thought. *Attitude. Lots of it.* "Sorry," he said. "I didn't see you clear down there."

Blue sparks flashed in her eyes. She tossed a disdainful glance at his expensive shoes. "I hope you didn't scuff your Guccis on my shin."

He raised an eyebrow. "I said I was sorry."

"Right," she said, "Forget it." She hustled past him and made her way to the ticket counter. "I missed my connection to Austin," she said to the attendant. "When's the next flight?"

Austin? he thought. *It's a small world after all.*

Mel looked her up and down. Her long hair was red as flame and pulled back into a loose ponytail. Her face would have looked almost elfin, except the eyes were a-crackle with worldly intelligence.

She wore jeans, running shoes and a travel vest, and she

had the air of knowing exactly what she was doing. She was breathing hard, but he was breathing harder.

He stepped up behind her. He was almost a foot taller than she was.

He said, "You were on the flight from New York."

She didn't bother to look at him. "Yes."

"You're going to Austin, too?"

"Yes," she said in a tone that meant *Stop talking to me.*

He wasn't about to stop. She rather intrigued him. She was the sort of little thing who thought she was a big deal, and he was just the man to bring her down a notch or two.

But he made his voice friendly, casual. "You must have got here right behind me. I thought everybody was eating my dust."

She cast him the briefest glance over her shoulder. "I got here before you. You ate *my* dust."

He laughed at her audacity. "I'm afraid you're mistaken. I was on my college track team."

This time her glance was longer and more dismissive. "So was I. I was the captain."

Again she turned her back on him. He looked dubiously at her. She was breathing almost normally now, but his heartbeat still labored, his lungs still burned.

She was built like a runner, he conceded, even if she was small. Her legs were long for her height, and she didn't carry an ounce of fat. While he'd searched for openings in the crowd big enough to get through, she'd probably dashed through like a rabbit through the forest.

How annoying. And she was apparently in better shape than he was. More annoying still. She probably ran ten miles a day, ate bean sprouts and drank only bottled water.

The attendant said to the redhead, "I'm sorry. There won't be another flight for at least two hours."

Mel heard the redhead mumble something under her breath. Then she said, "Is there a place around here to sit down and eat?"

"Up the escalator," said the attendant. "Then just keep going straight."

The redhead sighed and made her way toward the rest room, shouldering her carry-ons again. During her run, her hair had come partly undone. It hung down in tendrils along the nape of her neck and over her ears.

That neck was pale and slightly moist with perspiration. Mel wondered if her whole body was as flawless and damp as that ivory neck. He watched her disappear into the ladies' room, moving smoothly.

Two hours is a long time, he thought. *An enterprising man could make things happen.*

He made his arrangements for the next flight, then waited until he saw the redhead emerge from the rest room. Her hair was brushed neatly into place, and she'd added a touch of coral lipstick to that smart mouth of hers.

He watched her get on the escalator, waited until she was halfway up, then followed. A few people had got on between them. Once at the top he was surprised how quickly he had to move to keep up with her. Damn! She *was* fast, dodging in and out of the crowd as lithely as a cat.

It was a quarter past noon now, and the restaurants lining the concourse were packed. He saw her scan first one, then another, looking for an opening. She never broke stride until she saw one.

A harried-looking couple was leaving a tiny table at a bar and grill. The redhead spotted them before Mel did and veered into the restaurant without even a pause. As soon as the man stood up, she gave him a friendly smile and sat down in his place.

Perfect, Mel thought with satisfaction. *I've lived right.* He quickened his pace, strode into the restaurant and sat down across from her, beating out a beefy guy with a briefcase by a split second. "Mind if I join you?" Mel asked her cheerfully. "There doesn't seem to be another place."

She looked at him with suspicion. The place was crowded

to overflowing; she could hardly object. She shrugged the way one might shrug off a pesky fly.

Then she dug into her carry-on and pulled out a thick paperback book. The cover said *Guidebook to the Texas Hill Country* and bore a photograph of a myopic-looking armadillo. She opened it and began reading, ignoring him.

Mel Belyle did not easily suffer being ignored, but he never begged for attention, either. He didn't have to. He reached into his own carry-on and took out a book identical to hers, with the same beady-eyed armadillo. He opened it and pretended to read.

He saw her double take and pretended he didn't. He was aware the restaurant was overcrowded and understaffed. They could be at this table a nice, long time.

He'd noticed her back in New York, of course—he took note of all pretty girls. But he'd dismissed her: not his type. He liked his women tall and languid, not small and brisk.

Still, he'd noticed her again when he was sitting in first class, sipping a Bloody Mary. She boarded afterward, with the coach passengers, expertly shouldering her well-worn bags.

He hadn't been able not to watch her, but she hadn't cast so much as a glance his way. She seemed to have her mind strictly on business even though she wasn't dressed for it. She must not give a hoot for fashion. He liked his women fashionable.

"You're as bad as Fabian with his supermodels," his brother Nick had once taunted. "That last girl you took out looked like a giraffe in rhinestones."

The memory fell over Mel coldly, like a drop in the temperature. That was one of the last conversations he'd had with Nicky. They hadn't spoken since May.

The break wasn't over Nick's crack about the girl. Nick always teased, and about the model, he'd been right. She had looked like a giraffe, albeit an elegant one.

No, the rupture was over what Nick had done to Fabian. It was beyond ungrateful. It was treacherous, a betrayal too deep for Mel to forgive. He intended to settle the score, and if people wanted to call it revenge, let them. To Mel, it was justice. Nobody had more right to exact it than he did.

Yet in truth, he didn't like dwelling on it. He supposed that he'd loved Nick once, but now his brother was his enemy. It gave him a cold and hollow feeling in his gut, and he wanted distraction. He would distract himself with the redhead.

A roly-poly waiter in a striped vest appeared. "Afternoon, folks," he said. "Can I take a drink order?"

"Just a cola," said the redhead, barely looking up from her book. "And could I get half a turkey and Swiss cheese sandwich?"

"Well…" said the waiter, sounding perplexed.

"The same for me," Mel said quickly.

"Oh," the waiter said, his round face relaxing. "I see. Split it? Cola's cheaper by the pitcher."

"That'll be fine," Mel nodded. "Bring a pitcher."

The redhead glanced up sharply. "Those are *separate* orders," she said, but the waiter had already disappeared into the crowd.

Mel gave her an innocent smile. "Don't worry about it." He nodded at their twin books. "Coincidence, eh?"

Her blue eyes seemed to say *What's with you?* Her mouth, which was a very nice mouth indeed, said nothing.

He reached into his pocket and laid his card before her, in front of the napkin dispenser. "My name's Mel Belyle," he said. "Since we're sharing a table and a flight, we might as well be friendly. I'm sorry about bumping into you like that. Sincerely."

Her gaze fell to his card, and he saw her skeptical expression change. For a split second she was very still, and he studied her. She had a piquant little face, hardly beautiful, but arresting. She raised her eyes to meet his again. Her lashes were long, thick, and auburn.

For the first time she smiled. "Hello, Mel Belyle," she said. "My name's Kitt Mitchell."

She stretched out her hand in greeting. He shook it, enjoying the silky feel of her skin. He didn't marvel at the transformation of her mood, he simply congratulated himself. He guessed his charm was working, after all.

OH, THIS IS RICH, thought Kitt.

It was like the fly catching the spider. She recognized the name on the card and she recognized the firm he represented.

Melburn K. Belyle, Corporate Attorney
Castle Enterprises, Inc.
New York

Castle Enterprises was the corporation Fabian had created expressly to handle the Bluebonnet Meadows project in Crystal Creek. And Mel Belyle was the man Heywood Cronin had sworn would never speak to Kitt.

Yet here, in all his egotistical glory, was Mr. Belyle himself, trying to pick her up. She put her elbows on the table, laced her fingers together, and gave him her most admiring stare. She batted her eyelashes ever so slightly.

She pretended to be mildly flirting, but her practiced eye was taking his measure. He was actually an exceptionally good-looking man. Too tall for her taste, of course, but well built.

His hair was medium brown, thick and waving. Beneath straight, dark brows, his eyes were sapphire blue. He had a straight nose, a well-shaped mouth, and a square jaw.

He carried himself with confidence—too much for Kitt's taste. And, clearly, he had money. His blue sweater looked like cashmere, and its color matched his eyes. The dark slacks fit perfectly. His nails were manicured better than hers, and his haircut was more expensive.

She imagined him living at his elegant address, riding in limousines, dating those women whose pictures appeared in glossy magazine ads. His roots might have been humble, but nobody would ever guess. Maybe that was the point.

She began to sound him out. "Okay," she said with a demure smile. "We've made peace. So tell me about yourself. What takes you to Austin?"

"Business," he said. "What about you?"

"I'm going to visit my aunt," she said, which wasn't a lie. She paused for effect. "I haven't seen her in ages. It's a shame to be out of touch with family, don't you think?"

For a split second, almost imperceptibly, his smile wavered. He didn't answer her question. Instead he said, "So you're from Texas?"

"A long time ago," said Kitt. "I'm permanently transplanted to Manhattan now. What about you? Native New Yorker?"

"Transplant," he said. "I'm from Beaumont, originally."

She knew that already. "Castle Enterprises," she said. "That sounds familiar. What exactly is it?"

"Real estate development," he said, then turned the questioning. "And what do you do?"

She shrugged as if her job was of small interest. "I work for the Gilroy Group." This was misleading, she knew. The Gilroy Group owned six magazines, but it was far more famous for its other holdings, especially its television network.

His blue eyes kindled with mischief. "Gilroy? Are you connected with that *Uptown Girls* show? The sexy one?"

"I'm just a little-bitty cog in the Gilroy machine," she said flirtatiously.

He gave her a one-cornered grin. "That means yes, doesn't it?"

She gave a laugh meant to sound self-conscious. "Well…"

"It *does* mean yes," he said with satisfaction and leaned closer. "So exactly what do you do?"

She chose her words carefully. "Well, I guess you say I sort of—work around the editorial office."

His grin grew more wicked. "You mean like—a story editor?"

"Um. Kind of." She did, after all, work on stories. He just didn't suspect she was working on one right now and he was its central figure.

"So tell me," he said, leaning his chin on his hand. "Those plots? Are they based on real experience?"

He looked as happy as a man who has just fallen into a hutch of Playboy bunnies. *Uptown Girls* was the sexiest show on network television.

You lech, Kitt thought. *I bet you think I'm an encyclopedia of erotica.* She batted her lashes again. "That would be telling. I'm not going to discuss it until I know you much, much better."

He leaned closer still. "That can be instantly arranged. What do you want to know?" His dark blue eyes were fixed with happy predation on hers. For a moment her breath stuck in her chest.

"Everything," she said. "Tell me simply everything."

"No!" CAL CRIED as if in mortal pain. "She can't do that!"

J.T. sat at his desk. In his face, harshness mingled with resignation. "She can and she is."

"No," Cal repeated, then swore. "She's lived here since I was born. Since *before* I was born. Hell, she's family— she can't up and leave."

"I'm no happier than you are," J.T. said. In truth, he felt as if somebody had chipped a piece out of his heart.

"Hell," Cal said in frustration. He jammed his hands into the pockets of his jeans and stared moodily out the window of J.T.'s study.

J.T. gave a gruff sigh. Lettie Mae Reese, the cook, had given her notice this morning. In two weeks she would celebrate her sixty-second birthday. When she'd told him that she meant to retire, tears had brimmed in her eyes.

J.T. picked up a pencil and threw it down again. Hell, when she'd told him, tears had brimmed in *his* eyes. Lettie

Mae had come to work at the Double C when J.T. had married his first wife, Pauline, years ago.

He could not recall a major holiday or birthday without Lettie. He could picture her when she first came to the Double C, a young black woman so thin that her smile seemed wider than she did.

When Pauline had died, the only person who'd seen him cry was Lettie Mae. He'd stood in the kitchen and suddenly burst into sobs, making a noise like an animal in hopeless pain. She'd embraced him and held him fast, until he could stop. His outburst had been brief but violent, and afterward neither of them ever spoke of it.

Lettie had stood by him through everything, including his second marriage to Cynthia. When he became a father again, at fifty-five, Lettie Mae had looked at his new daughter as if the child was as precious as her own. "J.T.," she'd said, "you sure haven't lost your touch. After all these years, you still make a mighty good-looking baby."

Cynthia used to snuggle in his arms after lovemaking and repeat the words as their private joke. "J.T., you sure haven't lost your touch."

Cynthia hadn't been able to use that joke much in the past few months. Lord knew that J.T. liked sex, but by bedtime, he was so tired the need to sleep overwhelmed him. Then he had nightmares about bulldozers eating Claro County, chewing up the very graveyards and the bones of his ancestors.

Cynthia said she thought the stress was getting to him. This morning she'd said, "J.T., I know how much you love this country. But you're letting it eat you alive. Maybe the time has come for you to ease up."

Ease up? At first he'd been shocked. But was she right? J.T.'s lawyer, Martin Avery, wanted to quit lawyering and retire. His doctor, Nate Purdy, wanted to quit doctoring and retire. Even that old warhorse, Bubba Gibson, J.T.'s friend from boyhood, was starting to make threats about turning his ranch over to somebody younger.

Everybody else was retiring. Why not him? The ranch hadn't done so well lately. J.T. was even slightly in debt—to Cal, his own son. Borrowing money from his own child had made J.T. feel somehow diminished.

Cal still stood staring glumly out the window. "Is Lettie Mae gonna stay in Crystal Creek?"

With a jolt J.T.'s mind came back to the crisis at hand. He set his jaw. "I don't know. She's going to visit her cousin in Santa Fe. See if the climate helps her arthritis."

Cal turned, his face troubled. "Daddy, I can't imagine life without Lettie Mae here. What are you gonna do?"

"I'll find a replacement," J.T. almost snapped. In truth, he didn't know what he would do. When Lettie Mae went, it would be as if the best years of his life had taken formal leave of him.

"Well," Cal said with conviction, "what we gotta do is give her a party. Biggest damn party in the history of Crystal Creek."

While I go up into the attic and hang myself, J.T. thought morosely.

Maybe Cynthia was right. The ranch, the changes in Crystal Creek, the battle with Fabian that could drag on for years—maybe he should retire and try to get his life back.

But if he retired, what would become of the Double C? Tyler was consumed by the business of the winery. Lynn, J.T.'s grown daughter, only cared about raising racehorses, not cattle, and her husband wasn't a rancher. He was a dentist, for God's sake.

As for Cal, he had bigger enterprises than a ranch, and he still had his same old footloose streak. He'd been checking out investments all over Australia, and soon he'd head for South America. No. Cal was not one to be tied down to a piece of land.

Cal said, "Let's put the gals in charge of the party. That'll give 'em something to worry about besides this damn Blue-bonnet Meadows. Lord, what a name. Why didn't they just call it Cutesie-ville?"

"I don't care what they call it," J.T. said grumpily. "I just wish it'd disappear. Hole in the Wall was good ranch land once. I was just getting used to it being a dude ranch."

Cal shook his head and smiled. "It was a dude ranch for ten years. You don't adjust to change real fast, do you, Daddy?"

J.T. scowled at him. "No, I don't. And now I hear this Fabian's sending Belyle's own brother down here. Shelby Belyle told Lynn. Plus Nora says we'll have a reporter on our hands. Not local. Big-time."

Cal leaned against the wall and crossed his arms. "A reporter could be an advantage to us. *Exclusive* is a national magazine. It could stir up national sympathy."

"Sympathy? That and a dollar'll buy you a cup of coffee," J.T. said. "But don't try it without the dollar."

"The pen is mightier than sword," Cal observed.

"Fabian isn't using a sword," J.T. retorted. "He's using Uzis and flame-throwers and stealth bombers."

Cal raised an eyebrow. "How good is this lawyer that's coming?"

"Mel Belyle? I hear he's good. Very good. And motivated. He's got a score to settle."

Cal uncrossed his arms, hooked his thumbs in his belt and strolled to the fireplace. "How about the other one? The lawyer that deserted Fabian? And married the local girl?"

J.T.'s forehead furrowed. "Nick? He's good, too. And he's on our side. But he can't do much. Fabian's got him hog-tied."

"Exclusivity clause?" Cal asked. "Confidentiality clause? Corporate secrets, that kind of bull dooky?"

J.T. gave his son a long, scrutinizing look. It always surprised him when Cal said something knowledgeable about business or law. J.T. sometimes felt that Cal's wealth was a strange illusion, and that his younger son was still a rambling kid, without a serious thought in his head.

"Yeah," he admitted. "That kind of bull dooky."

Nick Belyle *had* revealed company secrets, and it had cost him. He lost his pension, his company stock, and he would probably never work at the corporate level again.

Nick was hardly poor—he could easily live on his savings and his own investments for years. He could also open a private practice, which he intended to do, right here in Crystal Creek.

What Nick could *not* do for one full year was get involved in any sort of business that ran counter to Fabian's. That included the Claro County Citizens' Organization. Nick wanted to help—but he couldn't even give free advice. If he did, Fabian could have him fined and disbarred.

"So Martin Avery's handling most of the legal eagle stuff right now?" Cal asked.

"Some of it," J.T. said. "With the help of some Dallas lawyers. But Martin's tired. He says this case is out of his league. He said—he said that he wanted your advice. That maybe you knew some high-powered people—but not too high-powered. I'm not made of money."

Cal nodded, his expression serious. J.T. had another surge of an emotion he couldn't identify—or didn't want to. It didn't seem fitting that a man as learned and careful as Martin should turn for advice to Cal.

Tyler had always joked that Cal had spent his formative years getting bucked off horses and landing on his head. There'd been times in Cal's wild years that J.T. could only agree.

"I want to meet Nick Belyle," Cal said. "Soon. Could you arrange it?"

"He wants to meet you, too," J.T. said, with the same unpleasant feeling. "He'd come over tonight if you're willing."

"I'm willing," said Cal. "In the meantime I'm going to talk to your better half and mine about Lettie's shindig." He paused, then gave his father a level look. "You told Tyler about Lettie Mae—that she's leaving?"

J.T. muttered yes. He had told Tyler first because it

seemed only fitting. After all, Tyler was the elder and he still lived on the Double C. He saw Lettie Mae nearly every day.

Cal said, "How'd he take it?"

"Hard," J.T. said, suddenly feeling bone-weary. Tyler took everything hard; it was his nature.

"Maybe I should talk to him," Cal said.

"He doesn't want to talk," J.T. said. "He's out in the vineyard, and he's not answering his cell phone."

Cal's normally playful eyes looked troubled. "Are he and Ruth getting along all—"

J.T. cut him off. "What goes on between them is their business. I don't interfere." *Neither should you,* was the unspoken message.

Cal's expression didn't change. "It's okay to ask Ruth about a party?"

"I suppose," J.T. said without enthusiasm. "And ask your sister. Don't leave her out."

"I wouldn't leave Lynn out," Cal said. "You know that."

"And another thing," J.T. said. "I want Lettie Mae to have a nice send-off. But don't go wild. We'll split the expense four ways—you, me, Tyler, Lynn. This is not some big show for *you* to put on, understand?"

Cal stood a bit straighter and looked him in the eye. For a moment, he didn't speak. Then he said, "I understand."

And his unspoken message was, *I understand better than you think, Daddy.* He turned and left the study.

CRONIN HAD TOLD KITT she didn't have a snowball's chance in hell of getting Fabian's Crystal Creek man to talk to her. Yet here that man was, ready and eager to tell her about himself. Delightful.

For once, Kitt didn't allow herself to dwell on journalistic ethics. After all, Mel Belyle had pursued her, not the other way around.

And, Kitt rationalized, she hadn't exactly lied to him.

He'd jumped to a conclusion, and she'd helped keep him jumping. He thought he was making a conquest. He didn't know he was becoming one.

She decided to pry slowly, not to stir his suspicions. "What kind of a name is Melburn?" she asked, just a hint of teasing in her voice.

"My uncle was named Melburn," he said, "My grandfather spent time in Australia when he was in the navy. He named him for the city."

Kitt looked again at his card and frowned. "Melbourne? It's spelled differently."

"My family wasn't known for its spelling skills." He gave her a self-deprecating smile.

She smiled back. "What were they known for?"

"Ah," he said, as the waiter set down a pitcher of cola and two glasses. "Refreshment. May I?" He offered to pour her drink.

"Please," she said. "You were saying about your family?"

He filled her glass as he spoke. "What were we known for? Nothing special, I guess." As he filled his own glass, his Rolex glinted in the restaurant's dim light.

She said, "You seem to have done all right for yourself."

"I was lucky," he said. He lifted his drink in a toast. "Here's to getting to know each other better."

She clicked her glass against his. "Much better."

He grinned. It was a charming grin, and he used it like a weapon of seduction. *Don full mind and body armor,* she warned herself.

He said, "I can't believe it. A story editor for *Uptown Girls.* You know who my favorite character is? Fleur. The one with red hair like yours. I bet she's based on you."

She wagged a finger at him. "Nope. I won't discuss it. Not until I hear about you. You were saying about your family?"

His face took on a look of mock resignation. "We were

just—a family. I don't remember much about my father. He died when I was four.''

"What did he do?" she asked.

"He was a roofer. He took a wrong step. He died three days later.''

Kitt winced. "And your poor mother?''

"She had three kids. She did what she could. Finally she moved us from Beaumont to New York. She had relatives there. They could help her find work that paid better.''

True, so far, thought Kitt. His story matched her sketchy notes about his past. "Go on," she encouraged.

"So she worked for this guy who was well-to-do,'' Mel said. "He liked her, took an interest in her, wanted to help her out. He was—generous. She was grateful. More than grateful.''

A shadow of moodiness passed over his face. He said, "I know you work with sexy plots and all, but this wasn't like that. This guy wasn't interested in my mom that way. She's a little Italian lady, round as a rubber ball. But she's got a heart as wide as the sky and personality to burn. She's got strong opinions and speaks her mind. But everybody loves her.''

He spoke of his mother with such affection that Kitt was impressed in spite of herself. "So how did he help her, this man?''

Mel rubbed his upper lip pensively. "He helped her mostly by helping us. Her sons. With education. Summer jobs. Training in his law offices.''

She studied him with increased interest. He gave few details, but he wasn't hiding his past. "So,'' she said, stroking the water beaded on the side of her glass, "this man put you through college?''

He frowned. "We all got scholarships. But he helped with other stuff. Books. Transportation. Medical. Clothes.''

He glanced down at the cuff of his expensive sweater. She was surprised he mentioned clothes. Maybe his tailored wardrobe and pricey haircut weren't all pure vanity, but symbolized something deeper to him.

She said, "This guy did this for you out of the goodness of his heart?"

"I think he did it out of the goodness of my mother's heart," Mel said. "His own mother died before he made any money. He never got to help her. My mother reminded him of her."

Kitt looked sympathetic. "And you—and your brothers—reminded him of himself?"

The dark blue eyes took on an unexpected wariness. "Some. And he saw we had potential. That he could help us, and we could help him."

She cocked her head. "Help him? In what way?"

"He had jobs for us when we got out of school. Good jobs. And we owe him the best we can give him. Without him, I don't know where we would have ended up."

She sensed complex emotions behind those words. His face, which she had first thought too handsome, was more interesting when he wasn't cocky. But why had he suddenly showed a hint of vulnerability? Was it because he was thinking about Crystal Creek and challenging his own brother?

"You said you had scholarships," she pointed out. "It doesn't sound as if you'd have ended up as bums in the gutter."

His sculpted mouth took on a wry crook. "We didn't exactly fit in, my brothers and I. Well, the youngest one, maybe. He was always more of a regular guy."

"You didn't fit in? Why?" She didn't have to pretend to be fascinated. She was.

"My older brother was a lone wolf." A trace of bitterness was in Mel's voice.

"You say that like it's bad. What's wrong with independence?"

His jaw tightened. "A man should have loyalties," he said.

"Your brother didn't?"

"That's talking about my brother. I don't want to do that."

She inched her chair a bit closer to the table, to him. "Fine. I'd rather hear about you. Why didn't you fit in?"

Mel gave her an odd look. "You know, you're really a good listener."

She shrugged modestly. "I'm just interested. You seem like the sort of guy who'd be captain of the football team, president of the student council, homecoming king, all that."

His smile went almost shy. He rubbed his upper lip again. "No. Track team. That's all."

She traced a question mark on the tabletop. "So. What were you running from?"

"I could ask you the same thing. You were in track. Were you running to something? Or from something?"

She shook her head. "No fair. The deal is that I learn about you first. So tell me. What made you feel different from other people? That your family didn't have money?"

"Lots of people don't have money," he said, a frown line deepening between his dark brows. "Most people don't."

"Then what was it?" she asked softly.

His frown changed from thoughtful to unhappy. "It's really no big deal. It just seemed so then. It doesn't—"

The waiter interrupted them. He set a plate with a sandwich and pickle before Kitt and an empty plate before Mel. "I'll let you two divide the goodies." To Mel he said, "Do you want the check now or later?"

"I'll take it now," Mel said.

"No, no," Kitt protested. "It should be checks, not check. We're not together. We're just sharing this table—"

The smile died on the waiter's round face. "I—I'm sorry," he said. "You looked like a couple. You acted like you belonged together—excuse me. My mistake. Sorry."

"It's been my pleasure," Mel said, "and it'll be my

treat.'' He handed the man two twenties. ''Keep the change.''

The waiter grinned and eased off into the crowd.

''No,'' Kitt said to Mel. ''Let me pay my share. I insist—''

''I said it's my pleasure. Maybe I can see you while you're in Austin. Does your aunt live in the city?''

''Um, no,'' Kitt said carefully. ''Kind of—outside it. But you were saying?''

''Nothing, really,'' he said. ''Put part of that sandwich on this plate, will you?''

Damn, she thought. He'd been about to reveal something. How could she steer this conversation back on track?

She heard the sound of a cell phone ringing. It wasn't hers. It was his.

He looked irritated at being interrupted, but his voice was pleasant. ''DeJames. How are you, my man?'' His face hardened and he gazed at Kitt. ''*Which* magazine?'' he asked. ''Her name is Katherine *what?*''

The change in his expression was both remarkable and frightening. Kitt felt a swell of foreboding.

''Repeat that description,'' he said into the phone, never taking his eyes from hers. As he listened, the set of his mouth grew harsher. ''Got it,'' he said. ''Thanks.'' He snapped the phone off.

His stare didn't waver. Kitt's face grew hot and her heartbeat speeded in dread.

''That was my office,'' he said from between clenched teeth. ''With a warning. About a reporter.''

''Well,'' she said, ''I'll be going now.'' She put her hand on the table to push her chair back and escape.

With cobra-like swiftness his arm shot out, his hand pinning hers in place. ''Stay put,'' he ordered. ''It's you. From *Exclusive* magazine.''

''Yes,'' she said. ''I never said otherwi—''

''You were pumping me.''

''Well, I—''

She squirmed, trying to slip away from his grasp, but he held her fast. "Visiting your aunt. Pathetic."

"I do have an aunt," she interjected.

"*Uptown Girls*. What a cheap ruse. Using sex to lead me on."

"You're the one who brought sex into—"

"You little liar," he said. He released her hand as if letting go of something hopelessly soiled.

"Look," she began, "*you* followed *me* in here. You assumed—"

It was too late. He had already risen and was disappearing into the crowd. Her face burned with shame and anger. She rose, stood on tiptoes, and cried out after him, "You haven't seen the last of me, you know!"

People glanced at her oddly. She sat back in her seat, feeling small and devious. She shouldn't have led him on. She wished she hadn't. But he *had* started it, and not from the purest of motives. To hell with him.

Her shame died. Her anger sank into a hot, hard ember that she could nurse for a long time and use against him.

She thought about what she had done, and she forgave herself. She ate her half of the sandwich. Then, with a philosophic shrug, she picked up his and ate it, too.

CHAPTER THREE

HER TAUNT RANG in Mel's ears: "You haven't seen the last of me...."

He vowed that she'd *heard* the last of him. He'd sooner cut his tongue out than talk with her again, the lying little minx.

Angrily he strode to the nearest Avis desk to rent a car. He'd be damned if he'd get on the same plane as Kitt Mitchell—she'd probably smirk all the way to Austin.

It was going to be rotten enough to be trapped in the same county with her. She'd be covering the Bluebonnet Meadows battle, and that meant she'd lurk, stalk, spy and breathe down his neck. Tough.

He could not only stonewall her, he could ruin her. Soothing himself with this pleasant prospect, he tossed his carry-ons into the back of the rented luxury car.

He should sic the most rapacious sharks in Fabian's legal department on that deceiving redhead. Have one of the media experts phone her magazine, threaten action and get her cute little butt fired—that'd teach her.

If Fabian wanted, he could get her blackballed forever from respectable journalism. She'd be lucky to get a job writing space alien stories for the cheesiest tabloid.

Obsessively he listed and relisted the sins of Kitt Mitchell. She'd solicited information under false pretenses. She'd used her pixyish face and wide blue eyes to lead him on. She'd shamelessly offered sex as bait—oh, yes, he'd have the office throw the book at her.

No, I won't, he thought in self-disgust as he drove. *Be*

honest. He was thinking like a bully and an oaf. What had happened was his fault, far more than hers. That's what made him sick with anger.

She hadn't set a trap for him; he'd set it for himself. Then, like a fool, he'd barged straight into it. He'd thought she was cute and feisty, and he'd heeded his hormones instead of his brain.

His disgust didn't disappear; it merely changed its target. Sure, he could punish her because he had the power—or Fabian did. But the author of Mel's shame was not Kitt Mitchell, but himself.

Still, she was a threat to the job he had to do in Crystal Creek. He needed to be on guard against her. He had reached a nearly empty stretch of highway. He pulled out his cell phone and called New York. He asked for DeJames Jackson, one of Fabian's top assistants.

"DeJames," he said, "That reporter you told me about— the Mitchell woman? She's already crossed my path. Get me all the information on her that you can. I want to know her better than she knows herself."

DeJames gave a deep, rich laugh. "You think she's that dangerous? Or are you interested in scoring? Those women over at *Exclusive* have a reputation for being smart—and lookers."

Mel felt a fresh sting of resentment. "She's not that great-looking," he said. "And yes, she's dangerous. Very sly." He thought about her deception and added, "Glib. Manipulative. Not above dirty tricks."

DeJames laughed again. "Why, Mel," he said, "it sounds like you finally met your perfect woman."

AT GATE AA1, the P.A. system crackled into life. An impersonal voice droned an unwanted message: the flight to Austin would be delayed for at least another hour.

Groans and mutters ran through the disappointed crowd, and Kitt, too, felt annoyed. But she was also puzzled. Where was Mel Belyle? He was supposed to be on this flight, but he was nowhere to be seen.

Forty-five minutes later, yet another delay was announced. Still no sign of the man. A mischievous smile teased Kitt's lips. Had she miffed him so much that he'd canceled his ticket? Maybe she'd dented his pride more than she'd thought.

Well, she told herself, a man as handsome and overconfident as Mel Belyle could use a swift kick to the ego now and then. Did he try to seduce every woman he met? What had he expected? For her to swoon at his expensively shod feet?

But he had looked great in that blue sweater, she must admit. It set off his wide shoulders and unexpectedly sensitive eyes. *Enough of that,* she scolded. She probably hadn't taken even a crumb off his self-esteem. He was avoiding her because he was avoiding the press, that was all.

He'd probably chartered his own plane or rented a Porsche upholstered in ermine. With Brian Fabian footing the bill, why not?

Kitt sighed. It didn't do to dwell on rich, good-looking men who moved among the power elite. She had been foolish enough to do that once, long ago. She would not make the same mistake again.

LATE THAT AFTERNOON, two men stood by the carved oak bar in the den of the McKinney ranch house. Cal poured two shots of whiskey. "Thought it'd be good for us to get acquainted-like. Have a couple words in private."

Nick Belyle nodded.

"Daddy'll join us pretty soon," said Cal. "He's givin' the kids a ride in the pony cart." He pushed the filled glass toward the other man.

"Thanks," said Nick.

"To those three pretty women out there," Cal said with

a nod toward the living room. "You married yourself a beauty."

"I'd be lying if I said I didn't," Nick said. The men touched glasses and drank.

Through the open door, Cal could see Shelby Belyle sitting with his stepmother, Cynthia, and his own wife, his own *gorgeous* wife, Serena.

Nick's wife was indeed a looker, thought Cal. She was curvaceous with richly dark hair and eyes. Beside Shelby sat Cal's stepmother. The two women were a study in contrasts. Shelby was a young brunette earth goddess, Cynthia a coolly blond aristocrat, still stunning at forty-four.

But in Cal's eyes neither of them could hold a candle to his beloved Serena. Her beauty was quieter, but deeper. Her green eyes still seemed to him the most mysterious in the world. She could give him a look from clear across the room that would shake him to the core with desire.

Just gazing at her now, his thoughts became carnal. He studied the way a strand of her long brown hair trailed over the delightful curve of one breast. Those lovely breasts were covered by a green silk blouse, and he wanted to unbutton it, part it, touch her and lower his mouth to taste her.

Tonight when they were finally alone in the guest bedroom, the first thing he was going to do to her was...

He heard the ghostly echo of his father's old question. *Do you always think with your dick?* J.T. had said it half a hundred times back in Cal's youth. The memory stung, and he hauled himself back to reality.

Nick Belyle smiled, as if he knew where Cal's thoughts had been and exactly how lascivious they were. Cal cleared his throat and poured them each another shot. *Down to business,* he told himself. He said, "This brother of yours that's coming—Mel. Tell me about him."

Nick's smile died. "What can I say? He's the last person I'd want in Crystal Creek."

"Is that from a legal aspect or a personal one?"

"Both," said Nick and downed his drink with one swallow.

Cal studied the other man. Nick Belyle was not conventionally handsome, but his face was interesting, or so women seemed to think. Serena had said he looked a cross between an angel and a street punk.

It was a complex face, and it suited him. He seemed like a complex guy. Going counter to Brian Fabian's orders had been hard on him. J.T. said so, and so did Cal's sister Lynn, and Nora said it, too.

Cal chose his words carefully. "Are you startin' to wish you hadn't got messed up in this?"

Nick pushed away his empty glass. "I don't regret what I did. It was the right thing."

Cal nodded. "We think so."

If Nick hadn't spoken out, nobody would have known what Fabian was up to. As it was, the McKinneys had been able to throw legal roadblocks in his way, and for the time, they had slowed him. The question was, could they stop him?

Cal met Nick's cool blue stare. "You think your brother's comin' to try to buy more land?"

Nick's gaze didn't waver. "What do you think?"

Cal tossed back the drink then leaned both elbows on the bar. "Hell, yes. I think we done made Fabian mad."

"*You've* made him mad?" Nick said with an ironic smile. "He doesn't like being crossed. I crossed him." Nick's eyes moved to the living room to rest on his young wife.

Cal followed his gaze. "You worried about her?"

Nick shook his head, but not with certainty. "This is hard on her. She loves this land. The worst thing Fabian can do to her is buy up as much as possible and 'doze it into housing lots. That'd break her heart."

That'd break a lot of hearts, thought Cal. He said, "What's the worst Fabian can do to you?"

The other man shrugged. "Professionally? He could

move to fine and disbar me. But he can't if I don't work against him for a certain time. I know the law.''

"That's about your work," Cal said. "What about personal?''

Nick paused before answering. "The worst? I guess what he's doing."

"Sending your brother down here?''

"Yeah." Nick's voice was toneless.

Cal slowly turned the whiskey decanter round on the bar, watching the light refract from the cut glass. He asked, "So how good a lawyer is your brother?''

"Damn good."

Cal kept twisting the decanter to make the light dance. "Is he a feller pretty much like yourself?''

"No," Nick said. "He's more of a company man. To me, working for Fabian was like a game. Sometimes the game was dirty. I ignored it as long as I could. My brother thinks differently. For him, it's a way of life. He's absolutely loyal.''

It was a loaded question, but Cal asked it. "Why?''

Nick's expression went cynical. "Somehow he needed that way of life more than I did. He and I never…" The words trailed off.

Cal's curiosity prickled. "He and you never what?''

"It's—private. But basically, he's coming here on a righteous mission. He wants to kick my ass.''

Cal lifted an eyebrow. "Meaning he also wants to kick *our* ass?''

"Precisely," said Nick.

"How do we stop him?''

Nick made a tight, exasperated gesture. "I can't do much. Fabian's got me in legal handcuffs for at least a year.''

"I understand," said Cal. "Daddy explained. He's hired lawyers in Dallas. What do you think of them?''

Nick's face became unreadable. "They're doing their best.''

Cal knew what the problem was. The central conflict was

a complex question over water rights. J.T.'s Dallas lawyers had forced Fabian to halt construction until it was resolved.

But Fabian had cleverly used the law to stop the work at a tricky stage. Now that stage threatened danger. The dam holding Fabian's artificial lake in place was temporary, a mere makeshift levee. With each rain that fell, it became an increasing hazard.

Fabian complained his hands were tied. The injunction against him forbade work on anything at Bluebonnet Meadows—including the dam. The Dallas attorneys dawdled and dithered and seemed incapable of solving the mess.

"The lawyers aren't doin' so great?" Cal persisted.

"I didn't say that," Nick murmured.

"I know you didn't," Cal returned. He reached into his shirt pocket and drew out a piece of notebook paper. "I got two names here. Other lawyers. Now Daddy probably can't afford 'em, but me and my partners can. I'd have to try to ease into doin' it. Not to put his nose out of joint. Would you just look at this for me?"

He unfolded the paper and laid it on the bar, smoothing it out. He could see Nick's reluctance. But Nick, grim-faced, looked down and read the names. Cal watched his expression. Slowly, disbelievingly, Nick grinned.

Cal said, "Now, I know you can't tell me if these folk'd be good. But you might make some little…remark. Chosen careful, I realize."

Nick looked at Cal with something like new-won respect. "Where'd you get these names?"

"I got connections here and there," Cal said nonchalantly.

"I see that you do."

"So—can you say what you think?"

Nick's smile grin became conspiratorial. "I think you're one smart cowboy."

"Naw," Cal said. "It was more my partners' idea. There's three of us. We call ourselves the Three Amigos. They're the brains. I'm just a simple country boy."

"Right," Nick snorted. He put his hand on Cal's shoulder and laughed. "Man," he said, shaking his head. "Man, oh, man. This is *something.*"

Cal laughed, too. Maybe Fabian and Nick's brother didn't hold the winning cards, after all.

KITT HAD NOT SEEN the Hill Country for twelve years— almost half a lifetime ago. She had convinced herself it would seem strange and was startled that it didn't. *Why does it still feel so familiar,* she thought with apprehension. *It shouldn't.*

Yet she knew the sweep of these hills with a primal, bone-deep knowledge. It was in her blood to know it—whether she wanted to or not.

The land had dramatic beauty. There were hills, cliffs and low mountains. Great expanses of sparse ground stretched between them. In the open spaces, only the sturdiest vegetation grew. The twisted mesquite trees crouched low to the ground, and the scrub pines were dwarfish.

Along the creeks and river banks, though, were lush green groves. Over this mixture of starkness and fertility arched the great Texas sky. It was gray today, threatening rain. In the distance, lightning glimmered like a ghost.

In her heart, she reluctantly admitted the land's grandeur. But her head asked: *What's it good for?* Cattle and little else. Raising cattle was a back-breaking struggle, and ranching often fell on ruinous times.

The memory of those hard times killed any nostalgia that might stir her. This land was beautiful, yes. But it was also cruel. She was here only because a story was here, and she happened to know the territory.

Yet when she reached the stone pillars that marked the entrance to the Double C, she paused a moment, letting the car idle.

As a child, this ranch had filled her with awe. In spite of herself, she felt a shiver of the old wonder. To her, J. T.

McKinney had been rich. Now she realized he'd never amassed the wealth people called "Texas *Big* Rich."

By Lone Star standards, his ranch, thirty-five thousand acres, was respectable. It was hardly dazzling. Kitt thought, *It's not a magic kingdom, it's only land.*

The Double C would have little importance if it wasn't so close to Austin—and Brian Fabian wasn't so greedy for it. She stepped on the gas and headed down the lane toward Nora's house.

Nora lived at the ranch in the foreman's house with her second husband. Ken was a fine and reliable man—unlike Nora's first husband, Gordon Jones. Kitt had despised Gordon.

She bit her lip in remembrance. Kitt had been considered a tough child, one who could hold her own in an argument, a wrestling match, or an all-out fight. She cried no more than did the most roughneck boys; she would not allow herself.

Yet when Nora had been forced to marry Gordon, Kitt had bawled like a baby. In secret, of course. In her bed and under her covers. She'd thought Nora's life was ruined. It almost had been.

Kitt passed the ranch house, which she'd known well. Her father had been a wrangler on the Double C, and the McKinneys used to give Christmas parties for the ranch hands and their families.

The house seemed just as impressive as ever. Lights blazed from every window, and the drive was full of cars, many of them expensive. But it was not the sprawling house that made Kitt's heartbeat speed.

Beyond the McKinneys' house, she saw another, more old-fashioned home standing on a rise. It was a tall, angular and white, a Victorian clapboard that more than a century ago had been the original ranch house.

A swing hung in the porch's shade, moving gently in the October breeze. Pots of mums marched up one side of the stairs and down the other, overflowing with fat-faced blossoms of bronze and jaunty yellow. On one side was a trellis with an ancient rose bush, still in pink bloom.

It was a lovely, old-fashioned house. It was *Nora's* house.

For the first time, feeling seized Kitt so hard she couldn't fight it off. She took a deep breath and pulled onto the house's graveled drive. She took an even deeper breath, then got out of the car. As she did, the front door of the house burst open.

Nora came half-running, half-skipping down the steps, her shiny brown hair bouncing against her shoulders. In her jeans and yellow-checked shirt, she still looked as young as a girl.

She raced toward Kitt and caught her in such an embrace that it nearly knocked Kitt's breath away. Nora was laughing and crying and talking all at once. "Kitt-Katt—welcome back! How was your trip? I was afraid you'd be stuck all night in Dallas. You haven't gained an ounce, not a single ounce—I'm going to have to fatten you up. Did you remember the way to the Double C? Does Crystal Creek look different?"

To Kitt's astonishment, hot tears pricked her eyes. And when she tried to speak, she couldn't. Her throat was too choked.

What's wrong with me? she thought, bewildered by the force of her emotions. All she could do was hug Nora back and hold her tight.

Vaguely, Kitt realized someone else had come out onto the porch. Nora drew back, laughing at herself for crying. Kitt fought down her own tears and found her voice.

"Oh, Nora," she said gruffly, "Stop the water works. This is like walking into a lawn sprinkler."

Nora shook her head wryly and wiped her eyes with the back of her wrist. "If you'd come back more often, maybe the flood wouldn't build up. I swear, I'm weak-kneed."

"So, Nora, your wandering girl's come home," said the man on the porch. Slowly he came down the steps.

Kitt had collected herself enough by now to look at him

with her usual cool detachment. Ken Slattery was long and lean—well over six feet tall and all sinewy muscle. He was older than Nora by almost seventeen years, but an attractive man. His pale blue eyes looked sharp enough to count the tail feathers on high-flying hawk.

Kitt recalled him from childhood, although she hadn't known him well. The years had not much changed him. Oh, weather had lined his face more deeply, and his brownish hair was going gray at the sideburns, but the strongly boned face was the same. The biggest change was that he walked with a noticeable limp.

"Little Kitt," he said, "we'd started thinkin' we needed to drive to Dallas and fetch you home ourselves."

He took her hand in welcome. His own was hard and callused, truly a cowboy's hand. She realized that he wouldn't embrace her or kiss her cheek. He had an air of reserve that bordered on shyness.

"I'm sorry," she said. "I missed my first flight, then they kept delaying the next one."

Nora took Kitt's arm and led her toward the house. "Come on in, stranger. I didn't make anything fancy for supper because I wasn't sure when you'd get here. You didn't even stop at the hotel?"

"Nope," Kitt said. "I made reservations ahead of time." She glanced down the slope at the McKinneys' house. "What's happening? A party?"

Nora shook her head. "Not really. Cal and his family are home. So it's a gathering of the clan. You remember Tyler and Lynn and Cal?"

Kitt stiffened. She remembered all of them, but most especially Cal. She hoped to God that he'd forgotten her.

"They're all married now," Nora said as they climbed the stairs. "And they're entertaining somebody you'll want to meet."

Kitt looked at her questioningly. Nora gave her a knowing look. "Nick Belyle. The first lawyer that Brian Fabian sent down here. The one you want to meet. Now Fabian's sending another lawyer—Nick's brother.''

"He's already here," Ken said from behind them.

The two women stopped and looked at him in surprise. "What?" Nora asked. "Since when?" Kitt's pulses inexplicably quickened.

Ken nodded. "He's at the hotel. Just got in about half an hour ago."

"How do you know?" Nora asked, looking puzzled.

"Phone rang just when Kitt drove up," Ken said laconically. "It was Cal. He said that Nick's brother just checked into the hotel."

"Well, why didn't you *tell* me?" Nora demanded.

"By that time, you were out the door. A-weepin' on your niece," Ken said.

Nora gave him a mock-angry look and pretended to jab him in the ribs with her elbow. He gave her a one-sided smile. Nora squeezed Kitt's arm as Ken opened the door for them. "That's coincidence, eh? You and he getting here the same day? Looks like the action's about to begin."

Kitt only nodded. She thought it best not to mention her little adventure in the Dallas airport.

They entered Ken and Nora's living room, and Kitt was struck by how homey and *right* it seemed. The overstuffed chairs and sofa seemed to beckon one to sit down and sink into soft comfort. Family snapshots crowded the mantel, and the walls were lined with overflowing bookshelves. On the coffee table were a vase of golden carnations and the latest copy of *Exclusive* magazine.

"Kind of spooky, isn't it?" Nora mused. "How fast news travels? That people already know he's here?—Nick's brother—what's his name?"

Mel, thought Kitt, but said nothing.

"Mel," Ken supplied.

"Come into the kitchen," Nora invited Kitt. "Yes. Mel,

that's it. His ears should be burning, us all talking about him this way."

Kitt smiled weakly.

BUT IF ANY EARS SHOULD have been burning, they were Kitt's.

Mel lay on the big four-poster bed in the West Gold Room of the Crystal Creek hotel. He was savoring, with sharp appetite, a smorgasbord of delicious details about Kitt Mitchell.

"Now wait," Mel said, "she was a homecoming attendant both years she was at this posh school in Dallas?"

"Both years," said DeJames, a grin in his voice. "Queen her senior year. And the Sweetheart of Phi Omega Phi."

"What in hell's Phi Omega Phi?" Mel demanded.

"The boys' academic honor society. She was also editor of the high school paper."

"And star of the girls' track team," muttered Mel. The redhead was clearly an overachiever. Not normal, a driven person.

DeJames said, "This is what they put under her picture in the yearbook. 'Some girls break records. Some break hearts. Kitt Mitchell breaks both.'"

"Cute," Mel said sarcastically. "What else does it say?"

"Most ambitious," said DeJames. "And most likely to succeed."

Mel envisioned her, a fiery-tressed Scarlett O'Hara, conquering by sly charm. Consumed by ambition, a schemer to beware of—even back then. He intended to have the full goods on her. He said, "But how did she get from Podunk High in Crystal Creek to the Snob-brat School in Dallas? I thought her father was just a ranch hand."

"The Stobbart School," DeJames corrected. "He was. And Stobbart was expensive. Very."

"Maybe a scholarship," Mel muttered. For track. Or academics. Or for just being disgustingly over-talented.

"Stobbart didn't give scholarships," DeJames said. "I haven't figured out yet how she got there. I will. The school itself's been closed eight years. But I was lucky—got a copy of one of its yearbooks with her in it.''

Mel's brow furrowed. ''Yeah. How did you do that?''

''Because,'' drawled DeJames, ''I am excellent at my work. And I also have mystical powers. You want me to fax that other stuff to you?''

''Yeah, yeah,'' Mel said. ''Send it on.''

DeJames had given him all the basic info on the redhead, where she'd gone to college, her job history, where she lived in New York, even who her last boyfriend had been, a writer who worked for *Celebrity Magazine.*

Mel glanced at his watch. ''You're working late, aren't you, DeJames?''

''It's how I'll get to the top. My excellence. My mystical power. *And* my legendary tirelessness.''

''Don't forget your becoming modesty,'' Mel gibed.

''That, too. You want me to send this yearbook? I can get it there tomorrow by courier.''

''Do that,'' said Mel. ''And keep digging. I want to get beneath this woman's surface.''

''I think you want to get beneath her skirt,'' laughed DeJames.

''It's time for you to go home now, DeJames,'' Mel said from between his teeth. ''To that pitiful, empty thing you call your life.''

''I happen to have a girlfriend who looks like Jada Pinkett Smith's prettier sister. A *steady* girlfriend, Don Juan. You should try it sometime.''

''Goodbye, DeJames,'' Mel said and hung up.

He sighed and rose from the bed. He'd kicked off his shoes and socks and was shirtless. He smacked his bare chest and padded to the window. It had luxuriantly full white curtains that matched the bedspread and the canopy over the bed. He was in a set of matched rooms called the Gold Rooms, with a sitting room in between.

The Plaza, it wasn't. Still, it was a decent enough place, with a window seat and hooked rugs and a surprisingly well-stocked minibar. There was a combination restaurant and pub downstairs. Its Scottish décor would have struck Mel as absurd in the heart of Texas if he hadn't known the hotel owner was from Glasgow.

Mel knew much about this town. He'd come to it as his brother had, armed with knowledge. Unlike his brother, he wouldn't let some woman make him into a turncoat.

He stared out the window. He could identify the buildings as easily as if he'd lived here for months. There was the bank, Wall's drug store, the Longhorn Coffee Shop, which was closed because it was Monday. Next to the café was the Longhorn Motel, where Nick had stayed.

It was nothing but an L-shaped row of units, not shabby, but clearly low-priced. It wasn't the kind of place Nick would have normally stayed on a bet. But he had done so because of the woman, Shelby.

Mel looked at the whitewashed motel units and shook his head in disgust. He rubbed his upper lip and thought of all Brian Fabian had done for the Belyle family.

Their mother still got teary when she tried to talk about how Nick had turned his back on such a good man. How Nick had given up everything. For a woman.

"I trust you won't make the same damn mistake," Fabian had hissed at him before he'd left.

"No problem," Mel had assured him. And he meant it. He was made of tougher stuff.

Behind him, the fax machine began to whir and click, receiving the first batch of data on Kitt Mitchell. She didn't interest him as a person, he told himself. Not a bit. All he wanted was to know his enemy.

CHAPTER FOUR

KITT HAD BEEN WORRIED. After all these years, would she and Nora have anything in common, anything to say to each other?

But they couldn't stop talking. One memory sparked another; each story unleashed a flow of more. The two found they could still complete each other's sentences—and make each other dissolve in hopeless giggles.

They sat at the kitchen table with Ken, who listened to them with wry amusement.

"And remember when we hiked up to Hermit's Cave—" Nora began.

"—we'd lugged tons of books up there—" Kitt put in.

"And a blanket to sit on. And potato chips and a canteen of limeade—"

"We were going to hide out all summer from my brothers—"

Nora grinned. "—and a *bat* pooped in my hair—"

"—and you screamed and ran halfway down the mountain—" Kitt snickered.

"—yelling, 'Bat poop! Bat poop!' and pouring limeade on my head. Oh, Lord! And you behind me yelling, 'It's okay! People use it for fertilizer!'"

Nora almost doubled up. Ken looked at his wife in wonder, as if he'd never seen her so giddy.

Kitt laid her head in her folded arms on the table and laughed until she cried. Nora told how she'd washed her hair four times and would never go back to the cave. Kitt had to carry all the books back down by herself.

This led to the story of how Reverend Blake's dog had wandered into the church one Sunday morning when the reverend was preaching a sermon on the virtue of obedience.

"Shoo, Spot," the reverend had thundered. But Spot wouldn't shoo. He sat in the middle of the aisle, ignoring his master and scratching a flea.

Nora went to the counter, took a paper towel and dabbed at her face. "And we didn't *dare* laugh. It nearly killed us."

"Whatever happened to that dog?" Kitt asked. Her ribs ached.

"He died of old age. They buried him in the backyard under a rose bush. Eva Blake still gets misty when she talks about that dog."

Nora sighed and added, "The Blakes are eager to see you, you know—Howard and Eva. They always ask about you."

Kitt's mirth vanished. An uneasy guilt filled her. She owed the Blakes a great deal, and she must visit them. But she didn't want to, not at all. They brought back memories that still gave her bad dreams.

But with false cheer she said, "Of course, I'll go see them."

Ken got to his feet. "You two look like you're just getting started. I need to catch some shut-eye. I've got a windmill to check out soon as the light comes up. Hope it doesn't rain again."

He kissed Nora. It was not a perfunctory good-night kiss. It was full on the lips and lingering—not long enough to be showy, but long enough to convince Kitt how deeply he cared for his wife.

"Good night, honey," he said in a low voice. Nora rubbed her nose against his.

Suddenly Kitt felt like an intruder. Ken wanted to make love, and Nora wanted it, too. "I should be going—" she began.

"No," Ken said. "You girls have catchin' up to do. You don't need me."

Nora was insistent. "I'm not letting you go yet. After all, it took twelve years to get you back here."

Ken kissed Nora's cheek and limped from the room. Nora looked fondly after him. "He's right," she said, turning to Kitt. "We have a *lot* of catching up to do. I'll make some cocoa?"

"He seems like a good man," Kitt said, gazing after Ken.

"He *is* good," Nora said. "The best. He's made a world of difference in my life. And Rory's. Lord, Rory. You should see him—he's six foot one now."

Kitt smiled the mention of Rory. He was the one good thing to come from Nora's marriage to Gordon Jones. But Nora's unplanned pregnancy with Rory was why she had to marry when she was only sixteen.

Kitt, eleven then, had been horrified. But she'd grown fond of Rory, and she knew how Nora loved him and how fiercely she had always protected him. And Rory had needed protecting. Gordon was abusive.

When Kitt was in college, she got word that Gordon had died—violently. In a haze of jealousy and drugs, he'd come after Nora and Ken. Cal McKinney had tried to intervene. There was shooting, and Gordon, fleeing, had been hit by a car from the sheriff's department.

Kitt said carefully, "Does Rory ever mention Gordon?"

"Not much. But he knows the truth. I didn't want him to find out by the gossip—which is still going around, dammit." Nora's frank eyes showed a spark of anger, but it quickly faded. "He's dealt with it fine, just fine."

"A freshman in college—I can't believe it." Kitt shook her head. "And he wants to be a professor, yet. He's your boy, all right."

Nora's smile was both happy and sad. "He was editor of the high school newspaper. Just like you. I wish Dottie could see him. She'd be so proud."

"She would." Kitt put her hand over Nora's and squeezed it. Dottie Jones had been a widow and Gordon's mother. She'd always loved Nora and stood by her, even when Nora divorced Gordon. Dottie had been the original owner of the Longhorn, and she'd left it in her will to Nora.

"How long have you been running the Longhorn now?" Kitt asked.

"Almost ten years, off and on. I've poured enough coffee to float an aircraft carrier."

"I thought," Kitt said carefully, "that when you got married again and went back to school, you were out of that place."

Nora tried to shrug as if it didn't matter, but she didn't fool Kitt. Nora said, "Ken saw that I finished my degree. He really wanted it for me...." Her voice trailed off.

"You *had* a job at the high school," Kitt said, still perplexed at what had happened to Nora. "The kids voted you Best Teacher."

"Ken got hurt," Nora said, going to the counter. "And that was it."

Ken had been trying to help unload an unruly Brahma bull bought at a stock auction. The brute had kicked and pinned him against the side of the truck, half-killing him. His leg was broken, his pelvis fractured.

"He couldn't work for a year," Nora said, stirring the cocoa. "J.T. did everything in his power to help. But at the same time, the school system was having money problems—no raises—and I could make better money going back to the Longhorn and managing it myself."

"What I've never understood," Kitt said with a frown, "is *why* the school system had money problems?"

Nora shrugged and filled two cups with cocoa. "The town's lost people. The tax burden on those left—it was getting out of hand."

Kitt crooked an eyebrow. "But Crystal Creek should have been growing. With this location? This close to Austin? Wasn't the town even trying to attract any kind of industry or business?"

Nora gave her on odd look. "We have an industry— cattle. We have the winery. We don't want things like that

yucky cement factory at Kelso. Or the dairy operations at
Bunyard—they both pollute something fierce.''

Kitt eyed Nora with surprise. Did she believe Crystal
Creek could survive without changing?

"I know what you're thinking," Nora said, a bit defensively. She carried the cups to the table and sat down. "That
Bluebonnet Meadows could actually *help* the town. We
don't see it like that. Our way of life is being threatened.
Our heritage. Our identity.''

*Your identity has got you back cleaning tables and flip-
ping burgers,* Kitt thought. But instead she said, "You plan
to keep working at the Longhorn.''

Nora shrugged. "Rory's in college. And business is
steady.''

But the conversation seemed to make Nora uneasy, and
she changed the subject. "What about you? I know about
your work—I read every sparkling word you write. But how
about life? Any love interest?''

It was Kitt's turn to be defensive. As a reporter, she was
used to talking about other people's lives, not her own. She
said, "I'm taking a break from that sort of thing.''

Nora raised an eyebrow in concern. "What about that guy
who wrote for *U.S. News and World Report*? Weren't you
living together?''

Kitt rolled her eyes. "Reese? For a while he was kind of
interesting. Then he became predictable. Then, finally, he
bored me to tears.''

Nora laughed. "They always end up boring you to tears.''

Kitt had the decency to blush. This was true. She had
never seriously dated a man for long. Any man who seemed
vaguely like a prince quickly became a yawn-inducing frog.

"Was he handsome?" Nora asked, leaning her chin on
her hand.

"Too handsome," Kitt said. "It made him conceited.''

An image of Mel Belyle flashed through her mind. He
was far better-looking than Reese. Yet Mel's looks were

somehow different from Reese's. Something deep in his sapphire eyes was complicated—and mysterious.

She reminded herself that Mel was also more conceited than Reese—far more. Yet something about his cockiness seemed forced, more assumed than genuine. She couldn't put her finger on it, which was maddening....

"You said he was quite bright," Nora said.

"Reese? Very bright," Kitt admitted. "But too serious."

"What's the matter with serious?" Nora asked.

"Nothing," Kitt said. "At first it was attractive. But he had no sense of play. He didn't have conversations, he gave lectures. Long, dull ones."

"Ugh." Nora wrinkled her nose.

"One day I realized that he was gorgeous, he was smart, the sex was great, but every time he opened his mouth, I wanted to scream."

Nora laughed. "You need a man with a little devil in him."

Kitt thought again of Mel Belyle, the wicked innuendoes, the playful sexuality of his words. She realized that he was staying at the same hotel she was, literally sleeping under the same roof....

"So there's nobody interesting?" Nora asked sympathetically.

Kitt pulled herself back to the moment. "Nobody interesting in the least," she said, almost believing it.

MEL BELYLE WAS NOT without potential friends in Crystal Creek.

There were people who looked at the rolling ranch country that Brian Fabian had bought and didn't see land about to be despoiled. They saw a crop of dollar signs pushing out of the earth, begging to be harvested.

Two who saw dollar signs were Ralph Wall, the town pharmacist, and his wife, Gloria. Mel had phoned them once he got settled, and Gloria immediately invited him over for a "little get-acquainted drinkee."

Mel went to see how much the couple would tell him and to gauge how grasping they were. They struck him as transparently greedy, and after two little drinkees, they were very talkative indeed.

"A smart man stands to make a lot of money out of all this," Ralph Wall said, doing his best to look like a smart man.

"You're exactly right," Mel answered. He smiled at Gloria Wall. "These are excellent hors d'oeuvres, Mrs. Wall."

Gloria beamed. She was a large woman whose hair was a crown of tight ringlets rinsed to an improbable shade of gold. She had filled a silver plate with things stuffed with ham, olives, anchovies and enough creamed cheese to supply Philadelphia for a week.

"We have five prime acres we inherited from Gloria's mother," Ralph said, leaning back in his flowered easy chair. "It's the ideal location for a strip mall. I thought I could lease it to Mr. Fabian for a hundred years—"

"Mr. Fabian doesn't usually lease," said Mel as pleasantly as he could. "This is an idea I'd have to run by him."

"He'll like it," said Ralph. "He's a man who thinks outside the box. I can tell that. Yessir. I'm a man who thinks outside the box myself."

"Mama's land is a select piece of property," Gloria said. "We were thinking of leasing it at oh, maybe, a million dollars. That's not very much, spread over a hundred years."

It's highway robbery, thought Mel. "Interesting. We'll have to do a feasibility study. That takes time. But I'll be sure to suggest it."

"Let me freshen that drink," she said reaching for the pitcher of margaritas.

"No more, thanks," Mel said. "But don't let me stop you. This is truly a festive spread."

Gloria refilled Ralph's glass and her own. "I lo-o-ove to cook. I want you to come for supper sometime this week. I'll invite my niece, Ladonna Faye. She's a lovely girl, a

natural blonde like me, and so interested in investments
We'll have such a nice cozy time."

When hell freezes over, Mel thought, suppressing a shud
der. But he smiled, told them he'd checked his schedule and
let them know. Now, when they were so friendly and thei
tongues growing loose, was the time to ask about Kit
Mitchell.

He had a thin stack of information on her in his hote
room, faxed by the tireless DeJames. He'd learned a few
things about Kitt—but not enough.

He said, "I need to confide something to you. I got word
today that *Exclusive* magazine's sending a reporter after me
A woman who grew up here. Her name's Katherine Mitch
ell."

Ralph and Gloria exchanged a significant look. Ralph
said, "Little Kitt Mitchell? She's coming?"

"She may already be here," Mel said. He knew she was
she had to be. It was eerie, but he could feel her presenc
in his marrow.

Gloria peered at him over the edge of her drink. *Ah*
thought Mel. *Gloria wants to gossip. It's shining out of he
face like a light.*

She said, "I'm surprised she'd lower herself. She couldn'
wait to shake the dust of *this* place off her feet."

Mel tilted his head in interest. "Really? What makes yo
say that?"

Gloria twirled her glass coyly, making the ice cubes clink
"Well…" she said. "Far be it from me to gossip…"

Mel stared into her slightly unfocused eyes. "This isn
gossip. It's intelligence. Business background."

"Give him the goods, Mama," Ralph said and reache
for another canapé.

Gloria seemed to puff up with importance. "I wish
didn't have to say it, but Kitt came from riffraff. They *bo*
did."

Mel's interest coiled up like an overwound spring. "*Bo*
of them? What do you mean?"

Gloria heaved a sigh of false sympathy. "She and that Nora Slattery. She's Kitt's aunt. She owns the café and motel."

Mel nodded solemnly, hiding his jubilance. So the little vixen had told the truth about having an aunt. And he recognized Nora's name; she ran the Longhorn, which was one of the town's main nerve centers.

"Excuse me," he said. "Why'd you call them riffraff?"

Gloria's small eyes narrowed to knowing slits. "Well, Nora's father was shiftless. Just a wrangler. He drifted all over the county. He worked for all of 'em at one time or another."

"All of them?" Mel reached for the pitcher and topped off her drink.

"All the money people," Gloria said with ill-disguised bitterness. "The big ranch folks. He dragged around a skinny wife and a passel of skinny kids. And the youngest was Nora. She was the 'caboose.' Her oldest brother—that was Herv—was sixteen—seventeen years older than her."

Ralph reached for another canapé. "Herv was already married when Nora was born. He worked for the McKinneys. Kind of a tenant-hand. There never was a Mitchell man who showed a lick of ambition."

"No," Gloria said sipping her drink. "And they all married young. Had to. Couldn't keep their pants on."

Mel frowned, wondering if this was supposed to include Kitt.

"Well," Gloria said with an expansive gesture. "When Nora's mother died, Nora was the only kid left at home. She was about nine. So her daddy dumped her on her brother. On Herv, at the McKinneys', and lit out for the panhandle. So Nora lived with Herv for—let's see—seven years."

Ralph heaved himself up out of the easy chair. "Those margaritas are so tasty, I'm going to make up another batch."

"Oh, goody," said Gloria. She gave Mel an almost flirtatious look. "What was I saying?"

Mel inched back from her slightly. "I asked about Kitt Mitchell."

Gloria finished her drink and set the glass on the coffee table with a loud clink. "Herv's oldest child was Kitt—the reason *he* had to get married. Then, like stair steps, there were three more little ones—boys—boom-boom-boom. Those Mitchells bred like rabbits."

Mel did some swift figuring. "So Nora and Kitt were actually kids growing up together."

"Right. And Nora was like a little mother to that child. Good thing, too. Kitt's own mother couldn't keep up with all those children. Ha! She didn't even try."

Mel felt an irrational desire to defend Kitt Mitchell. "Kitt did all right for herself. *Exclusive*'s a fine magazine."

"I never said the girls weren't *smart*," Gloria said with a sniff. "They were. But...blood will tell. Nora no sooner turned sixteen than she got pregnant by that no-good Gordon Jones."

Mel's face hardened. "What about Kitt?"

But Gloria's mind was on its own track and would not be derailed. She leaned forward conspiratorially. "There was something funny about how Gordon Jones died. It happened at the McKinneys' lake house. Cal McKinney himself was there. And so was Nora. And Ken Slattery—the man she married—the *McKinneys'* foreman."

Gloria looked at him with malicious satisfaction. He didn't like it. It was his job to find the weaknesses of Fabian's enemies, and the McKinneys were among those enemies. But where in hell was this leading?

With cool politeness he said, "I asked about the reporter."

The woman tilted her head knowingly. "And I'm telling you about her background." She jabbed her manicured finger toward his chest. "There was something *strange* about Gordon Jones's death. Cal McKinney and Nora and Ken were in it up to their necks. The McKinneys have enough money to buy their way out of anything.''

Mel looked at her in disbelief. ''You're saying they bought their way out of a killing?''

Her little pink mouth smiled, but her eyes were hard as ice. ''I'm pointing out things, is all. Suspicious things. You get my drift.''

Mel clamped his mouth shut so that he wouldn't swear. Ralph came in, bearing a pitcher of fresh margaritas. ''Woo, boy!'' he said. ''This is some party, eh? Well, how's my girl doing, Belyle? She giving you an earful?''

''I think I've shocked him plumb silent,'' Gloria said smugly. ''And I haven't but scratched the surface of what I know. Now Bubba Gibson—do you know he served prison time?''

Hell and damnation, thought Mel, who did this woman think she was? The Recording Angel of All Sins? ''Kitt Mitchell,'' he said. ''Was she even in town when this— Gordon Jones died?''

''No,'' Gloria said, holding out her glass to be refilled. ''She was at her fancy college. But I want to tell you about Bubba Gibson—he was cheating with this woman young enough to be his daughter—it was a scandal.''

Mel interrupted. ''How did a poor kid like Kitt Mitchell get to a rich school like Stobbart's?''

''I'm telling you about Bubba going to prison,'' she said. ''When you want to know something about somebody in this town, Mr. Belyle, you come to *me*. I know where *all* the bodies are buried.''

Time for my vanishing act, Mel thought grimly. He was sick unto death of this fat gossipy woman. ''I really have to go,'' he said rising. ''Long day. Had to get up early. Jet lag.'' He made his way toward the door and as he did so, he lied about having a nice evening and being grateful for their hospitality.

Gloria tried to follow him, but she wasn't quite steady on her feet. He'd just made it to the porch. She peered out through the screen door and added, "We didn't talk about your brother."

His spine stiffened, but he wouldn't give her the satisfaction of a response. She didn't notice. "And that woman *he* married. If you want to know the full truth about Shelby Sprague and your brother, ask me. I have the goods on her and him. Because I know—"

—*where all the bodies are buried, you bitch,* he finished mentally.

This last jibe, at his brother's wife, somehow offended Mel most deeply. He could not forgive his brother, and he did not want to. He had no desire to meet Nick's wife. So why did he resent Gloria Wall mentioning them?

He drove back to the Crystal Creek Hotel, smoldering with anger. He hadn't merely disliked the Walls, he detested them with vehemence.

And these people, God help him, were his allies.

KITT DROVE BACK to the hotel about ten-thirty.

The night was cloudy, drizzle fell, and the darkness seemed supernatural. Twice she had to swerve to avoid hitting white-tailed deer that suddenly bounded into the glow of her headlights.

Kitt had grown used to New York, where there were always nearby buildings and lights burned all night long. This black, vast space on either side of the highway almost frightened her.

She was restless and fidgety, too. This restiveness came from unpleasant truths that she didn't like to face. But Kitt was not cowardly about such things. She made herself face them.

In truth, she was surprised by Nora's marriage, maybe even a bit…jealous? When Kitt had heard, years ago, that Nora had married Ken Slattery, Kitt had thought: Another cowboy. Won't she ever learn?

As a girl, Kitt had paid little attention to Ken. He'd been attractive in an old-fashioned Randolph Scott sort of way—

but aloof. The sort of man who'd worked hard, kept to himself, and talked little.

She'd told herself that since he was foreman, Nora might have some security at last. She had never imagined that Nora could really be in love with him or that he would treat her as anything more than a hardy pioneer wife, born to do woman's work.

"Okay, so I was wrong," Kitt admitted to the darkness.

The man obviously adored Nora, and she adored him in return. Kitt had sensed the strength of their feeling every moment she was with the two of them. From the way they'd looked at each other when they'd said good-night, they were probably making love at this very moment.

The thought of Nora, naked and happily abandoned in Ken's strong arms, made Kitt feel like a voyeur. She quickly shooed the image away.

But still she felt unsettled. Kitt had always considered herself the lucky one, the one who escaped. She'd thought of Nora as trapped—and that sex was what had trapped her.

So why did Kitt feel suddenly lonely? She never felt lonesome; she never allowed it. And why did her series of safe, comfortable affairs suddenly seem empty, almost soulless?

Kitt wasn't promiscuous. She took her time between romances—in fact the time between romances usually lasted far longer than any of the romances themselves. Nora was right. Kitt seldom stayed involved with a man. She'd always thought it the fault of the men. But maybe it was something that was missing within her....

Thinking of the men in her life reminded her again of Mel Belyle. There was no sense in this linkage of thoughts; it just happened. All evening he'd haunted her.

She was above all a professional, but she had acted frivolously with him. That was a mistake. This assignment made them adversaries. That could not be helped. But at least he should see her as a worthy one.

Did she think of him as a serious opponent? She would be a fool if she didn't. Nora had told her that Nick Belyle was smart as hell—and that he himself had said his younger brother just might be smarter.

KITT PARKED in the hotel's back lot, picked up her laptop and backpack and went in the service entrance leading to the lower floors. She remembered it from years ago, when she and Nora used to deliver fresh eggs to the hotel kitchen. Kitt's mother had raised hens on her patch of tenant land. The yard around the house had always been pecked bare and smelled of chickens. Kitt still hated eggs.

She went down the long hall that led to the registration desk. The hotel had been spiffed up nicely, she thought with approval. She eyed the oak paneling and the spruce green carpet with its pattern of thistles.

At the desk she smiled at a blond woman with a Scottish accent. *She's a newcomer, I don't know her,* thought Kitt. The realization made her feel odd. This was her hometown, but she was a stranger in it.

She took the brass keys to the back entrance and her room—no plastic card keys for this old-fashioned place—thanked the blond woman, and picked up her bags. She turned from the desk and looked directly into a man's broad chest.

He smelled divinely of expensive aftershave, and the sweater looked like cashmere. Sapphire blue cashmere. She looked up and met the beautiful, enigmatic eyes of Mel Belyle.

Although she knew he was staying here, he'd caught her by surprise. Her heartbeat sped, and her breath felt just as stuck in her throat.

His perfect mouth twitched, as if he might say something. But he was silent, and almost self-consciously he touched his forefinger to his upper lip. There was something shy in that gesture, and it surprised her.

She swallowed and found herself saying, "I'm sorry for what happened this afternoon. You bought me a drink. I'd like to buy you one in return. After all, why not?"

The words sprang from her mouth before she had time to think of them. Instantly, she regretted them. He would of course say no. He would be scathing; she would be resentful, and they would dislike each other more than before.

He kept his finger resting on his upper lip thoughtfully. He looked at her such a long time that she thought he was not going to speak, only snub her. She was ready to spin on her heel and go.

But he said, "I could give you fifty reasons why not. Instead, I'll say it's a good question. Shall we start over, Mitchell?"

She looked up at him. For some reason she felt a smile stealing across her lips. "Let's," she said.

CHAPTER FIVE

NOW WHY THE DEVIL HAD HE said that? He wasn't supposed to talk to her.

But he already had in the airport, by accident, and the accident had turned out to be disastrous. Damage control was in order. Or so Mel told himself, looking into those blue eyes that were so lively—and so lovely.

He must change her image of him—not for his own ego. Of course not. For Fabian's sake and the sake of the assignment.

But part of him wondered if he didn't sympathize with her after listening to Gloria Wall dredge up the Mitchell family scandals. She had implied Kitt's own past was stained. Had the woman spoken truth? Or slander?

But finally, Mel admitted that he was with Kitt because he *wanted* to be. As a lawyer he could think of a hundred reasons to justify this urge. As a man, the desire was reason enough.

Besides, for years Mel had followed Fabian's whims and weird rules. He was smart enough to know when they could and should be broken. He certainly wasn't going to surrender corporate secrets to this woman. He was merely going to repair some wrong impressions.

He looked down at her—Lord, but she was a little thing. She came just to his collarbone. She had her laptop computer slung over one shoulder, her bulging backpack over the other. Its weight made her lean to one side.

"You're listing to starboard," he said. "Can I carry something for you?"

"No thanks. I can handle it myself." She shook her head for emphasis, and the ponytail flashed like silken fire in the lobby's subdued light.

I can handle it myself. He bet that was the motto of her life. She probably had it tattooed on her forehead under her bangs.

They paused at the entrance of the pub. The place was indeed a piece of Scotland transplanted to the Texas Hill Country. Tartans and crossed broadswords ornamented the paneled walls. The sound system played Scottish music. Mel recognized Andy Stewart's voice singing of pining for the love of an elfin queen.

A friendly waitress saw them and called, "Sit anywhere, y'all." Mel nodded. A booth in the far corner promised privacy. He bent to speak in Kitt's ear. "Back there?" Her minty perfume tickled his nostrils. He was both surprised and pleased at the old-fashioned scent.

She nodded. "Fine."

He put his hand on the small of her back to guide her. Although all he touched was her travel vest, it was as if sparks jabbed the palm of his hand, shot up his arm and struck him through the heart.

She stiffened and jerked away slightly, as if she felt the same instantaneous shock. He snatched his hand back, thinking, *What the hell?* He told himself they must have worked up a charge of static electricity crossing the carpet, but he knew it was a lie.

Without touching again, they moved to the booth and slid in gingerly, facing each other. Their corner was secluded and dim. A candle in a pewter holder threw a flickering glow over the table.

The candlelight danced on her face, emphasizing her delicate features, the marvelous hair. Suddenly Mel thought, *I shouldn't be doing this.*

She looked wary, as if she felt the same. He folded his hands on the table, locking his fingers firmly together. He gave her a smile he hoped was businesslike and neutral.

"What I say here is off-the-record, right?" he began. "Just between you and me. It doesn't end up in print."

"Absolutely," she said. "This is a truce."

"Temporary?" he asked. "Or permanent?"

"That's up to you."

He took a deep, uncomfortable breath. "Whichever, I think we need to do some fence-mending."

She tossed him a wry look. "Good fences make good neighbors."

"To help us wall each other out?" he asked. "It has to be done, you know. We have to maintain barriers."

"At least we can do it politely," she said, gazing at the candle flame.

"The bottom line is we're on opposite sides."

She met his eyes with a steadiness that made an odd quiver dance down his spine. "I want to cover *both* sides of the story. But I was told you won't talk to me."

He cocked a skeptical eyebrow. "You'd be fair? I doubt it. It'd be a first where Fabian's concerned. No. You might tell both sides. But you'll tip the scales against Fabian."

Her gaze didn't waver. "Try me. Defend what he's doing. My job's to be objective. I'm willing to listen. I want to."

He remained skeptical. "Then listen to the people around here who *like* the idea of Bluebonnet Meadows. There are plenty of them."

She took the challenge with a gambler's coolness. "Like who? Ralph and Gloria Wall? You were there tonight. I know."

He nodded in appreciation. "Ah. See? You must have an excellent intelligence network already set up here."

"It's a small town," she said. "People talk."

"It seems they do. So tell me—what do you think of the Walls?"

Her expression hardened. The change was subtle, but he saw it. "The Walls? As I said, people talk. And some talk too damn much."

The waitress appeared, order pad in hand and pencil

poised. She had a round face and a ready smile. "Something to drink?" she asked. "The kitchen's closed, so all we've got are chips and salsa, but they're on the house if you want them."

Mel thought of the orgy of cream cheese he'd just escaped at the Walls'. "Food? No thanks. Just a scotch and water."

"A glass of white wine," said Kitt. "The local Chardonnay, please."

"You got it," the waitress said and bustled off.

Mel leaned closer to Kitt. "Who told you where I was tonight?"

Kitt tilted her head. "There's a vineyard nearby. I heard it through the grapevine."

"Cute," he said. "And where were you? At your aunt's? That's the one honest thing you said this afternoon. That you have an aunt."

She folded her arms on the table nonchalantly. "Ah. I suppose Gloria Wall told you that."

"Her name's Nora. She's not much older than you. She owns the Longhorn café and motel. She's married to the McKinneys' foreman."

Kitt maintained her cool. "Hmm. So you're a detective. I hear there's a giant hound hanging around the Baskerville place. You ought to check it out."

"I thought we were mending fences," he said, leaning closer.

She sighed. "Look, the way I treated you today? That wasn't professional. I'm sorry."

"I accept your apology," he said.

"But," she added, spirit glinting in her eyes, "you were *really* obnoxious."

He gritted his teeth. She was right, dammit. "Yes. I was. I apologize, too. I'm not usually like that."

She smiled as if she didn't believe him.

"I'm not," he protested. Good grief, he had all the women he wanted, prettier and more cooperative than she was. He certainly didn't make a habit of picking up strange ones in airports.

She looked him up and down. "You weren't yourself?"

"Exactly," he said. "So just wipe it from your memory, all right?"

"What was wrong with you? Worried about facing off against your brother?" His muscles tensed. How in the hell had she known that? She'd thrown the question into the conversation like a grenade and hadn't even blinked.

"No comment," he said sharply. He was relieved when the jolly waitress reappeared and set down their drinks. "Last call," she said. "Anything else?"

Mel shook his head. Kitt said, "No thanks. And put it on my bill, will you? Room 203."

"You got it, hon." She turned and trotted away.

Mel squinted at Kitt in disbelief. "Room 203? That's right next to me. Did you do that on purpose?"

"Hardly," she said. "How come you're so touchy about your brother?"

"Because he's my brother. I don't talk about him. Period."

She toyed with a strand of hair, winding it around her finger. She said, "This is off the record, remember?"

"On or off," he returned. "I don't talk about him. We're not part of your story."

"That remains to be seen," she said. "How come you're so loyal to Fabian when he wasn't?"

Mel straightened, drawing back in his seat. "You want to talk family? Why don't you tell me about your aunt? I hear you used to be very close. So how come you didn't come back to see her for twelve years?"

It was Kitt's turn to stiffen uneasily. Her face went wary. "My aunt's not part of this story."

He raised his chin skeptically. "Isn't she? The McKinneys sure as hell are. She lives on McKinney property. She's married to their top hand. That café of hers is practically the hub of this town. Everybody on the McKinney side meets there for informal powwows.''

''The Longhorn,'' Kitt countered, ''is where your brother met his new wife. I hear she's a lovely woman. You'd probably like her if you met her. But you don't plan on it, do you?''

He sighed in exasperation and said, ''Let me explain something.''

She narrowed her pretty eyes. ''What?''

''I'm supposed to avoid talking to the press. I'm trying to explain that nicely.''

She raised her chin. ''Do you always do what you're supposed to? You strike me as more independent than that.''

''You used the word 'professional,''' he returned. ''Your profession is to ferret out information. Mine, at present, is to withhold it. Don't knock me for doing my job.''

She gave a sassy shrug. ''Why is Brian Fabian so set on secrecy?''

''It's his nature,'' Mel said. ''And his right.''

''So you're a mouthpiece with nothing to say,'' she said.

''To you. I've got nothing to say to you. And I'm sorry for that.''

''Sorry?'' she said with a little laugh. ''Why?''

''Because under different circumstances—'' He didn't finish the sentence, not even in his own mind. Instead he took a long pull on his drink.

''Under different circumstances, what?'' she challenged.

He set down his glass. ''Nothing. You want the latest information on Bluebonnet Meadows?''

She sat up straighter. ''Of course.''

''I'll give you a brochure. We've got new ones.''

''Really?'' Her voice was sarcastic. ''What do they say?''

''I'll slide one under your door tonight. You can read it in bed.'' His tone was suggestive; he couldn't help it. ''Do you read in bed?''

''Oh, look,'' she said. ''Your airport self is back.''

''Maybe you just bring out the worst in me,'' he said.

"The grapevine says—" she began.

"—the grapevine from the local vineyard?"

She nodded. "It says that you've come to buy more land."

"I don't see any for sale signs up," he said.

"That didn't stop Fabian before," she countered. "He managed to buy up four thousand acres."

"No comment," he said.

"The grapevine also says that when your brother defected, Fabian took it personally. That he's got a vendetta against him. And the people opposing Bluebonnet Meadows."

"No comment," said Mel.

"Why would he bother?" Kitt persisted. "A man that rich? Why does he care if a bunch of ranchers and townspeople throw a few legal roadblocks in his way? Why did he offer all those inflated prices in the first place?"

"No comment. I'm glad we mended fences. Our lines of communication are much more open now." He stood. "Thanks for the drink."

She shot him a baleful glance. "Thanks for all the information."

He turned to go, then paused. Over his shoulder he said, "By the way, *do* you read in bed?"

"You'll never know," she said.

"Pity," he said and walked away.

But he could feel her there behind him in the candlelight, her anger almost crackling in the air. It struck him that if he never learned what she did in bed, it would, indeed, be a pity.

SHE WAS GETTING READY for bed, putting on her nightshirt with the cartoon picture of the Tasmanian Devil. She heard a gentle rustling in the hall. She whirled, looked down and saw a color brochure inching under her door. *Damn.* She stamped to the door and snatched up the brochure.

Its cover photograph showed a kaleidoscope of Texas

wildflowers. A red banner ran across the top of the photo, and white letters spelled out an invitation. CLAIM YOUR PART OF THE TEXAS DREAM...

Smaller black print announced *Bluebonnet Meadows, The Lone Star State's Premiere Planned Community.*

The paper was thick and glossy, the photo perfect, the design excellent. She sat on the edge of the bed and opened the pamphlet. With a start, she realized she did *not* want to read this in bed, on the bed, or near the bed.

She rose and sat instead at the room's small oak desk. She reopened the brochure and read the sales pitch: prime location in the Austin vicinity, beautiful Hill Country scenery, man-made lakes for boating and fishing, golf courses, swimming pools, a clubhouse, even a community stable.

Kitt was surprised to find herself bristling protectively. A map showed how Fabian planned to carve up the land. Three handy sizes of lots, for the well-to-do, the extremely well-to-do, and the obscenely rich.

The hills that had seemed so eerily familiar this afternoon would be studded with houses and mini-ranches. There would be the gated "Golden Community" with lots of an acre apiece. It would cover more than half of the former Hole in the Wall Dude Ranch.

The "Platinum Community" would consist of mini-ranches, 20 to 50 acres. And lastly, the "Diamond Community" would be an exclusive group of small ranches between 75 and 200 acres.

The Best of Texas—At the Right Prices, boasted the text.

Sure, thought Kitt, the right prices—if you happened to have a lot of gold, platinum or diamonds lying around.

Nora had said several model homes had been built on the one-acre lots, the first golf course laid out and graded, the first lake gouged out.

She knew the lake, with its makeshift dam, was a particular source of contention. "With all the rain, people are afraid of flooding," Nora had said. "And Fabian's torn up the land until it looks as if it's been bombed."

But, Kitt thought, Fabian must be confident of winning this turf war. The new brochure had cost him big money— and it *was* new. She had a copy of the older one in her research folder.

She looked at the last page and tensed. It contained an unpleasant surprise. There was another photo of wildflowers and the announcement: *The Miracle Begins! Bluebonnet Meadows—The First Offerings. Phase One.*

Kitt sat up straighter. First Offerings? Phase One? This was a clear indication: Fabian *did* scheme to buy more land.

Why had Mel refused to admit the fact, then put this brochure into her hands? She knew he must have a motive and couldn't stand not knowing. She snatched up the receiver and dialed his room number.

Through the wall, she could hear his phone ringing. It rang six times. She heard the click of it being picked up. His voice was lazy when he said, "Mel Belyle here."

"And Mitchell here," she shot back. "Listen, barrister, I've got some questions for you."

"Sorry to take so long answering," he drawled. "I was getting out of the shower. Oops. Dammit. Dropped the towel. Excuse me a minute."

You over-sexed fiend, she thought in resentment. But she could not quell an image of him, naked and glistening with water. She pictured the wide chest, the broad shoulders, the narrow waist—then her inner censor kicked her and made her stop picturing.

"Ahh," he said. "There. I'm decent again."

I sincerely doubt that, she thought. She said, "Has anybody else in town seen this brochure?"

"Actually yes," he said. "Now that you mention it. I have."

"You know what I mean," she retorted.

"Everyone in town will have seen it by tomorrow," he said. "There's a mass mailing to Realtors all over Texas. And the whole shebang goes on our Internet site at midnight. In about—oh—six minutes. If you're going to make a scoop out of this, you'll have to act fast.''

"You dodged every question I put to you," Kitt accused. "Then you get cute and slide this under my door. Why?"

"A picture is worth ten thousand words," he answered. "Oops. Towel's slipping again. Dammit."

She cursed him under her breath. "Stop telling me about your towel."

"Do you happen to have a safety pin over there?"

"This *thing*—" she waggled the brochure in impotent anger "—clearly says 'First Offerings,' and 'Phase One.' That implies Second Offerings and a Phase Two."

"Does it?" he asked with feigned innocence.

"That must mean Fabian's planning to get more land," she said from between her teeth. "A *lot* more land."

"Pure guesswork on your part."

"Whose land does he think he's going to get?"

"No comment," Mel said.

"And how does he plan to get it when there's none for sale and the ranchers are united against him?"

"I wish this was the kind of hotel that gave you bathrobes. I'm getting chilly. Brr."

"Stop harping on your bare bod," she snapped. *Stop thinking about his bare bod,* she scolded herself. But she couldn't. She imagined him tanned, fit and muscular. He would smell of soap and his skin would be cool and damp to the touch.

"It's not my fault I'm nearly buck naked," he said. "You're the one who got me out of the shower."

"I want to know about Phase Two," she said grimly.

"So far it's a figment of your imagination. But while we're on the phone, let me ask you a question."

"What?" she demanded.

"What quality do you most prefer in a man?"

She sighed in exasperation. What was he getting at? He was maddening. "Straightforwardness. I wish you had an iota of it."

"Ah. My answer would be loyalty. And I hope I have more than an iota. Good night. Sweet dreams."

Click. She grimaced with displeasure. He'd hung up on her. Gritting her teeth, she snatched up her laptop and plugged it into the phone line. She switched on the machine, pulled up her favorite Internet search engine and typed in "Bluebonnet Meadows."

The computer labored in silence for a moment, then her screen filled with a fiesta of color: the yellow, red, and blue of wildflowers. "CLAIM YOUR PART OF THE TEXAS DREAM…"

It was exactly the same as the cover of the brochure. She glanced at her watch. It was two minutes after midnight.

Mel Belyle was toying with her, the fiend. She resisted the desire to throw the brochure at the wall that divided her from him. She could almost hear him laughing.

CAL SLIPPED HIS ARM around Serena's warm, bare shoulder and drew her close. She laid her cheek against his chest, over his still-hammering heart.

They'd just made love so lustily that the headboard of the bed had slammed repeatedly against the wall. Serena had muffled her laughter and warned him to be quieter, but he'd been beyond considering quiet.

"You're awful," she whispered and kissed him between the pecs.

He sighed with pleasure. "Is that an estimate of my performance? Or my character?"

"Your character," she said, her voice almost a purr. "Your performance was fairly spectacular."

"Only fairly?" he asked with mock horror.

"On a scale of one to ten, tonight you were only a twelve," she teased.

"It'll have to do," he said, nuzzling her silky hair. "I'm done spent. Lord, I'd been wanting to do that all night."

"Me, too," she admitted. "I love your brother and sister and their families but…"

"...but it seemed like they'd never go to their own houses," Cal supplied and cuddled her closer to him. "Well, they get to talkin' about this Bluebonnet Meadows mess, and they don't stop. And me with lechery drivin' me up the wall."

"You nearly drove the headboard *through* the wall," she admonished, but stroked his naked chest. "I bet your parents heard. They had to."

The main guest room was next to J.T. and Cynthia's bedroom. Cal had forgotten this fact when his libido eclipsed everything except Serena.

"Well, hell," he answered, "it's not like they don't know we do it. Those twins didn't get brought here by a stork. Mmm, you smell good. What kinda flower is it you smell like?"

"Lily of the valley." She kept stroking his chest. "Cal?" She said it with hesitancy.

"What, sugar?"

"Your father seems edgy with you. Why?"

"Daddy always gets edgy with me," he said. "He's always glad to see me the first day, the second day he gets critical, the third day he still thinks I'm eighteen and a dropout. It's habit, is all."

She raised herself on her elbow and looked at him. He could just make out her face in the dim glow of the nightlight. Her long hair hung like a thick veil, tickling his bare arm.

She said, "It's more than that. You came here to help. He sounded as if he *wanted* you to come help. He *needs* you. But sometimes he acts almost—resentful."

A pang twisted Cal's heart, but only briefly. He was not his father's favorite and never would be. He'd accepted this from boyhood. He tried to reassure Serena, who always took things harder than he did.

He touched her smooth cheek. "This Bluebonnet Meadows gripes him, sugar. He'd like to wade in and fight it out single-handed. He don't want to admit he could use help. He's proud.''

"Sometimes I don't think he likes it that you have more money than he does," Serena said, bending closer.

"Aw, it's just he's always been the alpha wolf. You know.''

"It's not like you lord it over him. And it's not as if he hasn't benefited. They all have—Tyler and Lynn, too.''

He laid his finger on her soft lips. "Shh," he said quietly. "Don't say such things.''

He had loaned his father money; he had refinanced Tyler when the winery had trouble; he had helped Lynn to increase her string of beloved horses. He begrudged none of them, and he didn't give a damn if they ever paid him back. What good was money if you couldn't use it to help people you loved?

Cal wasn't introspective, but he wasn't blind to nuance. Neither his father nor his brother liked to be beholden to anyone. Perhaps *especially* to him.

"I have to say it," Serena objected. "Your father should be grateful to you.''

"Honey, he's grateful in his way. He's just touchy. When this Fabian fella gets stopped, Daddy's gonna be fine.''

"You," she said, caressing his collarbone, "are an incurable optimist.''

"I'm getting optimistic now," he said. "Why don't you move that hand a little lower? Maybe I'm not so spent as I thought.''

"Cal, I'm serious. Tyler's mood seems dark, too. And Ruth's not herself. Do you think they're having trouble again?''

This sobered him. "I don't know. Did she say anything?''

"No. She just seems—subdued. And so does Cynthia.''

He twined his fingers in Serena's soft hair. "Cynthia's worried about Daddy. She always has since he was sick.''

"Cal?" she said his name with such sweet earnestness that a fresh surge of love went through him.

"What, sugar?"

"You talked to Nick Belyle. Do you think you can stop Fabian?"

"I sure as hell aim to try. He's got a whole lot of money, though. Which puts me in a damn strange position. I'm just rich enough to make my family uncomfortable, but not rich enough to be sure I can help them. Fabian's pretty much out of my class."

"You're in a class by yourself," she said fondly.

He drew her nearer. "Remember what I asked you about movin' that hand?"

She laughed. "This time don't make the bed bang the wall."

But he got carried away, as usual. The headboard thumped and thudded and thumped.

J.T. HAD ALMOST BEEN ASLEEP, then the damn racket next door snapped him wide-awake again. He lay in the darkness gritting his teeth.

How long could those two keep at it? This was the second time tonight—Cal was randy as a stallion.

Cynthia lay beside him, motionless and silent. Her back was to him, the sheet and cover pulled tightly around her body as if insulating herself from him. He didn't blame her.

She'd come to bed in her expensive ivory colored nightgown with the see-through lace top. It was his favorite. She'd put on the perfume he'd given her, the French stuff that usually drove him crazy.

She smelled wonderful, a complex fragrance of flowers and exotic spice. She felt wonderful, her skin smooth and warm, and the fabric of her nightdress so silky it was slithery.

Snuggling intimately against him, she'd whispered, "It's nice to have you to myself at last. Umm."

Her voice was full of invitation, but he was dog-tired. Desire didn't stir in his blood or his imagination or anywhere else. He loved his wife, but he'd responded to her as if he had ice in his veins instead of hot red blood.

She rubbed her nose against his shoulder, ran her hand over his chest. Her fingers toyed with the top button of his pajama shirt. "Why'd you start wearing pajamas?" she teased. "You never used to."

"I get chilly," he said. "And I'm tired. It was a long night." He faked a yawn, although in truth he *was* tired, bone weary and wracked by apprehension.

Her hand went still. She no longer toyed with the button. "J.T.," she said in concern. She put her hand on his arm. "What's wrong? You're not yourself lately."

You're not yourself lately. He knew what that meant. It was criticism. *You've got no interest in sex lately. You're not the man you used to be.*

"Nothing's wrong," he muttered. "I said I'm tired. I shouldn't have had that last glass of wine."

At that point in the conversation, the bed in the guest room began bumping against the wall—for the first time.

In former times J.T. would have grinned ruefully, and likely as not reached for Cynthia. He would have said something ironic such as, "Only amateurs make that much noise. Behold—the Master."

Now each thud sounded like mockery of the man he used to be. J.T. would love to take his wife in his arms, to be driven wild by hunger for her. His sexual desire had been fading steadily over the last two months, and tonight it seemed to have vanished completely.

Maybe his drive was gone because his manhood was failing. The thought sickened him. What if he got Cynthia excited, then couldn't satisfy her? He could not face risking it.

She had taken her hand from his chest. Now she lay beside him in the darkness, listening to the damnable bumping and thudding from next door. The longer it lasted, the worse J.T. felt.

Finally, mercifully, it ceased. Silence fell. He imagined

his son and daughter-in-law giggling and cuddling in the intimate quiet. Beside him, Cynthia sighed. "Maybe you should see a doctor."

J.T. tensed. "I'm not due for a checkup for months," he almost snapped.

Cynthia lay gazing up at the ceiling. "I don't mean Nate Purdy. I mean a specialist."

J.T. bristled. "A specialist? What's wrong with Nate Purdy? He's been my doctor for forty years."

Cynthia didn't even turn her head to speak. "I don't know how frank you'd be with Nate. You're so—macho. You always hate to admit anything's wrong."

"Nothing's wrong," J.T. countered. "I told you. I'm *tired,* dammit." He shouldn't have sworn, but he felt cornered and defensive.

"You're taking too much on yourself," she answered. "You're wearing yourself out. You're anxious. You're on edge. Tonight you just picked at your supper. I worry about your heart."

J.T. didn't want to think about his heart. He'd had a heart attack almost eight years ago. He'd taken good care of himself since then. Nate Purdy had told him he could live to be a hundred if he was careful.

Cynthia said, "You were eager for Cal to come home. Now that he's here, you're touchy as an old bear. Why don't you just sit back and let him handle this thing with Brian Fabian? You and I could go away for a while, even have a sort of second honeymoon—"

"Cal doesn't live here anymore," J.T. retorted. "He hasn't even lived in this country for the past six months. He's been in *Australia,* for God's sake. I've been involved in this thing from day one, and I plan to stay involved."

"Cal has a network of connections," Cynthia argued. "That partnership of his, Three Amigos—those men are powerful. They can put him in touch with people who are expert in these matters. He—"

"Look," J.T. said with impatience. "I know you were a

big high muckity-muck banker in Boston. And I'm a lowly cattleman. But I'm not so ignorant and feeble that I have to turn over the reins yet. And why are you talking just about Cal? Tyler's got a share in this, too. Lynn, as well.''

"There," Cynthia accused. "See how edgy you are? All I'm trying to say is that I love you and I'm concerned about you.''

"If you're concerned about me, let me sleep," J.T. said, more sharply than he should have. "I've told you three times, I'm *tired*."

"J.T.," she said, "sooner or later we're going to have to talk about this.''

"Make it later, will you?" he said. He turned his back to her and pulled the sheet up to his ears.

"I mean it," she said, her voice tremulous. "We *have* to talk.''

"Good night, Cynthia," he said with weary finality. She got up and swept into the bathroom. He heard the sound of running water and knew she was taking a sleeping pill. She came back to bed, but she slept on the opposite edge, as far from him as possible.

At last her breathing became even, and her body seemed to relax. He thought of all the things that preyed on his mind. He *hadn't* felt well lately. His sex drive had diminished to nothing. He was facing the fight of his life, and his temper was frayed to tatters.

Sometimes it scared him. He *should* talk to Cynthia. But there were some things a man didn't admit, and there were things he didn't talk about. A man had to act like a man, dammit.

It was then that the noises next door had started the second time. J.T. lay there and listened to the sound of his son doing what he feared he could no longer do himself.

CAL FELL BACK against the pillow exhausted. "Oooh," he said in happy exhaustion.

Serena cuffed his bare shoulder in mock punishment. "You promised you'd be *quiet* this time."

He caught her hand and laced his fingers through hers. "Sugar, I'd've had to concentrate on two things at once to do that. And the only thing on my mind was you."

"Your parents will think we're terrible," she said, but she settled beside him, snuggling close. "And that we do this every night."

"We pretty much do," mused Cal.

"Not twice," she said with a wicked little laugh.

"Sweetheart, the spirit is often willin', but the flesh is weak."

"Tomorrow," she said, "I want you to move this bed. I feel like we have a kettledrum for accompaniment."

"Oh, I think Daddy and Cynthia get it on pretty regular."

"I hope you're right," she said. "Your father does look tired this trip."

"Daddy?" Cal said sleepily. He'd noticed it himself, but he'd decided not to pay mind to it. "Yeah. But he's the original iron man."

"He'd like to think so," Serena said. "He's pushing himself awfully hard. Maybe too hard. I think Cynthia has reason to worry."

"He'll be okay." Cal dropped a drowsy last kiss on her forehead and began to settle into sleep. But sleep didn't come. He mused on Serena's words. He'd never worried deeply about J.T. In his mind his father was immortal and eternally strong.

But of course he was mortal, and strength had its limits. *I've got to do something,* Cal thought. *I've got to help. Whether he likes it or not.*

CHAPTER SIX

MEL'S SLEEP TEEMED with frustrating dreams that he couldn't recall on waking. He shook his head to clear it, threw back the sheet and staggered to the window.

The sun was just rising, tinting the eastern sky pink and golden. The buildings of Crystal Creek seemed at rest, as if content to drowse through the dawn. The streets were empty, the sidewalks deserted.

He turned, stretching and running his hand through his hair. He was dressed in blue silk briefs and a T-shirt. He'd never slept naked. In boyhood he'd felt too shy, and it was an ingrained habit.

"What's the matter with you?" women sometimes asked when he got out of his bed to slip back into his shorts and shirt.

"I can't fall asleep undressed," he'd say, trying to laugh it off. "It's my only fetish." One of the models he'd dated had spent time in therapy. It miffed her that that he always put clothes back on after making love.

"What's your problem?" she'd demand. "I think you've got intimacy issues. You fear being uncovered. What are you ashamed of? You've got a nearly perfect body. I know bodies."

Well, she hadn't known him. Finally she'd said, "You've got to choose. Me or your shorts." He chose his shorts. They didn't try to psychoanalyze him.

He walked into the bathroom and splashed water on his face. He'd shave later. This morning he was going to run.

He hadn't run all summer—it had been too hot, he'd gotten out of the habit. And now in the mirror his "nearly perfect" body looked a few pounds too heavy around the middle.

Worse, yesterday he'd been outsprinted in the airport by a woman—a very small woman, at that. Afterward, still fuming from the shame of it, he'd stopped at a mall in Dallas. He'd bought running shoes, shorts and a few extra T-shirts—items he hadn't bothered to pack. The redhead was a wake-up call from the gods of fitness. It was time to get back in shape.

Besides, he was becoming antsy about taking up Fabian's business where his brother had abandoned it. For the first time, he felt a wave of true uneasiness about Nick.

Quickly he dressed. He would run until he burned away all doubts and misgivings. He'd do a few miles out in the country, and he knew exactly where he wanted to go—the freshly cut main road that ran through the Bluebonnet Meadows development.

He'd see firsthand exactly how far Fabian had gotten before the local yokels shut him down. And he wanted to look over the controversial dam. He snatched his wallet and car keys and headed for the parking lot.

The western sky was clouding up, but the sun was still visible. As he drove, it rose higher, and he watched as the hills changed color, brightening under the gold of full morning.

A few solitary hawks cruised beneath the mounting clouds. Then a far larger bird flew out of the scrub beside the highway and flapped across the road—a wild turkey.

He smiled to himself. He'd never seen a turkey in the wild before. Then, in a stony field, he saw a small herd of longhorn sheep. They fled as the car approached, nimbly trotting up a narrow limestone shelf and disappearing among the boulders.

Beautiful country, all right, he told himself. No wonder everybody wanted a piece of it.

But then, the billboards loomed into sight. "The Future

Site of Bluebonnet Meadows!'' One trumpeted. Another announced: ''Austin's Finest Planned Community!''

The signs sprouted out of the land as if planted there by aliens with a rotten sense of decor. Lots for Sale! Tour Our Model Homes! Prices For Everyone! Share the Dream!

Somehow, the billboards irked Mel. They marked Fabian's victory so far and promised of greater triumphs to come. But against the subtle hues of the landscape, they looked garish and out of place, and there were too damn many of them.

He'd have to tell Fabian. *Memo: billboards need to be rethought. They make plastic flamingoes look good.*

A barricade blocked the entrance to the main road into Bluebonnet Meadows. More signs. Not inviting, but hostile: KEEP OUT! TRESPASSERS WILL BE PROSECUTED! AUTHORIZED PERSONNEL ONLY!

He considered himself Authorized Personnel. He parked beside the barricades and got out. Beyond the sawhorses and yellow tape, he saw the new road stretched across the landscape like a barely healed scar.

The ground on either side was still raw and churned. Heavy equipment had gouged a confusion of tracks into the denuded earth. The road took a curve and disappeared between a pair of low, stony mountains.

Mel stared at those mountains as he stretched before running. Beyond them lay the first of the model homes—and the last of the Hole in the Wall Dude Ranch.

Fabian's planners had ordered most of the ranch's outbuildings torn down. The wrecking ball had smashed them, the bulldozers had flattened their remains. All would be replaced with structures that matched the architectural overview.

Only the original lodge and ranch house would stay—as a rec center and sales office. But they would be gutted and redone to conform to the master plan. Everything in Bluebonnet Meadows must match.

Mel stepped over a sawhorse and started down the road

at a medium jog. On either side of the concrete ribbon, the muddy earth was stabbed with surveyors' flags, orange triangles wagging in the breeze.

But the morning air was cool and sweet in his lungs, and the faint sunshine warmed his bare arms and pumping legs. The muscles in his calves and thighs tingled pleasantly.

He followed the road's curve. A surprised jackrabbit sprinted off into the nearest patch of mesquite. *Sorry, buddy,* Mel thought in amusement. *No harm meant. This place is big enough to hold us all.*

But the curve took a sharp bend, and the view worsened suddenly, almost violently. Mel slowed. Before him was a broken vista of construction mixed with destruction.

Oh, hell, he thought. He stopped, breathing heavily. For a stretch of twenty acres, the countryside looked as if it had been shelled. Ragged sockets of ground were littered with the debris of shattered buildings.

The injunction must have stopped work before these pits could be filled. Steam shovels and bulldozers stood idle, like great yellow dinosaurs rendered motionless by the spell of the law.

High on one mountain slope, the ranch house stood. Its empty windows looked like dead eyes, and only the skeleton of the porch remained. On a plateau below it, the lodge had a similar air of mutilation.

Mel shook his head. Anybody who had loved this place would be sick at the sight of it. He wiped the sweat from his forehead, then put his hands on his hips. On the flat, in the valley below the lodge, stood five houses, only one of them finished. Each reigned over its own muddy acre. No trees graced the yards, and no grass.

The wind had risen, making a sound like mourning.

Then he heard the sound of quick, light steps behind him. He turned to see Kitt Mitchell. Her running shorts and sleeveless T-shirt were bright yellow, and so was her terry headband.

She pattered toward him with lightning speed. Drawing

up to him, she stopped, not even out of breath. She stood with one hip cocked and her arms akimbo. He looked into her blue, mocking eyes.

Perspiration gleamed on her skin, and although her fiery hair was pinned atop her head, tendrils had escaped and danced insouciantly in the breeze.

"Hi," she said with bright, false innocence.

He glared as fiercely as he could. "You snuck up on me."

She wasn't fazed. She looked around the ravished landscape. "Nice rock pile," she commented. "Who did it? Fabian's convict labor?"

He crossed his arms. "You're trespassing."

"Am I?" she asked.

"Yes. This is private property. Leave."

"Let me rest a minute," she said, although she clearly wasn't a bit tired.

"Did you follow me here?" he demanded.

"No. I followed the pretty signs. There were so many of them. All pointing this way. Where I found you surveying the work of your master. He's done wonders with the place."

Mel resisted grinding his teeth. Moments before, he himself hadn't liked the look of Bluebonnet Meadows. Yet he felt compelled to defend it. "You can't build up without tearing down first."

"Did he have to tear down so *much?*"

He looked her over. She seemed so full of life and spirit that she practically sent electrical sparks popping into the air. He remembered the words DeJames had quoted: "Some women break records. Some break hearts. Kitt Mitchell does both."

He bet she had broken hearts, all right. He envisioned them as an endless string of torn red valentines trailing behind her, and he should take the image as a warning.

"I'm not talking to you about this," he said.

"Okay," she said lightly. "Let's just take in the view."

She looked off at the five model houses in the middle

distance. Each had a deep hole gouged into the earth behind it. She said, "I love to see the way the morning sunlight hits an open septic tank. Don't you?"

"No comment," Mel muttered. The pits had been dug for the tanks, but they hadn't yet been placed. It was another action the Concerned Citizens of Claro County had stalled.

She brushed a strand of gleaming hair from her forehead and kept her gaze on the houses. "Nice the way they're all going to resemble one another. Just a little difference here and there. Individualism is vastly overrated. Conformity—it's a good thing."

"No comment," he repeated.

"I can't wait to see five hundred of them," she continued. "Like clones. Marching in lock step across the landscape. There will be a landscape, won't there? Will Mr. Fabian allow grass to grow?"

"No comment," he said for the third time. He studied her legs. Nice. Too nice. He crossed his arms more tightly and looked away.

"That was a pretty brochure you gave me," she said. "There were designer's drawings of the five types of houses allowed. They seemed to have grass in the yards. Or was it Astroturf? So much tidier. It doesn't do sloppy things like grow."

He stared at the land around them. It looked like a cross between a battlefield and a moonscape. Most construction sites did at some point, and she must know it. She was trying to needle him into replying.

He turned and stared at her. "You got straight A's at Stobbart. And straight A's at Georgetown. Except for chemistry II. What happened?"

She stiffened slightly. Her eyes flashed into higher alertness. "How do you know that?"

"I've read your transcripts," Mel said with a smirk. *That ought to slow her down,* he thought.

It didn't. "And I've read yours," she said. "At Yale you

got straight A's. But only an A minus in world geography. What was the problem?''

The problem had been a blonde. She'd had topography more interesting than any country. A beautiful girl. *Very tall,* he reminded himself. *Unlike this sassy elf.*

''Probably a blonde,'' she said. ''I've read that you're partial to blondes. Tall ones. Models.''

He shot her a killing glance. He didn't know who all her boyfriends or lovers had been, but he'd know soon. De-James was as thorough as he was tireless. ''Look,'' he said, cocking his head. ''This has been delightful. But I have to go. So do you. Off the property.''

Her eyes traveled to his feet. ''Your shoes look new. Shouldn't you break them in before you run?''

He pointed east. He did it with a great deal of authority. ''That's the way back to the highway. Take it.''

''If you're going to keep running, I should go with you,'' she said, tossing her hair from her eyes.

''No, you shouldn't. Scat. Scram. Begone. Avaunt. Shoo.''

''I've got Band-Aids,'' she said, patting the pouch fastened to her belt. ''And water. I *always* carry emergency supplies. You could die of thirst out there in the man-made wasteland. Nothing but swamp mud to drink.''

He stretched, getting ready to head west, toward the model houses and past them to the lake. ''I could call the sheriff to come get you, you know.''

''No,'' she pointed out. ''You don't have your phone. You left it in your car. I peeked.''

''I can get a court order to keep you away from me,'' he warned.

''Not now, you can't,'' she said with a smile. ''Where are you going? To see the dam? I know Fabian's engineers swear it'll hold. People around here aren't so sure.''

He turned from her, his patience nearly gone. ''Goodbye,'' he said and set out down the road at a brisk trot.

She followed, her legs pumping swiftly, and she was at his side, smiling up at him. "I'll go with you."

He'd started relatively slow, but he'd show her. "You can't keep up," he jibed.

"Yes, I can," she said with infuriating confidence.

Impossible, he thought. He opened his stride and took off like a cheetah.

KITT PUSHED HERSELF to keep up. She guessed him for a long-distance runner, and he couldn't keep going at that pace long. He was clearly out of practice and already favoring his right foot.

She had a killer sprint, and she used it to close the distance between them. She grinned at him, although it took effort. "Hi, again," she said.

He didn't answer, only increased his pace. She did, too, though it hurt. Her lungs burned, her thighs and calves strained. She gave him a sidelong glance. He was angry. Goody.

A film of sweat glistened on his bare skin, and very nice skin it was. He was one of those smooth, golden men who wasn't all fuzzy with body hair. He was tanned, and so muscled that his arms seemed sculpted.

The wind tousled his dark hair over his forehead and frowning brows. His expression was rigid with the intensity of his desire to shake her off. But his breath was growing more ragged, and his gait less smooth.

I'll stick with you if it kills me, she thought. He was so much taller that she had to take two steps for every one of his, but she could do it. She *would* do it. She was a competitor.

Unfortunately, so was he. Suicidally so, she began to fear. Her heart drummed crazily, and her pulses banged in her temples. But then she got a second wind, a kind of glow, a sense of freedom in motion.

A lightness filled her, and her legs began to move of their

own accord. A glow of well-being seemed to surround her. For a moment, it seemed she could run forever.

It was at this very moment Mel broke down. His stride wobbled, then broke. They were by the last model house, and he stumbled, nearly fell. He slowed to a lurching walk, forcing air into his lungs with great gasps.

He clamped one hand to his ribs, as if a stitch ripped his side. He hobbled to the concrete porch of the unfinished house. He sat down heavily on the lowest step, grimacing with pain.

Kitt slowed until she was running in place and watched him. He doubled up, one hand still clutching his side, the other rubbing the calf of his left leg. Sweat had soaked and darkened his burnt-orange shirt so that it plastered against his torso, showing every muscle.

He was clearly so miserable that Kitt had to feel sorry for him. She jogged over to him. He groaned and folded himself over in anguish. She paced back and forth in front of him to cool down. But she kept her eyes on him, worried. At last she said, "Are you okay?"

He glanced up at her, his face glistening with perspiration, his wet hair hanging over his brow. "I'm just dandy," he rasped, then his face twisted with new pain.

"Stitch in your side?" she asked sympathetically. Well, she thought, a stitch wouldn't kill him. He'd be fine in a few minutes. But he also had a death grip on his left leg, and the calf muscle looked rigid as stone.

"Charley horse, too?" she asked, still pacing. She'd seen such cramps reduce strong men to tears. His eyes were dry, but his jaw muscles were tightened with the effort not to show the full extent of his pain.

She dropped on her knees beside him. "Here," she said, massaging his calf. "Let me do it. I'm an expert."

"Go away," he ordered, his teeth gritted. But after she kneaded the cramp for half a minute, he stopped resisting and let her take over.

Kitt had strong hands, and she'd massaged hundreds of

leg cramps in her time, her teammates', her running friends' and her own. She knew how to press and deeply massage the spasming knot.

"Oh, God," he finally said in relief and collapsed backward onto the concrete stairs, his arms spread out. His chest still heaved up and down, but not as spasmodically. His muscle had relaxed under her probing and stroking, but she kept working on it.

He had good legs, lean and strong, with not an ounce of spare flesh. Then she glanced further down and saw that his foot twitched oddly. She took it in her hands and turned it slightly.

"You idiot," she scolded, "you're bleeding, too." Dark blood was creeping up the back of his sock.

"I like to bleed," he panted. "It's a hobby of mine. I did it on purpose."

"You're insane," she said, unlacing his shoe. "I bet you've got a blister the size of a poker chip."

"A dinner plate," he corrected. "Stop undressing me. I'll call a cop."

"Call away," she retorted, pulling off the shoe. The inside was stained with blood. She rolled down the sock and winced at the sight of the blister. It wasn't as big as a poker chip, but it would do. "Good grief," she grumbled, "you had to *feel* this. Why didn't you stop?"

"It would have given you too much satisfaction," he said, still lying on his back. "Go ahead. Gloat."

In truth she felt no satisfaction, only concern. And a bit of mild wonder. *She* couldn't have run like this. She unzipped her belt pack and ripped open a foil packet containing an antiseptic swab. It made a small metallic tearing sound.

"What was that?" he asked. "A condom? Now you're going to take advantage of me? Oh, God, the shame of it."

She fought back a smile. "No such luck. This is going to sting. Try to be brave."

She washed his wound, and he didn't flinch. He only muttered, "The joys of masochism."

The blister was large but not deep. She took out a Band-Aid, tore off its wrapper and put the strip on the back of his ankle. "Sit up," she ordered. "I'll give you a drink." He raised himself gingerly to a sitting position, while she took her water bottle from her belt. She uncapped it and handed it to him. "Don't drink too fast," she warned.

"I know, I know," he groused. He took the bottle from her and took several small, slow swallows.

He handed the water back to her, and their fingers brushed. His eyes met hers. "Happy now?"

Again the mystery in his eyes jolted her. Looking into them was like falling into something so deep and paradoxical that it was endless. A woman could get trapped there forever.

Her stomach muscles tensed, as if she were standing on the edge of an abyss. She looked away quickly and shrugged. "Happy about what?"

"You won. You ran me into the ground. You are victorious. I, supposedly, am humbled."

"I'm not happy you're hurt," she muttered. She took a swig of the water and stared at the barren mud. "I'm just surprised you'd be so stupid."

"It wasn't stupidity. It was a matter of pride."

"Male pride? Same difference," she said, offering the bottle again.

"Touché," he said, taking it from her. "I was stupid." He tilted it back and took another swallow, a longer one.

She stole a sideways glimpse. He was recovering fast. He didn't look like an exhausted Manhattan lawyer. He looked like a classic Greek athlete catching his breath after a well-run race.

He set the bottle between them and started putting on his stained sock.

"You're speedy," he said grudgingly. "But you're a short-distance runner. You couldn't have kept up."

"I didn't have to, did I?" she said sweetly.

"So what did you run?" he asked, lacing up the offending shoe. "I'd guess you for dashes. And relays."

She capped the water bottle and thrust it back into its holder. He was right on both counts. She only nodded in reply.

She turned to him. "What about you? Long distance?"

"No comment," he said, tying the knot.

So we're back to that, are we? Stonewalling. As usual. She wasn't put off. "I'd take you for a long-distance man. You've got that air. The loneliness of the long-distance runner."

He looked at her sharply. "What's that mean?"

His defensive tone surprised her. Had she struck a nerve?

She lifted a shoulder, feigning indifference. "*The Loneliness of the Long Distance Runner.* It was a movie. British. I saw it on TV a long time ago. It was about a kid who was an outsider. Poor. In reform school. But he was a great runner. So the powers-that-be gave him privileges."

He no longer met her eyes. She followed his gaze to the horizon, the rim of the earth was still green. Fabian's crews hadn't struck there—yet.

Then she gazed up at the steeper of the two mountains, the one opposite the Hole in the Wall house and lodge. She blinked in surprise. "The shape's changed. The top is flat. It didn't used to be. Good grief, they must have dynamited it. Is he going to build even up there?"

He didn't answer. She stared in consternation at the mountain, once so familiar to her. It was the place where she and Nora had carried all the books that long-ago summer. She could still see the narrow natural path that led to the hermit's cave, although the cave itself was hidden by foliage.

She shook her head. "Fabian beheads mountains. He creates lakes. Who does he think he is—God?"

Mel stood up. "I wish I'd made it to the lake. I'd jump in it. Which would suit you just fine, I know."

Kitt squinted up at him, again puzzled by his reaction. "Is that one of the things you're here to do? Fight that suit about the water rights?"

"No comment," he said, his gaze still fastened on something far away.

"That lake fills by diverting a major underground stream," she said. "The ranches downstream suffer. I can't believe Fabian really thought he could pull it off."

"No comment." Weariness mixed with impatience in his voice. He took a few steps, favoring his right foot.

"Are you starting back?" she asked. "Maybe you should rest longer."

"Thanks for the first aid," he said. He turned his back on her and began to limp toward the highway. His tall figure looked like a dark cut-out against the swiftly clouding sky.

She bit her lip, concern mixed with frustration. She rose and caught up with him. "I'll walk with you," she said.

He sighed in exasperation. "You've done quite enough."

"Your leg might cramp up again," she said, undeterred. "You might fall down here and bake to death in the sun."

A garter snake slithered across the road and into the bleak waste of mud. "I envy snakes," Mel grumbled. "Their shoes never hurt."

"Snakes. That brings us back to your boss. Does Fabian *really* think he can claim that water underground?" she persisted. "Jeez, how many political contributions will that take? And how many high-priced lawyers like you?"

He didn't answer. He didn't even say "No Comment." Looking both stoic and disgusted, he stayed silent all the way back to the cars.

She pretended not to notice. She kept asking him questions, hard ones. How had Fabian gotten as many permits as soon as he had? Whose palms had he greased? If he intended to buy land, whose did he want? How much would he pay for it? How hard would he fight? Why was he always so damn secretive?

But Mel obstinately said nothing. His mouth set at a grim

angle, he just kept walking, staring straight ahead. He walked faster than she could have imagined, given his raw heel. Sometimes she had to break into a little trot to catch up, but catch up she did.

When they reached the cars, he unlocked the blue sedan's door, then stood and gazed at her a moment. Smiling ironically, he gave her a mock bow of farewell.

"See you soon," she promised.

He made no answer. He got into the car and drove off, leaving her in a drift of dust. She stared after him, vowing she could be just as stubborn as he could. She knew that this was absolutely true.

What she didn't understand was why, now that he was gone, she suddenly felt so lonely.

MEL SWORE as he pulled into the hotel parking lot. He could see her, a block behind him, just rounding the corner. She'd followed him the whole way, even when he'd speeded.

He slammed the car door shut and stalked, limping, to the hotel's private back door. He unlocked it and took the back stairs to the second floor.

He wanted to get into his room before she caught up with him again. Good lord, she was like one of those Furies out of mythology that would pursue a man to his death.

He climbed the steps two at a time even though his legs ached like hell. He should have been able to outrun her. He was out of practice, that was all. In a few days he'd have his edge back.

She'd never overtake him again. She'd collapse in defeat, and they'd carry her off on a stretcher. To rub it in, he'd bring her flowers in the hospital. She would lie wanly on her bed and apologize. "I'm sorry," she would say. "You're so much better than I am."

This pleasant fantasy was interrupted when he reached the second floor. He saw a man standing by his door, waiting.

Recognition seared through Mel like a fatal bullet.

He could not smile or sneer. His face felt paralyzed. The initial shock fled, but a coldness like death filled him.

But his brother could smile, just like always—that engaging, innocent choirboy smile.

"Hello, Mel," said Nick.

CHAPTER SEVEN

"So," MEL SAID. "This is your new job? You clean the halls here?"

"No," Nick said. "I came to see you. We should talk."

Mel was tired, out of patience, and his whole body ached. The sight of his brother sickened him. It was as if a claw seized and twisted his stomach. Yet there stood Nick, oozing the old charm as if that would fix everything.

"Move," Mel ordered. "We've got nothing to say. I don't know you any more."

Nick, still leaning against Mel's door, crossed his arms. "I heard you went out dressed for running. Still on the run, Mel-Boy?"

Mel had always hated that nickname. "Get the hell out of my way."

"I figured you'd be back around now," Nick said. "I didn't want to buttonhole you in a public place. So I came here."

"You have somebody spying on me here?" Mel challenged.

"It's a small town," Nick said. "News moves at the speed of light. People are watching you. Yes. They watched me when I came."

"Fine. Now move. Am I going to have to *throw* you out of my way?"

"Ask me inside," Nick said. "Talk to me. How's Mom?"

"She's heartbroken, you bastard. Move, or I swear to God I'll hit you."

Nick smiled his seraph's smile. "Go ahead. I won't hit back."

Mel swore to himself. Of course not. The old trick. Nick never hit back; he knew nothing infuriated Mel more. Still, Mel doubled his hand into a fist, aching to take a swing at that smug, knowing face.

"Don't make a scene, Mel-Boy," Nick purred. "We've got an audience."

Nick's head whirled and he saw, to his disgust, Kitt Mitchell at the top of the stairs. She stood motionless, her alert blue eyes taking in everything.

How long has she been there? How much has she heard? Mel seized Nick by the shoulder. "All right," he snarled, "get inside, say what you've got to say, then get out." He jammed the key into the lock, shoved the door open and half-pushed Nick inside.

He stole one last look at Kitt, her headband off now, her hair loose and tousled. He slammed the door.

"Cute redhead," Nick murmured. "One of your conquests? She doesn't seem like your type."

"She's a reporter," Mel said from between his teeth. "I don't talk to her. You shouldn't, either. You signed nondisclosure agreements."

"I know what I signed," Nick answered. He put his thumbs in his pockets. He was wearing black boots, jeans and a white shirt of Western cut with the sleeves rolled up. Very urban cowboy.

"You signed. But you disclosed information anyway," Mel accused. "You put Fabian in a vulnerable position."

Nick shrugged carelessly. "I said why he wanted the land. It didn't stop him from getting it. It didn't alert the competition. There *was* no competition. Nobody else was crazy enough to offer the prices he did."

"There's competition, dammit, and you know it," Mel snapped. "You're part of it. You *married* into it. Now all these cowboys are throwing monkey wrenches into the works."

Nick cocked his head, unimpressed. "They'd have done it anyway."

"Not as soon," Mel hissed. "You gave them warning. A head start. I saw Bluebonnet Meadows this morning. Everything's at a standstill."

A shadow of regret crossed Nick's face. "Looks like hell, doesn't it?"

Mel warned, "If you spill any more, if you work with these people, you'll be disbarred and fined. You could even go to prison."

Nick raised one dark eyebrow philosophically. "I know. Fabian's got me tied up for a year. After that, Mel-Boy, I'm my own man. It's a good feeling, being your own man. You'll never know it, though, will you?"

A cold fury spread through Mel. "You can't blab about Fabian, *ever*," he said. "That's one confidentiality clause you signed for a lifetime. You *ever* talk about him, and he'll crush you like a cockroach."

"Why would I want to talk about him?" Nick countered. "He's not very interesting. He's got his money and his women and his ventures and his vendettas. Every interest he's got—you can count on four fingers."

"That's not how Ma sees it," Mel argued. Mentally he kicked himself for using their old childish name for Minnie.

Nick, of course, caught it. "Is *Ma* proud you've come out here to put me in my place?"

Mel turned away in distaste. "I came out here to finish what you wouldn't. This was one of Fabian's pet projects."

"Yeah," Nick sneered. "And I could never figure out why."

"You know why," Mel retorted. "This location is pure gold. Fabian had the vision to see it. And Mom's humiliated that you turned on him."

Nick only smiled. "Mom's a great gal. But with Fabian, she sees only what she wants to see. He's like a son to her, one of us."

"What do you mean 'us'?" Mel shot back. "You're not family anymore."

Nick gazed at him mildly. "Did Mom say that?"

"I said it, and it goes."

"Mom would like my wife if she met her. She really would."

"*If* she met her. But she didn't come to the wedding, did she?"

"She was sick," Nick answered.

"She was sick, all right," Mel said with vehemence. "Over you. Physically ill, Nick. She felt you dishonored us."

"Dishonored," Nick said contemptuously.

"Fabian saved us." Mel's voice shook with passion. "He made us. What would we have been without him?"

Nick's nostrils flared. "We weren't stupid, any of us. We would have made something of ourselves."

"You, maybe," Mel countered. "Me? I'm not so sure. Jack? Jack would have probably married that girl from Missouri if Fabian hadn't—"

"Jack *loved* that girl from Missouri," Nick flung at him. "Fabian had no right to meddle in that. Neither did Ma."

"Jack was eighteen years old, for God's sake. And what about when Ma needed a pacemaker when we were in college? Could we have taken care of her? No, it was Fabian. We owe him, Nicky. We owe him big. But you kicked him in the teeth."

Nick made a sound of disgust. "I didn't want this to be personal."

"Tough," Mel said. "It's personal."

"You can come after me if you want," Nick said. "You don't scare me."

"I'm not coming after you unless you screw us again. You do, and you're roadkill."

Nick raised his index finger and shoved it in Mel's direction. "You try to hurt me—fine. I'll take you on. But if you do one *bit* of harm to my wife, I'll break your neck."

"I don't care about your wife," said Mel. "To me she's nothing."

"Oh? She's from Beaumont," Nick said. "I knew her from years ago. When you were about fourteen."

Nick paused to let it sink in. Mel tensed, scowling.

Nick said, almost lazily. "Don't worry. She doesn't remember you. You were in your *Phantom of the Opera* stage back then. I haven't told her about you. But somebody back in Beaumont might. You never know, do you? Nope. You just never know."

Mel felt the blood drain from his face, and he was light-headed with rage. He clenched his fists again, wanting to hit.

"I'm not talking to anybody about Fabian," Nick said. "And I'm not talking to anybody about you. Isn't that enough?"

"Get out," Mel said, his stomach churning. "Just get out, will you?"

"Tell Mom I love her," Nick said. "Someday I hope she'll understand. Jack does. You—probably never."

"Never's right. Go. Before I hurt you."

"Gladly. You look like hell by the way. What's the matter? Out of practice? Was your little reporter tagging along? Looks like she gave you a run for your money."

"Out!" Mel shouted. "And stay away from me, dammit!"

"So long, brother."

Nick turned, opened the door and was gone, pulling it smoothly shut behind him. Mel swore and kicked the wall as savagely as he could. He wanted to follow after Nick, grab him and break his face. Instead he jerked off his sweaty shirt and sat down on the settee to yank off his shoes.

The phone rang. He swore again and snatched up the receiver. "What?"

"Mr. Belyle," said a woman with a soft Scottish burr, "this is Rose at the main desk. We have a package here that just arrived by courier."

The yearbook that DeJames sent. I forgot the fool thing. "I'll be down in a few minutes," he said. He forced himself to say "Thanks" and to set the receiver down easily.

Still sitting on the edge of the settee, he put his elbows on his knees and cradled his pounding forehead in his hands. He was breathing too fast, and his heart hurt in a way that wasn't physical.

IN HER ROOM, Kitt had resisted the childlike desire to lay her ear against the wall to try to eavesdrop. From the hostile gleam in Mel's eye, she didn't expect the two men to be making peace.

Mel's shout startled her. The cry sounded as if it had been torn, raw, from his throat. And she heard him kick the wall so hard it must have knocked the plaster loose.

She wanted to peek out the door to watch Nick Belyle leave. The minute she'd seen the two men together, she'd known they were brothers. They had the same foreheads and high cheekbones. Both were dark-haired and blue-eyed, though Mel's eyes were darker and more intense than his brother's.

Mel was taller, leaner, and his features were more even. Nick's nose was broader and slightly crooked, as if it had been broken. His mouth was wider and not nearly as well-shaped.

She'd taken in these details in a few seconds' observation, as a good reporter should. She'd also sensed that the trouble between the brothers went deeper than their rift over Bluebonnet Meadows. Far deeper.

Her stomach growled, an inelegant reminder that she was hungry. She would hit the shower, dress and march over to the Longhorn. Nora had promised her breakfast.

Kitt had a list of people set up to interview today. That was her outline for procedure, the formal one. But she would also check out things informally. The Longhorn was the live, throbbing pulse of Crystal Creek. She was eager to take its measure.

AT THE LONGHORN, Kitt suffered being hugged by the gossipy Shirley Jean Ditmars, who asked her why she wasn't married yet.

She enjoyed an embrace from old Dr. Purdy—until he reminded her that he'd brought her into the world and slapped her naked backside. "I never heard a child howl so loud," he laughed. "You had a redhead's temper clear back then."

Kitt extricated herself from her welcomers as gracefully as she could. "I have to talk to Nora," she said. She moved to the counter and took the stool on the end farthest from the crowd.

"Hi," Nora said, setting a mug of coffee before her. "Do you see Martin this morning?"

Kitt nodded. Martin Avery was a lawyer and the town's former mayor.

"And J.T. tomorrow afternoon?"

"Right," said Kitt. She worried about the McKinney interview. J.T. would grudge her only half an hour's time. He'd seemed singularly unenthusiastic about talking to the press.

"Don't worry about J.T.," Nora said in encouragement. "He's passionate on the subject. Once he gets going, he'll probably talk your ear off."

Kitt held up crossed fingers. "I hope. Let me ask you something—"

But the door burst open and Bubba Gibson swaggered through. "Looky who's back in town," he crowed. He made for Kitt with widespread arms. "That little redheaded cousin of Nora's."

He enveloped her in a bear hug. "Niece," Kitt managed to say. "I'm her niece."

"Hell," he said, sitting down beside her, "there was so

many of you in that little house, I never could keep you straight. But you done all right for yourself, huh?''

"I've done all right," she said. "You know, Bubba, I was going to—"

"How many brothers did you have, darlin'?" Bubba asked.

"Three," Kitt said.

"Whoo," he said. "Seems like more. Kids crawlin' like cooties all over the place. You stay in touch with 'em?"

"Christmas cards, mostly," she said. Her brothers were all younger than she was and spread across Texas. One was a ranch foreman, one a bartender, and the youngest, Toby, her favorite, was a track coach.

Bubba squinted at her, frowning. "Wasn't there a bunch of step-brothers, too?"

Kitt tensed. "Just two," she said. "Not a bunch."

He snapped his fingers impotently, trying to jar his memory. "Johnson? Jameson? Was that their name?"

"Jasper," Kitt said tightly. Her father and mother had divorced when she was thirteen. Her father had drifted off, and her mother remarried almost immediately to Bull Jasper, another of the McKinney ranch hands.

Before Bubba could ask more, she said, "That marriage didn't last, either. They broke up after they moved to San Antonio. I didn't stay in touch with any of the Jaspers."

Bubba's face softened. "I was sorry to hear about your mama. She got the blood ailment?"

"Hodgkin's Disease," Kitt said, growing more tense by the moment. She felt a desperate need to take charge of the conversation. "So, Bubba," she said, "when can I schedule an interview with you? I hear you're quite the prosperous ostrich rancher now."

His big face went somber. "I'm an ostrich rancher. I ain't so sure about the 'prosperous' part."

"I've never seen an ostrich operation," she persisted. "Will you and Mary give me a tour?"

"Sure thing," he said. "Come anytime. How 'bout Sat-

urday night? Come for supper. Bring your appetite. You
ain't got no more meat on you than a sparrow bird. Mary
serves supper 'round seven o'clock. Come at five and I'll
give you the grand tour.''

"It's a date," Kitt promised. Bubba's role in the land
wars interested her. He could turn out to be the wild card,
and she very much wanted to hear what he had to say.

Then she heard the tinkle of the bell that signaled the
door being opened. She turned automatically and without
thinking. The man who had entered was Cal McKinney.

Her heart cartwheeled through her chest; she had the sensation of falling. *You knew this moment would come,* she
told herself. *You knew it all along.*

But she had not expected the sight of him to hit her so
hard. *He's a husband and father now,* Kitt told herself. But
it didn't seem possible.

He was still lean, broad-shouldered and as handsome as
she'd remembered. A wedding ring gleamed golden on his
left hand. For a split second, the glint of that ring seemed
almost blinding.

"Cal!" Bubba called, waving him over. "Come here. See
who I got!"

Kitt sucked in her breath in panic. *Don't be stupid,* she
ordered herself. *It was years ago. What happened between
us was nothing. Not anything—not really. Not anything last-
ing.*

Cal nodded at Bubba. He made his way toward the
counter, his step as jaunty as ever. "Howdy, Bubba. How's
Mary?"

"Fine as frog hair," Bubba said, throwing arm around
Kitt's tensed shoulders. "Looky who's home. You heard she
was comin', didn't you? Kitt Mitchell. She's a reporter now.
You recollect her, don't you?"

Cal gave her a calm, cursory glance. He touched his hat
brim and smiled. It was a careless smile, the kind that meant
nothing. "I heard you were coming," he said. "But I can't
say I remember you. Sorry."

Kitt's chest tightened. Did he mean that? *Could* he mean it? She had feared he'd be embarrassed to see her. But he didn't even seem to recognize her. Stunned, she tried to smile back.

Bubba squeezed her shoulders even more affably. "Kitt, you 'member Cal McKinney? When he was a young rascal on the rodeo circuit? Believe it or not, these days he's almost respectable."

Kitt looked for a flash of recognition in Cal's hazel eyes. But she saw nothing. He acted as if he was meeting her for the first time. Her mouth had gone desert dry and her heart banged.

But she managed to shrug. "I—can just barely remember you," she lied. "It's been a long time."

Bubba's eyes narrowed in mirth and he chuckled. To Cal he said, "See? This one was too sensible to pay mind to your sort. She had a brain in her head. She was immune to the no 'count likes of you."

No, thought Kitt. *I wasn't. Oh, I wasn't immune at all. For me, he was the only one. Cal. Always and only—Cal.*

MEL STRETCHED OUT on the couch in the suite's sitting room. It was a comfortable, old-fashioned room, but he didn't feel comfortable.

He had a few minutes until he needed to leave for his first appointment. It was a secret appointment, far too sensitive to keep in Crystal Creek. It was set up in Fredericksburg, a forty-minute drive away.

To while away the time he opened the book that DeJames had sent him. It was the Stobbart yearbook, a dark blue volume stamped in fake silver. He went straight to the book's index and looked up Kitt's name. It appeared over a dozen times. A popular girl, he thought, unimpressed. He had no affectionate memories of popular high school girls.

He turned to the first picture: student council. There was a teenage Katherine Mitchell, junior representative. She looked impossibly young and impossibly perky.

Her hairdo seemed dated and a bit untidy. Her clothes looked cheap. She wore no makeup. But she was all smiles and sparkle—Miss Personality.

And yet, he thought, *and yet…didn't the smile seem forced?* Just a trifle? Didn't the sparkle seem almost aggressive? As if she was using it as a disguise?

He flipped to the next page. Katherine "Kitt" Mitchell on the track team. Exactly the same smile, as if she'd rehearsed it and could produce it on demand.

Still, the same air of scintillation seemed to radiate from her. It made the other girls seem like dim background figures. She was a little thing, but vitality showed in every line of her body.

Mel came finally to her class picture. Other girls on the page might be more beautiful, but he didn't notice them once he saw her. Under her portrait was the legend DeJames had read him: "Some girls break records, some break hearts. Kitt Mitchell does both."

"Hey, kid," he muttered to her photograph, "what's your story?"

KITT WAS SPARED any further conversation with Cal by the entrance of old Horace Westerhaus.

Horace hobbled into the Longhorn fuming and brandishing one of the new Bluebonnet Meadows brochures. "Has anybody else seen this?" bellowed Horace. "Or am I the only lucky one?"

Horace owned Crystal Creek's radio station and weekly newspaper. He said he'd come to the radio station this morning, and the mailman had handed him the envelope containing this goddamn brochure.

People crowded around him, including Bubba and Cal. Kitt was momentarily forgotten—and grateful for it.

"That brochure, what is it?" Nora asked Kitt. "Do you know?"

Kitt told her what she knew. "Mel Belyle said it would

come in the mail today. Why did Horace get it first? Because he runs the media here?''

''No. It's just his place is first on the town mail route,'' Nora said, looking worried. ''Did you bring your copy?''

''No,'' Kitt said. ''My job's to report the news, not stir it up. I didn't want to be the first to flash it around.''

''I understand,'' Nora said. ''But it actually says 'Phase One'? As if Fabian plans to expand even more?''

''Well…that's what it sounds like,'' Kitt said, careful not to exaggerate.

Then Cody Hendricks, the bank president, burst into the café with an identical copy of the brochure, and the hubbub in the Longhorn grew.

''What I don't understand,'' Kitt whispered to Nora, ''is where does Fabian think he'll get more land? There are patches here and there. But the McKinneys own the most, and they'll never sell—never.''

''Neither will Carolyn Trent,'' Nora said softly. Carolyn was the sister of J.T.'s first wife, Pauline. She owned the Circle T ranch, and her land was precious as heart's blood to her.

J.T. and Carolyn, the two most powerful landowners in Claro County, would fight against Fabian to the end. The other ranchers and farmers had pledged solidarity with them. Nobody would sell out, they had all declared.

''If somebody does break ranks, who would it be?'' Kitt asked.

Nora bit her lip. ''I couldn't say. I *wouldn't* say.''

But her uneasy gaze went to Bubba and rested there. Kitt's eyes followed and she thought, Yes. *If there's a weak link in the chain, it could be Bubba. It wouldn't be the first time he scandalized the town. But would his wife let him sell? She's the steady, strong one.*

People crowded around two tables, staring at the brochures, their voices merging into babble. Unhappy emotions stamped their faces: anger, bewilderment, alarm, indignation, fear.

Cal McKinney stood taller than all the others, and his expression was uncharacteristically somber. He shook his head at the brochure and seemed lost in deep thought. Then he raised his eyes so that, briefly, they met Kitt's. His glance was impersonal, a man barely noticing a stranger.

He's forgotten me. He really has. But how could he? How? The thought cut through her like a blade slicing open an old wound.

But he had already turned his gaze away, his face still solemn. He murmured something to Dr. Purdy, pulled his hat brim lower over his eyes, turned on his heel and left the restaurant.

Shaken, Kitt forced herself not to stare after him. She knew what she'd once felt for him had been only a girl's crush, silly and desperate. But seeing him had been a greater shock than she could have imagined. And all the old pain had come flooding back.

A FEW MOMENTS LATER, Bubba cried out, "Jehoshaphat! My damn watch is stopped." He shook his wrist as if to punish the offending wristwatch. He glared at the big clock on the wall, which said it was nine-thirty.

"I thought it was near an hour earlier," he grumbled. "I got an appointment!"

Kitt's interest prickled. Bubba and Nate Purdy were close enough to her that she could hear them clearly. "Where?" Nate asked with frank curiosity.

"A business appointment," Bubba muttered. "In Burnet County. Hell, now I don't got time for breakfast."

"Console yourself that greater tragedies have befallen the lot of man," Dr. Purdy said out of the corner of his mouth.

Bubba, not amused, hitched up his belt and made for the door. Nobody paid much attention to him. Shirley Ditmars was clearly thinking of something else altogether. "I wonder why Cal didn't stay. He acted peculiar. He's usually so friendly."

Shirley stole a sly glance at Kitt. Shirley was Gloria

Wall's biggest rival for the crown of the town's gossip queen. Who knew what old rumors or new speculations were stirring in her fertile mind?

Calm again, Kitt stared her down.

Nate Purdy said, "Cal? He's worried that J.T.'s going to be upset by this blasted brochure. And he will be." With one spotted knuckle he tapped the brochure on the tabletop. "This is pretty damn cheeky. It's like that Fabian fella's throwing down the gauntlet."

The others muttered in agreement, and the conversation swung back to what fresh evils Fabian might be brewing.

Kitt rose from the counter and drifted toward the window. She saw Bubba backing his pickup truck out of the parking lot. She watched as he drove down Main Street, and her reporter's instincts began to hum.

If Bubba was going to Burnet County, as he claimed, he was heading in the wrong direction. Burnet County was due north. Bubba was driving west.

She stood, brooding on this, letting the opinions and arguments in the room swirl around her. She wasn't due to see Martin Avery, the former mayor, for another forty-five minutes. If needed, she could call him and push back the time.

"We can handle Fabian *and* his fancy lawyer," Nate said. "It doesn't matter what they try. Just so long as we stick together."

A mumble of agreement went through the crowd.

At that moment, Kitt saw Mel Belyle's car come down the street, heading west, just as Bubba's pickup had done. She felt an irresistible rush of curiosity.

Where was Mel bound? Was it a mere coincidence he and Bubba were going in the same direction at the same time of day? She could not resist the temptation to find out. And she needed action. Only action could exorcise the ghosts of the past that Cal had awakened in her.

CHAPTER EIGHT

An Austin radio station was playing the score of *Smokey Joe's Café*. Mel drove, humming along with "Love Potion #9." Stupid lyrics—about magic and instant love. But still a catchy melody, an irresistible beat.

Casually, he glanced up into his rearview mirror. A mile or so behind him was a white compact car. It was familiar.

He blinked hard, as if to clear his eyes of illusion. But when he looked in the mirror again, the car hadn't vanished. He swore and smacked the steering wheel with the flat of his hand.

Kitt Mitchell? The crazy little redhead was following him? She was truly insane. Nobody could follow someone on a back highway like this. The road was straight and empty—except for the two of them. She couldn't stay hidden if she'd camouflaged her car with twigs and cactus plants.

He speeded up. She sped up. He pushed the sedan up to a hundred. She fell back a little, but not much. This was stupid and dangerous, and he didn't like handling a car this big. He wished he had his agile little Aston Martin. He'd hit warp speed and leave her behind in a slower universe.

He changed his tack, slowing to a tortoise's pace. She, too, slowed. He crept. She crept. He stopped. She stopped, still keeping a mile between them.

He swore again. There was a junction ahead. He would dawdle up to it, then smash the gas pedal to the floor, fake an escape onto the other route, then as soon as she followed, cut a fast U-turn and flash past her.

He might not be able to outrun her, but he could sure as hell outdrive her. If she ran off the road and crashed into a Brahma bull, it wouldn't be his fault. But then, like an omen of warning, a sheriff's department car appeared on the horizon, approaching them.

Do no evil, the car seemed to warn. *Or you will see the fateful lightning of my terrible swift ticket.*

Mel swore again. The cruiser had slowed; the deputy had noticed that two cars were crawling surreally down the highway like huge metal snails.

Mel hit the accelerator and brought the sedan up to exactly the speed limit. Behind him, Kitt did the same. The cruiser passed them.

When he's out of sight, I levitate, Mel thought, setting his jaw in grim determination. But the cruiser did not continue toward Crystal Creek.

It pulled over, turned and began to follow them. *Great,* thought Mel, *now he's suspicious. I'm leading a damn parade.*

This was not the way to go to a clandestine meeting. Mel picked up his cell phone and tapped out a number. A man answered.

"This is Belyle," Mel said. "Where are you?"

"I'm on the outskirts of Fredericksburg. I'm almost to the museum."

Mel had planned the meeting to take place at the Nimitz Museum, a nice, roomy place, not too crowded on a Tuesday morning in autumn. Two men might seem to bump into each other, strike up a quiet conversation. That had been the scheme. Kitt Mitchell had tanked it.

"Listen," Mel said from between gritted teeth. "We've got to abort this mission. I'm being tailed."

"Tailed," the other man said in disbelief. "Who?"

"The reporter," he said, glancing again at the mirror. "The redhead."

"Kitt Mitchell?" the other said in the same tone.

"I can't shake her. There's a deputy behind us. We're going to have to arrange another time, another place."

There was a pause. Mel could sense the man's frustration. He could hear the resentment in his voice when he asked, "When? Where?"

"I'll call you tonight. After eleven."

"But—"

"It's the best I can do," Mel retorted. "Be patient. There's a lot of money at stake here."

"But—"

"Tonight. After eleven." Mel snapped the phone shut. He saw another junction, leading to the main highway. He took the turn as decorously as a preacher setting an example for others.

Kitt followed, abiding just as strictly to the laws. The deputy followed Kitt. "I feel like a goddamn mother duck," Mel grumbled.

When he saw a rest stop, he signaled and turned into it. He parked and waited, tapping his fingers on the steering wheel. A few moments later, Kitt wheeled in. She stopped at the other end of the lot, her motor running. The deputy pulled in and parked between them.

The deputy got out. He was a big man with a proud belly riding over his sheriff's department belt. He had three chins, a Smokey the Bear hat, and the rolling gait perfected and patented by John Wayne.

He strolled up to the driver's side of Mel's car. Mel sighed and rolled down the window.

"Could I see your license?" the deputy said. It was more of a demand than a request. Mel took his wallet, extracted his license and handed it to the big man.

"New York City," the deputy said, in the tone one might say, *I see that you're a lower life form.*

"Yessir," Mel nodded. "Would you mind telling me if I've broken a law? I wasn't aware of it."

The man fixed him with a gaze of piercing intensity.

"You were driving funny. When I first saw you, you were going about five miles an hour. You mind telling me why?"

Mel shrugged, wondering if he should tell the truth or concoct the most cunning lie he could.

Then Kitt appeared at the deputy's side, her red hair tossed by the breeze. She barely came to the man's shoulder, and she smiled up at him in seeming delight. "Hi, Hugo. I thought that was you behind me. Got a problem?"

Mel could have sworn that the deputy blushed with pleasure. "Hey, Kitt. I heard you were in town."

She positively beamed up at him. "Is this character in trouble?" she asked with a nod toward Mel.

Hugo struggled to regain his dignity. "I saw you two driving down the road slow as turtles. Now, I have to say my suspicion was excited. So I proceeded to question Mr. Belittle."

"Belyle," growled Mel.

"That was my fault," Kitt said airily. "He thought I was following him."

"Yes," Mel interjected. "And she *was* following me. I slowed down so she'd have to pass. She wouldn't do it. Officer, can I file a complaint against this woman?"

"Oh, grow up," Kitt said with maddening playfulness. "It's not like I was going to hurt you or anything. Do I scare you? Boo!"

"I have certain business I have to conduct in confidentiality," Mel complained. "She's interfering with my appointed duties, and she's infringing on my privacy."

Hugo shook his head so that chins waggled. "You shouldn't ought to follow him, Kitt. Him driving slow like that, it could be a hazard."

"Going too slowly is a hazard?" Mel objected.

"I've got a job to do, too," Kitt said, looking up at Hugo. "After all, freedom of the press. Want to see my press card?"

"No, Kitt. I know you." He turned to Mel, leaning down

to look him in the eye. "Now I think you should settle your differences with this lady—"

"Me settle with her? She *caused* all this."

Hugo's eyes became steelier. "You ought to settle your differences with this lady in private, not on the highway system of the state of Texas. Now I could give you a ticket—"

"Me?" Mel said in affronted disbelief.

Kitt put her hand on Hugo's sleeve. She seemed incredibly tiny beside this mountain of a man. "Oh, Hugo, no," she pleaded. "Give me the ticket. It really was my fault. And I was only trying to do my job."

Hugo sighed. "So am I."

"And so am I," snapped Mel. "This woman is *stalking* me, dammit. Make her stop."

Hugo glared at him. "You're the lawyer, aren't you?"

Mel was taken aback. The fabled grapevine had twined him in its tendrils again. "Yes, I am."

Hugo looked at him pityingly. "Then you ought to know that I can't do nothing but warn her. You want her stopped? You need to go to court and get a restraining order. Or don't they teach you that in New York City?"

A red haze danced before Mel's eyes. Hugo faced Kitt again. "Consider yourself warned, Kitt."

Her expression became fetchingly contrite. "I do, Hugo. Thanks for your concern. I'll work it out with him. I promise."

"You do that," Hugo said with a nod, and his chins nodded with him.

"Sure thing," she promised. She took his hand in hers. "*Good* to see you again. We'll have to have coffee. Talk over old times."

"I'd like that," he said.

"Goodbye, Hugo," she said.

Hugo thrust Mel's license back through the window. "Watch how you treat her," he said. "She's a good girl." He smiled again at Kitt, then went back to his car in stately stride. He got inside, took up his microphone and held a conversation with someone.

Kitt leaned against the sedan's door, peering at Mel coolly. "Aren't you even going to say thank you?"

He glowered at her. "That was one of the most disgusting things I've ever seen. You had that poor shmuck wrapped around your little finger. There ought to be a law against women like you."

"You're a lawyer," she smirked. "Make one."

He wasn't amused. "You give feminism a bad name. My God, what goo-goo eyes. I'm a victim of rank sexism."

"Oh, settle down," she said. "And act nice. Or I'll call him back."

"I can do it, I can get a court order," he threatened.

"Bull." She laughed. "The best you could do would be to keep me fifty yards away. After all, you're news. And the news is my job. Where were you going, by the way?"

"No comment," he snarled.

"Your brochure made a big hit at the Longhorn this morning. Well, maybe 'hit' is the wrong word. It stirred up a lot of talk."

He said nothing. He wished Hugo would leave and go patrol elsewhere.

"The big question is if Fabian's going to buy land, whose land would he buy?" Kitt said. "I have a few ideas about that. Do you want to hear them?"

"No," he said. Lord, he thought irritably, but she was pretty. It was hateful of her to be so pretty. He decided not to look at her any longer. He stared at a mesquite tree instead.

She said, "There are five major landowners in this county. J.T., Carolyn Trent, Brock Munroe, Dan Gibson and Bubba Gibson."

Mel glanced in exasperation at Hugo, still sitting in his cruiser talking on his two-way radio.

"Are you listening to me?" asked Kitt.

"No," said Mel.

"Now, by the process of elimination, I'd say the person who'd be most tempted to sell is Bubba. He's getting on in years, and he has only one daughter. Her husband's wealthy. She doesn't want or need the ranch. Bubba could sell and retire in style. So I bet that you're courting Bubba."

He'd been studying the animation in her face. Oh, clearly she loved it, analyzing, probing, second-guessing. Her blue eyes were lit with the liveliness of it all.

"Was he in love with you?" he asked, gesturing at the cruiser. "Officer Oaf? Did he sit in study hall and pine for you in high school? Did he waste away to a mere three or four hundred pounds?"

"Don't be mean," she said sternly. "He had a crush on me, that's all."

"What made me guess that you reduced him to a pathetic puddle of schmaltz?"

"I was nice to him, that was all," she said, tossing her head. "Kids can be mean. People used to tease him. It made me mad—and sad for him. He's a nice person."

"I felt that. I looked into his eyes, as friendly as razor blades, and said to myself, behind that hideously murderous stare is a nice person."

"Which is neither here nor there," she answered. "The question is are you working to cut a deal with Bubba Gibson?"

From the corner of his eye, Mel saw Hugo's car finally backing out. The cruiser stopped by the sedan, and Hugo rolled down the window. His face appeared in it like a framed picture of the moon. "Everything okay, Kitt? Situation in hand?"

"Everything's fine," she beamed at him. "Thanks for your help, Hugo."

"That's what I'm here for," he said. He gave her a mock salute and drove off.

"Now," Kitt said, leaning her crossed arms on the window, "back to business. Bubba's sworn up and down he won't sell his land. But what if you make him an offer he can't refuse?''

Hugo's car reached the intersection that led back to the county road. He took the turn and the car disappeared.

Mel grasped the door handle and opened the door. Kitt, startled, moved back. ''What are you doing?''

''Your protector is gone.''

He got out and stepped toward her. She held her ground. He towered over her, and it was a pleasant reversal, this position of power.

''You don't dare do anything to me,'' she said defiantly. ''If you try to hurt me, damage my car—the entire *country* will read about it.''

He stared down at her, his emotions in a turmoil he barely controlled. ''I'm not going to hurt you.''

''You'd better not,'' she warned. ''Now. Here's my theory about Bubba. I've heard he's never really liked ostrich farming. That was his wife's brainchild. So the biggest pressures for him to keep his land are her and peer pressure. What will the people of Claro Country think—''

Mel stepped closer still. ''You know what?'' he asked.

A sudden wariness came into her eyes. The breeze stirred her hair.

''Somebody ought to stop your smart little mouth,'' he said. ''And I'm just the guy to do it.''

Then, before he quite realized it, his arms were around her, and he was kissing her the way he'd wanted to kiss her from the first.

AT FIRST HIS LIPS CLAIMED HERS with something like fury. Kitt was shocked. It was as if he was not only angry with her, but angry with himself for wanting her.

If he had used the kiss only to punish and dominate her, she would have broken away. She wouldn't stand for it, and she knew how to protect herself. She might be small, but she was a fierce and cunning fighter.

But she didn't have to fight him. Something in his touch

changed almost instantly. For a fraction of a second his mouth went still against hers, he gasped, and his body tensed.

His hands moved to her shoulders, gripping her so that his body remained tight against hers. His face raised slightly from hers, and he stared down at her. Regret and hunger warred in his eyes.

Kitt stared up at him, more than a little dazed. Her heart pummeled her breastbone, making it hard to breathe.

"I didn't mean to do that," he said in a low voice. His breath was warm and caressing against her parted lips. "I meant to do this."

His hands moved up to frame her face. He bent and brought his lips against hers just as hungrily, but without the edge of aggression. He kissed her with a thoroughness that dazed her.

His mouth lingered and teased. Her lips parted. He trailed one hand down the side of her throat and clasped her shoulder. His other arm went round her waist, his hand splaying just above the curve of her hips.

Ooh! Kitt thought in confusion. *I shouldn't like this. But I do. I do.* His arms were strong, and he knew how to hold a woman.

His tongue flirted and teased. She found her own doing the same. She fought the urge to put her arms around his neck, to arch against him.

But then he broke the kiss, gazed down at her, one eyebrow lifted. "Well," he said. "Now we know what that's like. So where does it go from here? Do we go back to my room? Check into a motel? Or do I keep flirting and do you keep teasing?"

The question brought her back to her senses with a painful jolt. She should have drawn away from his first touch. But she hadn't, and that was foolish.

Now she stepped back, and he let his hands fall away from her. She felt oddly incomplete and alone. And she also felt ashamed of herself.

"It goes nowhere," she said. "It can't." She moved farther away. She turned and stared out at the hills and smoothed her tousled hair back from her forehead.

"Then don't let me do that again," he said quietly.

She tossed him a glare. "Don't *let* you? As if it's *my* fault it happened? From now on keep your hands to yourself."

"From now on don't follow me."

She turned to face him and put her hands on her hips. "It's so like you to make this a sexual issue."

He stepped back to his car, opened the door. "Is that so?"

"Yes, it is."

He gave her an ironic smile. "But you're irresistible. 'Some girls break records. Some girls break hearts. Kitt Mitchell does both.'"

She jerked her chin up in surprise and defiance. "Where'd you hear that?" she demanded.

His smile grew more sardonic. He got back inside the car. "Stay away from me, Mitchell. I might find out a lot more than that." He started the car, turned it and gunned it out of the parking lot.

She stood staring after him, her fists clenched and her heart pounding. "And I'll find out about *you*," she vowed. "Wait and see, pretty boy."

CAL DROVE BACK to the Double C. He pulled into the driveway at the same time Tyler did in the winery truck. Tyler looked in a dark mood, and Cal wondered if it was because of Fabian's latest mischief.

"Has the mail come yet?" Cal asked as they walked up the porch steps.

"No. Why?"

"Have you seen this?" Cal thrust out the new brochure.

Tyler's black eyebrows lowered in a frown. "No. What is it?"

Cal folded the pages back and showed Tyler. "Look at

this. 'First Offerings.' 'Phase One.' Sounds like he's just gettin' started.''

Tyler gritted his teeth in exasperation. He swore. "The bastard's already got four thousand acres. He thinks he's going to get more? Why's he so sure of himself?''

"I don't know. He's up to something. I'd bet money on it. I came to warn Daddy. I don't want him hittin' the roof.''

"Yeah?'' Tyler said, scanning the page. "Well, if you're betting money, bet that he'll get riled. Hell, I don't need this. On top of everything else.''

Cal narrowed his eyes and studied Tyler's taut face. "What's 'everything else?'''

"That's why I came over here. I need to talk to you. Alone.''

Cal had a sudden sense of foreboding. He knew Tyler well enough to know something serious was looming. "Talk? About what?''

"Later,'' Tyler muttered. "Let's show this thing to Daddy before he sees it on his own.'' The two men went inside, but the house seemed deserted. Serena and Cynthia had taken the twins to the Austin museum. No one was in sight, and the quiet seemed unnatural.

Then a harsh noise, a heavy screeching, came from down the hall. Tyler frowned harder, and Cal cocked his head, puzzled. The same noise, along with a thump, came again. The sound issued from the guest room.

"Daddy?'' Cal called. He jammed the brochure in the hip pocket of his jeans, went to the door of the guest room and shoved it open.

J.T. was struggling to move the king-size bed by himself. His face was flushed with the effort, and he was pushing with all his might, the veins in his neck bulging.

"Lord, Daddy,'' Cal said, "what you tryin' to do?''

"I'm moving this goddamn bed,'' grunted J.T. "What's it *look* like?''

"Like you're givin' yourself a hernia,'' Cal answered.

"Let us do it. You're gonna pop a blood vessel. C'mon, Tyler."

"Why're you moving the bed?" Tyler asked.

"I decided to, that's all," J.T. said from between clenched teeth.

"Where you want to move it to?" Cal looked around the room. It had no free wall space.

"I'm putting it where the dresser is," J.T. muttered.

"Good God, that dresser weighs three hundred pounds," Cal said. "You couldn't move that by yourself."

Cal and Tyler took charge of the bed and moved it easily away from the wall and to the middle of the room. "Now this," Cal said to Tyler, nodding toward the dresser. "Then we can go out and lift tractors for a rest."

"I can do it myself," J.T. protested. "I'm not such an old fart I have to have my children come and move a few sticks of furniture." Still, he paused and leaned against the wall, tired but too proud to sit down.

Tyler groaned at the dresser's weight. "Jeez, what's this thing made of? Lead?"

"Yes," Cal ground out. "And it's full of cast iron underwear." At last they had wrestled the two pieces of furniture into place.

"I don't see the point," Tyler said, rubbing his arm. "It doesn't look any better than before. I don't think it looks as good."

"Well," Cal said artlessly, "that bed's real noisy when you're makin' whoopee with the little woman. Did we keep you awake, Daddy?"

"No," J.T. snapped. He gave the bed a disapproving look. "Let's get some iced tea or something."

He led his sons down the hall and into the kitchen. Cal noticed that his father limped slightly. "You hurt yourself, Daddy?" he asked. "You look a little gimpy."

"It's nothing," J.T. answered. "A little arthritis."

"You seen Nate Purdy?"

"Hell, he's got it worse than I do," J.T. grumbled. "The old coot."

"Maybe you ought to see a specialist," Cal said. "Take care of yourself—"

J.T., opening the refrigerator, scowled at his younger son. "Having a touch of arthritis doesn't mean I'm at death's door."

"I didn't say it did," Cal argued. "I got some myself—in my back. Got bucked off too many broncs."

"You're lucky you can still walk," Tyler said dryly. "We used to think they'd bring you home in a body bag."

"Ah," said Cal, "but I had fun while it lasted."

J.T. set the pitcher on the table and took three glasses from the cupboard. "Fun," he snorted. He gave Cal a sharp glance. "You were in town this morning. Anything up?"

Cal knew it was his duty to break the news. "Yeah. Fabian's sent out a new brochure. The way it's worded, it sounds like he's set on expanding."

J.T. stiffened in displeasure. "You got a copy?"

Cal pulled it from his pocket and handed it to his father. Tyler pointed out the ominous words.

J.T. sat down heavily at the table and bent over the brochure, studying it. His shoulders slumped, and as he read, his face seemed to age five years. Cal felt a frisson of alarm.

J.T. slapped the table in disgust. "It's that new lawyer. Nick Belyle's brother. He's going to start flashing money around. So much that somebody'll cave in and sell."

"Maybe it's inevitable, Daddy," Tyler said. "You know, there may come a point where it's foolhardy to fight him any longer."

J.T. shot him a fierce glance, and Cal looked askance at his brother. Tyler would never have dared say such a thing to their father in public.

Tyler's jaw jutted out. "What if Fabian offers so much money *nobody* can resist? Even you?"

"Even he hasn't got that much money," J.T. said stonily. "I'll eat this land before I sell it."

Cal sat down across from his father. "Daddy," he said carefully, "I been thinking. I asked my partners about lawyers who handle cases like this. We can get you some heavy cannons."

J.T.'s eyes narrowed. "My lawyers aren't just popguns, you know."

Cal put his hand on his father's clenched one. "I'm just sayin' you can't have too much help. A couple of attorneys owe me and my partners favors. They're willin' to help. It can't hurt."

"Where did these hotshots come from all of a sudden?" J.T. asked suspiciously. "And why do they owe you and these partners favors?"

"They come from here and there," Cal said. "We helped some folks. They're grateful."

Tyler sat down, looking unconvinced. "What's in it for you and your partners?"

Cal gave his brother a cool smile. "If Fabian's forced out, somebody's got to buy that land. My partners think it might be a good investment. Could be."

"For what?" J.T. demanded.

"Somethin' better than Bluebonnet Meadows," Cal said.

Tyler raised an eyebrow. "Ha! You can't play in Fabian's league. You'd have to hock everything you own."

Cal only shrugged. "It's an idea, that's all."

J.T. frowned. "I hear that Fabian's going around picking Texas legislators and commissioners like they were daisies. Throwing money at everybody—campaign contributions, fund-raisers, lobbyists…"

"That's right, Daddy," Cal said. "All that and more. So better be ready to roll in the heavy artillery. A couple phone calls, and it's done."

J.T. shook his head. "I need—I need to talk it over with the other members of the Concerned Citizens group before bringing in more lawyers."

"Why should they care?" Cal shrugged. "It won't cost 'em nothin'."

"And Cynthia," J.T. muttered. "Cynthia's smart about these things."

"She'll tell you to do it," Cal said. He knew Cynthia would agree.

"And the lawyers," J.T. said. "Martin Avery. And the ones in Dallas. They can't just be—replaced. I've known some of these men a long time."

"You're not replacin' 'em," said Cal. "You're *augmentin'* 'em."

"I still have to consult folks," J.T. said. "I have to—consult folks. How many more lawyers you talking about?"

Cal held up two fingers.

J.T. cocked an eyebrow skeptically. "And they'd work for nothing?"

"They're mostly environmentalists. They can write it off as pro bono."

J.T. shook his head wearily. "This is giving me a belly ache. I've got to take some of Nate's damn pills. Then I'm going to saddle up, take a long ride and mull over this mess. 'First Offering.' 'Phase One.' *Damn.*"

He got up and walked toward the bathroom, rubbing his stomach. Cal and Tyler looked after him. When J.T. disappeared, Tyler turned to Cal, his lip curled. "I never heard anybody who could shovel bullshit like you."

Cal feigned innocence. "I got no idea what you're talkin' about."

"You don't have any free lawyers owing you favors. There's no such thing as a free lawyer. That's just talk."

"Believe what you want," Cal said. "Believe the world is flat if it makes you happy."

Tyler leaned across the table, his dark gaze grim. "You're paying for some dream team to come here because you think we can't afford lawyers good enough to fight Fabian."

"How's Donna?" Cal asked, stirring sugar into his tea. Donna was Tyler's older daughter. "Daddy said Ruth was takin' her to the new pediatrician. She okay?"

"It's only allergies," Tyler said. "Don't change the subject. You're going to pay for these legal eagles and lie about it. To spare Daddy's feelings. And everybody else's.''

"I ain't lyin','' Cal lied. "And even if I was, what's wrong with sparin' Daddy's feelin's? This deal has got under his skin bad.''

Tyler leaned closer. "I know that. I'm here every day. I *see* it. It's wearing him down. Ruth and I talked about it a long time last night.''

Cal tipped back his chair so it balanced on the back two legs. "Oh? And what'd you and Ruth say?''

Tyler suddenly looked defensive. "That maybe we're all fools to fight Fabian. That maybe it's inevitable he'll win. Why should Daddy fret himself into the grave over it?''

Cal crossed his arms and nodded skeptically. "I see. This is a brand new song you're singin'. You have done changed your tune. Why?''

Tyler stood and started pacing the kitchen. He stopped when they heard the front door slam. J.T. had gone out. Tyler hooked his thumbs in his belt and stared at his brother. "Cynthia's worried about Daddy. So are Ruth and I. He's going to work himself into another heart attack.''

"I'm trying to take some pressure off him,'' Cal said, still balancing the chair on its hind legs.

"Maybe you're putting more on him,'' Tyler retorted. "What if Fabian made Daddy an offer? Enough money to set him up for the rest of his life?''

Cal laughed. "Daddy wouldn't take it.''

"What if Cynthia wanted him to?'' Tyler said, almost combatively. "What if Ruth and I agreed? And what if Lynn did, too?''

Cal let the chair settle back on all four legs. He frowned at Tyler. "Why're you talkin' like this? A couple of days ago you were ready to fight to the death for the old homestead. What changed your mind?''

Tyler turned his back on Cal. He leaned his hands on the sink counter and gazed out the window. "We got a call last night,'' he said shortly.

Cal studied his brother's tall, tensed body. Again he sensed trouble was afoot, and it was big. He rose and walked to Tyler's side. He put his hand on his shoulder. "What's wrong, Tyler?"

"I've got choices to make," Tyler said, not looking at him.

Cal grasped his shoulder more tightly. "What choices? Tell me. Don't play games, Tyler. We're too old for that."

Tyler sighed harshly. He shook his head. "You've noticed Ruth's been quiet? She's going back to California tomorrow. She's taking the kids."

Cal was stunned. "She's leavin' you?"

Tyler swallowed and shook his head. "No. Nothing like that. It's her father. We've got word he's—bad sick. He's not going to make it."

Cal's emotions spun unpleasantly. He was relieved for Tyler, but at the same time sorry for Ruth. He loved his sister-in-law. "I'm sorry."

A muscle twitched in Tyler's cheek. "He's got maybe three months to live. Ruth wants to be with him."

"I don't blame her."

Tyler gripped the counter more tightly. "We've been afraid of this. It's not like it came out of left field. But it—changes things. Like I said, there are choices to make. Hard ones." He paused. "I'm going with her."

Pieces began to fall into place for Cal. He stared at his brother. "Ruth's an only child. Her father's winery…"

"…is one of the best mid-size wineries in Napa Valley," Tyler said. "It's his life's work. Ruth loves it, too. She grew up there. She'll inherit it."

Cal waited uneasily. He could see the stress in his brother's face.

Tyler took a deep breath. "She doesn't want to sell her father's place. She can't stand the idea. It makes her cry. But I don't know that I can run two. Not when they're so far apart."

Cal felt a rush of disbelief. His brother had slaved to

establish the vineyard on the Double C. "You don't mean you'd leave Texas for good? Well, *hell!* What about all you've built up here?"

Tyler's gaze met his, his dark eyes bleak. "That's a damn good question, isn't it? I don't know. She wants us to try to keep both. But if we can't handle two, we should keep the one in California. It makes twice the money."

"You'd sell everything here?" Cal asked in disbelief. "After all the sweat you put in it?"

"Sell it," Tyler said grimly. "Or lease it. To you. Or—whoever."

Cal swore. "Me? Is that why you've been actin' jumpy ever since I came home?"

The muscle jerked in Tyler's cheek again. "Yeah. That's why. You already own twenty-one per cent. You set up the import thing from Australia. Why shouldn't you own it all? You're the rich guy."

"Because it's *yours,* dammit," Cal retorted. "And I only own twenty-one per cent until you can pay me back."

Tyler gave a sarcastic laugh. "How can I pay you back? I can sell ours and settle up what I owe you. Or I can try to make Ruth sell her father's property and pay you. It doesn't work out too well either way, does it?"

Cal swore more colorfully. "She can't ask you to choose between your own winery and her daddy's."

"No," Tyler said evenly, "she hasn't. Not yet. But it could come to that. I need to go out with her and see if we can handle both places. If it stretches us too thin—we may end up staying there."

"You can't leave Daddy," Cal argued. "It'd kill him. You've always been his right hand."

"I love my wife," Tyler said with bitter simplicity.

"And what do you mean, if I don't buy it, you can sell it to 'whoever'? For God's sake, you don't mean Fabian, do you?"

"If I have to, I will. I don't want to. But…"

"Dammit," Cal said. "Would Ruth let you do that?"

"I don't think she's making distinctions," Tyler said. "She's a woman who's hurting for her father and wants to go home."

Cal, who was seldom angry, felt resentment surge through him. "*This* is her home, dammit! She can't turn the whole family upside down because she's got a bad case of homesick blues. I'm gonna speak to that woman. Talk some sense into her—"

Tyler grabbed him by the arm. "You're going to say nothing, cowboy. She's *distraught.* She loves her father, and he's dying."

"Well, our father don't look so good himself," Cal challenged. "You just gonna turn your back on *that?*"

Tyler tightened the pressure of his grip. "What's the matter. Cal?" Tyler taunted. "Won't all your money fix things the way you want this time?"

Cal stared at his brother, breathing hard. He clenched and unclenched his fist, but made no other move.

Tyler said, "The best I can hope for is that I run *two* wineries. It's going to be hard. I'll be back and forth all the time. I can't look after all that business and Daddy's, too."

Cal's eyes narrowed. "You'd walk out on him?"

Tyler's mouth quirked into an acidic smile. "Look who's talking. You walked out on him years ago. Did you think I'd always be around to watch out for him, for the whole ranch? Maybe it's your turn—finally."

A punch to the stomach couldn't have knocked Cal harder. He felt the blood drain from his face, and he blinked hard at Tyler's accusation.

"I never meant—" he said, but he couldn't find words to finish the sentence. Tyler was right. Dependable, unfailing, he'd always been the one who stayed at J.T.'s side. Always. And Cal had taken it for granted.

"So just what," Tyler asked with the same smile, "do you have to say, prodigal brother? Prodigal son?"

CHAPTER NINE

MEL TURNED toward Fredericksburg even though his appointment was canceled. He'd weave in and out of every back road to throw Kitt off his trail. He'd lay down a path as intricate and serpentine as a Celtic knot.

When he thought he'd lost her, he almost relaxed. But in a troubling sense, he could not put distance between her and himself. She stayed with him—or he couldn't let her go.

He knew that the body has memories, just as the mind does. The physical memory of her was so keen it hurt. He remembered the feel of her, small and vibrant, in his arms. She had fit against him as perfectly as if he had been destined to hold her.

The memory of her kiss pulsed in his blood. Her mouth had been warm, pliant, and giving. She hadn't resisted. After the first split second of surprise, she'd been caught in the same dizzying sensual spell as he.

He had more than just wanted her; he'd wanted her beyond reason. And she had wanted him back, he knew it. Crazy. But true.

The ring of his cell phone jangled his nerves and made him drop back into reality. "Hello," he snapped. "Mel Belyle here."

"Mel Belyle, God's greatest gift to models since the catwalk?" The voice, deep and irreverent, belonged to DeJames.

"Ah," Mel sighed in resignation. "It's you. How are things at the National Sarcasm Institute?"

"We're all crying because you're gone. Listen. Fabian

didn't like your news about Cal McKinney being back. This partnership he's in—Three Amigos?"

Mel frowned. "Yeah?"

"It's something new. McKinney just joined up with them. These guys he's with? They're smart, they're connected—and they're mavericks."

"Mavericks? How so?"

"They just stalled a monster condo deal in Hawaii. Now they've got the property themselves. Claim they're going to do some wussy 'environmentally friendly' developing."

Mel wasn't impressed. "So they say. Who are they?"

"Jocks. Outdoorsmen. One's a rodeo rider turned stuntman turned investor. The other's got a wilderness gear company."

DeJames told him their names. Mel had never heard of them, so still wasn't impressed. "They sound bush league—amateurs."

"They've got great lawyers. And Fabian thinks Cal McKinney's sniffing after his land down there."

Mel sneered. "If McKinney mortgaged everything he owned, he couldn't afford a third of that land."

"That's what people said about the other two guys in Hawaii. But they did it. It's a nuisance. Fabian doesn't like it."

"DeJames, I've got two things to do down here," Mel said. "One, I try to buy land. Two, I try to turn public opinion in Fabian's favor. I've got my hands full. What more does he want?"

"Dirt on McKinney and his clan, for one thing."

Mel tensed. "What kind of dirt?"

"The kind that can make tabloid headlines. Fabian says he's tired of these people. That maybe they'd like to take on a couple of national scandal sheets."

Mel didn't like it. "Even Fabian's never sunk to that level."

"Who says he will? Anyway, I've got a possible lead for you. A woman named Trina Gilroy. She wrote a few weeks back. Claims to know a lot about the McKinneys, especially Cal. She's married to a lawman, and she'll talk—for money. She sounds like she's got a grudge. A big, nasty one.''

''Where do you find these people?'' Mel asked in distaste.

''I picked up a rock. I looked under it. Something wiggled. It was her.''

Mel glanced in the rearview mirror. The road behind him was empty. He said, ''Any more on Kitt Mitchell?''

''I'm working on it,'' DeJames said. ''In the meantime, call this Gilroy woman. Before she changes her mind.''

KITT SAT in Martin Avery's private office. Her pen hovered in frustration over a virginal page of her notebook.

Lawyers, she thought in exasperation. *There've been too many lawyers in my life today.*

Like Mel Belyle, Martin Avery gave few straightforward answers.

Kitt tried to bait him with the Phase One page of the brochure. ''Phase One implies Phase Two is coming. Some people think the Fabian forces are going to make a move soon. A big one. What do you think?''

Martin shook his head. ''Anything I'd say at this point would be mere speculation.'' His smile was kindly, but not encouraging.

She tried again. ''If Fabian becomes more aggressive, are the Concerned Citizens ready to do the same?''

Martin made a vague gesture, palms up. ''What can I tell you? We'll cross that bridge if we come to it.''

How did attorneys do it? Each morning did they gulp down magic pills to prevent them from saying simple things like *yes* or *no* or *we'll sue their pants off?*

Yet, to be fair, Martin was a far cry from Mel Belyle. He was amiable and courteous, soft-spoken to a fault. He had an air of old-fashioned chivalry, a quaint formality.

Kitt remembered Martin from her childhood. Even in middle age, his hair had been snow white. He had always radiated civility, but never aggression—or sexuality. That lack of raw vigor and sexuality was completely different from Mel Belyle.

"I wish I could tell you more, Kitt," Martin said.

So do I, she thought, and took another run at breaking down his defenses. "Fabian's got another lawyer in town, Mel Belyle. Why do you think he's here?"

Martin's left eyebrow made a decorous arch. "A good question. I don't know the answer."

"Some people think there are going to be more offers made for land. What do you think?"

He shook his silvery head. "Anything I say would be a guess."

She persisted. "He's here for *some* reason. Is his purpose to read people, see what it takes to lure them into the Fabian camp?"

"It's possible," he said with his impeccable vagueness.

She fought back a sigh. "There are already people in his camp, right?"

"Some might put it that way," Martin said.

"Like Ralph and Gloria Wall?" she asked.

"You'd have to ask Ralph and Gloria about that."

She touched her fingertips to her brow, where a tension headache had started to throb. "Martin, I understand your position. I really do."

"I'm glad," he said. "Could I get you a cup of coffee? Tea? A cold soft drink? Anything?"

The world's biggest aspirin, she thought. *And a crowbar to get answers out of guys like you.*

"No thanks," she said. "Tell me. Will you try to talk to Mel Belyle? Has he tried to make an appointment to talk to you?"

For the first time, Martin looked troubled. But he quickly recovered his polite blandness. "Talk? We may at some point."

She clapped shut her notebook, shoved her pen back into

her vest pocket. "Let me ask you something off the record. May I?"

He laced his manicured fingers together. "You may. I may not be able to answer."

She blew a wayward strand of hair from her eyes and slouched in her chair, giving him her best gunslinger's stare. "I'm not going to get any straight answers out of you, am I?"

He met her stare as coolly as she gave it. "No," he said.

She tapped the arm of her chair. "So if somebody in town *would* give me straight answers—really straight, objective answers—who would it be?"

He thought for a moment. "Reverend Blake. He's as fair and forthright a man as you'll find in this town."

Kitt's muscles tensed. She'd known it was inevitable she would have to face Howard Blake. She'd hoped to postpone it as long as possible. But she took a deep breath and said, "How soon do you think he'd see me?"

Martin glanced at his desk calendar. "He's been out of town. He'll be back this afternoon. He might see you this evening. I'll give you his cell phone number."

"Great," she said, forcing a smile.

"I don't want to get your hopes up," Martin said, neatly writing a phone number on his memo pad. "Howard may not want to be quoted. He's an honest man, but discreet."

Kitt kept her artificial smile in place. *Oh, I know. Howard Blake's discreet. He can keep a secret. For all these years, he's kept mine.*

TRINA GILROY'S HOUSE was on the outskirts of a little town named Bee Tree. Mel sat in her living room. It was shabby and cluttered.

The Gilroy woman settled back in an easy chair with flowered upholstery, her slippered feet on a plaid hassock. She wore a pink muumuu, her hair was in yellow curlers, and an evil-looking Chihuahua lay in her lap.

She had on no makeup except a slash of scarlet lipstick,

carelessly applied. Charming this woman would be like charming an asp.

"You want to hear about Cal McKinney?" she asked.

"That's why I came," Mel said.

"You're recordin' this, ain't you?" She had a sly crook to her mouth.

He only smiled. She was right, of course. A small tape recorder was running in his pocket. In Texas it was legal for him to tape a conversation without consent. As a lawman's wife, she must know it.

"I want a thousand dollars," she said.

He kept his smile and tried to make it as sympathetic as possible. "I'd be a fool to pay before I've heard anything."

"And I'd be a damn fool to talk before I got any money." She blew out a stream of blue smoke that swirled into a shifting cloud between them.

Mel had stopped at the bank in Johnson City, the last city of any size before Bee Tree. From his pocket he drew an envelope. He took out two fifty-dollar bills.

"Let's do this by installments," he said. "You said this was about the McKinneys. Particularly Cal. What do you know?"

Her eyes stroked the money. "There's a death that people say was accidental. Gordon Jones. J.T.'s son and foreman were involved. Cal McKinney and Ken Slattery. There was a cover-up."

She held out her hand, but Mel pulled the money back slightly. He'd already heard that rumor from Gloria Wall. "Sorry," he said. "That's not news. It's not worth a hundred."

Her hard face went even harder. "Gordon's wife, Nora, divorced him. She was chasing Ken Slattery. Gordon went after both of them with a gun. Cal McKinney got mixed up in it. He had a gun, too. Cal got shot, and Gordon ended up dead—'accidentally.'"

Mel raised an eyebrow. "You're saying McKinney killed him?"

"I'm saying he's dead. Shot by McKinney's gun. That was never in the papers. Nobody printed Cal got shot, neither. My Len was one of the first men on the scene that night. My Len *knows* what happened."

Mel studied her. She stared back with absolute confidence. "Gordon Jones was *shot*," she said. "But the McKinneys covered it up. Paid off the law. And Ken married Nora so she wouldn't talk."

"Are you saying she blackmailed him into it?"

"Oh, the McKinneys made it worth his while. Bought him a new pickup truck. She got what she wanted—him—and she kept their dirty secrets. Cal got off scot-free. Money buys you anything."

He didn't believe her story, but he laid the two fifties on the hassock and drew out another two. He held them up. "Will it buy me more information?"

She scooped up the first two bills and stuffed them inside her robe. Mel had a glimpse of the top of a grimy brassiere. She shut the robe and took another drag of her cigarette.

"You want to know another thing about Cal? That reporter who showed up here? That Mitchell girl? She's a relative of Nora's—and not one bit better. Cal got her pregnant when she was sixteen. Marry *her?* Hell, no. The McKinneys sent her off that summer to have the baby, then paid her way to that fancy school so she'd stay away and keep her mouth shut."

Mel's face stiffened in disbelief. "How do you know this?"

"Before I married Len, I was a nurse in Dallas. I was *there* when she had that baby. I held it myself. It looked just like Cal McKinney. The spitting image. She gave it away. It was a little boy."

The woman talked on. She talked and talked. Her stories grew wilder, and everything she said was ugly and hurtful. It was the sort of thing that, if made public, would cause damage whether true or not.

He paid her only two hundred dollars, which made her

swear at him and order him to leave. He was glad to go. It was like escaping the untidy web of a spider whose fangs dripped venom.

MEL DROVE BACK to Crystal Creek in a black mood. Much of what the woman said was preposterous, and he didn't want to believe any of it. But he was worried. Fabian had never stooped to planting stories in the tabloids. If he couldn't find a damaging truth about the McKinneys, would he settle for a damaging rumor?

Mel had a sudden, almost irresistible urge to smash the damn cassette and throw it out the window. He didn't. He kept it in its case, safely tucked into the car's glove box.

He phoned DeJames, he said, "The Gilroy woman? She's lying through her teeth. But I want you to check out some things for me. First, death reports on a Gordon Jones. I've heard twice that Cal McKinney's implicated. Get me everything on it you can."

He said, "Second, check out Trina Gilroy herself. Get her background. I especially want to know if she was a nurse in Dallas twelve years ago."

He squared his jaw. "And you're not getting me enough on Kitt Mitchell. I want to know when she left Crystal Creek and started Stobbart."

"I've already got the last for you," said DeJames. "I tracked down a teacher from Stobbart. Mitchell went there in the middle of September, three weeks into the fall semester."

Mel's heart missed a beat. "You mean she went straight from one school to the other, no break in between?" *No time to have a baby. Gilroy had lied.*

"Right," said DeJames. "The second week of September she was in the Crystal Creek paper for being made captain of the girls' gymnastic team. The next week she was in Stobbart. Boom."

Mel heard the rustle of paper. "Let's see," DeJames said. "She got sidelined in gymnastics a month later with a broken wrist. Began to seriously concentrate on track. She stayed with a family named—Coolidge.''

"Were they relatives?''

"No. They were both teachers at Stobbart. From time to time they'd take in a kid from a troubled home. That's the scuttlebutt I got on Mitchell. Her home situation wasn't good. I can't get anything more concrete than that. Did Trina Gilroy say anything about her?''

"No,'' Mel said, realizing this was the first time he'd ever lied to DeJames. "Keep trying for details on Mitchell.''

"Will do.''

Mel hung up and frowned. DeJames's news seemed to knock Trina Gilroy's story into a cocked hat. DeJames, on the other hand, was nearly infallible. The real reason Kitt left *must* have been her family. But why?

MEL DROVE to Bluebonnet Meadows to look at the controversial dam.

Kitt was still on his mind as he walked the same road he'd tried to run yesterday. He didn't believe the Gilroy woman's story about her, but Gloria Wall had also hinted of something dark in Kitt's past.

And Trina Gilroy puzzled him. Was the woman simply vicious? Had everything she'd said been a lie? Or was there, somewhere, a grain of truth in her tales?

It was hot, humid, and starting to drizzle when Mel reached Fabian's man-made lake. It was nameless, at this point called only Lake Number One. Its water was dark and lifeless except for a coating of sickly green scum.

Number One covered almost twenty acres. It was protected from overflowing downstream into its old creek bed by a crude dam. In truth, it was more an earthwork or levee than dam, and sloppily built, at that.

It was a makeshift thing, an embankment formed by the piles of limestone and dirt gouged out when the lake bed was dug. Stone and gritty soil had been bulldozed into a thick wall to hold the water in place.

He knew that the levee had been meant to be a temporary impoundment, in place only until a permanent dam could be erected. Nobody had meant for the thing to serve all summer and into the autumn.

And the water was dangerously high. It lapped within a few feet of the levee's top. How many more days of rain could this thing withstand?

The original engineers must have seen the impoundment was unstable. They had started to erect a second levee downstream in the dry creek bed in case water should seep through the first. And water *was* seeping.

Only a trickle, here and there, but it was dribbling into the old creek bed, which already held half a foot of standing rainwater.

Mel swore. No wonder this thing spooked people. Fabian needed to reinforce it, no matter what the court order said about no more work.

HE WENT BACK to the hotel to change out of his damp clothes. The drizzle stopped, started, stopped and started again. He thought about every drop that hit the unnamed lake, raising its level higher and higher. It made an uneasy feeling creep along his backbone.

He was putting on a fresh shirt when DeJames called. "My man," he said jovially, "pull up your e-mail. I've got a pot of gold for you. The medical examiner's report on Gordon Jones. Claro County doesn't have its own medical examiner. Jones's body had to be taken to Austin."

"So give me a summary," Mel said.

"Okay. Ken Slattery and Nora Jones were at the Mc-Kinneys' lake house. Gordon Jones was high as a kite on pills and came after them. He had a gun. Cal McKinney tried to warn them. He gave Slattery a gun. Jones started shooting, and Slattery shot him in the right hand. Clearly self-defense. When Jones heard sirens coming, he bolted. Got killed by a police car. Hell of an ironic way to die, if you ask me."

"That's official? He got shot only in the hand? The car killed him?"

"That's official. There wasn't much news coverage at the time. Gordon was linked to a federal case, and Feds took over the investigation. A couple of months later, they busted some gun runners. I talked to one of the ATF agents myself."

Mel grinned. "You're a genius."

"Yes, I am. The agent said Gordon took a potshot, but only grazed Cal McKinney. The ATF kept a lid on most of the information at the time. You know the Feds."

DeJames sighed. "McKinney's clean. No dirt there. Not a speck. Fabian's going to be so-o-o disappointed. Can't you find something else on the guy?"

Mel's grin died. He thought of the claim that Kitt had borne Cal's child. He said, "What about Trina Gilroy?"

"I called the constable in Bee Tree. He's not the brightest bulb in the chandelier. I fed him a line and he took it."

"And?" Mel prodded.

"Gilroy was born and raised in Crystal Creek, never finished school, married young. She moved to Bee Tree fourteen years ago. Only job she's ever had is driving the school bus. She was never a nurse in Dallas or anywhere else."

Mel felt a deep, secret jubilation at this news. Trina Gilroy had never held that baby in her arms. That baby, he was certain, had never existed except in the woman's malicious imagination.

"Why the curiosity about Gilroy?" DeJames asked. "I thought you said she was a waste of time."

"Just double-checking," Mel said. "She had nothing."

"You sure?" DeJames sounded disappointed.

"Absolutely." He fingered the cassette tape. "I stopped taping her after five minutes," he lied. "She's a nutcase."

"Well," DeJames said philosophically. "I tried. You can never tell."

"That's right. Thanks, Big D. Can you connect me with Fabian?"

"He's feeling bad. He's not taking business calls."

Mel ground his teeth. Fabian was always feeling bad. He had serious health problems, and his chronic ailments caused much of his waspishness. "This is an emergency. Tell him to disobey the injunction and get somebody to shore up that dam, pronto. Or it could cause him big trouble."

"His engineers have guaranteed him that dam will hold. You know that."

"Tell him to get a second opinion fast. It is, I repeat, an emergency."

"I'll do what I can," said DeJames. "But no guarantees."

When Mel hung up, he picked up the cassette tape and tapped it against his palm. He didn't want DeJames to know about it because he didn't want Fabian to know. In a mean enough mood, he might use it, for spite if nothing else. Mel decided he needed to protect Fabian from himself. He was almost sure that everything Trina Gilroy had said was false. But why had she done it? Money? Malice? A combination of both?

She had claimed that Nora had blackmailed Ken Slattery into marriage—most certainly another lie. Yet, he'd like to know more about Nora and Ken, to judge for himself. And he'd also like to know why Trina Gilroy so hated these people—including Kitt Mitchell.

Kitt Mitchell. He wished like hell he could get her off his mind. He couldn't. He touched his mouth, remembering her kiss. *Keep your distance from her,* he warned himself. But he wasn't sure he could do that, either. Not sure at all.

AT NOON Kitt found the Longhorn packed.

Disappointed, she supposed she'd have to go back to the hotel pub, which was never as crowded. Here, every seat was filled.

But then she saw an opening—only one.

Mel Belyle sat a table for two in the far corner, his head bent over a folder. He held a mug of coffee.

Her stomach took an odd, swooping dip. Both her legs went strangely jelly-like. A faint but pleasant humming filled her head, blocking the hubbub of voices in the room.

The last time she'd seen this man, she'd ended up in his arms. Not only that, but she'd enjoyed it shamelessly. If she had any discretion, she'd turn and flee.

No. He'd like that. Discretion *wasn't* the better part of valor. She would march right up to him as if she was unfazed. She was not some fainting maiden to be fended off by a kiss.

Kitt collected herself, squared her shoulders, and thought, *No guts, no glory.* She made her way through the maze of full tables, smiling and greeting people. Then there she was in the back corner, standing across from him.

He didn't look up. "Hello, Mitchell," he said, resignation in his voice.

She was taken aback. "I didn't think you saw me come in."

"I didn't," he said in the same tone. "I *felt* it."

"Are you saving this seat for someone?" she asked.

"Only my own privacy," he said. He finally glanced up and the deep blue of his long-lashed eyes jarred her, as always.

"Odd to try to preserve your privacy in the busiest spot in town," she said lightly. "The truth is nobody wants to sit with you. Right?"

"Think what you like," he said.

She thought that there were people who would sit and gladly talk business with him, all right. They just wouldn't do it in public. Ralph and Gloria Wall were in the café, and so was Bubba Gibson. Each carefully avoided looking Mel's way.

"May I join you?" she asked, pulling out the empty chair.

He slapped his folder shut so she couldn't see its contents. "Didn't I warn you not to follow me?"

"Who's following? This is the only free seat. You joined *me* in a crowded restaurant in Dallas."

He sighed in resignation. "I was under the mistaken impression that you were a normal human being."

She sat down. "I never had such delusions about you."

"Remember what I said about your smart mouth?" he asked.

Her face burned at the recollection. For a moment she relived the sensation of his lips on hers, his arms enfolding her body. But she lifted her chin in disdain. "You overestimate the power of your hot lips. I'm still talking."

He gave her a look that clearly said, *Maybe I'll have to see what I can do about that.* It gave her that odd, fluttery feeling in her stomach, but she forced herself to speak as blithely as possible. "So—what did you spend the rest of your morning doing?"

"Losing you," he said. "And you?"

"An interview," she answered. She didn't add that it had been a highly unsatisfactory interview. "And what brings you to the Longhorn? For a guy like you, isn't this slumming?"

"Hiya, sweetie. Welcome," Nora said as she swooped Kitt's side and set down a mug of coffee. She placed a steak and salad before Mel. Then she put one hand on her hip and looked down fondly at Kitt. "Half a turkey and Swiss cheese sandwich, just like old days? Lettuce, tomato, dill pickle?"

"Exactly," Kitt grinned. "I can't believe you still remember."

"Coming over tonight?" Nora asked. "I'll make pizza, just the way you like it."

"I'd love to. But I have an appointment with—" Kitt saw the naked curiosity in Mel's eyes and caught herself. "I have an appointment at six. I might be late."

"So we'll eat late," Nora said. "No problem. Give me a call when you're on your way."

"Is that an open invitation?" Mel asked, startling both women.

Nora's blue eyes widened. "I beg your pardon?"

"I asked if the invitation to your place is open. I know I'm a stranger, but Kitt and I have been getting to know each other—" he gave Kitt a look freighted with meaning "—better and better."

Clearly he'd flustered Nora. Kitt was both appalled and intrigued by his boldness. Nora looked at her for guidance, and Kitt raised her eyebrows and gave a helpless shrug that said *I have no idea what to tell you.*

Nora, ever resilient, recovered herself. "You're welcome to join us," she said. "But it won't be anything fancy, I'll warn you."

"There are better things than fanciness," Mel said, gazing at Kitt.

Nora, watching, smiled an odd little smile. "About eight o'clock? Can you make it by then, Kitt?"

"I—I think so," Kitt said, trying to read the look on Mel's face. She saw conflict in his eyes, as if contrary emotions warred deep within him.

"Nora!" Bubba called loudly, "Hey, girly—I need more coffee."

"Duty calls," Nora said. "So I'll see you both tonight?"

"I'll be there," Mel assured her.

"Absolutely," Kitt answered. But as soon as Nora had scurried off, she clenched the edge of the table and leaned across it. "You've got your nerve," she accused. "What do you mean, inviting yourself like that?"

He ignored her tone and cut into his steak. "You asked what I was doing in the Longhorn. I'm not slumming. I wanted to check the place out."

"Why?" Kitt demanded. "Does Fabian want to buy it, too? Is that his secret desire? To get away from his vaults of money and become a fry cook?"

He tasted the steak. "Mmm," he said with an approving tilt of his head. "Good. This is a busy place. Your cousin must work hard at it."

"My *aunt*," she corrected. "She does work hard. Too darn hard."

"She doesn't seem old enough to be your aunt," Mel said. "Excellent food, though. I can see why this place is an institution."

"And why do you want to come to Nora's house?"

"I have my reasons," he said with his old maddening vagueness. "Now, you tell me. Who are you going to see at six o'clock?"

"No comment," she replied with satisfying malice. "And I know better than to ask where you'll be spending the afternoon."

"Very good," he said. "You're catching on."

"And how will you make conversation at Nora's?" she challenged. "Since you make a career of never saying anything?"

"That," he said, "you'll have to wait and see. By the way, why did you leave high school here and transfer to Stobbart in Dallas? Just a few weeks into the new school year?"

She straightened up and felt herself go pale. "No comment," she said, again using his own line against him.

"Okay," he said. "I won't push you on the subject. If you'll do a little something for me."

Her head jerked higher and she eyed him with suspicion. "What?"

"Let me take you to Nora's tonight. You ride out there with me—and back."

She straightened in her chair, her face suddenly wary. "Why?"

He looked at her steadily, as if drinking her in. "The truth is I don't know why," he said. "I guess I want to find out."

CHAPTER TEN

KITT'S AFTERNOON PASSED in a jumble of frustration.

Mayor Douglas Evans postponed his appointment for two days. This both worried and puzzled Kitt.

When she'd phoned Evans from New York, he'd seemed friendly, eager to talk. Now she sensed he was dodging her. But why? What had changed? Was Mel Belyle the one who changed it?

Dan Gibson, Bubba's nephew, politely declined an interview. He and his wife didn't like being in the public eye, he said. He wished Kitt luck, but had nothing more to say.

Lynn McKinney Russell also declined to talk. "I don't completely agree with Daddy on this subject," she said over the phone. "I don't completely disagree, either. It's best I don't speak out. I might say the wrong thing and hurt him. I love him too much for that."

Blood is thicker than water, Kitt thought with resignation. Especially McKinney blood.

She had hoped Dr. Claire Turner, the pediatrician, would give her the viewpoint of a newcomer to Crystal Creek. But no, the good doctor said, very nicely. She wasn't an expert on the town, and she'd liked to stick to what she knew: doctoring. She was pleasant, but firm.

Kitt sighed and scratched the woman's name off her list. She was going to have to count on Howard Blake.

REVEREND HOWARD BLAKE HAD AGED WELL, thought Kitt. The blue eyes still sparkled, his bass voice was just as thrilling, and he was still strong enough to give her a bear hug in welcome.

Now they sat in the Blakes' cozy living room, drinking ginger ale.

"So people don't have much to say to you, eh?" he asked. He was settled into the big, flowered sofa, his latest fox terrier asleep in his lap.

Kitt shook her head. "Nobody was discourteous. It was just clear—they weren't comfortable talking to me."

Howard settled his glasses more firmly on his nose. "That doesn't surprise me. And it won't surprise me if J.T. won't open up. He's a very private man. He'd rather that the lawyers did the talking."

"The problem is that lawyers talk lawyer-talk," said Kitt. "I want to hear people talking people-talk."

He smiled at her. "My dear, you're a woman of the world. Surely you understand that you're not an ordinary listener. You're a reporter. For a national magazine. It makes people nervous."

"Does it make you nervous?" she asked, hoping he would say no.

"Yes," he said wryly, "it does, I'll admit. We're not sophisticated folk here. Nobody wants his or her words distorted by the media."

"I wouldn't distort," Kitt said. "It's not my way."

"I know it isn't," he said. He leaned sideways and tapped the magazine rack. It was neatly filled with back issues of *Exclusive*. "I read your pieces," he said. "They have integrity—because you do."

She smiled, touched by his compliment.

"But even the honest press can beget monsters," he said. "You know that."

"Will *you* talk to me?" she asked.

His face went solemn. "I'll answer as frankly as I think seemly," he said. "I'd like to speak under anonymity—"

"That's easily arranged," she said.

"—but it wouldn't be right. A minister shouldn't speak his opinion if he's afraid to put his name to it."

The unvarnished honesty of the man made her feel chastened. She had bent the truth lately—only a little, here and there. But Howard Blake was a man who would never do so.

"I should have known you'd say that," she murmured.

"Do you want to use a tape recorder?" he asked. "I don't mind."

"I'd like that, yes. I was going to ask you." She took the recorder from her backpack, switched it on and set it on the coffee table between them.

She took a deep breath, then said, "Reverend Blake, the Texas media's heard about the Concerned Citizens' side of the controversy. But few people outside the county have heard about townsmen who take the other side. There are such persons, aren't there?"

He nodded. "Yes. There are."

"Which side are you on?"

"I haven't taken sides," he answered. "I have parishioners in both camps. I don't want people to think the church is endorsing one view or the other. I don't want to polarize folks."

"I know why people *don't* want Bluebonnet Meadows. But why are some people in favor of it? What do they have to gain?"

He smiled, as if he knew her question was falsely naive and that she didn't fool him. "Ah, my girl," he said. "What do you think?"

"Profit," she said. "There's money to be made. Certainly by property owners. That's clear. A man like Bubba Gibson could be a millionaire, many times over."

Howard nodded and petted his sleeping dog. But he said nothing.

Kitt continued. "And the merchants here would profit if Bluebonnet Meadows is built. Crystal Creek has seven thousand residents, right?"

"Seven thousand and fifty-seven," he supplied.

"A thousand new families would mean a lot of new customers for people like Ralph Wall," Kitt said. "For the grocery stores and the bank. For the hardware store and beauty shops and restaurants—"

"Including the Longhorn," commented Howard.

Kitt nodded reluctantly. Nora already had as much business as she could handle. What would she do with more? Expand? Or stubbornly keep the Longhorn as it always had been?

She pressed on. "A thousand new families would make huge demands on the water and power companies. On the schools, the hospital, the fire department…"

"True," the minister agreed. "And those families would also pay the taxes to upgrade the very same things."

"Right," Kitt said. "And there'd be more construction, more jobs. That could be good. This town has hardly grown in twelve years."

"It's a hold-out," Howard Blake said, watching her expression closely. "The Hill Country around Austin is transforming. Every day. But not Crystal Creek. It's resisted change."

She asked him the question that was at the heart of the story she must write. "Yes. It's resisting change. Is that good or bad?"

He picked up his glass and swirled his ginger ale so that the bubbles danced. "That, my dear, depends on your perspective."

A fruit bowl sat on the coffee table. He took an orange from it and placed it on the latest copy of *Exclusive* magazine. He said, "On one hand, we have a beautiful countryside, a slow-paced and old-fashioned town. It's friendly, it's familiar. It has little traffic, less crime, no pollution. It's a bit of Texas paradise, almost perfectly preserved. Who'd want to spoil such a thing?"

Resentment tightened in her throat. *Brian Fabian wants to. And Mel Belyle's here to speed the destruction.*

Howard reached into the fruit bowl and took out a shiny red apple. He set it beside the orange. "On the other hand," he said, "the town hasn't prospered because it *hasn't* grown or changed. It's lost population. There are few jobs for young people—or anyone else. The teachers are overworked and underpaid. So are doctors, nurses, the police—on and on."

He paused and sighed. "Heaven knows this town's had its share of money woes. But has it ever worked to attract more business and industry? No. Never."

He studied the two pieces of fruit he'd placed on the magazine. "So some will say that Crystal Creek has been wise. It's hung onto its past. Others will say it's foolish, because it hasn't provided for its future."

Kitt looked into his kindly blue eyes. "Then which side is right?"

He smiled sadly and picked up one piece of fruit in each hand. "That's what I'm getting at, my dear. Who can say with certainty? It's like comparing apples and oranges."

"What do *you* think?" she asked. He was a fair and kindly man, and she wanted to know his opinion.

"Quite truthfully," he said, "I see both sides." He set the pieces of fruit back on the copy of *Exclusive,* side by side.

She said, "Right now the people who want to save the old ways are more organized. And more vocal."

"Yes," he answered. "Nobody in the county has tried to built a coalition to support Bluebonnet Meadows."

Kitt frowned. "But the Concerned Citizens group has members who could profit if Fabian wins."

"Yes," Howard nodded. "For instance, Douglas Evans. His pub and hotel could profit. So could his real estate business. But he came to Crystal Creek because of its old-fashioned charm. He wants it to keep that charm."

Her brow furrowed, remembering how oddly Douglas Evans had acted toward her this afternoon. Slowly she said,

"Has anyone done a study of how much money Bluebonnet Meadows might bring the town?"

"Not to my knowledge," Howard said.

But Brian Fabian is smart enough to do it, she thought. *He can convince the town that Bluebonnet Meadows is the goose that can lay golden eggs. And that only a fool would kill it.*

She said, "So Fabian's biggest enemy here is the Concerned Citizens group," she said.

"Exactly."

She leaned forward in her chair earnestly, her fingers linked together. "Reverend Blake, if you were Fabian, how would you fight them?"

"I'm a minister, not a strategist," he said with a wry smile. "But I've read Aesop's fables, and I know the truth of the morals. If the town and country stand united against him, he'll lose."

"You really think so?" she asked, raising an eyebrow dubiously.

"I said 'if,'" he cautioned her. "It's a small word that casts a big shadow. So if I were Fabian, which thankfully I am not, I would set out to divide—and conquer."

"And how would you do that?" she asked.

"By setting people against each other," he said. "Lines of division are already showing. He might do everything in his power to widen them."

"But again, how?"

"From what I've heard of the man, he might do anything."

She pondered this, staring at the apple and the orange, so futile to compare. She desperately wanted to ask Howard Blake something else: what he thought of Fabian setting one brother against another. And what he thought of Mel for taking up a vendetta against his own blood.

But she could not quite bring herself to utter the questions. The silence grew long.

At last Howard Blake said in a gentle voice, "Enough

about the land. What about you, Kitt? Are you happy? Are you fulfilled? Do you feel that life's been good to you?''

She raised her eyes to meet his and gave him an uncertain smile. ''I love New York. I love my job. Yes, life's been very good to me.''

''So we did the right thing by sending you to Dallas?''

She bit her lower lip and looked away. ''Yes,'' she said. ''It was absolutely the right thing. It made everything else possible.''

''It's good to hear you say that,'' he said with a strange note of sadness. ''I've hoped so. I've prayed so. You seem to have done well materially.''

''Oh, yes,'' she assured him. ''I live in the most exciting city in the world, I live comfortably. And I practically have a promotion guaranteed.''

''Materially, you're well-off. But what about the inner Kitt? Still carrying scars? Or do you feel healed?''

It was wrong to lie in general, she thought. It was worse to lie to a minister, especially one who'd been as kind to her as Howard Blake. ''A few scars,'' she admitted. ''But no gaping wounds. I'm fine. Really.''

''You haven't married,'' he said. ''Is it because of—well, you know?''

''I've had no desire to get married,'' she said. ''I'm happy just as I am.''

''Ah,'' he said. ''Maybe someday a fine fellow will come along who'll change your mind.''

''Maybe,'' she said, but she didn't believe it. She'd allowed no room in her life for any kind of real commitment. For the first time she could remember, the fact depressed her.

Perhaps Howard sensed her darkened mood. ''I saw Nora late this afternoon,'' he said, the tone of his voice more cheerful. ''She said you and she took my name in vain the other night. That you laughed yourselves silly over my—embarrassment—when Spot tried to get himself saved.''

''Oh!'' Kitt gasped, caught out. But she looked at the dog

in his lap and smiled. The animal was a double for the infamous Spot. ''You haven't learned your lesson, eh?'' she teased.

He scratched the dog's brown ears. ''Yes, I have,'' he joked. ''When I go to church, this fellow's locked tight in a fenced-in yard. The good Lord invented dogs, but He didn't intend them to trot in to church during the middle of a sermon and scratch their fleas.''

When Kitt had to leave, he walked her to the door, and the sleepy terrier walked behind them, its nails clicking on the tiles. It didn't seem to want to leave the man's side for a second.

Howard took her hand between his large ones. ''It's good to have you home, Kitt,'' he said. ''Eva will call you. We want you to come to supper one of these nights. Nora will have to be generous and share you.''

She promised she would, then left. He watched her make her way back to her car, he and the dog standing on the porch. She felt great warmth for the man, yet he made her also feel oddly empty and defenseless. Almost as empty and defenseless as when she'd been sixteen years old.

Suddenly she wished with all her heart that she hadn't agreed to be with Mel Belyle tonight.

MEL SAT on the hotel bed, holding the receiver to his ear, his knuckles pale.

''I know where you are,'' his younger brother, Jack, said. ''Thank God Mom doesn't know about it. Why didn't you check with me before you did this?''

Mel's jaw squared dangerously. ''I don't have to ask you what to do.''

Jack's voice was taut with accusation. ''Mom would never want you to pull something like this. It's like you're gunning for Nick.''

''Mom isn't speaking to him,'' Mel retorted. ''She's done everything but disown him. He's shamed her. He's shamed us all.''

"She'll get over it. For God's sake, don't make it worse."

"This is between Nick and me. You stay out of it. How in hell did you even find out? This is a confidential mission."

"Some woman called my office," Nick flung back. "Her name was Tawny or some damn thing. She said she wanted to get in touch with you, but all she knew was that you were in Texas. Somewhere around Austin. I put two and two together. It wasn't exactly rocket science."

Mel cursed under his breath. Tawnee Phipps was a model who was gorgeous, but as predatory as a barracuda. Before he'd left, she'd phoned him in the middle of the night, wheedling him about where he was going, he'd been too groggy to lie well.

Now he had Jack on his case. "What's going on in your head?" Jack challenged. "Why'd you let Fabian send you? Aren't things bad enough?"

Mel allowed himself a small, crooked smile. "Fabian didn't send me. I volunteered."

"You're crazy," Jack muttered. "Leave it alone. Nick nearly broke Mom's heart. You're going to make things worse."

"I'm going to make things right," Mel countered. "Nick screwed up. He sabotaged the whole operation. I'm here to undo the harm he's done."

Jack said nothing for a moment. Then in a bitter voice, he muttered, "Mom could forgive Nicky if you'd just stay out of it. You should forgive him, too. He's your brother."

"No," Mel contradicted. "Not any longer, he's not."

"And he's not Fabian's number one man any longer, either," Jack shot back. "You want his place. That's it, isn't it? You were always afraid that Fabian wanted Nick on his work force the most. And that he played on Mom's feelings about you to get him. You've resented Nick, and now—"

Mel hung up on him. He could imagine the scorn on his younger brother's chiseled face. Of the three brothers, Jack was the most intense and the most volatile.

Swearing again, Mel rose from the bed. He paced to the mirror and studied his image. He was a handsome man, and he knew it. He saw behind the looks, though. He knew who really lived behind that face.

I'm grateful. I'm loyal, he told himself. *I'm not like Nick. I didn't resent him. He resented me.* He forced Jack's words out of his memory. What did Jack know? Things had always come easily for him. Too easily.

Mel straightened the collar of his blue silk shirt. He was dressed well for his evening with Kitt and the Slatterys. The irony was that Kitt wouldn't care. She'd probably be in her cargo pants, her vest of many pockets and her well-worn shoes.

She simply didn't seem to give a damn about appearances. He ran his finger critically over his upper lip. He wondered if he should have shaved again. Maybe he'd just slap on a few more drops of cologne; he hadn't put on any since this morning.

Just as he unscrewed the bottle cap, a knock rattled his door. He glanced up in bemusement. He expected nobody. Kitt was supposed to phone when she was ready.

He walked to the door, swung it open, and there stood Kitt in all her tousled glory.

She'd swept her hair back into a ponytail, but already tendrils were hanging loose, trailing in front of her ears and at the nape of her neck. Her only makeup was a touch of coral lipstick.

She leaned one hand against the door frame. ''Hi,'' she said with exaggerated casualness. ''I'm early. I thought I'd just stop by. I didn't realize I'd catch you while you were still primping.''

She looked pointedly at the bottle of cologne in his hand. She was garbed just as he'd expected: the plain white turtleneck, the khaki pants, the unflattering vest. Still, she looked terrific to him. She looked pretty and brimming with life.

And she was teasing him, as usual. He looked her up and down, pretending to be unimpressed by what he saw.

"Do you always wear that same damn outfit?" he asked. "The vest and all?"

"This is a *great* vest," she said. "It holds everything— pens, markers, tablets, sunglasses, cell phone, flashlight, sewing kit."

He shook his head. "Don't you get tired of it?"

"I like to be prepared. And to travel light," she said. "I rinse things out at night. All I need is a couple shirts, a change of underwear—I'm set."

He swallowed and tried not to think of her underwear. He was sure it was plain and utilitarian. He was also sure she'd look great in it, much more intriguing than if she'd opted for the blatant sexiness of Victoria's Secret.

She frowned as her eyes swept him, measuring him as he'd measured her. "But you're your usual *Gentleman's Quarterly* self. Where'd you keep all those clothes? You were carrying hardly anything in the airport."

"I had my clothes sent ahead. It's a special travel service."

"Wow," she said. "So that's how the other half lives. Well, I'm ready to go. Whenever you finish anointing yourself."

He screwed the cap on the bottle and set it aside. "You're a sassy little thing."

"I am," she admitted. "And a walking fashion disaster. I'm surprised you let yourself be seen with me."

"It's either you or another night with the Walls," he lied. "You're the lesser of two evils."

"We'll see about that." An impish smile curved her lips.

His heart banged crazily as he looked at that beguiling mouth. He thought, *I want you. I want you so much it makes me half-crazy.*

CHAPTER ELEVEN

KITT AND NORA STOOD at the kitchen counter, chopping vegetables to garnish the pizza. Ken had taken Mel to the ranch's hangar to show him J.T.'s Cessna and his army surplus helicopter.

"So J.T. flies emergency cases into Austin sometimes?" Kitt said.

"Yup," Nora said. "He's a godsend."

Through the window Kitt saw the men returning from the hangar. As Mel neared the house, the porch light fell on his high cheekbones, his straight nose, his maddeningly perfect mouth. Kitt's midsection tightened in excited longing. She tried to fight down the feeling.

Nora noticed him, too. "Great googly moogly, he *is* the best-looking thing. How do you keep your mind on your work?"

"No problem. I just wish he hadn't invited himself here," Kitt grumbled. "What's he thinking of?"

"You," Nora said with a laugh, pelting her with an olive. "Can't you see, you ninny? He *likes* you."

Kitt neatly caught the olive and popped it in her mouth. "Ridiculous," she said. For emphasis she spit the pit into the garbage.

"He keeps stealing looks at you," Nora countered. "When he thinks nobody's watching. *Such* looks. Like he's eating you with his eyes."

"He's just getting even," Kitt muttered, chopping with a passion. "I've been shadowing him, giving him a hard time. He wants to give me a taste of my own medicine."

"He likes you, all right." Nora gave her a wise, sidelong smile. "And you like him. You like to tease each other. You strike sparks."

Kitt laid down the paring knife and put her hand on her hip. "He and I couldn't get involved if we wanted to. Our jobs forbid it."

Nora laughed. "Shhh. Here they come."

Ken swung open the back door, and he and Mel entered the kitchen, as Nora slid the pizza into the oven. "Well, did you two inspect the air force?"

Ken shook his head. "Something's leaking in the Cessna's engine. Looked, but couldn't find it. I'll try again tomorrow. Right now I'm ready to wash up and have a beer."

"Sounds good," said Mel.

"Oh, rats, look at you," Nora said, moving to Mel. "You've got oil on that beautiful shirt. Men and motors—yech!"

Kitt stole a covert look. A dark smudge stained the shoulder of his blue shirt. She almost flinched. He was the kind of man who looked sexy with his sleeves rolled up and a bit of grime on him.

"It's no big deal," Mel shrugged. "The cleaners'll get it out."

"No, no," fussed Nora. "Let me have it—please. I'll put some spot remover on it. If you let it set, it'll be ruined. It'll drive me nuts all through supper. Do an obsessive lady a favor and hand it over."

Ken fought back a grin. "Better do what she says. Once her mind's made up, that's that. Nora, pop us a couple of cold ones, will you, honey?"

"Sure enough, hon," Nora said.

The two men made their way down the hall, and Nora pulled open the refrigerator door, plucked out two bottles of Lone Star beer, and neatly uncapped them. "You want one, too?" she asked Kitt, "or would you rather have Chianti?"

"Chianti, thanks. But I'll wait for supper."

"You've got it," Nora said. She pulled a glass plate of appetizers from the fridge, then bumped the door shut with her hip.

In almost one movement, she set the plate on the kitchen table, spun, opened the freezer and drew out two chilled mugs. She filled them expertly and set them on the counter for the men.

"You have *that* down to a science," Kitt said moodily.

"Lawsy, I ought to, after all these years of slinging hash."

"Doesn't it bother you?" Kitt asked. "Waiting on people all the time? Even here at home?"

Nora gave her a peculiar look and started to set the table with professional efficiency. "I'm not waiting on people here. I'm having supper with my husband and guests. It's fun."

"Yes, but at the Longhorn all day—"

"That's different," Nora said.

"But it's not what you really want to do," Kitt persisted. "Don't you ever wish you were still teaching?"

"I wish a lot of things. But I've got no complaints. I'm a lucky woman," Nora said. "Where'd I put that blasted spot remover?"

Kitt crossed her arms. "Why clean his shirt? You're not his maid. And he's probably got a thousand shirts."

"Why let the life work of some poor silkworm go to waste?" Nora asked blithely, reaching for a bottle.

"He's probably got a thousand silk shirts. I'm just saying you don't have to wait on him. You didn't even invite him."

"Look—I don't mind. It'll make for an interesting night," said Nora. She glanced at the kitchen clock. "I wonder if Rory's going to call tonight? Sometimes he calls on Tuesdays. I wish he would. He sounded like he had a cold this weekend. He doesn't get enough rest. I'm not sure he's eating right, either."

You worry about everybody but yourself, Kitt thought,

watching Nora bustle. *It's not right.* But she said, "I'm sure he's fine. He's a great kid."

Rory, Nora's son by Gordon, was a freshman at Tulane, majoring in journalism. Kitt was flattered he'd chosen the same field as she had and was almost as proud of him as Nora.

She was about to ask about Rory's work on the newspaper, when Mel returned, his shirt slung carelessly over one T-shirt clad shoulder. The T-shirt hugged his chest and revealed the hard bulges of his biceps.

"Here," Nora commanded holding out her hand. "And your beer's on the counter. Have a seat and an appetizer."

With a half-shy smile, Mel gave her the shirt. "A woman like you could make a man like domesticity," he said.

Nora blushed prettily, and Kitt felt both inadequate and rebellious. *She* wouldn't have cleaned his shirt for a thousand bars of gold bullion. She crossed her arms more stubbornly and looked away from him.

HE FELT AT HOME.

How unexpected. How stupid. How nice. How painful.

These impressions chased each other through Mel's mind like insane squirrels that dived, swooped and jumped without aim or logic. He tried to fight off the feelings and kept his expression under control. Expertly he wielded his smile, and with precision he utilized his charm.

He usually did not give a damn if people liked him. If he needed them, he beguiled them as best he could. He used them, then moved on, and afterward he didn't look back.

He had a low opinion of human nature. Most of the people he met were on the make, one way or the other. If he had no access to power, they wouldn't give him the time of day, and he knew it.

But Nora and Ken Slattery didn't seem like wheeler-dealers or hustlers. They didn't ask sly questions; they didn't smirk and gossip; they didn't try to impress him or curry his favor. They spoke well of the people they respected. They spoke ill of no one.

The four of them sat round the oak table in the tidy kitchen. Mel couldn't remember the last time he'd eaten in anybody's kitchen except his mother's. His mother had ended up living in a fancy condo in Atlanta, but she could never get used to its dining room. When her boys came home, they got fed in the kitchen, and for some reason, Mel liked that.

Nora wasn't Italian like Minnie Belyle, and she didn't look like her in the least, but she reminded Mel of a younger version of his mother. It was partly because of the books. Her living room was lined with books, and so was the hallway, floor to ceiling—all sorts of books, from classics to best-sellers. It was like she lived in her own well-loved little library.

Minnie had worshipped education, yet never had a chance to get one. She'd married young, as soon as she'd finished high school. First she was a young wife with a baby coming every year, and then she was a young widow struggling to support three sons.

But she'd loved books, and she passed her passion for learning on to her boys. That, along with her irresistible cheer and fierce loyalty, had won her what many people coveted, but few earned: Brian Fabian's respect—and his affection.

The comparison gave Mel an eerie feeling. It was as if he understood, for the first time, how a solitary and complex man like Fabian might hunger for simplicity and lack of pretense.

There was nothing formal about Nora's house. For a centerpiece, she'd stuck a humble bouquet of wildflowers in a blue earthenware vase. A black and white border collie wandered in and out of the kitchen at its leisure. Sometimes it flopped beside Ken's chair and gazed up at him worshipfully.

Nora was a pretty woman, Mel thought, the kind who

grew prettier the longer you looked at her. And she was smart. She tried to keep the conversation on neutral and pleasant ground.

"—and so that's why we have a carousel on the lawn of the courthouse," she said, finishing the story.

"It's a beautiful thing," Mel said, but he looked at Kitt when he said it.

Ken pushed away his emptied plate. "Great meal, honey. Did you make spumoni?"

"Of course," Nora answered. "You'd feel downright persecuted if you didn't get your spumoni. Everybody ready for dessert?"

"Sounds great," Mel said. He still felt the same weird contentment. The sky outside had darkened, and the overhead light in the kitchen cast the room in a warm, golden light.

The Slatterys were nice people, genuine, generous and intelligent. And they were clearly in love. He tried to imagine them marrying for cold calculation, the way Trina Gilroy had accused. He couldn't.

Nor could Mel picture them conspiring to cover up a crime. No. These were not people who lived a lie—for Cal McKinney or anyone else. Any rumors about them, he suspected, sprang from jealousy of them.

As SOON AS the last bite of spumoni was eaten, Nora rose and briskly began to clear the table.

"Let me help," Kitt offered, but Nora gestured for her to stay seated.

"Nope. You're company," she said firmly.

"I'm family," Kitt argued.

"You're both," Nora said. She nodded at Ken. "And I've got well-trained help here. Make us some coffee, handsome?"

"She's got me well-trained all right," Ken said, pushing back his chair and hoisting up his long body.

Nora was putting the ice-cream bowls in the sink when

the phone rang. "Rory," Nora said, breaking into a smile of pure joy. "I'll take it in the living room. Ken, you take the bedroom extension. Excuse us a minute, please?"

She raced for the living room, and Ken ambled down the hall, the border collie following, slowly wagging its plumy tail. Kitt and Mel sat alone at the table. Kitt felt atypically self-conscious.

To do something, anything, she stood, went to the sink and began to rinse off the dishes. But Mel, too, got up. He came to her side and started to help by scouring the pizza pan. This gesture both surprised and oddly touched her.

She gave him a startled look. "I—didn't think you knew how to do things like that."

"I didn't grow up rich," he muttered. "I've scrubbed pots and pans before."

Kitt turned her gaze to her work and kept it there. "The phone call—it's Rory. He's her son. *Their* son. Ken adopted him."

"I know," Mel said.

"He's a very bright kid. They did a fine job raising him."

"I can see that they would. They're good folks."

It felt strange to be doing such a humble task side by side with him. It gave her an almost pleasurable pang in her chest. But she was too aware of his physicality, of his height, of the play of muscles that the T-shirt showed, the bareness of his arm so close to hers.

Defensively she said, "Why did you want to come here tonight?"

"Curiosity," he said. "That's all."

"Professional curiosity?" she asked, still not looking at him.

"Partly." He reached for a sponge, and his hand brushed hers. They both jumped a bit and edged slightly farther apart. Her little finger tingled where he had touched her.

Kitt took a deep breath to steel herself. There was a subject she didn't want to bring up, but she feared she must.

She said, "If you've heard rumors about Ken and Nora, I know what they are. And you can forget them."

She wondered how he would answer. He kept scouring the pan as if it was more interesting than their conversation. He said, "If you're talking about the death of Gordon Jones, I know I can forget it. I've seen the medical examiner's report."

Suspicion flared through her. Her head snapped up, and she stared at him, her eyes flashing. "Gordon's death was an *accident*," she said from between her teeth.

"I know," he said as calmly. "I told you. I saw the report."

"*Why* did you see it?" she demanded. "What's it possibly got to do with Bluebonnet Meadows? Or have you descended to collecting rumors for Fabian?"

His face hardened, and the deep blue eyes grew colder. "If I hear a rumor once, I ignore it. If I hear it twice, I start to wonder. I checked it out. You'd have done the same."

She dried her hands and put one fist on her hip. "Is that why you came here tonight? To see if Ken and Nora act like MacBeth and Lady MacBeth?"

For a split second, displeasure registered on his face, and she thought she'd hit a nerve. But his expression became impenetrable, and his eyes more unreadable than before. He said, "The person most seriously implicated wasn't Ken or Nora. It was Cal McKinney."

Kitt felt suddenly chilled. *If he'd heard that rumor, he might have heard others…including the one about her…*

"This is a small town," she said defensively. "People talk. And some people gossip. And some people just flat make up things."

"It also happens in New York," he said, "which is a big town."

Her thoughts raced. "You mean Fabian. All the stories about Fabian."

"Yeah. That's what I mean." He laid aside the cleaned pan, and put the scouring pad in its dish. He dried his hands.

He leaned one elbow against the cabinets, but all the sense of domesticity, of homey intimacy, had fled the room.

His eyes flicked her up and down. "You wouldn't be on this story if Fabian wasn't in it. If it was just some ordinary corporation coming here, doing what he's doing, *Exclusive* wouldn't give a damn—would it?"

She set her jaw, uneasily remembering Heywood Cronin's words: "Brian Fabian. He's *always* news. He sells magazines, by God."

She said, "Fabian's different. He's famous, a national figure, not like Ken and Nora. They're ordinary people. They shouldn't be subjected to—to low snooping."

"But Cal McKinney might enter the fray. Is he an ordinary person?"

She looked away, offended and not knowing what to answer.

Mel persisted. "When you write your story, how will *you* describe him? Mr. Average Guy? Will you check out his background? List his virtues? And his sins, great and small?"

Ignoring the hammering of her heart, she gave him her coolest look. "No comment," she said.

From the living room, she heard Nora laugh, then say, "No, Rory, that's the *point*. They fall in love, but they both know they should never, ever get together. If they do, nothing but disaster can come from it."

Ken came into the kitchen. If he sensed the tension between Mel and Kitt, he hid it well.

"Nora's talking to Rory about his paper on the Knights of the Round Table—or something. I'm out of *that* conversation. Once a teacher, always a teacher, I reckon," he said. "Lord, she loves to rattle on about that stuff."

He looked at the two of them and said, "Ready for coffee?"

THE RAIN HAD STARTED again, and both Nora and Ken cautioned Mel to be careful driving back to Crystal Creek. The water drummed on the car's roof and streamed down the windows. The windshield wipers thumped hard and monotonously.

Mel had to squint to see the highway. "It's like being on the edge of a hurricane," he muttered, remembering Beaumont.

Lightning slashed the sky to a blinding blue white. At the same instant thunder roared so loudly that he felt it vibrate his breastbone. He swore under his breath.

Kitt twisted in her seat nervously. "So," she said. "Did you enjoy having pizza in a plain old kitchen?" She tried to sound flippant, but he heard the anxiety in her voice.

His fingers tightened on the steering wheel. "Yes. I told you. They're nice people."

"Yes," she said. "They are. And there's no scandal about them. None."

The lightning flared again with even more punishing brightness. Mel held his hand up to shield his eyes. The rain poured down with a force that had turned violent.

"Maybe you should pull off the road until it slows down," Kitt said, her voice even tighter with worry.

He gritted his teeth, not wanting to agree. But he could barely see the road through the flood of water washing over the windshield. He felt the tires tugged at by the greedy pull of rain gushing in rivulets down the road.

He wasn't a coward or a quitter, but he wasn't a fool, either, and she was clearly nervous. He slowed, pulling to the side of the road by a deer crossing sign.

She gave a tense sigh. "I forgot how hard it can rain here."

He kept the motor on, the lights and windshield running. "What do they call this? A gully washer?"

She nodded, her profile outlined by the dashboard lights. "Or a toad strangler. It's enough to drown a fish."

He unfastened his seat belt. "I remember a hurricane once in Beaumont… Unbelievable…"

He and his mother and Jack had taken refuge in the upstairs

bedroom. Minnie had sat on the bed, hugging the two younger boys to her, fearing the rising water and roaring rain.

But Nick, always fearless, had stood at the window, fascinated by the storm's rage. Mel had resented him doing that like very hell. It had upset Minnie, who kept saying, "Come away from the window. Get away from the glass. Nick—Nick—do you hear me?"

Kitt seemed lost in her own memories. "There was a flash flood on the old Hammerschmidt spread," she said softly. "The next day, after the water went down, we found a dead steer—in a tree. In the top branches of an oak tree. A big oak tree. He'd been swept there by the high water and drowned...."

She shivered and wrapped her arms around herself.

"Cold?" he asked, leaning nearer.

She shook her head. "It's just I can still see it. My little brothers laughed—a steer in a tree. But I was horrified. The vultures circling...the sky was dark with them—" She shuddered again.

He bent nearer. He could smell the sweet, summery scent of her hair. "Your brothers," he said, "you and Nora never mentioned them. Not once."

She turned her face to his. "You never mentioned yours, either."

"That's different," he said. The rain drummed down harder. He and she seemed isolated in their own shadowy, safe little world.

"My little brothers had each other," she murmured. "And Nora and I had each other. We were one unit, and they were another. We had nothing in common."

She gave him a smile that hinted at her usual mischief. "They were *boys,*" she said with mock repulsion.

He looked at her lips. By the dim light they looked soft as velvet.

"You must have missed Nora when she got married. She got married young, didn't she?"

The smile fled from her face. She turned her gaze to the

windshield. It was as if she were gazing out at a dark sea. "I suppose Gloria Wall told you all about that," she said, her contempt barely veiled.

The steady beat of the windshield wipers thumped like his heart. He said, "She didn't tell me anything I can't see. Nora's not much older than you. Still, she has a son in college."

Kitt tilted her chin up, but didn't meet his eyes. "He's the light of her life. He's a wonderful kid."

"But he was an accident—wasn't he?"

Her head whipped back to face him again. Even in the subdued light he could see the flash of her eyes. "You don't answer questions about your family," she countered. "And I won't answer questions about mine. Is *that* really why you invited yourself tonight? To pry into Nora's life?"

That was part of it, of course, and he had to lie about it. But he didn't have to lie about everything.

"I wanted to know more about you," he said, and that was true.

"Why?" she demanded. "Is that your strategy? If I check up on you, you check up on me? Is this supposed to drive me away?"

The rain hammered on the roof; it covered the windows, sealing them in waves of darkness. "No," he whispered, touching her hair, "it's supposed to bring you closer."

He kissed her. Her mouth was as velvety soft as it had looked. It was warm and sweet. But it was reluctant. She did not want to respond to him, he knew.

His hand moved from her hair to her cheek, then the smoothness of her throat. Her old-fashioned perfume made him dizzy with the oldest fashion of yearning.

"I liked being with you," he said against her lips. "I liked sitting across the table from you in a real home. I liked being alone with you in a kitchen. I liked looking at you, listening to you, seeing you with someone you love."

She put her hand to his chest, pushing him away, but without conviction. She shook her head, and her hair brushed his face like the faintest, most beguiling touch of silk.

"We can't do this," she said, her breath uneven. "*I* can't do this."

She undid her seat belt and slid as far from him as she could. Her back was against the door, and she kept her hand braced against his chest to ward him off.

He could see the conflict in her face, the unhappy resolve in her eyes. He wondered if she could feel how hard his heart beat beneath the touch of her hand.

"We can't do this now," he said, taking her hand in his. He smiled in sad irony. "And we can't do it here. Not like this, like two teenagers in a car. But I promise you something."

She looked at him, her eyes wary and questioning.

"When this is over, and we're back in New York," he said, "I'm coming for you." He lifted her hand to his mouth and kissed her smooth knuckle. "I promise you that," he said.

The rain, mercifully, was slowing. She turned and laid her forehead against the glass of the window on the passenger side. "You aren't what you seem," she said.

There was a surprising weariness in her voice.

"No," he said. "I'm not."

"Why are you so loyal to Fabian?" she asked, as if she were asking the night. "So loyal that you'd even go against your own brother? Why do you think you owe him so much?"

"We'll talk about that in New York," he said.

She did not move. For a moment the only sound was the rain, not as fierce now. She said, "You hide your feelings most of the time. Very well."

"So do you," he said.

She was silent again, for the space of half a dozen heartbeats. He stared at the faint glitter of her fiery hair. He wanted to touch it again but did not.

"The rain's easing up," she said. "Please take me back."

The thunder rumbled, but more softly and farther in the distance.

CHAPTER TWELVE

BACK IN HIS HOTEL ROOM, Mel tried to forget that only a
wall separated him from Kitt Mitchell.

He had a job to do, and he couldn't afford to think of
how she would view that job. He dialed Bubba Gibson's
number. Gibson would be waiting for the call, he knew. Just
as he had been ready to meet him in Fredericksburg, before
Kitt sidetracked him.

Lord, she was a woman designed to throw a man offtrack,
to highjack his thoughts, scramble his plans, confuse his
priorities. And his first priority was to get Brian Fabian land.

If Bubba took Fabian's offer, J.T. would be sold out by
one of his oldest friends. Bubba might not cave in immediately. But he was itching to hear Fabian's new offer. He
couldn't disguise that curiosity, no matter how hard he'd
tried.

The phone rang a strangely long time before Bubba answered, and when he did, he was terse as the crack of a
whip. "I don't want to see you, after all," he snapped. "I
told my wife you were after me. She said don't even talk
to you—you're leadin' me into temptation."

Mel scowled. "All I'm doing is trying to make you rich.
You haven't heard our offer yet, and—"

"And I don't want to," Bubba said combatively. "I'm a
weak man, but God gave me a good wife. She sees through
you like you were a pane of window glass. I was born on
this land, and I will by God die on it."

Mel swore inwardly. The wife, of course. Mel had always

known Mary Gibson would be a problem. It was child's play to tempt Bubba, but Mary was made of sterner stuff.

"I thought you wore the pants in the family, Bubba," Mel chided. "You'd let a *woman* decide this? So you die on your precious land. Then what happens to it? Is she going to run it alone—a woman nearly sixty?"

"She's run it before," Bubba retorted. "And she ain't alone. We got a grandson who's comin' of age to take my place. There will *always* be a Gibson on this land. And we got a topnotch foreman. He and me got a deal. I ain't backin' out on it."

Dammit! "Just listen to me," Mel argued. "I'm going to name a price. Think about this price. Think hard. Then talk to the little woman again, and talk some sense into her. You can't—"

"I don't want to hear your price," Bubba roared. "You ain't tryin' to buy my land. You're tryin' to buy my soul. Get thee behind me, Satan."

He hung up. Mel swore as he smashed down the receiver. He'd gambled that Bubba's weakness was greater than Mary's strength. But no, she'd made Bubba have a fit of integrity. What a waste—a perfectly fine traitor ruined by the love of a good woman.

To hell with *that* scheme. Well, Fabian had an arsenal of other tricks ready; he never entered a fray with only one weapon. Tomorrow Mel would arrange for the heavier artillery to rumble in.

He heaved himself up from the bed and paced to the window. The rain still beat down outside. He stared at it and remembered Kitt's lips beneath his own.

J.T. HUNG UP the phone, heart pounding dangerously. Cal had just strolled, uninvited, into his study. Did he know what was happening? Maybe he did, because he looked uncharacteristically serious.

"Hi, Daddy," Cal said. "You all right?"

J.T. sank against the back of the leather sofa. He had a

half-empty glass of bourbon in one hand. "That was Bubba. Mel Belyle's been after him, trying to make him another offer. Bubba just told him to go to hell."

Cal's familiar grin flashed. "Good for him. I been scared he wouldn't hold out. Old Bubba loves money."

J.T. gave him a dark look. "He loves the land more." *Not like you,* he thought, then felt guilty for thinking it.

Cal's grin died. "I knocked, but you didn't answer. I guess you were on the phone. Cynthia said I could come on in."

Cynthia. J.T. sighed and took a stiff slug of bourbon. "Where's *she?*" he demanded.

"She said she was goin' to bed," Cal said.

Going to bed. Thank God. J.T. could wait until she was asleep then slip in beside her undetected. He finished his drink, rose and poured another. He put his foot on the brass rail and stared morosely at the framed map of the Double C behind the bar.

Cal moved to his side. "Mind?" he asked. J.T. grunted in answer, and Cal poured himself a shot of bourbon. J.T. could feel his son eyeing him, studying him, and he clamped his lips together to hide his emotions.

"I know what's wrong," Cal said quietly. "I just talked to Tyler. He said he talked to you about him and Ruth leavin'."

J.T. gave him a resentful glare. "Tomorrow. They're leaving *tomorrow*—out of the blue. He suspected this might be coming. He's known for weeks it might be coming. He's even arranged for somebody from Fredericksburg to come manage the winery. But he never mentioned a word to me—until tonight—when he's packed and ready to go."

Cal gazed into his glass. "He was hoping it wouldn' happen. That it wouldn't come to this. They'd hoped he father wouldn't get sicker, but he did. You can't blam Ruth, Daddy. She needs to be with him."

J.T. felt sickly himself, but it was mostly with deep dis appointment. He was overwhelmed by abandonment, eve betrayal. Tyler had mentioned that Ruth's father was ailing, but he'd never hinted at how serious the situation was. Or, if he had, J.T. had not allowed himself to hear it.

He muttered, "She's going to inherit that winery."

Cal shrugged, as if it was an inevitability and not to be fought. "It's a good one. It tops a lot of lists of Californian wines."

"What's wrong with the one here?" J.T. snapped. "Tyler's put damn near ten years work into it. Now he talks like he might—might just walk off and leave it. California. Leave Texas for *California*."

J.T. couldn't help himself. He spat out the word California as if it were the worst obscenity. Cal looked at him with pity, and he hated that.

"He don't know how this is going to come out," Cal reasoned. "He'll see if he can run two places—"

"He's had trouble running one place," J.T. said in frustration. "Now he'll handle two? He says if he can't, he's asked you to buy the winery here. Is that true?"

Cal looked him in the eye. "Yessir."

"And would you?" J.T. demanded. "If you don't, it'll go to some outsider. Maybe even Fabian."

Cal stood straighter. "I'd have to talk it over with Serena. But if he wanted me to buy it, I'd do my best."

J.T. looked at him askance. "But you wouldn't stay around to run it. You're too busy—elsewhere."

"I'm not a winemaker, Daddy. Hell, I can hardly make Kool-Aid."

"You can't stay put in one spot, either," J.T. grumbled. "I always thought that Tyler would. California. *Hell.*"

"He might not stay in California. Nothin's settled. He may be back here for good in six months. Ruth's emotional right now. She probably don't know what she really wants. Her father—"

"Her father is my *friend*," J.T. interrupted, his voice righteous. "A good friend. I feel rotten about losing him, too. They should have told me sooner. Warned me. Tyler springs this on me all at once.''

''You had enough on your mind,'' Cal said, putting his hand on his father's arm.

''Enough on my mind?'' J.T. said with an angry glance. ''Do you two think I need protecting? Has it come to that?''

''No sir,'' Cal said, his face going stiff with control. ''It's just that Ruth hated talking about it, and Tyler—''

J.T. hardly heard him. ''Too much is changing. Too much is—slipping away.'' He turned to face Cal, his expression almost combative. ''What about you? Where do you slip away to next?''

''South America,'' Cal said. ''There's cattle land in Argentina that—''

''There's cattle land *here*.'' J.T. hit the bar with his fist for emphasis. ''Oh, hell, what do you care? Just leave me alone for now, will you?''

Cal tossed down the rest of his drink and set the glass on the bar. His usually lively face had gone impassive. ''Sure, Daddy. I understand.''

He turned and left. When the door closed, J.T. put his elbows on the bar and stared at the map again, his face taut. Tyler—dependable Tyler, always his right hand—was leaving. At a time like this. And Cal would never stay. It wasn't his nature.

WEDNESDAY KITT STAYED busy—news kept breaking. Mel Belyle had tried to cut a private deal with Bubba Gibson, but Bubba had refused. It was the talk of the town.

But then came word from the Double C that Tyler Mc-Kinney was leaving for California with his wife. Her father was seriously ill, and rumor said they might stay and run the Napa Valley winery. Tyler leaving? The townsfolk were stunned.

J.T. canceled his interview with Kitt. Clearly he didn't want to talk about the situation. And like sinister background music, thunder rumbled and rain poured down all morning, all afternoon, all evening.

Kitt didn't see Mel. She was grateful, yet wondered where he was, what fresh mischief he was up to. That night she and Nora and Ken talked into the small hours about what might happen next. And the rain fell relentlessly.

Kitt stayed out so late that Thursday morning she overslept. She awoke with the foreboding that strange weather could sometimes bring. Even in the hotel room, she could feel a heaviness in the atmosphere, a closeness and an unpleasant electrical charge.

A glance at her watch told her that she had no time for a run. Her first appointment, with Mayor Douglas Evans, was at nine-thirty, only an hour away. She decided to go to the Longhorn to have a cup of coffee with Nora.

She showered and dressed, then examined herself in the mirror critically. Her travel clothes were practical, not pretty.

So what? she thought defensively. It was how she always dressed on assignment. Once, an angry boyfriend had called her clothes asexual. He'd taunted her, demanding to know why she was so frightened of her own femininity.

Again she thought, *So what?* She knew she wore these clothes as a sort of armor. Mel Belyle had pierced the armor, and now he was making her doubt both its power and worth. To hell with him.

I'm as tough as he is, Kitt thought stubbornly. *And just as much a loner. I can't let him play mind games with me. And I won't.*

SOMETHING HAD HAPPENED. Kitt sensed it as soon as she walked into the Longhorn.

The air crackled with tension. At each table and booth, people hunched in tense, unhappy discussions. At the corner booth, Bubba Gibson stood up, his face brick-red with anger. He jammed his hat more tightly on his head and stomped out of the café, slamming the door behind him.

Nora stood behind the counter, her face strained. She met Kitt's eyes, and her expression said, *There's trouble, big trouble*. Nora tilted her head in a signal to meet in the kitchen.

"What's going on?" Kitt asked once they were alone.

Nora reached into her apron pocket. She handed Kitt a business-size envelope, thick and important looking. "This came from New York this morning. By special delivery, no less. I think everybody in the blooming county's getting a copy."

Kitt withdrew the document, unfolded it and scanned the first paragraphs. A sudden queasiness rocked her stomach. "Good grief," she breathed.

"An Open Letter to the Citizens of Claro County:

"The Bluebonnet Meadows project has suffered *undeserved abuse* from a group calling itself 'Concerned Citizens of Claro County.'

"These so-called 'Concerned Citizens' have used every possible legal ruse, no matter how dubious, to stop work on Bluebonnet Meadows.

"Yet who forms the core of this organization? Typical, hardworking citizens like most of you?

"No. The leaders of these self-styled 'Citizens' are the power elite of Claro County. They are the families who have monopolized the land for generations—for one reason: their own profit. They have enjoyed this privileged monopoly at the expense of others, people like *you*.

"LOOK FOR YOURSELF at the growth, income and jobs Bluebonnet Meadows can bring to the city and the county!

"SEE FOR YOURSELF how a stunted town can bloom into a prosperous city—a city with unlimited opportunity for you and your children!

"THINK FOR YOURSELF how Bluebonnet Meadows can make your future brighter and more secure!

''The following statistics show the growth that Bluebonnet Meadows will create for *you and yours*...''

Kitt was no expert at economics, but the charts and graphs
and lists were clear. Almost every business in the county
would grow and prosper. New businesses would spring up,
more jobs would be offered. Money, money, everywhere.

Kitt saw that it was a convincing argument. But was it
true? Or only Fabian's clever propaganda? She looked at
Nora. ''These statistics—are they right?''

Nora made a gesture of mock helplessness. ''I'd need a
crystal ball to answer that. It's what everybody's arguing
about.''

''Mel Belyle did this,'' Kitt said bitterly. ''He sat in your
house night before last, so charming, so down-to-earth. But
then he tried to buy Bubba, and when that didn't work, he
pulls this, the bastard.''

''It's not from *him*,'' Nora reminded her. ''It was mailed
from New York. From a public relations firm.''

''Owned by Brian Fabian,'' Kitt said, her eyes narrowed.
''I'd bet money on it. And Mel knew it was coming. He
had to.''

''Maybe he wasn't allowed to say,'' Nora ventured, her
voice hesitant.

Kitt stared in surprise. Was Nora defending the man?
Why? Did she want to believe all this wealth would really
flow into the town, plating the streets with gold?

Nora said, ''It says those figures were computed by a firm
that specializes in predicting economic change. Henderson
and Associates.''

''Fabian probably owns them, too,'' fumed Kitt. ''They'll
say whatever he tells them to say.''

Nora shrugged and pointed to the bottom of the letter.
''It also says this information's going to be released to the
media tomorrow.''

''Damn!'' Kitt said. ''This is inflammatory. It makes the

major landowners sound like a bunch of medieval barons oppressing the serfs.''

"That's why Bubba's so angry. Yesterday he was a hero for not selling. Today he's a selfish thug."

"Has J. T. McKinney seen this? Or any of the ranchers besides Bubba?''

"I don't know. If they haven't, they'll hear about it soon enough."

"Can I borrow this?" Kitt asked, giving the document a little wave. "I want a copy for myself and to fax one to *Exclusive*. The research department can see if these figures are valid."

"Of course," Nora said. She shook her head worriedly. "Oh, J.T.'s going to be furious. All the McKinneys will."

"I've got to see the mayor," Kitt said. "And then I'm going to track down Mel Belyle and rake him over the coals. *God,* this is underhanded."

Kitt stuffed the envelope into her vest pocket and left by the back door, stalking out almost as angrily as Bubba had. The document was designed to split the townspeople into warring factions.

Reverend Blake had guessed right. If Fabian wanted to win, he needed to divide and conquer. It was exactly the ploy he was using, and Mel Belyle was his instrument of division and conquest.

KITT WASN'T SURPRISED when Mayor Evans wouldn't see her.

His secretary was a plump little woman with curly white-blond hair and a frilly white blouse. "I'm sorry," she said. "The Mayor will try to schedule another appointment with you. Something unexpected came up."

And I know what that something is, Kitt thought ruefully. It was the same document that was folded in her vest pocket. She could feel it there over her heart, like some malignant packet emitting poison rays into her.

"I'll try again tomorrow," Kitt said.

"Fine," said the secretary. The phone rang and she answered. "Mrs. Trent?" she said in a perky voice. "The mayor's on another line. Do you want to hold or leave a message?"

Kitt turned away. She knew the caller had to be Carolyn Trent, J. T. McKinney's sister-in-law. She was a prime mover in the Concerned Citizens of Claro County.

Now, according to Fabian's insinuations, she was also an enemy of the people. Like J.T. and Bubba and the others, she was privileged and powerful—and selfishly standing in the way of a brighter future for those less fortunate than she.

It sickened Kitt that Carolyn, an honorable woman, was suddenly cast as a villainess. She clenched her jaw more tightly and strode out of the courthouse and headed back to the hotel.

She used the hotel's machine to fax the document to *Exclusive*. Then she ran up the stairs to her room. Picking up the phone, she flopped onto the bed and dialed the number of the research department. She asked for the department head, Gideon Hammer.

"Gideon," Kitt said. "I just faxed something I need you to check out. It's important. I've got to know if the statistics are reliable."

Gideon vowed to do it as soon as possible. "But that might not be soon," he warned. "It sounds like a complex piece of work. We'll do our best."

"I know you will," she said. As she hung up, she heard footsteps in the hall, the sound of a nearby door opening. *I think he's here—right now. I'm going to pounce on him so hard it'll rattle his teeth.*

Like a shot she was out of her room and rapping on his door so fiercely her knuckles stung. Her heart banged, rat-a-tat-tat.

The door eased open. Mel stood there looking down at her skeptically. He was shirtless. The sight of his tanned and sculpted chest took her back.

"To what do I owe this honor?" he asked.

She pulled out the envelope and brandished it under his nose. "To this. You did this to start trouble, didn't you?"

"I didn't do it at all," he said. "A public relations company did. Blackmun and Fielding."

"Don't play word games," she retorted. "Fabian's behind it, and you're his point man on this project. Do you think this is ethical?"

He sighed and swung the door wider. "If you want to talk, come inside. I don't want to have this conversation in the hallway."

Reluctantly she eased inside. He'd barely moved, so she had to squeeze by carefully to avoid brushing against him. A yellow shirt hung over the back of the armchair.

He moved to the chair and flipped the T-shirt onto the bed. "Have a seat," he said.

He leaned against the dresser and crossed his arms over his bare chest. The movement made his arm and shoulder muscles undulate distractingly. He wore low-slung gray jeans and black cowboy boots that made him even taller.

"I ran again this morning," he said. "It wasn't the same without you. Nobody to shadow me and enjoy my pain."

She ignored the remark. She waggled the envelope again. "Would you please explain this?"

He shrugged one naked shoulder. "I thought it was self-explanatory. What do you want to know?"

She yanked the document out of the envelope and unfolded it. "These so-called facts. These projected figures. It's mostly propaganda—isn't it?"

He raised one dark brow as if in sardonic pity for her naivete. "Why would Fabian be such a fool? Why would he lie?"

"Because it serves his purpose," she answered, her chin tilted defiantly.

"One of the finest economic consulting firms in Texas did the statistics," he said. "They specialize in economic impact analysis. Want to see their qualifications?"

He picked up a blue folder and handed it to her. She

opened it suspiciously. But just the opening page stunned her. It listed the firm's recent projects and clients—and they were stellar.

"Not too shabby, eh?"

"Statistics can lie," she argued.

"Not at this company," he said, nodding at the folder and crossing his arms again. His biceps bulged, and she wished to hell he'd put on his shirt.

"If you're so proud of this, can I copy it?" she challenged.

"Take it," he said. "Copies have already been mailed to all the major newspapers and broadcast stations in the area." He smiled. "Including Horace Westerhaus. Right here in Crystal Creek."

"Horace is against Bluebonnet Meadows," Kitt said defensively.

"Horace *was* against Bluebonnet Meadows," Mel countered, his smile growing more smug. "I spent most of the morning talking to him. He's a convert. He's seen the light. Bluebonnet Meadows will be buying a *lot* of media advertising in Crystal Creek—from good old Horace."

Oh, hell, Kitt thought, her spirits plummeting. She met Mel's gaze and held it. "You really do fight dirty, don't you?"

"It's business," he said. "That's all."

She pointed to the document she'd got from Nora. "This isn't clean business. It's a plain old-fashioned smear campaign."

His brow arched higher. "A smear? But it's true, isn't it?"

Kitt tossed her head angrily. "This says that the people fighting Fabian are—are practically robber barons. It calls them the 'power elite.'"

He gave a short, ironic laugh. "You're saying they're not?"

"Certainly not," she shot back. But she knew she had to

qualify her statement, for part of what he said was true. "At least, not all of them."

"Like who?" he gibed. "The good mayor? Douglas Evans? He could make a lot of money from Bluebonnet Meadows. He's a Realtor. He's got this hotel—he could only prosper from a larger population."

She rose to the bait. "He could. But he wants to keep the town as it is."

"Exactly," Mel said, his smile fading. "He came here because it was a sleepy, old-fashioned place, unchanging, stuck in the past."

"It has its charms," Kitt said stubbornly.

"Does it?" he asked, his voice edged. "Not for you. But for someone like Doug Evans—yes. He can *afford* the luxury of no change. He owned the lion's share of a major distillery in Scotland. Why should he worry about bringing more money to the town? *He* doesn't need it. He's rich."

Kitt stiffened in the armchair and her hand tightened on the document. She'd known Doug Evans was from Scotland. She hadn't known he was independently wealthy. How had she missed *that* fact?

"There's Dan Gibson," Mel said silkily. "You probably remember him as a hardworking young farmer. Just making ends meet. But he married well. A millionairess. He's got thousands of acres. She's got millions of dollars. If that doesn't make you the 'power elite,' what does?"

"J. T. McKinney?" Mel asked. "For seven generations his family's owned most of the county. He's like a king. Was your father like a king, Kitt? Was Nora's?"

Kitt struggled not to squirm. Uneasily she remembered how awed she had been by the McKinneys as a child, struck by their land and wealth.

Mel's eyelids lowered almost seductively. He glanced at another folder on the dresser and picked it up. He flipped it open and drew out a photograph. He held it up for her to see.

She sucked in her breath sharply. It was an old snapshot

of the tenant houses on the Double C. They were mobile homes, six of them. J.T. had leased them to his married wranglers.

Perhaps the homes had once been nice. But Kitt remembered only shabbiness. The Texas rains had rusted them and warped them. The Texas heat had scorched them until their paint peeled. No grass grew in the yards, and the children had played in the stones and dirt.

Her breath stuck in her chest. "The wranglers were responsible for the upkeep," she managed to say. "That was part of the—the arrangement. But most of them didn't hold up their end of the deal."

"What?" Mel asked. "Still defending the great J.T.? Was it programmed into you? His kids were living like royalty."

He sighed and dropped the photo back into the folder. He held up another snapshot. It showed the McKinneys' patio, the three good-looking McKinney children lounging by the pool.

"Not quite the same as where you grew up," he said.

Her sensation of suffocation grew, and she felt almost dizzy with anger. "Our fathers didn't take care of our places—" she began.

He cut her off. "Why should they? They didn't own them. J.T. did. He owned everything."

"Those trailers are gone now," she countered. "It was an experiment that didn't work. Nora says there are some nice little houses there now—"

"Yes," he said, dropping the picture of the McKinneys back into the folder. "Nice little pre-fab houses. For the have-nots."

Kitt knotted her left hand into a fist. "You make us sound like sharecroppers or slaves—it wasn't like that, dammit."

He raised both brows innocently. "I said there are 'have-nots' in the county. Isn't it true? Let's talk about Nora, for instance. Nora and Ken."

"Leave Nora out of this," she ordered. She was sure he

was about to make fun of Nora and Ken, and she wouldn't tolerate it. If he did, she would slap his face.

"Nora's a good woman," Mel said. He straightened and uncrossed his arms. He inched closer to Kitt. "She's symbolic of this whole situation."

Kitt shook her head. "She's a person, not a symbol."

"Listen to me," he demanded. "Where'd she grow up? In one of those damn trailers. Who owned it? J. T. McKinney. Where's she live now? Well, she *has* moved up in the world. She lives in the foreman's house. But who owns it? J. T. McKinney."

Kitt's head buzzed from the pounding of the blood in her temples. "She *loves* living there. It's a great old house. It's got charm, history—"

"—but it *isn't* their house, is it?" Mel retorted. "And the land they live on isn't their land. All this great, beautiful land—and how much of it do *they* own?"

Kitt, breathing hard, refused to answer.

He answered for her. "They own a tiny lot with a tiny house in town, right? It used to belong to Dottie Jones. And Nora owns the Longhorn. Or maybe it's the other way around. The Longhorn owns Nora."

"What do you mean?" Kitt felt he was pushing her toward the edge of a steep precipice.

"She's not doing what she wants, is she?" Mel challenged.

"They—they had setbacks," Kitt stammered. "And they have Rory to put through college."

He threw the folder back onto the dresser. He stepped to the chair, looming over her. "Setbacks. She lost her teaching job—why?"

"The school had to cut back," Kitt answered, pressing against the back of the chair.

"Right," he said, leaning over her. He put one hand on each arm of the chair, effectively trapping her. Kitt looked away from him, staring at the curtained window. The scent of his cologne muddled her thinking.

"And *why* did the school cut back?" He almost purred the words.

"The town was low on money."

"And, my dear, sweet, smart, informed Kitt, *why* was it low?"

His face was only inches from hers. She made the mistake of looking into his dark blue eyes. "Crystal Creek was losing population," she breathed. "The tax base shrank...."

Her voice trailed off, but his took up the explanation. "And what did the town do for itself? Did it try to attract business? Industry? Create jobs? Housing? Did it do *any* of those things?"

Kitt turned her face to avoid that sapphire gaze. "No," she admitted in a little voice.

"No other county this close to Austin is this undeveloped." His breath was hot and tickling against her cheek. "None. Nobody here wants to look ahead. They're too busy looking back—at a past that nobody will admit is gone forever."

"Get away from me," she said. His nearness overwhelmed her.

To her surprise, he stepped away. She felt both relieved and strangely disappointed. He walked to the closet, took out a clean white shirt. He slipped it on but didn't button it.

He went to the window and pushed back the curtains. He stared out at it. "There it is. Charming—but unchanged for almost forty years. On weekends and holidays, they crank up the town carousel, and the animals move in the same old circle, going nowhere. Just like the town."

He turned to face her, his smile mocking. "If the town never changes, Ken and Nora can probably still make enough to live comfortably. They'll get the boy through school. Someday they'll retire to Dottie's little house in town. Maybe some days Nora'll be called in as a substitute teacher—if the school's still open—and she has energy left to try."

Kitt rose, pressing the folder against her chest. "I'm going. I've heard enough."

"No, you haven't," he said. "If the Bluebonnet Meadows project goes forward, do you know the value of the Longhorn would skyrocket? She just manages now—the motel's repairs will eat up her whole year's profits."

Kitt had meant to move, but now she stood as if paralyzed. She stared at him.

He nodded. "She could make plenty if the sale was handled smartly. In the meantime, a thousand families in Bluebonnet Meadows would bring more students. That would mean more teachers, better salaries."

He paused, letting his words sink in. "Finally she'd be doing what she loves. She'd be dealing with poems and novels, not burgers and fries. She'd be teaching kids, not making sure Horace Westerhaus has his eggs cooked right or Bubba Gibson's coffee cup is filled."

He walked to her, looked her up and down. "Think of it, Kitt. She wouldn't have to carry the responsibility of that restaurant around on her shoulders six days a week."

She took a deep breath and held her ground.

Mel's smile grew more ingratiating. "She'd have real vacations. She and Ken could go places. She could even visit England, see the London of Shakespeare and Dickens. The moors of *Wuthering Heights*."

He reached out and stroked a wayward strand of hair from her cheek. He said, "And if Bluebonnet Meadows went to Phase Two—if two *thousand* families moved in—who knows how much Nora's property might bring? She could go back to the university, get a master's degree—even teach in a college or junior college."

He took another strand of her loose hair between his fingers. He held it as if it were a ribbon he enjoyed touching. "With Bluebonnet Meadows, so many good things might come to Crystal Creek. So many."

She squared her jaw to keep it from trembling. "You're a devil," she accused. "That's what you are."

"Am I? Devils tempt. Do you feel tempted?"

"No," she lied, dashing his hand away. "I don't want anything you've got to offer. And neither does this town."

She wheeled, her heart thundering, and flung open the door to escape.

"We'll see about that," he said from behind her. "Won't we?"

CHAPTER THIRTEEN

SHE WAS GONE, slamming the door behind her.

Her absence seemed to suck all the oxygen from the air. Mel was breathing hard, and the pulses in his temples hammered. What he'd told Kitt was *true,* dammit.

And she was smart enough to understand, if only she'd admit it. Bluebonnet Meadows could be very good for Nora and her family. How could Kitt be against anything that was good for Nora?

True, Kitt might *write* against it, but her heart wouldn't be in it. If public sympathy turned in Fabian's favor now, he'd hold all the aces. The Hill Country around Crystal Creek could no longer belong only to the very rich few. The town itself would profit from it.

Mel's fax machine began to clatter. He tried to push Kitt from his mind. But the message wouldn't let him. It was from DeJames.

"Mel—Call ASAP. Cal McKinney has some hotshot lawyers investigating the possibilities of getting a court order about the dam. Working at this end to stall them. Find media outlets to emphasize dam's condition is fault of Concerned Citizens of Claro County. Repeat: emphasize *their* responsibility. DeJames."

Mel gritted his teeth and dialed Fabian's private number. There was no answer. He phoned DeJames. "I need to talk to Fabian. Where is he?"

"He's spending the day at the clinic. He's been having a bad time of it lately," said DeJames.

Mel sighed. Fabian was not well. He had never been well.

He was plagued with arthritis, and a mild case of Asperger's syndrome. He was a small man, with twisted limbs and a nerve disorder that gave him facial tics and made his hands tremble and flap. He might have seemed pathetic, except that his drive and irritability had made him powerful, and when he chose, he could be venomous as a hornet.

Mel said, "Look, DeJames, I *have* to talk to him. About this dam. He's got to stop fighting the lawyers and fix the bloody thing. He should beat McKinney's lawyers at their own game and head them off at the pass. It's been raining for two weeks here. If that thing gives, there's going to be hell to pay."

"Fabian hates backing down. You know that."

"He's spent a fortune down here trying to make himself sound like a hero. Tell him it's time to *act* like one. Fix the damn dam."

"I'm not saying *that* to him," DeJames laughed. "He'd have my head on a plate. I'll tell him to call you."

"Do that," said Mel.

KITT HAD AN APPOINTMENT with Shelby Belyle, Nick's new wife. Kitt knew the woman would be careful what she said; she could not compromise her husband.

Still, Shelby had a degree in biology and had worked for two years as a nature guide at Hole in the Wall Dude Ranch. Now she was working on her master's. She knew a great deal about the land Fabian had bought and the impact he would have on it.

Shelby had asked Kitt to meet her at Rimrock State Park, at the scenic overlook above the Claro River. Kitt, eager to escape Crystal Creek and thoughts of Mel, arrived early.

Yet early as she was, Shelby was already there. She sat at a cedar picnic table by the overlook's low stone wall. Before her was a stack of folders and a map weighted down at the corners with pebbles.

Shelby rose when Kitt got out of the car. She was a beautiful woman, dark and lushly pretty. She offered Kitt her hand and said, "Thanks for coming clear out here."

"It's kind of you to meet me at all," Kitt said.

"I can't say anything that might jeopardize Nick," said Shelby. "He has nothing to do with this. Whatever I show you is data I got from the University and the Environmental Protection Agency—on my own."

Kitt nodded. "I understand. I can make that clear."

"In fact, it'd be better if you didn't use my name," Shelby said nervously. "Just call me an 'anonymous source.'"

Kitt promised that she would, and the two women sat at the table side by side. The air was still and humid. It seemed pregnant with more rain, and dark clouds covered the sun. Kitt looked out at the Claro River and the hills beyond. Far below, the river twisted and flashed with foam.

"The river's high, and so are the creeks," Shelby said. "That's part of the problem. The most serious issue's water. J.T. wasn't going to take on this fight until it involved the water."

On the map Shelby circled the land that Fabian owned. She pointed at a Y-shaped line. "Here's the complication, at this fork." She explained that both a small creek and an underwater stream fed into Lower Crystal Creek. Fabian had diverted both to fill his lake.

Kitt nodded. "And the lower creek's an important water source to everyone downstream. Especially J.T."

"It *was*," Shelby said, tapping the map with her pen. "And back when Fabian dammed the water, we were having a dry spell. The lake itself was half full. But the lower creek went dry."

Shelby's brow furrowed as she explained how intricate Texas law was about surface water and underground water. "So," she said, "is Fabian within his legal rights, diverting this water? Only the courts can say. But in the meantime, with all this rain and only a temporary dam—who knows what could happen?"

Kitt studied the map. "Where would the flooding hit if it came?"

"It would sweep right through Fabian's construction site, for starters," Shelby said. "Which would serve him right. But it could do damage farther downstream, starting with the Double C. It would cover mostly grazing land, but it could affect roads and bridges, too."

Kitt bit her lip. "Can I have a copy of this map?"

"I brought it for you," Shelby said. "And these reports, too. I wish—I wish I could talk more frankly. There's more I'd like to say. But I can't."

Shelby looked so pensive that Kitt knew she was thinking of the rift between Nick and Mel. Impulsively Kitt put her hand over Shelby's. "I'm sorry, too. I hope things work out."

"So do I," Shelby said with a sad smile. "But I don't see how."

J.T. SAT in Dr. Purdy's office fervently wishing he could disappear. "All I want," he said gruffly, "is some of that Viagra stuff. Just write the prescription, will you?"

Now in his sixties, Nate Purdy had been a doctor and a colonel in the Vietnam War. He had steel-gray hair, a steel-gray mustache and steel-gray eyes. Over the tops of his glasses, he gave J.T. a reproving look. "Not so fast. I don't pass this stuff out like Halloween candy. I need more details."

Details were the last thing J.T. wanted to give. "You said I'm healthy. And I said I want some Viagra. I'm—getting to a certain age."

Nate's eyes narrowed. "You passed your physical with flying colors last spring. You seem healthy enough now— except your blood pressure's up. Now what's this problem about sex?"

J.T. fought not to flinch. He had never enjoyed talking about sex. He only liked having it—or he *had* liked it—up until now. "It's not really a problem," he hedged. "I mean,

I've read that everybody has some, eh, times they don't, eh, well, you know.''

Nate Purdy was a frank man. ''Can't get the old pecker up?''

To his humiliation, J.T. felt his face redden. ''No!'' he said. ''I've just kind of—lost interest,'' he muttered. ''Got other things on my mind.''

Nate nodded, but he knew he wasn't getting the whole story. ''You and Cynthia getting along all right?''

''Yes,'' J.T. insisted. He loved his wife passionately. She loved him. There was no trouble in their marriage. But if there was no trouble in their marriage, why was he in Nate's office, feeling like a bug pinned, squirming, to a board? Chagrined, he said, ''She's not—happy with me.''

''Because of sex?'' Nate asked.

J.T. made a dismissive gesture. ''She hasn't said much about the sex. But I know she wonders what the matter is. Hell, I used to be horny as a Brahma bull. And now...I know she wonders, that's all.''

Nate crossed his arms. ''You don't talk about it?''

''Um. Not much,'' J.T. said.

''You mean you don't talk to her about it at all,'' Nate said out of the corner of his mouth. ''Right?''

J.T. felt trapped. ''I'm not worried about *talking*. I'm worried about *doing*.''

''The talking would help the doing,'' Nate said. ''I guarantee it.''

He leaned against his counter and stroked his mustache wisely, as if it were a thing that gave him magical powers of perception. ''I know your type, J.T. Real men don't talk about their feelings. Especially real cattlemen. What do you tell her—you're too tired?''

''Mostly,'' J.T. said dismally.

''Afraid you can't perform?''

J.T. felt more insect-like than before. ''I *can* perform— if I feel like it. I just don't feel like it. Can't you just give me the damn pills?''

"No, I can't," Nate retorted. "You're afraid you're going to try to have sex and fail. That's what it is, isn't it?"

J.T. didn't like having it stated in such bald terms. "I just want a little insurance, that's all. I want to keep my wife satisfied."

Nate's stern features looked almost sympathetic. "Tell me about Cynthia. You said she's not happy. If it's not the sex, what is it?"

"She thinks I work too hard," J.T. grumbled. "She's nagging me to retire."

Nate arched one gray brow. "You're sixty-five. She *should* nag."

A small sense of righteousness surged through J.T. "Who'd run the ranch? Tyler can't. He's leaving. Cal's not interested. Lynn's got her horses, and she's still recovering from that failed pregnancy…"

Nate cut off his litany of excuses. "Who are you married to, J.T.? Cynthia—or the ranch?"

"That ranch has been run by a McKinney since 1837," objected J.T.

"Spare me the history lesson," Nate said. "I know how long it's been there. It's how long *you're* going to be here that worries me."

J.T. bristled defensively. "You said I was healthy."

"I said you were healthy as far as I could see. I can see only so far. I'm a doctor, not God. You might blow an artery tomorrow for all I know. You might get hit by a truck. An asteroid might fall on you. Then where's the McKinney to run your precious ranch? Will Jennifer do it? A big job for a ten-year-old girl."

J.T. blinked in displeased surprise. "Some day—maybe Tyler can take over. When this California nonsense is out of Ruth's head. But that time's not now. For now he can't be here."

Nate picked up J.T.'s chart, studied it, then set it down with an air of impatience. "Let's get back to your talley-whacker problem," he said. "I'm going to draw some blood and get a test on your testosterone level. But I don't think your problem's too little testosterone. It's too much stress. This fool Fabian business is wearing you down.''

J.T.'s spine stiffened in resentment. ''It's a fight that's got to be fought.''

''Not by you alone. And you act like the whole thing's on your shoulders. You *think* like it's on your shoulders. You know that you've lost five pounds since last spring?''

J.T. snorted. ''That's good, isn't it? With my ticker, I shouldn't be carrying around spare weight.''

''You didn't *need* to lose it,'' Nate said sternly. ''Ranching comes with problems built into it—big ones. They'd run down a younger man than you. You've had one heart attack. The last thing you need is extra stress. And that, my friend, is what your pecker is telling you.''

J.T. fought back a grimace. ''Look, all I want is a prescription—''

''You're not getting it until you talk about it to your wife,'' Nate said. ''And I'd like to talk to Cynthia myself. Maybe the two of you should see a counselor about this. I can make an appointment.''

''A counselor?'' J.T. practically yipped. ''My God, next you'll have us on some afternoon TV show, talking to the whole country about my penis—''

''Oh, settle down,'' muttered Nate. ''I've seen this coming since August. I didn't know it'd show itself as a sexual dysfunction, but I knew *something* was going to give. This damn land war is eating you up. It's affecting your health, and it's affecting your marriage.''

''I can get a prescription from somebody else,'' threatened J.T. He felt he was protecting the essence of his masculine pride.

''Fine. Be a damn fool,'' said Nate. ''You've got a beautiful wife who loves you. You've got a darling little girl. Take care of yourself, you can watch your daughter grow up. And you can have your sex life back.''

He sighed, uncrossed his arms and moved to J.T.'s side.

He put one hand on J.T.'s shoulder. "Or you can fret your-self to a frazzle. You can lose your health, ruin your mar-riage, never see your girl become a woman. You need to lighten up, J.T."

J.T. felt a wave of abysmal dismay. "But I—I— Some-body's got to spearhead this fight against Fabian—I can't—I can't…"

Nate squeezed his shoulder. "J.T., the land will be there forever. But you won't. Let somebody else lead the fight. Cal. He's young and scrappy. He came home to help you."

"Cal doesn't care about it the way I do," J.T. said with passion. "He wouldn't bring the right fire to it—"

"He'll bring his own fire," Nate said. "Don't sell him short. You know, sometimes a man in a fix like yours, well, he starts to kind of resent a young buck of a son. Cal's been waiting all his life for you to trust him with something. Maybe it's time."

J.T. shrugged and stood. "I'll think about it," was all he said. His throat was too choked to say more. He might have trusted the fight to Tyler. To Cal alone? He wasn't sure he could bring himself to do such a thing.

MEL'S CURIOSITY HAD got the best of him, and he did what he hadn't wanted to do. He phoned Gloria Wall.

He gritted his teeth and said, "You hinted Kitt Mitchell had a secret in her past. I need to know. Then maybe we can make that supper date."

Gloria, stone-cold sober, wasn't as elusive as she'd been under the influence of margaritas. "Well, some people says Kitt had a baby by one of her stepbrothers, one of those Jasper boys. Reverend Blake fixed it so she could get away and go to school in Dallas. He told J.T.'s wife, and she fired Jasper. He and that brood of his left town."

Mel's brow furrowed. Same basic rumor but an interest-ing variation. "When was she supposed to have this child?"

"After she went away," Gloria said airily. "I don't *know* it's true. *Anything* could have happened in that Jasper house.

There was Bull Jasper and his two big sons—just lunks—
and that slutty sister of his, Trina.''

''*Trina?*'' Mel's nerves went on high alert. ''Where's she
now?''

''Bee Tree or somewhere,'' Gloria said. ''I don't know
what her last name is. She got married a bunch of times.
When she was here, she *threw* herself at Cal McKinney.
Then at Gordon Jones. But *he* upped and married Nora, and
Trina got pregnant by—let's see—Ollie Pollack—and
then—''

Mel listened, but he didn't need to hear more. Trina Gilroy hated Nora for marrying Gordon Jones. She hated Cal
McKinney for spurning her. And she hated Kitt because
something concerning Kitt was bad enough to get Trina's
brother fired from the Double C.

He promised Gloria to come to supper at some vague date
in the future. He hung up the phone and stared at it. Then
he took the cassette of Trina Gilroy, smashed it, tore the
tape and threw it in the trash.

He could never tell Kitt he'd checked on her this way.
And he might never really know what had happened to her
in the Jasper house.

Suddenly he wanted out of the confines of his room, to
sit alone at a bar and drink a lonely beer. And think on girls
like Kitt, who had suffered and struggled to heal themselves,
in spite of the long infection of rumor.

BY EARLY EVENING, Kitt needed to move. Heart-thumping,
blood-pounding, physical, sweaty movement.

She hadn't been able to run that morning. Now she felt
a primal need for it, a yearning in her bones, a twitching in
her muscles. All afternoon she'd sat in her hotel room,
studying Shelby Belyle's folders and maps until both her
mind and body rebelled.

It was five-thirty, and she wasn't due at Nora's for two
hours. She shucked off her working clothes and slipped into

her yellow shorts and tank top. She laced up her shoes and pinned her hair atop her head.

Crystal Creek was small but had a large city park. She would run there, until all tension was driven from her body and her brain was clear again. She left the hotel and set off at a slow jog toward the park. The sky still hung low and dark; the air was still thick with humidity.

She skimmed along First Street, past businesses that had been there since her childhood: Schwartz's Barber Shop, Keller's Appliances, Andy's Handy Hardware. There was only one new business, Hutch's Chili Parlor.

She reached the residential section and came to the little house where Dottie Jones had once lived. Nora owned it now and rented it out. It was the house in which Mel predicted Nora and Ken would end up retiring.

Kitt didn't remember the neighborhood being so modest or the house so tiny. Would Nora work her heart out at the Longhorn only to end her days here? She had lived here with Dottie before she married Ken. For all her labor, would she go only in a circle, coming back again to Dottie's place?

Kitt began to jog faster and was relieved when she reached the park. It was a pretty expanse of land, rolling and dotted with trees. She took a path that led to little Lake Arden and began to run.

Thunder rumbled, and she ran harder. She didn't want to think of the swelling creeks, the makeshift dam, or Shelby Belyle's troubling charts and maps. As she reached Lake Arden's edge, fat drops of rain began to fall.

She kept pounding down the path. But by the time she was halfway round the lake, the rain poured down with such vehemence she could hardly see. Lightning cracked the sky open, and the thunder made her ears ring.

Suddenly a bolt of lightning brighter than the others slashed down and struck a pine tree, splitting it in half like a giant ax. It shivered, sent a shower of chips and splinters through the air and fell so hard that the earth shuddered beneath Kitt's feet.

This storm had gotten dangerous, and she was in the most dangerous place possible, next to the water, which drew lightning as a steel draws a magnet.

Damn! I need to get out of here! She knew the park had pavilions, roofed shelters for picnickers, and she headed for the nearest. She was drenched and half-blinded.

Again lightning struck nearby. It dazzled her eyes, making her see bright spots, and she caught a whiff of brimstone. She fought her way to the shelters at the park's north end.

There were two of them between the playground next to the park's main road. She took cover in the one nearest and sat down on a concrete bench, dripping and shivering. The water drummed on the roof's shingles; it whipped in past the cedar supports. She hugged herself, cursing Texas and its Texas-sized weather.

It might have been an eternity, or five minutes later that a pair of headlights appeared. They looked ghostly and wavery through the curtains of rain, and they slowly approached the shelters.

Kitt squinted against the unexpected brightness, putting her hand to her eyes to shield them. Then the car crept abreast the shelter and stopped, a dark hulk with two great yellow eyes. *Some other fool got caught out here,* she thought miserably. *He's lucky a tree hasn't blown down on him.*

The lights suddenly blinked out, and she heard the slam of a car door. Why would anyone leave the snugness of a car in this deluge? But a figure appeared at the pavilion's edge, and a voice called her name. "Kitt?"

It was Mel. A shudder that had nothing to do with cold ran through her, fluttering her stomach. She hugged herself more tightly. "What are you doing here?" She struggled to keep the quaver out of her voice.

"Looking for you, you idiot," he said scornfully. He moved nearer until he stood in front of her. His height made him seem to loom. But when he spoke again, his voice was unexpectedly concerned. "Are you all right?"

"I'm fine," she said. "I'm dandy. I'm hunky-dory. The only thing that would make me feel better would be gills."

He sighed in disgust and sat down next to her. In the dim light she could see that his hair was damp with rain. A dark forelock hung over his brow, and his white shirt was splotched with wetness. He said, "I guess the classic question applies. Don't you know enough to come in out of the rain?"

"I guess the classic answer applies," she said. "Go to hell." But then her body betrayed her, because such a chill went through her that her teeth actually chattered.

"Oh, come here," he said. He put his arm around her and drew her close. His body heat was not just comforting, it was delicious. Sinfully so. She tried to fight enjoying such forbidden pleasure.

"Don't," she protested feebly. "You'll get all wet."

"I'm already wet," he muttered, pulling her more snugly against him. "My God, what a drowned little rat you are."

"Enough of your slick flattery," she tried to say, but her jaw twitched and her teeth chattered again.

He sighed against her hair. His breath made her first warm, then cold. He said, "I should have come with a keg of brandy around my neck, like a St. Bernard."

A lightning flash and another blast of thunder made her flinch. She heard the crash of another tree toppling to the ground. "Steady," he said, stroking her back.

"How d-did you know I was here?" she asked.

"I was having a beer at Hutch's place. You jogged by, headed this way. It's the logical place to run. I almost came here myself this morning."

She shivered again, and he brought his body more fully against hers. She shouldn't let herself drink in his warmth this way, but couldn't stop herself. She let her arms slip around his waist so she could nestle closer.

He said, "I was leaving Hutch's when the sky opened

up. I was getting in my car, and I thought of you. I came looking.''

It had been kind of him, and she should thank him. She was afraid to. She just rested against his chest, feeling guilty for liking it so much.

He said, ''When the lightning started, I figured you'd be smart enough to take cover. I drove from one shelter to another. This was the last one. I was getting ready to start over. I was lucky to see you. You're such a runt.''

She jerked back sharply and gave him a killing look.

''Ah,'' he said, drawing her back against his chest, ''I thought that'd get your blood pumping again. No, you're little, but you're wearing bright yellow. Easy to see.''

She settled against him, grateful for his heat and strength, ashamed for wanting it. ''I shouldn't do this.''

He stroked her wet hair back from her face. The motion was so tender that it nearly undid her. In her ear he whispered, ''Yes, you should. So should I. I meant what I said about New York. When this is over, I want to be with you.''

This is impossible, she thought. Resignation to that impossibility chilled her more than the cold. ''No.'' She pulled back from him with more determination. ''I can't afford to let this get personal. I have an assignment. Part of it's to watch you. I don't like what you're doing here.''

''Change has to come to Crystal Creek some time,'' he said, taking her hand in his. ''The time is now.''

''Not this way,'' she said. ''Not Fabian's way.''

But she found she was clinging to his hand in spite of herself. It was as if she couldn't sever the link between them. Not completely.

''Fabian's way is better than some,'' he said. ''He doesn't just want to create a development. He wants to create a community.''

''Create a community by tearing this one apart?'' she said. ''Turning people against each other? And their own heritage?''

He bent nearer, his voice earnest. ''Who's going to own

the Hill Country, Kitt? A handful of privileged ranchers? Or the people? Couldn't a piece of it ever belong to somebody like you? Or Nora? Or Rory?''

It was a question that nagged her, but she dodged it. ''I don't want to own a piece of it. I wouldn't have it if you gave it to me.''

''No,'' he said, more gently, stroking her knuckles with his thumb. ''And why not? What happened to you here that soured you on this place? I know *something* happened. And that's why you went to Stobbart.''

A deeper, more painful cold pierced her, and she snatched her hand away. She turned from him to stare out into the darkening streams of rain. As often, when she felt threatened, she went on attack. ''This isn't about me. It's about other things—including this rain. Bad things are happening to the land. You and Fabian are letting them happen.''

''You mean the water rights and the temporary dam?''

She whirled to face him. ''Exactly. I talked to Shelby Belyle today—your sister-in-law.''

His manner went stony. ''The noted tree-hugger?''

''She knows what she's talking about. And Fabian's not going to create a happy community if he makes all the landowners around it despise him. They'll hate him and everything he stands for if he causes a flood. And they'll hate the people that move onto the land.''

''The water rights can be settled,'' Mel said.

''And the temporary dam?'' she challenged.

''The Concerned Citizens brought that one on themselves. When they brought the injunction to stop working. But I've got a call in to Fabian. I'm going to tell him to make the dam safer, even if he has to violate the injunction. Even if he's fined for it.''

Kitt looked at him in disbelief. He had told her more in the past minutes than he had ever before. ''Can you convince him to do it?''

''Yes. I think I can.''

''Can I print that?''

"Not yet. But when he answers, yes."

"Why the change of heart?"

"Maybe I've decided you're too powerful as an enemy. I'd rather cooperate with you."

She studied his face, unreadable in the dim light. "Does Fabian know about your decision to 'cooperate' with me?"

"No comment," he said. "You're starting to shiver again. Let me take you back to the hotel. You need a hot shower. And probably a good meal. Have you eaten?"

"I'm going to Nora's," she said.

"You should wait until the rain slows," he said.

"I intend to."

He stood. He offered her his hand, but she ignored it and stood, careful to keep her distance from him. She was conscious that the wet, skimpy fabric clinging to her body made her feel almost naked.

"Thank you for coming to find me," she said. "But you didn't have to. I can take care of myself."

"I know you can," he said. "But will you ever let anybody get close enough to help you do it? Or is that too dangerous for you?"

She stared up at him. Lightning briefly illuminated his handsome face. His expression was hungry and intent.

Why's this happening? I'm a lone wolf, and so is he.

"That's a strange question for somebody like you to ask," she said.

"Yes," he said, an edge of self-mockery in his voice. "Isn't it?"

CHAPTER FOURTEEN

BACK AT THE HOTEL, Mel stripped off his soaked clothes. He wanted a hot shower, but he took a cold one. He needed to drive away the too-vivid memory of Kitt's body pressed against his.

He'd accused her of fearing closeness with another person. This was ironic, for he'd always feared the same thing himself, yet now getting close was precisely what tempted him. He didn't want to possess merely Kitt's body, but her mind, her manner, her vivacious spirit, her very soul.

Mel's problem, he saw, was to stay loyal to Fabian yet break down Kitt's defenses. He would need every scrap of his skill and guile to make Fabian relent about the dam. He had come here prepared to be as cutthroat as any pirate. Now he was turning into a mediator, a man eager to make peace.

It was a hell of a thing. Nick would laugh his ass off.

Nick would also laugh about Mel's infatuation with Kitt. Let him. Mel couldn't help himself. When he stepped from the shower, he wondered if next door Kitt was doing the same thing. He imagined her compact body, her long hair hanging in shining streamers clear to her bare breasts.

Stop it, he commanded himself. Tonight she would be going again to her beloved Nora's. He wished he was going with her. Instead he had quietly set up a meeting with a group of small landowners, including the noxious Walls.

Fabian had decreed that if he couldn't buy a big bundle of land like Bubba's, he would snatch up all the small parcels he could. Mel was to flirt at negotiating for them, to get the owners excited. Fabian wanted word to get around—people in Crystal Creek who cooperated with him could become *very* rich.

KITT HAD JUST SWALLOWED her last bite of apple pie at Nora's when the telephone rang. Ken went into the living room to answer it.

"I *know* the town needs progress," Nora said over her coffee cup. A copy of Fabian's statistics lay on the table between her and Kitt. "I know it as well as anybody." She wrinkled her nose with repugnance. "The problem is I *hate* Fabian's master plan. It's so—so phony, so plastic. A thousand doll houses, nearly identical—ugh."

Kitt agreed. She didn't love the Hill Country as Nora did, but Fabian's plan did seem soulless. The land had its own beauty; it was unique. Why turn it into the same sort of gardened golf courses one could find anywhere? Why drown it under artificial lakes and stud it with look-alike houses?

Ken limped back to the table, his expression solemn.

"*A thousand* new houses," Nora repeated. "It's *Attack of the Clones*."

"There might be more than a thousand," Ken said, shaking his head.

Nora looked appalled. "More? *How?*"

Ken gave a sigh of disgust as he sat. "That was J.T. He got word something's up. Mel Belyle's meeting with a lot of small landowners tonight. He's most likely trying to cut a deal with them."

Kitt's mind raced. Lots of people in the county who owned small chunks of land. Gloria Wall loved to brag of her five acres. There were folks with less, others with much more. "How much land could he get that way?"

"A couple hundred acres," Ken said. "Over three hundred."

"But that could be—ye gods!—three hundred more houses," gasped Nora.

"Yeah," muttered Ken. He tapped the papers on the ta

ble. "J.T. says since these damn stats came out, half the town is willing to sell out."

"What will he do?" Nora asked. "He and the others?"

Ken shrugged. "He doesn't know. Hold to his course. Keep Fabian tied up in court. Especially about that dam."

Inwardly Kitt winced. *The dam. Mel would plead with Fabian to give up on the dam.* She hadn't told this to anyone. It might build false hopes. Yet, if Fabian surrendered about the dam and the water rights, he'd take away J.T.'s strongest arguments in court. Fabian could lose a battle, but win the war.

Nora put her elbow on the table and her chin on her fist. "Ken, what's Cal say about all this?"

Ken frowned. "Cal thinks the best bet would be to back Fabian into a corner and buy him out. Three Amigos wants to make him an offer."

"But he'd never take it," Nora objected.

"If they keep him tied up over the water rights—and more—he might have to," Ken said. "What else can he do? Let the land just sit there?"

Kitt felt the guilty desire to squirm. *There it is again. The water rights. The dam. It's like a game of cards. And the water is the trick that's crucial.*

But again, she said nothing. Mel's promise might be empty; maybe he wouldn't even try to change Fabian's mind. Or the promise might be futile. Perhaps he *couldn't* change Fabian's mind.

Nora looked both disturbed and puzzled. "Can Cal afford to buy that land?" she asked. "Can Three Amigos?"

Ken said, "No. And no. Lord knows how much they'd have to spend in legal fees to pull it off. They'd be in hock up to their necks."

Nora cocked her head in frustration. "But if they spend that much to get the land, what will they *do* with it, to make it worth what they've paid?"

"That's the catch," Ken said. "They'd have to develop it."

"Yi-yi-yi," said Nora. "J.T.'s having none of that, I'll bet."

"You're right. He's having none of it." Ken drained his coffee cup.

Nora drummed her fingers on the tabletop. She took a deep breath. "So J.T.'s set on doing it his way? Just try for an endless legal standoff?"

"That's right," said Ken. "With a little help from Cal."

"Emphasis on the *little*," Nora said glumly. "And you know where that leaves us?"

"Where?" Kitt asked.

"In a quandary." Nora gave the papers a sharp flick with her finger, as if she could punish them for the trouble they'd created. "It can't come out right. J.T. can't win. I don't think Cal and his friends can, either. Fabian has too much money. They shouldn't even take the chance."

"Cal's always taken chances," Ken said. "That's his strength."

Nora didn't look convinced. "It could also be his fatal weakness."

When Kitt left, the conversation haunted her all the way back to town. She wondered if Mel was still at his meeting, buying pieces of the county, fragment by fragment. And she wondered for the dozenth time if he'd been sincere about changing Fabian's mind.

The issue of the water controlled the entire future of Crystal Creek. But who, ultimately, would control the water? Would Mel decide the balance? Could he?

It struck her suddenly that she had listened to talk about Cal McKinney all night without cringing. It was as if he had at last become an ordinary man to her; the spell was broken. The man she had been unable to forget, for even a moment, was Mel.

CAL AND HIS FATHER WERE at loggerheads. The two men stood at the bar, J.T. glowering at his son.

"I can do it," Cal vowed. "I've talked to my partners

They're willing. We make Fabian a standing offer. If he balks, we turn up the pressure.''

J.T.'s glance was sarcastic. "With your *free* lawyers?''

"Okay,'' Cal said, holding up his hands. "I admit it. The lawyers aren't exactly a hundred percent free. They are only somewhat free.''

"Ha!'' said J.T. "I knew it. What does 'somewhat' free mean?''

"I don't know,'' Cal said gruffly. "Just 'somewhat.' Not altogether free-for-nothing.''

J.T. pointed an accusing finger at him. "It means, you're footing the bill—and not telling me.''

"Well, I'm telling you now,'' Cal retorted. "Hell's bells, so what if I pay—my partners are willin' to help.''

"You and your partners,'' J.T. said scornfully. "And what do you and your partners get out of it? A chance to take over the development yourselves? The point is that the ranchers here do not *want* a development.''

"We wouldn't do it the way Fabian would,'' Cal argued. "We'd do it different. We'd do it right.''

J.T. repeated himself. "The ranchers here do not want a development. Are you deaf, boy?''

Cal pulled himself up to his full height, which was one inch taller than his father's. He looked J.T. in the eye. "Daddy, Crystal Creek is gonna change. Whether you like it or not. The question is how it's gonna change and who's gonna do it.''

Cal picked up the pages of statistics from Fabian's PR firm and thrust them at J.T. like an indisputable piece of proof. "You've seen the numbers, and they work against you. People are going to want more population in this county. And it will happen. One way or the other, it will happen.''

It will happen. The words seemed to hammer through J.T.'s brain like three sharp nails. "It won't happen while I've got a goddamn breath left in my body.''

He tried to stare Cal down, but couldn't. "And how long

do you think that's gonna be, Daddy?'' Cal asked quietly. ''At the rate you're goin'?''

J.T. looked in his son's eyes and saw a stubbornness that matched his own. Had it always been there, that steeliness? Had he somehow never noticed it before, or was it something newly forged in the flame of conflict?

Cal's gaze grew even harder. ''I mean it,'' he said. ''How long are you gonna last, drivin' yourself this way? Cynthia's worried about you.''

Cynthia. J.T.'s resolve faltered, almost fell. This afternoon he had been utterly humbled in Nate Purdy's office. He had wanted nothing so much as his old life back, and for things to be normal between him and his wife again. He was ready to do anything, to make any concession.

But where was Cynthia now? In their bedroom, alone, probably lulled to sleep by a pill again. She had retreated there, close to tears, earlier tonight, when he and Cal had begun to go at each other.

Serena had slipped away as if by magic, taking with her those rambunctious twins, for once miraculously silent. Even Lettie Mae, who had weathered every sort of family storm, had fled before the gathering force of this one.

Cal seemed to sense he'd hit a nerve. He hit it again. ''Who you married to, Daddy? Her or a patch of land?''

It was nearly the same question Nate Purdy had asked, but put more relentlessly. J.T. felt as if his son had struck him.

Cal pressed on. ''If you had to choose between them, which would it be? I think Cynthia's afraid it'd be the land. And it's tearin' her apart. If you won't think of yourself, think of her. And Jennifer. And me and Tyler and Lynn.''

J.T. tried to recover himself. ''You've got no right—'' he began.

''I got every right,'' Cal said. ''I love you.''

Oh, God, thought J.T., feeling battered. *Why did he have to say that?* Cal was the only adult male McKinney who could say those words without having them extracted from him like a battlefield bullet.

J.T. tried to defend himself by charging. "I forbid you to meddle in this. I forbid you and your fool partners to put in some crazy bid and—"

"You're too late," Cal countered. "I meddled. My fool partners faxed him this afternoon. Promised to stand behind your lawsuit with everything we got. Forbid all you want. What's done is done."

J.T. felt his jaw going slack. He stared at Cal in disbelief. Cal's eyes flashed in defiance and something else that J.T. could not even start to name. "You—you're crazy," he managed to stammer. "You can't wade into the middle of this mess that way. It isn't your fight."

"It is if I say it is." Cal paused and looked into J.T.'s eyes again. "And I'll make you a promise. If we get that land, I'll buy a piece of it. Build a little place. Settle down, sort of. Right next door to you."

"My God," J.T. said, stunned, "you don't have to risk everything on a crazy gamble like this. If you want land, I'll give you all you need—"

"Daddy," said Cal. "You gave me life. You raised me up. You want to give me something, let me help. It's time you learned to receive."

Cal's eyes welled, and J.T. was alarmed. Cal was the most mercurial of his children, the only truly light-hearted one, and the most emotionally open. Was he going to *cry?* God forbid.

But Cal saved him. "I've said what I got to say," he muttered. He kicked at the carpet with the toe of his boot, then turned and left the room.

J.T. stared after him with churning emotions.

CAL STRODE into the bedroom where Serena sat in bed, pale-faced and waiting. "How'd he take it?" she asked, her smoky green eyes wide.

"He was mostly struck dumb as a fish," Cal said. He shook his head. "Lord, but he is obstinate."

"Cal," she said softly, "don't you worry about this? About plunging in on this? It's such a gamble...."

He came to her, threw himself down on the bed beside her, and grinned. "Hell, sugar. Don't worry. It's not a gamble. We're gonna win. We're gonna win because Fabian won't ever give up on those water rights. And on that point, we *got* him. We'll win. It's in the bag."

AT THE HOTEL, after his meeting, Mel frowned and tried for the sixth time to call Fabian's home number. There was no answer.

He had checked for messages when he got back. Fabian hadn't returned his call—damn. He'd hoped, foolishly, for a call from Kitt. There was none, of course. If she'd heard about the meeting tonight, she probably wouldn't talk to him. He'd have to scheme a way to get in her good graces in spite of his night's work.

The only message was to phone DeJames. When DeJames answered, he sounded uncharacteristically cranky. "Hell, it's time you got in," he said. "You know what time it is in New York? I'm seriously sleep-deprived."

Mel felt no sympathy. "The natives were restless. They wanted to know why they couldn't have their money *now*. It was a long night. You were supposed to have Fabian call me. He didn't. What's up?"

"He was having tests all afternoon. He's got more in the morning. He's not to be disturbed."

"Disturbed, damn," Mel snarled. "This is important. What kind of tests?"

"Allergies," DeJames said. "They think he's got allergies. He itches."

Mel swore more colorfully. DeJames only laughed. "I've got to talk to him, too. Guess what happened today? He got an offer for the Crystal Creek property. From California. The Three Amigos."

Mel sat on the edge of the bed and rubbed his forehead. "How much?"

"Forty-three and a half million," DeJames said with a laugh. "Exactly what Fabian paid for it. Cash."

"They're idiots," Mel said scornfully. "And McKinney can't afford a deal that size. It'd bankrupt him."

"I don't know," DeJames reflected. "The others pulled it off in Hawaii."

"They weren't dealing with Fabian. Look, DeJames, I've got to get through to him. If he lets the locals have their way about these water rights and the dam, he wins. He takes away the one good case they've got against him. He'll start construction again—within weeks."

"Man, you *know* he wants that lake. Bart Knox has lakes, so Fabian wants lakes."

Mel nearly swore again. Bart Knox was a real estate mogul that Fabian wanted to rival. He wanted Bluebonnet Meadows to torture Bart Knox with envy. It was stupid, it was petty, and Mel needed to talk him out of it fast. "There could be a problem with that dam—if it gives way."

"There's no problem with the dam," DeJames said confidently. "The engineering firm guarantees it."

"I'm telling you," Mel said between his teeth, "all he has to do is concede the dam and water rights, and he's got the whole shebang. It's a sure thing. He'll win. No contest. It's in the bag."

"I'll try to get word to him," DeJames said wearily.

MEL COULDN'T SLEEP. He tossed. He turned. He thought of Kitt. DeJames had found no more information on her years at Stobbart, but was trying to trace another former teacher or classmate who'd talk.

Kitt. One room away. But more than a wall of beams and plaster separated them. Brian Fabian, in all his power and complexity, his generosity and meanness, stood between them like a colossus.

Mel threw back the sheet, rose and paced to the window.

Looking out, he saw the streetlights in a blur of haze. The rain had stopped. Puddles shimmered dimly in the streets. In the distance, lightning glared, then faded.

If Mel could convince Fabian to yield on the water and the dam, Kitt might think him a hero. If he couldn't do it, what would she think? That he had never tried, that he was a liar or a weakling?

He raked his fingers through his hair. After she heard about the meeting with the minor landowners, she'd be set against him again. And he had much, much more to do that she wouldn't like.

He had to show her that he wasn't evil simply because he worked for a man who sometimes seemed evil. Fabian was a flawed and driven being, but a strangely vulnerable one, sometimes like an aging child in pain.

Mel needed to prove to Kitt that he cared for her with an intensity that transcended their differences. He stared out the window, pensively, his gaze going from building to building.

And suddenly, he *knew*.

His heartbeat speeded, and he grabbed the phone. He dialed DeJames again. DeJames was groggy and disbelieving. "What do you want now? It's three o'clock in the morning here. What *is* your problem?"

Mel gripped the phone more tightly. "It's only midnight in California. Get me Sheila MacCauley."

"Sheila MacCauley? You're *crazy,* man."

"Like a fox," said Mel.

KITT GOT UP EARLY the next day and went to the park for a run. Again the sky was gray, the humidity high, the air still. By the morning light she could see how much damage the storm had done. Lightning had struck down two big pines, and a dogwood tree had been uprooted. The autumn foliage, stripped and sodden, lay on the beaten grass.

Kitt ran past the shelter house where Mel had held her in his arms. She kept her head down, so she wouldn't have to look at it. She tried not to think of the feel of his arms around her or of his promise to come for her in New York. She wondered for perhaps the thousandth time about the water rights.

She jogged back to the hotel, showered, changed and went to the Longhorn. Like yesterday morning, she could sense tension as soon as she walked in the door.

But today the tension was different. It was anticipatory, excited and righteous. None of the major landowners, like the Gibsons or the McKinneys, were in sight. In a corner booth old Horace Westerhaus was holding forth.

"Fabian's people are right, dammit! We're living in the dark ages. Gillespie County's got an Economic Development Commission. Do we? No. It's time for folks like us drag this county kicking and screaming into the twenty-first century."

"Look!" Gloria Wall said, pointing at Kitt. "It's the reporter. Well, she *calls* herself a reporter." She gave Kitt a challenging stare. "Why weren't you at that meeting last night? Why weren't you covering *that* news?"

"Because it was a private meeting, and I wasn't asked," Kitt retorted. "I don't know what was said."

Ralph Wall leaned across the table and shook his index finger at her. "I'll tell you what was said. Fabian's interested in buying our land. But he won't buy while he's being sued."

Gloria nodded indignantly. "He'd pay almost twice the market price. But we can't get it because of the lawsuits. We're being *robbed*."

Kitt was more astonished than before. "You mean as long as people like the McKinneys hold out, he won't buy?"

"That's exactly what we mean," Ralph snapped.

"So the clock is ticking, and *we're* losing money," fumed Gloria.

"The big landowners are holding the small ones hostage," said Horace. "I'm writing an editorial about it—a masterpiece of fiery rhetoric."

"But a few days ago you were on the other side," Kitt protested.

"Consistency is the hobgoblin of little minds," Horace said pompously. "I am not afraid to admit I can have a change of heart."

Kitt thought he was a hypocrite, but she wasn't going to argue with him. "This is all fascinating," she said, "but I have to find Nora."

"We want to tell you *our* side of the story," Gloria said, trying to lay her hand on Kitt's arm.

"Later," Kitt said, dodging her. She zigzagged between tables and made her way to the kitchen. Nora stood by the counter, looking stricken.

"Good grief," Kitt said, "what's happening? You look like a deer caught in the headlights."

"I feel like one," Nora said. "Gloria Wall practically *attacked* me. She called Ken one of J.T.'s 'henchmen.' I don't want to go back out there. I might smack her upside the head with a skillet."

"Make it a cast-iron one," said Kitt.

Nora managed to smile.

Kitt said, "And Mel Belyle made this proposition?"

"It's a fiendish thing to do," Nora said angrily. "I heard two Austin TV stations are sending crews here to interview—people. I bet Gloria Wall can't wait to be on the six o'clock news. And have you seen the papers?"

When Kitt shook her head, Nora snatched up a fat stack of newspapers. "Every major Texas paper has an ad—with Fabian's stats about how much bloody money Bluebonnet Meadows will make for us. Every single one."

She thrust them at Kitt. Kitt stared at a headline on the Fort Worth front page: "Billionaire Wants to Enrich Claro County: Ranchers Object."

"Take them," Nora said. "I can't stand to look at them any longer. I feel like closing the place for the day. It makes me sick to listen to people run down J.T. and the others.

For years J.T.'s been the most respected man in the county. Now, all of a sudden, he's the enemy."

Nora paused. "And yet…" she said, her brow furrowing "…and yet…"

Kitt said, "And yet, you understand that people like the Walls see this as the only chance they may ever have to strike it rich."

Nora nodded sadly. "Minnie Wallenhaupt has four acres. She's a widow and could use the money. And she'll never get a higher offer. Ever."

Kitt understood. A chance indeed to grab the brass ring, to claim the prize. The carousel on the courthouse lawn was turning into a fitting symbol of Crystal Creek. The town was turning into a merry-go-round, whirling with dizzying madness.

KITT SPENT part of the day watching a media circus parade into Crystal Creek. Two television news crews came from Austin, and one from San Antonio. Radio people showed up as well, and newspaper journalists from all over the state.

At three o'clock, Mel Belyle was to hold a short news conference in one of the hotel's two meeting rooms. Kitt wasn't invited, and she would have loved to crash it. But she could not.

At three she was due to meet in Austin with an engineer who was an expert on water resources. She hoped he could clarify the legal tangle over the water on Fabian's land. When she returned to Crystal Creek, after five, a light rain started to fall. Kitt hoped another cloudburst wasn't about to drench the county.

At the hotel, she was surprised to see Hugo standing outside Mel's door. He was dressed in a different uniform and had a badge that announced "Security Officer."

"Why, Hugo," Kitt said. "What are you doing here?"

"I'm off-duty," the big man answered with a blush. "I'm moonlighting. As a security guard."

"For Mel Belyle?"

"To keep away the press. I'm not supposed to let anybody near this door. For any reason."

Kitt gave him a questioning look. "Does that include me?"

Hugo looked sheepish. "I'm afraid so, Kitt. Sorry."

Kitt positively itched to talk to Mel. Her interview with the Austin engineer hadn't been encouraging. He said the case was so complex it could go to the state supreme court—and beyond. It could stretch out for months or even years unless one side or the other yielded.

Kitt sighed. "All right, Hugo. I'm not going ask you to do anything that would get you in trouble."

She went into her own room. She tried phoning Mel, but she could hear no ringing next door. He must have unplugged his phone, the coward. She resisted the urge to pound on the wall that separated her from Mel and to shout for him to come out and fight like a man.

Instead she switched on the television. She was just in time for the local news from Austin, and she saw a clip of Mel's earlier press conference. He sounded polished, brilliant and disgustingly sincere.

And she had to admit that he looked handsome and sexy as hell standing at that podium. The camera loved his features, the strong cheekbones, the straight nose, the perfect and masculine shape of his mouth.

She remembered the feel of that mouth upon her own, and an erotic tickle ran through her body. Her stomach fluttered and her heartbeat speeded.

Those lips can also lie, distort and manipulate, she told herself sternly. *Those blue eyes are deceptive. You don't notice how they're always alert, always watching, searching out other peoples' weaknesses.*

She picked up the phone again and called Gideon Hammer. It was after hours, but if she knew Gideon, he would still be there. She was right.

"I'm sorry to call so late," she told him. "Have you had

time to check those figures Fabian gave out about Bluebonnet Meadows?''

"I was about to phone you," Gideon said, sounding tired.
"I got lucky. There's a convention of economists in town.
I found a professor from Baylor who got interested in Bluebonnet Meadows when the story first broke. He's made
some projections.''

Kitt's heartbeat skittered in anxiety. It would be wonderful to prove Fabian's statistics were a pack of lies. "So
what's his opinion?''

"That Fabian's projections are fairly accurate. Once that
development is up and running, my God, the money'll roll
in.''

She clenched her fist in frustration. "New jobs?''

"Plenty," Gideon said. "There's going to be a demand
for more services of every kind—cops, nurses, teachers—''

Teachers. Nora.

"—oh, yeah. Claro County will definitely be more prosperous.''

Kitt said, "But what about the environment? He claims
he's not making a negative impact on the environment, but
that *can't* be true. Have you checked those statements?''

"Sorry, Kitt. I was lucky to get what I have so soon. The
environmental questions? At this point I can't tell you anything.''

She thanked him and hung up. She sat on the edge of the
bed feeling oddly dejected. Fabian had told the truth about
the money. Crystal Creek and the rest of the county would
be richer, much richer. Shouldn't that be good? Shouldn't
she be glad?

She'd skipped lunch, so went downstairs to get a candy
bar and a can of cola from the machine. When she came
back upstairs, Hugo still stood by Mel's door. She put her
fists on her hips. "Is he still hiding in there?''

Hugo laughed at her combative stance. "Nope. He went
out the back way. I'm supposed to stay here, just in case.''

"Where'd he go?''

"He didn't say. No place fancy. He had on jeans and running shoes and one of them windbreaker things."

Hmmm, though Kitt. Maybe he'd gone out to Bluebonnet Meadows again. The engineer in Austin had told her troubling things about Fabian's water scheme and the temporary dam. "An accident waiting to happen" was how he'd described it. "But the ironic thing," he'd said, "is it'd do most damage to his own land."

It'd serve him right, she thought. She made a bit of small talk with Hugo, then went into her room. Just as she finished her candy bar, the phone rang. It was Nora, and she sounded distraught.

"Nora!" Kitt said in alarm. "What's wrong?"

"I—I don't even know how to say it," Nora stammered. "When I got home this afternoon, I got a call. It was from a—a Realtor. A man from Austin. He was *here,* in Crystal Creek."

Something deep inside Kitt cringed. Somehow she knew what Nora was going to say. "He—he asked me if I'd sell the Longhorn," Nora said. "He had a buyer. He told me what the offer was, Kitt—it's a *fortune.* It's twice what it's worth. I—I don't know what to do."

"Do?" Kitt said. "*Grab* it. Good Lord, Nora, get rid of the place. Get your life back."

Kitt paused, suddenly worried that she might stir up domestic trouble. "What's Ken say? Doesn't he want you to sell it?"

"That's not it. He does. He actually said it hurt him to see me working there—I never knew he thought that. He was too proud to say it—*damn.*"

"Then what's the problem?" Kitt asked, puzzled.

"I don't know who's made the offer," Nora said, a catch in her voice. "The real estate agent would only say it's a company—Hometown Restaurants. I've got forty-eight hours to answer. He said he'll give me an extension if I need it."

"You think it's one of Fabian's companies," Kitt guessed.

"That's what I'm afraid of. But Kitt, why would he pick on *me?* Is it just another way he's trying to demoralize the town? By changing the Longhorn? By closing it? Why on earth would he want it?"

"I don't know," Kitt said from between her teeth. "But I intend to find out. I'm going to buttonhole Mel Belyle and shake the truth out of him."

"Is he there? At the hotel?" Nora asked.

"No. But I think I know where to find him," Kitt said.

She told Nora to stay calm, that she would phone her as soon as she knew anything. She snatched up her fanny pack and went out the door. Hugo was no longer guarding Mel's door. Another man stood in his place, one she didn't know. She nodded to him, but didn't speak.

She ran down the back stairs, got into her little car and set off to confront Mel. The rain was pounding down harder. A faint flicker of lightning shone in the darkening sky. Kitt didn't care. She was ready to drive, literally, through hell and high water to find him.

CHAPTER FIFTEEN

MEL HAD PARKED at the barricade, then half-walked, half-jogged past the model houses. They stood forlorn in the rain, their windows dark and their yards bare and sodden.

He paid no attention to the chill or the wet. He wore a blue windbreaker, but didn't bother to put up its hood. He was too preoccupied.

He'd finally reached Fabian. And the call had been a failure. Fabian wouldn't budge about the water rights, and he acidly denied that the dam was a problem.

Mel had argued like hell. That afternoon he'd had a call from Martinson Engineering, the independent consultant he'd contacted. Enoch Martinson himself had phoned. "We're concerned," he'd said. "You could have big trouble on your hands. And soon."

Fabian wouldn't buy it. "The dam will hold. My engineers guaranteed it, so shut up about it."

"What if your engineers are wrong?" Mel had challenged.

"They aren't. Drop the subject. I've got bigger problems. I'm allergic to everything in the world. Why is this happening to *me?* Who am I, Job?"

"Look," Mel had pleaded, "consider it. You're winning the PR battle on every other front. Concede on the dam and water rights, and you're a hero. The McKinneys and their pals won't have a leg to stand on."

"I've got hives the size of eggs. I've got hives *because* of eggs. And milk and wheat and every kind of meat but goat meat. Am I supposed to live on goat meat for the rest of my life? *Goat,* for God's sake.''

''Make the concession. Be the hero. The peacemaker. You're doing this for public safety. You want to show you're a good neighbor. You're as nice as Mother Teresa. Nicer. Do it and you've won. You don't worry about anybody—including Three Amigos.''

''Three Amigos—ha! I laugh in their faces.''

''Don't say no outright,'' Mel countered. ''You pay a lot of money for my advice. Promise at least to consider it.''

''I'll consider considering it if you'll shut the hell up.''

Mel had to settle for that. But he'd sent Fabian a terse fax restating his case as strongly as he could. Now, restless, he decided to take another look at Bluebonnet Meadows and see how the dam was holding.

Immediately Mel saw that the water in the lake was high, all too high. The rising wind tossed its dark waters until they rippled in little white caps against the makeshift wall of dirt and stone. Some of the bigger waves already spilled over the levee's edge.

And the water no longer merely trickled through the stones and rubble that formed the dam. It leaked in steady streams. The old creek bed that was meant to be dry was instead dangerously close to full. Hundreds of gallons of water had oozed through the wall, forming an uneasy channel that was swelling up between the two levees.

Mel stared at it with foreboding. As he stared, the rain began to pelt down harder. He walked to the first dam and stepped out on its uneven surface. The lake was only inches from its top. The dirty wavelets struck at it like an army of foaming claws.

The stones beneath his feet felt solid, yet the steadiness struck him as illusory, undependable. He sensed a sort of tremor pulsing through the wall, a tiny but ominous vibration.

From behind him, a voice spoke. ''If there's a flash flood

upstream, this stupid dam will never hold. You know that, don't you?''

Kitt. Her voice went through him like a blade. He swung round to face her. She stood at the edge of the embankment in her cargo pants and a yellow windbreaker, the hood up. Her running shoes were thick with mud.

"Another sneak attack," he accused. His heart beat fast at the sight of her, and he resented the power she could so easily wield over him.

"I walked out here in plain sight," she said with a shrug. "It's not like I covered myself with tumbleweeds and tiptoed up on you."

"I had my mind on other things," he said. "I didn't think anybody would be knuckleheaded enough to follow me out here. Even you."

"Feeling guilty about this miracle of engineering?" she asked tartly. "You should. I talked to a man in Austin today who says Fabian's flirting with disaster here. Your sister-in-law said the same thing."

"Leave her out of this," he said in disgust and faced the tossing lake again. He could still sense the subtle shuddering of the stones beneath his feet. Was it his imagination, or was the tremor growing?

"She's a smart woman, your sister-in-law. You should get acquainted. She could tell you a thing or two about watersheds and water tables."

He set his jaw. A sudden flash of lightning split the clouds, and thunder blasted with deafening force, shaking the air. The sky opened up, and rain roared down like a waterfall. At the far end of the levee, a pile of stones fell with a rumble, and a stream of water coursed over the gap.

Mel swore and grabbed Kitt's hand. "Let's get out of here."

For once she didn't argue. She put her free arm up to shield her face from the blinding rain. They jogged back to the road, which streamed with brown rivulets. Mel glanced at the water trapped between the two levees. It was rising with a great, rushing sound.

The water on the road was covering the asphalt; their feet splashed at every step. "Are you up to running in this?" Mel asked from between his teeth.

"Yes!" she said with fervor and gripped his hand more tightly. Heads down, they sprinted in the direction of their cars.

She was small but fast, and she managed to keep up with his longer strides. But just as they had reached the first of the model houses, she stumbled, cried out and fell to her knees in the streaming rain.

The water swirled along the road more wildly now. It was nearly to Mel's ankles. He hauled Kitt to her feet, but she winced when she tried to put her weight on her foot. She grimaced. "My ankle. I felt something—tear or snap."

He hoisted her into his arms. "Hang on," he ordered.

She obeyed, wrapping her arms around his neck. As he held her against his chest, he glanced nervously at the creek bed. It meandered only fifty yards or so from the paved road.

When he'd jogged to the dam, just minutes ago, it had been like a long, deep, quivering puddle. Now brown water coursed down it, spilling the banks and swiftly spreading.

"My God," he said.

His heart hammering, he held Kitt tighter. The torrent in the creek bed was growing higher, wider and wilder, and that could mean only one thing. The first makeshift dam was breaking down fast. And when it gave way, the second, weaker one would go, as well. A wall of water would come crashing like a juggernaut through this valley.

Kitt saw, too. "We've got to get to higher ground," she screamed in his ear. She pointed at the steeply sloping mountainside. "Go up! Go up!"

He swore and veered toward the mountain. The rain poured, and the slope was steep and slippery. He could barely keep his footing. From behind them came a deafening rumble, a hundred times louder than the thunder. He knew it was the huge, weakened wall of stones of the first levee giving way. He climbed more desperately, half-dragging Kitt, supporting her with one arm and using the other to pull his way up by bush or root or outcropping.

"Higher," Kitt cried. "There's a path, if you can get higher."

He couldn't answer her. His breath tore his chest. His lungs burned, and his legs ached. He was a swift runner on a straightaway, but this incline challenged all his energy.

Slick with rain, the ground was a treacherous quagmire of mud studded with stones. He lost his footing, slipped. For a terrifying second, he thought they would both plunge back down the hillside. But he kept tight hold of Kitt and dug his heels in until he found enough purchase to stop them from sliding back toward the valley.

He regained his footing and hoisted Kitt into his arms again. He started to climb again, then turned to look down. He stopped as if paralyzed. He held her more tightly and both of them stared in disbelieving horror.

Water came roaring through the valley, an immense foaming brown wall of it, twenty feet high and broad as the valley itself. The flood wave seethed and rolled forward like some great dragon uncoiling to strike.

The creek disappeared beneath it. The land, boulders, cactus, trees disappeared. The road disappeared. Two bulldozers vanished, and an empty yellow truck was swept along like a toy.

Mel swore in awe and dread. The wall crashed into the white houses and knocked them from their foundations. It was as if they were the toy houses on a game board, and a giant hand had sent them spinning into the whirling water. Two of them crashed together, and the splintering of their timbers was like the snapping of tiny sticks in the tumult of the flood's rush toward the highway.

One house toppled onto its side, another simply split apart and sank before their eyes. Kitt clutched Mel more tightly. Stunned, holding on to each other, they stared down as the water spread and grew. They were safe. But everything that had once been Bluebonnet Meadows was gone.

KITT WAS A REPORTER; she'd seen disasters before. She'd covered train crashes, plane crashes, car crashes. She'd seen what fires and floods and explosives could do.

But she'd always seen the aftermath. She had never before watched, helpless and horrified, as such a thing happened before her eyes.

She wasn't the person who reported action news from its white-hot center. She did not deal with the chaos of violent events in the present. She probed the forces that caused them, the human consequences that followed them.

Even as she clung to Mel, soaked and aching, the rain pouring down on them, she fought to make sense of what she'd seen. The water had not oozed up over the landscape like a normal flood, steadily rising. It had not come rushing in a straight, high burst down the creek bed, overflowing the banks as it came.

No, this had been a churning, crashing mass of water that changed its shape like some creature of evil enchantment. It did not slowly cover what lay in its path. It drowned all obstacles or swept them away.

The houses still intact bobbed as forlornly as cardboard boxes tossed about by a monstrous tide. The yellow truck zigzagged off in the swirling froth like a child's sinking plastic toy.

The wall of water moved not straight forward, but crookedly. It surged along the snaking bed of the creek, and its height loomed or sank as the floor and walls of the valley channeled it.

It lashed against first one side of the valley, then the other. When it had smashed into the houses it had been a mountain of water, but now as it reached the highway, it lowered, flattening and spreading.

From the heights, Kitt and Mel saw the wave wash away the barricades as if they were toothpicks. It carried off both their cars. It covered the highway as if it had never existed, and it rolled on, with a sound like a hundred jet engines.

She watched as her own car sank from sight. Mel's was dashed against a huge limestone boulder, then both the boulder and his car disappeared under the surging waves.

"Good Lord," Mel said in a ragged voice.

She understood. They were lucky not to have made it as far as the cars. If they had stayed on their course, they'd be dead or dying now. She laid her face against his chest. For a moment, she wanted not to see the destruction below them. But she did not cry. She would not let herself cry.

"Come on," Mel said in her ear. "Let's try to get to higher ground. I don't feel safe even here. Can you take being moved any more?"

She raised her head and nodded. "We should call the sheriff's department. Warn people."

"I lost my cell phone," he said. He stared down into the valley, the swift, tumbling water surging between the hills. "It's down there, somewhere."

She groped for hers, belted to her waist. But it was cracked and useless. She must have smashed it against a rock when they fell.

Mel frowned at the southern horizon. The water was still swelling forward, spreading like a great stain across the countryside. "How many people live downstream from this?"

"Nobody for miles," Kitt said. "It's mostly J.T.'s ranchland. Beyond that? Some isolated farms. But a settlement? Not for twenty miles…"

Her voice quavered, trailed off. There was no town for twenty miles, but there were roads with people traveling on them. There were bridges that could wash out as drivers tried to cross them. There could be wranglers riding out in the storm, trying to bring in cattle.

She looked into Mel's eyes pleadingly. "Surely to God people heard it. When that dam gave way, it sounded like—like hell cracking open."

Her head still rang with the sound. She knew she would hear it in her nightmares for the rest of her life.

"Yes," he said, his jaw muscles tight. "People heard. Surely to God."

CAL MCKINNEY HEARD IT. He'd been riding out toward J.T.'s most northeastern section. He'd been glad to get out of the house. His father was still disgruntled about Three Amigos; he'd been glum and silent all day.

Jennifer's pony, a renowned escape artist, had slipped out of its paddock early in the afternoon. Cal had tracked her down and was leading her back through the drizzle. He'd decided to ride up Stony Hill, where he'd have a good view of how the creeks were running.

He'd reached the hill's summit just as the sky opened in a ferocious cloudburst. "Hellfire," muttered Cal, moving his horse and the pony beneath the shelter of a ledge. "Ain't riding back in *this*."

He pulled his hat lower. Looking through the rain was like squinting through a watery curtain. Fabian's stupid lake was hidden by the ridge. His five houses looked like white pinpoints. Cal gazed at the scene idly. He wished he was back at the house with his wife and kids, J.T.'s dark mood be damned.

Then the air was rent by a rumble unlike anything Cal had ever heard. Did he imagine it, or did the solid stone that sheltered him seem to groan and vibrate with the din?

Suddenly, from the direction of Fabian's lake, he saw a mass of water, a shimmying wall of it, coming like a tidal wave. He saw the houses flicker, then spin away, like tiny flakes in a torrent. His heart nearly stopped in his chest.

The dam broke. The flood's covering the highway. It'll go for miles, clear to the river.

Cal whipped his cell phone from under his slicker and punched 911. The dispatcher, Margaret, answered. Cal's horse began to dance and kick, rebelling at the danger it sensed. Cal hung on and fired his words into the phone,

"This is Cal McKinney. I'm on the Northeast section of the Double C. The dam at Bluebonnet Meadows gave way. It took those five houses down like they was sledgehammered. You got a flash flood coming right down the whole of Lower Crystal Creek—"

"Flash flood?" Margaret asked. He could barely hear her over the rain and the roar of the great wave drowning the valley. "Has it reached the highway?"

"Yes." Cal yelled to be heard. "This is an emergency, Margaret. Get word out, for God's sake."

"Was anybody on the road?" she asked.

"I can't tell," he practically screamed. "Get out the word, dammit!"

Serena and his children were safe, he knew, because J.T.'s house was out of the flood's path. J.T. and Cynthia were with them, and safe. His sister's place in town should be fine.

But who else was out there in the path of that man-made tidal wave?

J.T. WAS PROFOUNDLY GRATEFUL to have his family all in one place. His daughter Lynn and her family had come as soon as they heard the news.

But Lynn was grim-faced, and so were her two adopted daughters, sitting on either side of her. Allie looked nervous and Sandy angry as they all listened to radio reports of the flood.

In three hours, the crest of the flood had plunged along the path of Lower Crystal Creek until it had begun emptying into the Claro River. It had hurled and twisted for twenty-one miles. The water lowered as the valley widened; its velocity slowed.

But the damage was done. And nobody knew how much. Fifteen buildings at the water's farthest edge were flooded, in a little community called Baswell. So far nobody was reported killed, but there were people unaccounted for.

No one could speculate on the amount of physical damage. Trees had been uprooted, crops drowned, cattle killed, roads washed out, bridges collapsed. Roadblocks had been set up, and the Crystal Creek water supply was compromised; nobody was supposed to drink from it.

"I wish we'd kept protesting last summer," eighteen-year-old Sandy muttered. "We should have stood up to Fabian *then*. We never should have backed down."

Lynn stroked the girl's long, fine hair. "We decided to settle it legally."

"Legally," Sandy scoffed. She stood and tightly crossed her arms. "Look where *legally* got us."

J.T. had to agree with the last part. If they hadn't blocked Fabian, he'd have had time to build a real dam at his lake. He sighed and stared out the picture window. Beyond the rivulets of rain that streaked it, he could see only blackness.

Cynthia came to her husband's side and put her hand on his arm. "J.T.," she said, "you don't blame yourself for this do you?"

Dear Cynthia, he thought. He turned to her, taking both her hands in his.

"We fought. Maybe we shouldn't have. But we tried to fight fair."

"I know you did," she said. She rose on tiptoe and kissed his jaw.

"Daddy," Cal said with a frown, "you *had* to take him to court. He can't mess with the water rights the way he did. It affects everybody downstream. You. Aunt Carolyn. Mark Devlin. Jake Zangwell… You had no choice."

Sandy said, "He stopped construction even though he knew there was danger." She said it with great bitterness. "If that creek ran a little farther west, this flood would have taken out most of Tyler's vineyard."

Her father, Sam, patted her arm. "It didn't. It took a few acres, that's all." But Sandy had thought about it too much and started to cry softly.

"*Damn* Fabian," she choked out. She laid her face against Sam's chest, and he wrapped his arms around her.

Cal moved to the window beside his father and step-mother. "Those fancy houses of Fabian's washed away like paper boats," he said. "So far he's hurt himself more than anybody," he said.

"Only so far," said Sam. "Not everyone's accounted for."

J.T. nodded and drew Cynthia closer to him. He and his were all right. His hands and their families were accounted for. He'd heard from Carolyn; she and Vernon were fine. So were Ken and Nora. Bubba and Mary Gibson were okay except that they had a lot of very wet ostriches, and Bubba, enraged, was sputtering his head off about suing Fabian.

Every five minutes, it seemed, the phone rang with some-one else reporting in and asking if they were all right. Right now Serena was talking earnestly with Tracey Hernandez, who'd called long distance from Abilene. No sooner had she hung up than it rang again. This time J.T. picked it up himself. "Double C. J. T. McKinney speaking."

"J.T., it's me again," said Ken Slattery. "I'm sorry to bother you, but Nora's worried. She hasn't had any word from Kitt since about five-thirty. They talked, and she told Nora she was going to find Mel Belyle."

J.T. tensed. He'd been concerned about family, friends, neighbors. The little redhead had completely slipped his mind. "Belyle? Where was *he?*"

"Kitt didn't say," Ken told him. "She said she'd phone after she talked to him. That's the last we heard of her. I called the Sheriff's Department. State Police, too. Nobody knows anything about either of them."

J.T. swore under his breath. He wouldn't give a damn if Mel Belyle got swept into the Claro River and turned into fish food. But Kitt Mitchell? She was such a little thing—a wall of water like that could have carried her off as easily as if she were a child.

Ken said, "Nora's getting frantic."

"Kitt's got a good head on her shoulders," J.T. said. "She seems like the kind who can take care of herself. But

I'll put the word out. You and Nora want to come over here?''

"No. She wants to stay close to the phone here. But thanks.''

J.T. said goodbye and hung up. The others looked at him expectantly. ''Nora hasn't heard from her cousin. Kitt Mitchell.''

Their faces went wary, and Sandy looked as if she might cry again. Nobody said anything. All they could do was wait.

"MY GOD,'' Mel said in Kitt's ear. His voice was hoarse. They'd reached the ledge that formed a narrow path that led upward. The ground beneath them was stony and muddy— but blessedly level.

He'd nearly crawled the last few yards to the ridge, pulling Kitt with him. Now they lay, collapsed, on the ledge. They held each other, and Kitt could feel his heart hammering next to hers. Her breath came in torn gasps.

Kitt wanted to weep with relief. But she had no strength for weeping. All she could do was lie beside Mel, stunned at still being alive. She didn't know how he'd managed to toil up the steep slope until he reached the path. In places it was nearly as sheer as a cliff.

The sky had turned black, the rain blinding.

He'd stumbled too many times for her to count, he'd slid backward, he'd fallen twice, but he never quit. And he never loosened his grip on her. Sometimes he had her slung inelegantly over his shoulder. Sometimes he clutched her against him protectively as he crawled and clawed his way higher.

Now she lay pressed against him, her own heart pounding and the blood ringing in her ears. She raised herself weakly and tried to look over the ledge. A distant flash of lightning briefly lit the sky a dull blue.

Far below she glimpsed a black swirling sea, valley wide. The unleashed water rushed and roared. If Mel had really fallen—or if he'd lost his hold on her just once...she wouldn't think about that.

She turned away, tears stinging her eyes, and fell back against the wet earth. Her ankle throbbed. She felt scratched, bruised and battered all over.

Beside her Mel moaned and swore. He raised himself on his free elbow. "We've got to get out of this rain. You said there was shelter somewhere? How do we get there?"

She stayed where she was, protected in the crook of his arm. "I don't even know where we are."

With a groan he sat up. He pulled her up beside him, wrapping both arms around her so she could lean against his chest. Lightning flickered on the horizon again, a series of dull flashes. Mel hugged her tighter. "Are you okay? Are you in shock or something?"

"I've felt better," she said. "I'm just—stunned. I feel—all shaky."

"It's gotten so damn dark," he said. "I don't know if we can get any farther."

"I—I might have a light," she said. "If it still works. I forgot about it until now. Maybe I am in shock."

She rummaged in her vest and found her pen light. It was no larger than a fountain pen. But it worked. Its beam lit a circle of light around them.

Mel took her face between his hands and kissed her. "You're wonderful."

"I just feel stupid for forgetting it," she admitted.

"I've got a fanny pack with nothing in it but my wallet and car keys," he said. "Neither of which helps at this point. Can you tell where we are?"

"Not by this," she said, regarding the light's thin beam.

"Shut it off. Save it," he advised. "Try to see a landmark during the lightning."

She obeyed and snapped off the light. When lightning next flashed, she stared down at the black valley. It was like staring into a maelstrom of darkness.

"The landmarks are gone," she said in a small voice.

It was true. The road was gone. The houses were gone. In the distance the very highway was gone. Kitt bit her lip, fighting down a surge of hysteria.

"Steady," Mel said in her ear. "Next time—look across the valley. I think the original ranch house is still there. It was up in a grove of oaks, right?"

"Right," she said, then bit her lip harder. She waited for the light to shimmer again. She tasted the salty warmth of her own blood. When the next ghostly glow shuddered over the world, she strained her eyes. Then her heart bounded.

Across the water pitching in the valley, she saw a dark grove of trees on the high rise of the opposite hill. And—barely visible—the rust-red shingles of a roof—the lodge of Hole in the Wall. And above it, the Harris's old house!

She could have wept with happiness. Something man-made still remained solid and surviving in this ruined world. "My God," she breathed. "We could have gone *there*."

"No," he said, his breath warm on her neck. "We would have had to cross the creek bed. We would have never made it."

She shivered and drew nearer to him, her back against the dependable hardness of his chest. She tried to keep her voice steady. "If that's the house, then we're north of it, right?"

"Right." He swore again. "So how do we get out of this bloody rain?"

She thought back to her childhood, to the careless summer days when she and Nora had climbed this path with their books and blanket and limeade. She struggled to remember.

"About a quarter mile farther north," she said, "there's a place we called the Hermit's Cave. My father told us not to go there. He said it wasn't safe. We went anyway."

"Why isn't it safe? Do they have mud slides around here?"

"Rock slides sometimes. But mostly he said it because the path was so steep. We could fall and break our necks."

"What are our other choices?" Mel asked.

"On this side? Nothing."

"Then we'll go for the Hermit's Cave," he said. He stood and drew her to her feet. "Want me to take the light? Can you walk?"

She handed him the light, then tried to put her weight on her foot. Pain speared through her as her ankle crumpled. She nearly fell, but he held her.

"I'll need to lean on you," she said. She put her arm around his waist.

"You'll have to get us there," he said, wrapping his arm around her shoulders. "We'll lean on each other."

Below them, the flood waters rushed on in the darkness.

CHAPTER SIXTEEN

HOW SHE DID IT, he didn't know, but somehow she found the way through the storm to shelter. The only illumination was the ridiculously small beam of her tiny pen light and the inconstant lightning.

After a seeming eternity, they reached a wide spot in the ledge, and she said, "We're here." She shone the light on a dark tangle of vines and scrubs that cloaked the hill's stone face. When she pushed back a screen of rain-battered branches, he saw the edge of the crevice. She said, "Follow me."

He kept his arm tightly around her as she led him inside and toward the back. "It's warmer in the rear," she said. "And there used to be a spring, a little one."

"A spring?" he said sarcastically. "Just what we need—more water."

"It's small, but it's *warm,*" she said. She shone the weak light far into the shadows. The cave went back for another fifteen or twenty feet, its ceiling growing lower until it met the rubbled floor.

He heard the trickle of water from somewhere. Not the plunging rush of the rain outside, or the muted growl of the flood below, but like a tap left gently running.

Then he saw it: a tiny stream glittering in the light's beam. The rivulet sparkled as it ran down the wall into a small natural basin. The water swirled there a moment, then sank through a crack and disappeared into the rocks.

Kitt kneeled before it, setting the light on a stony outcropping. Mel watched her shadowy profile as she scooped up water and washed her face. "Mmm," she said with sensual happiness. "It's some kind of a hot spring. Lord, that feels good." She turned to him. "Come here."

He crouched beside her. She dipped her hands in the water and brought it to his face. He almost gasped with pleasure at the warmth. He put his hands over hers and held them against his flesh.

"That felt almost as good as sex," he said with something near reverence.

She laughed and pulled her hands away. "We can take turns washing up. I wish it was bigger."

So did he. The thing was no larger than a punchbowl, but to him it looked as tempting as a hot tub. She stood, drawing herself up by clinging to a ridge of rock. He rose and put his arm around her. "You're still shaky on the ankle. Give me the flashlight. I'll take a look at it."

She gritted her teeth, nodded and gave him the light. She sat down on a stone. "Nora and I used to come here and pretend to camp."

He flashed the feeble light around the interior. He narrowed his eyes and sucked in his breath. "Somebody still does."

"Does what?" She wiped her wet hair back from her eyes.

"Comes here and camps," he said in a low voice.

Her gaze followed his. "Good grief," she breathed.

The feeble beam of light gleamed on a long shelf of rock. And on that shelf of stone flashed man-made objects. Glass. And metal. And plastic. He grinned as his heart speeded in happy disbelief. On the stone was an old-fashioned lantern, its chimney glass blackened with soot. Beside it, a red can of kerosene. Stacks of canned goods—soup, orange juice, beans, green chilies, a tin of tuna. Clear plastic zippered bags held—*blankets?*

"We've died," he said. "We've gone to heaven."

She laughed giddily, as if she didn't believe the sight

either. "Somebody still uses this place. Who'd have thought it?"

He swept the beam of light toward the back wall. On the floor was an inflated mattress, the kind used in sleeping bags. An old checkered oilcloth partly covered it. There was a half-empty wine jug beside the mattress.

"Somebody still comes up here and camps out," she said in wonder.

No, Mel thought. *Somebody comes up here and makes love.*

The light glittered on something trodden into the rubble of the floor. He recognized it as the foil wrapping of a condom. This spot wasn't some boyish Tom Sawyer hideaway. It was somebody's secret love nest.

From the plumpness of the air mattress, he'd guessed the place had been used recently. He wondered who, but didn't care. They'd left the mattress and blankets, and for that, he considered all their sins forgiven.

Kitt shone the small light past the mattress, where stones circled a heap of ash and half-burned sticks. Nearby was a haphazardly stacked pile of wood. "Mesquite," she said. "They've built fires here. Oh—*fire.*"

She said the word with the same wonder and satisfaction with which some women might say "diamonds."

"Matches?" Mel asked dubiously.

"There have to be," Kitt said, turning the light back to the stone shelf. "There's everything else. Look—a can opener, even a corkscrew." She rummaged purposefully among the booty until she found a tin box. She grinned up at him and held out the box. "Waterproof matches," she said. "And there's still kerosene in the lantern."

She lit the lamp, her hand shaking with excitement. "Just in time," she said, shutting off the little flashlight. "These batteries are almost gone."

They stood in the glow of the lamp. Her shadowy face was wet, mud streaked her neck, and her left cheek sported a bruise. But her expression was beatific.

He couldn't help himself. He bent and kissed her. After what they'd been through, how could he not kiss her? They had trusted each other with their lives. They had depended on each other utterly, and neither had failed the other.

She put her arms around his neck. Her mouth was icy, but when her lips parted, her tongue was warm, as life-nourishing as fire. Still, the skin of her face was wet and chill, her clothes were drenched, and so were his. He felt a shudder quake through her, and didn't know if it was the cold of the rain or the heat of desire, or both.

He drew back, shaking his head. His wet hair hung in his eyes, and his hands were stiff with cold. "You're trembling like a little leaf. Get out of those wet clothes. Wash in the spring and put on a blanket."

"You're as cold as I am," she protested.

"You go first."

"We should build a fire," she said. "We'll need it. To get through the night." She fought back another shudder. "Come on. Or we'll die of hypothermia. Can you build a fire?"

Mel's grin was close to a grimace of pain, and like her, he was fighting bone-deep chills. "No," he said. "I'm a city boy. But I'll try."

"Never mind," she said with determination. "I think I remember how. God, this is wonderful. It's like finding a hotel." He helped her limp to the fire circle. She knelt painfully, piling sticks on the ashes. "Drat," she muttered. "This wood's damp. We need tinder."

Mel spotted the edge of a small plastic bag, tucked under the oilcloth draping the mattress. He pulled back the cloth and opened the bag. It contained a worn paperback book. It was dry. But it was also unexpected.

He cleared his throat. "Er—do you mind using a few pages from the *Kama Sutra*?"

"What?" Her head snapped up in surprise, and he handed her the book. It was subtitled "A Photographic Guide to The Most Intimate Arts of Love."

The cover picture was clear even in dim light: a naked couple, the man kissing the woman's breasts. "Whatever," Kitt said, gritting her teeth against the cold. She began ripping out pages and crumpling them.

Nothing fazes her for long, was Mel's first thought, and a strange emotion flooded him, bewilderingly powerful.

And then he knew. *Good Lord, I love her. That's what this feeling is. I love her.* Struck dumb by the realization, he watched as she set fire to the missionary position.

ONCE THE FIRE STARTED, Kitt basked in the life-restoring heat. She held out her hands to it, she hugged herself, she turned her back to warm it, then faced the flames again, unzipping her windbreaker and vest to better feel the warmth.

Mel sorted through items on the stone shelf. "An old beach towel," he said in a wry voice. "Kind of ratty. But dry." She heard the rattle of plastic as he searched the bags. "Two blankets and a pillow. Somebody's really set up house here," he said.

She frowned. "I wonder who? This is a long way from everything."

"Maybe that's its charm," he said. He moved to her and helped raise her to her feet. "Come on," he said. "Out of those wet clothes. We've got warm water. Use it. Then you can wrap up in a blanket."

He helped support her so she could hobble to the little basin of stone. "Strip down. We can lay out our clothes and hope they dry by morning."

The idea of being naked in front of him filled her with conflicting emotions. "Take 'em off," he said, toying with the top button of her shirt. "This is no time for false modesty."

He was right, but her throat was tight, and her heart pounded. "I can undress myself." She moved his hand away from her shirt.

"Then do it," he said in a low voice. "I'll turn my back if it makes you feel better."

"Yes," she said. "Please." She leaned against the stone and shucked off her windbreaker and sodden vest. True to his word, he turned away. Swallowing hard, she unbuttoned her top and let it drop to the stones. She struggled out of her shoes, then her socks and cargo pants. Her ankle was swollen so grotesquely that she didn't want to look at it.

She set her jaw, unfastened her bra and stepped out of her panties.

The cool air assaulted her bare skin, and her nipples tightened. She sank to her knees and began to rub the warm water over her face, her throat, her body. At first touch, the water was like bliss, then it cooled, but she kept stroking it over herself, feeling warm and chilled at the same time.

At last, shivering, she felt almost clean again. She felt a rough cloth cover her shoulders. Mel had draped the towel about her. She stared up at him. The lantern's glow made light and shadow dance on his face, and in its inconstant flicker, she couldn't read his expression.

"You said you wouldn't look," she said, her heart beating harder.

"I didn't look much," he said. "And what little I saw was lovely."

She tried to rise and pull the old towel more tightly about herself. But pain shot through her ankle; it wobbled, and Mel caught her. "Turn around and lean against the wall," he said. "I'll help dry you off."

"I'm not so sure that's a good idea," she breathed, tightening the towel across her breasts protectively. But she faced away and leaned one hand against the wall to support herself. She let him help her dry her shoulders and back.

He did it with such firmness he was almost rough. But it felt wonderful. It felt right. He was getting her blood circulating again. He took her by the arm and gently pulled her to face him again. "Finish the job," he said gruffly. "I'll bring you a blanket. Then sit by the fire. I've pulled the mattress close to it so you don't have to sit on the ground.''

When he took his hands from her, she missed his touch. A kind of anxious heaviness settled in her chest, and her flesh tingled. She finished drying and didn't resist when he took the towel and wrapped an old red blanket about her. It smelled fusty, but it was deliciously dry and warm.

His arm around her shoulders, he walked her to the fire. He helped settle her on the air mattress, then knelt beside her and helped towel her hair. ''Lord,'' he murmured, ''when your hair reflects the fire, it's like fire itself.''

He got up and gathered her dropped clothes, spread them next to the fire to dry. ''You have a comb in this vest of many pockets?'' he asked.

She smiled a bit shakily. ''Yes. On the inside left top.''

He retrieved it and handed it to her. ''I'm going to wash up.''

''I won't look,'' she promised. It seemed a childish thing to say, but she couldn't help saying it.

''I don't care,'' he said. He chucked her under the chin affectionately. ''I might like it if you did.''

Mel picked up the other blanket and moved to the basin. She thought she heard the wet rustle of his shirt sliding free from his body. She knew she heard him kick his shoes off and unzip his jeans.

Kitt combed her hair and tried not to imagine him naked in the lantern light. She couldn't stop herself. ''Argh!'' she heard him cry. ''For two seconds it feels great, then you're cold again.''

She kept combing. ''Do it fast,'' she recommended. ''And rub hard.''

''Argh!'' he said again. ''Part of me's warm and part's freezing.''

She laughed and pulled the blanket more snugly around her. Discreetly, she stole a glance over her shoulder. He was a gold and semi-dark figure, kneeling on one knee before the basin, scrubbing his face. He had a fine body, broad of back and shoulder, long of leg. His muscles were hard, and as the light played on them, shadows threw them into high relief, their curves changing intriguingly.

Quickly she looked away, but his image seemed branded on her mind. She combed her hair and tried not to think of what might happen next.

"Oof!" he huffed. "Enough is enough." She imagined him standing, drying himself as best he could in the already damp towel. She heard the flutter of the other blanket being flung open.

Then he was beside her, wrapped in a faded blue blanket. He carried his wet shirt. She was stroking the last of the tangles out of her hair. He smiled at her. "You look like a mermaid sitting and combing her hair."

"I should have *been* a mermaid. It would have been safer to be half fish."

"Down there, it would have been safer to be *all* fish. But since you've got legs, let me see your ankle."

She made a face, but stuck her foot out from beneath the hem of her blanket. It was swollen and discolored. He picked it up and set it on his lap. "You think it's a break or a sprain?"

"A sprain or strain, I'm pretty sure. Maybe a torn ligament."

He massaged it. "Does that hurt?"

"Yes!"

His hand went still, then stroked her shin. "It's too late for a cold compress. You're probably as swollen as you're going to get. I'll wrap it. Lie down."

She clenched her teeth and obeyed, stretching out on the mattress. She felt vulnerable and dangerously close to naked. She heard the sound of something ripping and said, "What's that?"

"My shirt," he said. "We need a bandage. Shh. Lie still." She could feel him tying the torn cloth firmly first around her ankle, then under her instep, then round the ankle again. "Tell me if it starts to feel too tight," he said.

"I will," she said. His hands were sure and gentle.

"Okay, try not to move your foot. Rest it all you can. We're going to have to get down from here tomorrow."

"Yes." The descent wouldn't be bad if the rain would stop.

"The water should be mostly gone."

She knew. It would have rushed on, lowering as it went, emptying finally into the river. It would leave behind silt, mud—and wreckage. "Those houses are all gone." She said it almost sadly, even though she hadn't liked them.

"Yes." He propped her foot up, then slid beside her and put his hand on her shoulder. "Hungry?" he asked. "I can rustle up some food."

"No," she said. The reality of what they'd been through was starting to sink into her consciousness. "I couldn't eat anything."

"Lost your appetite?" She could hear the concern in his voice.

"Terror tends to do that to me," she said with grim humor.

"You? Terrified? Never. You never faltered. Not once."

"There wasn't any time then," she said unhappily. "Now there is."

"Some wine's left in that bottle," he said squeezing her shoulder. "Would it help? I wish there was coffee, but there isn't."

"Wine sounds wonderful," she said with feeling.

"There's a couple of metal cups. Stay put. I'll pour you some." He rose, stoked the fire, then filled two enamel cups. He sat beside her, handing her one. "Prop yourself up," he said. "You can lean against me."

"I've been doing a lot of that lately," she said worriedly. But she raised herself, then leaned back against his chest. He slipped one bare arm from his blanket and put it around her, drawing her more securely to him.

Oh, she thought, *He's warm. He's strong. He feels just*

right. He feels like home. The idea of feeling at home jolted her, even frightened her. She raised the wine to her lips.

"Wait," he said, clicking his cup against hers. "A toast. To survival."

"To survival," she repeated and took a drink. It was cheap wine, sweet but strong. It went down her throat like a gentle liquid fire, and she took another sip.

"Not exactly French champagne," he said in her ear.

"I don't care," she said. "I wonder who lugged all this stuff up here."

She felt him shrug. "Who knows? Probably some couple who shouldn't be together."

"Like us," she said pensively.

"Why shouldn't we be together?" His mouth was even closer to her ear. His breath was warm against her cheek.

She stared into the fire and listened to the rain. She took another sip of wine to fortify herself. "You and I are on different sides," she said at last.

"It's gone beyond being on sides," Mel said. He drew her nearer to him.

The movement shifted his blanket. She rested now against his partly bared chest. She had the bizarre desire to turn and kiss it. She struggled not to think of the forces that pulled them together, but only of those that split them hopelessly apart.

She took a deep breath and said, "I followed you here because of Nora. Somebody made her an offer on the Longhorn. Some outfit called Hometown Restaurants. But it's Brian Fabian, isn't it?"

"No," Mel said. "It's not. It's an outfit in California. They're legit. They made the offer. For me."

She blinked in astonishment. "*You? Why?*"

"Because Nora deserves to get out of there and do what she wants with her life," he said. "You know it as well as I do."

Kitt touched her fingertips to her brow. The wine was going to her head.

"You made the offer? I don't understand. Why?"

His arms tightened around her. "Because Nora's not at the Longhorn out of choice. She has no choice. Can you deny it?"

"No." She rubbed her forehead. "It broke my heart when she had to go back. She never complains. But it bothers her. I know."

"It doesn't have to bother her any longer," he said.

"But—what would you do with it? Do you think it would make money? Would you change it?" Kitt asked. She knew how Nora felt responsible to keeping the standard that Dottie Jones had set.

"Make money?" Mel asked with a wry laugh. "It might. Change it? No. I'll probably forget I own it except at tax time. There's a philanthropist of sorts in California. Sheila MacCauley. Her hobby is buying and preserving small-town restaurants. She'll find somebody who knows how to manage it, keep it in character. Somebody like that other waitress—what's her name?"

"Kasey?" Kitt said. "She'd love the chance. She could use the money. She's got a little boy to support."

"So then everybody's happy, right?"

Kitt shook her head in confusion. She took the last drink of wine. "I still don't understand. You thought this up on your own?"

"Yes."

"But why? You hardly know Nora. Why would you bother to help her?"

"Because you love her," he said, his voice suddenly gruff.

She twisted to look at him. His face was so close to hers she could feel the warmth of his skin. He touched her chin, traced his fingertip along the curve of her lower lip.

"You did it for *me?*" she asked softly. Somehow she knew he spoke the truth. She could see it in his expression, as the fire's golden light flickered on his face.

"I had to do one thing to try to prove to you I'm not completely rotten."

She put her hand on his jaw. "I don't know what to say."

"Don't say anything," he whispered. He bent and kissed her.

Oh, yes, she thought, half-faint with desire for him. *Yes. Yes. Yes.*

She wound her arms around his neck, and the soft blanket fell away from her. The cool air hit her flesh like a mild shock, but then all she was aware of was the warmth and strength of his body.

He deepened the kiss. She was dizzied with wanting him and wanting to give herself to him. His tongue flirted boldly and expertly with hers. She reveled in tasting him and being tasted. Both their mouths were tangy with wine, and the air was fragrant with woodsmoke and rain.

His hands stroked her bare arms as his lips traveled down to the hollow of her throat. He kissed one of her breasts until it throbbed, then the other. She gripped his shoulders. They were hard and powerful beneath her fingers.

He drew back and knelt beside her, letting his own blanket fall away. He stared at her, bare to the waist, with fierce hunger in his eyes. Her nipples were peaked with yearning to be touched again, and her breath was thick in her throat.

"Good Lord," he said, his voice raspy with pleasure. "What an exquisite little thing you are." His hands closed over her shoulders, and his eyes traveled up and down her body.

She let herself look at him. His naked body was gilded by the firelight, and he was the most beautiful man she'd ever seen. She ran her hands over the planes of his chest, savoring the feel of his muscles.

His stomach was flat, his belly lean, his thighs long and sinewy. She let her hands caress the sides of his hips, the strength of his legs, and, at last, touch his erection, stroking it.

He gasped and lowered her to the mattress. He drew back

the blanket that still covered her. And for a long moment drank her in, one hand moving from her breasts to the cluster of red-gold curls between her legs.

She bit her lip to keep from crying out. Her body began to tremble with need for his. He gasped again and turned away. "I have a condom in my wallet. I—I'm sorry. I mean, it shows what a conceited bastard I am. But—but—"

"Get it," she said. "Hurry."

He rose and lifted up the fanny pack drying by the fire. She looked at him without shame now, how tall he was, how masculine, how aroused.

He came back to her and lowered himself beside her. "You're shivering again," he said in concern.

"I think it's because of you," she said, putting her hands on his waist, wanting to draw him nearer.

"I'm not going to let you freeze," he said.

He seized up both blankets, and drew them around them as he lay down beside her. He kissed her on the mouth again. Their hands explored each other greedily, passionately. Their legs commingled. Kitt lost awareness of everything except the two of them, wild and tender and aching with longing.

At last he entered her, and waves of pleasure swept through her, more and more strongly until they completely engulfed her. She was conscious of nothing except the sensations that rippled through her with such power and pleasure that she held onto him as if he were the secret to life itself.

HE LAY WITH HER in the crook of his arm. Her hair, still damp, tickled his chest. They both gazed at the fire. "I'm going to have to get up in a minute and put more wood on," he said. The idea of leaving her, even for only moments, filled him with regret.

"Not yet," she said, snuggling closer to him. She was good at snuggling. He'd like to grow old being snuggled up to that way.

He stroked her shoulder. "I mean it about the condom. I was carrying it out of habit, that's all. I didn't think that you—that I—that we—"

"Don't apologize. I know you haven't exactly lived like a monk." He thought he heard a note of sadness in her voice.

He drew her closer. He'd had dozens of beautiful women, and he'd never so much as pretended to make a commitment to one. He used them for sex and for his vanity.

But Kitt was different. Kitt was—Kitt. She was a person with fire and intelligence and bravery and integrity.

She stirred uneasily. "What happens now to Bluebonnet Meadows?"

He tensed. He'd thought she was going to ask *What happens now to us?* But perhaps the two questions were the same.

He said, "Fabian lost his chance to make good on the dam. I failed. I couldn't convince him. My guess is that Bluebonnet Meadows is stalled for a long time. Maybe for good. Who knows?"

She twisted so that she could face him. Her hand rested on his bare chest, over his heart. "What do you mean?"

He put his hand over hers. "Fabian's going to be sued. He'll countersue. But he can outlast everybody because he's got the money to do it. He's capable of hanging on for pure spite. Years, if he has to."

"Years?" she asked. She settled against him again, but he sensed she didn't feel as secure as before. Her voice sounded worried. "Then you'll still be fighting J.T. and the others?"

"No," he said. He was certain of this. "I'm not a court-room animal. He'll send others. He'll assign me somewhere else. This damn land doesn't have to stand between you and me any longer."

"I want to believe you," she said. "But it's not that simple."

His hand ran down her bare back, savoring the smoothness of her skin. "We'll make it simple. You had an assignment. So did I. We did our jobs. We go back to New York. And Crystal Creek will be behind us."

She made a sound of doubt, but he whispered, "Shh."

He kissed her cheek, then her ear. "Tomorrow we go back down that path. Back into the real world. I file my report. You write your story. And we get on with our lives—far from here. And together."

She sighed and nestled closer.

"It's true," he insisted. He wanted to say *I love you*, but he couldn't bring himself to say that, not yet. He had never said it to another human being in his life, not even his brothers or mother.

But he thought of Kitt, so small and warm in his arms, and he was overwhelmed with feeling for her. "Your ankle," he said, "does it hurt?"

"Yes," she said. "But you made me forget it for a while."

He smiled. "Go to sleep. Rest. Tomorrow we'll get it fixed."

She murmured, "Mmm. Tomorrow."

His throat tightened. "Right." He held her, feeling her body finally relax, her breath become even. When he was sure she was asleep, he whispered, "I love you."

The words were soft on the damp air. The fire crackled. Outside the rain had slowed to a steady drumming. But he liked the sound of the words, so he said them again. "I love you."

By tomorrow the flood waters would have drained away. He meant what he said: he'd carry her all the way back if he had to, and from then on, he intended to protect her from hurt for the rest of his life.

He pulled the blankets more snugly about them. He slept.

Outside the thunder growled. The rain redoubled its force. The wind wailed like a mad thing. Somewhere outside a rock tumbled down, striking the ledge outside. But neither Mel nor Kitt heard. Exhausted, they were lost together in dreamless sleep.

A RUMBLE AWOKE HIM. A thunderous growl almost like the levee breaking, only closer, as if this time Mel and Kitt were at its roaring center. There was a hellish clatter of stones falling, great and small.

A pebble hit Mel. A gigantic groan of rock moving against rock filled the air. Another pebble struck, then another. "What?" Kitt asked sleepily.

Dust and pebbles came raining down from the cave's ceiling. Mel saw a larger one strike the fire, sending sparks and coals leaping. He swore. *Cave-in!*

Outside, the rumble grew to a roar, the clattering became a series of crashes, and the ceiling shook. Instinctively he grabbed Kitt and half-dragged, half-shoved her beneath the shelter of the rock ledge.

He pushed her down so that he could angle his body above hers, shielding her. Kitt clung to him, burying her face against his chest. Pebbles pelted his shoulder. Noise deafened him; vibrations shook every cell of his body.

It sounded as if the whole damn mountain was coming down around them, closing in on them like a great stone vice.

CHAPTER SEVENTEEN

LATE THAT NIGHT, Sheriff Wayne Jackson had to break the same bad news to two separate families. First he told Nora and Ken.

Two crushed cars had been found, their remains wrapped around the same bridge abutment. One was Kitt's rented compact, its roof crumpled flat, its hood smashed like that of a toy car by a giant hammer. There was no sign of Kitt.

The other car had been Mel Belyle's. It was rammed even more cruelly around the abutment. Its wreckage was twisted almost inextricably with Kitt's car. There was no sign of Mel Belyle, either.

"We're calling in the National Guard, Red Cross, volunteers," he said. "We don't know how many people are missing. We can't really start searching until light. I'm sorry."

"We understand," said Ken Slattery. He held his wife's hand tensely, his other arm around her shoulders.

"She went off to find Belyle because of *me*." Nora's voice shook. "She must have followed him to Bluebonnet Meadows. She must have been there when the flood—when it—" She couldn't finish the sentence.

"It's not your fault," her husband told her.

But tears spilled down Nora's face. She looked at the floor and shook her head. "She was trying to look out for *me*."

Ken wrapped his arms around Nora. "She's a smart girl. She thinks fast. She may be fine."

But Nora would not be comforted.

SHERIFF JACKSON WENT THROUGH much the same scene with Nick and Shelby Belyle. They had come to the Double C, which had become a sort of nerve center for news.

Shelby gazed in agonized sympathy at her husband. But Nick Belyle's face was harsh and unreadable. He asked an ugly question. "If he's dead, how long will it take to find him?"

Jackson saw Shelby flinch. "I don't know," he said. "Maybe right away. Or it could take—days."

Nick swore and turned away from them. "He should have never come here," he said in a bitter voice.

In another room a phone rang. The sheriff heard Cynthia answer it, heard her talking in a low voice.

"My mother's been calling from Atlanta," Nick said in the same relentless tone. "She heard about the flood on CNN. She's been trying to reach Mel. She can't. His cell phone's dead."

Cynthia came to the doorway. She spoke to Nick and Shelby. "That was Ken. He and Nora are coming here. Nora's in bad shape. He thinks she needs people around her."

She paused, staring at Nick's rigid face. "J.T. and Cal will go out looking tomorrow, as soon as there's light. They'll take the helicopter. You can go with them if you want."

"Nick?" Shelby said, touching his arm. "It might be a good idea…"

Nick nodded, but he kept his back to the others. With more sadness and less rancor than before he said, "He never should have come here. The damn fool."

And Jackson knew what was going through the man's mind.

Nick was angry and sick with helplessness over his brother. He was thinking, *What if Mel can't wait till morning? What if he's in trouble now? What if tomorrow's too late?*

KITT CLUNG to Mel, hiding her face against his chest. The world sounded as if it were ending. The air was choked with smoke and falling sand. The walls trembled, the floor shuddered. Kitt's very marrow shook in her bones, and her eardrums seemed to be bursting.

Then the noise stopped. It was eerie. It simply stopped. Once more there was only the constant murmur of the rain.

Kitt coughed. Her lungs ached from smoke and the musty downpour of pulverized stone. Her hands tightened on Mel's shoulders. "Is it over?"

"I don't know," he said, still shielding her body with his. "Maybe."

"Wh—what was it?" She coughed again.

"Rock slide," he said in a raspy voice. He coughed, too.

But he sat up, drawing her up next to him. His arm was comfortingly firm around her shoulder. She leaned her head back against the stone. She dared, at last, to open her eyes.

The fire was broken and guttering out in smoke. The lamp had fallen on its side and gone out. The shadows in the cave danced strangely, and she sensed the walls closed in on them more tightly than before.

"Let me try to fix the fire," Mel muttered. "That's what's causing the smoke." He let go of her, and half-crouching, made his way to the fire. He kicked a few sticks of kindling back into the fire circle. He fed the dying flames a new branch. The fire hissed and sputtered, but flared higher.

He swore. "I feel like a caveman. I'm putting my pants back on."

She almost smiled, but her face felt stiff as the stone around them. Suddenly the thought of being naked as a worm repelled her, made her feel weak and vulnerable. "I want my clothes, too."

"Right," he said, zipping up his jeans. He picked up her shirt, cargo pants and vest and brought them to her. He knelt before her, his hand skimming over her hair. "Are you all right?"

"I was too frightened to be frightened. If that makes any sense."

"I understand perfectly," he said.

The fire was still unsteady and behind him, but even by its uncertain light, she saw his face was badly cut and bleeding. His left arm, too, was gashed, his shoulder darkened by a bruise.

"You're hurt," she said in concern. She reached to touch his face. The cut ran from the top of one cheekbone and half across his upper lip.

"It's okay," he assured her. "It could have been a lot worse."

The realization sickened her. "Part of the ceiling caved in, didn't it?"

"Yes." He drew back, picking up what was left of his shirt. He shook the dust and rubble from it and wiped it first across his face, then his arm. He swore again.

"I need to wet this outside," he said. "Let me see if I can get the light back." He squatted by the lantern as she slipped awkwardly into her clothes. They were damp and prickly with grit.

Among the debris Mel found the box of matches. He struck one. By its light she could see just how ugly the slash across his face was. Blood dripped from his cheekbone.

But something like a smile touched the harsh line of his mouth. "Amazing," he said, setting the lamp upright. "There's a chunk knocked out of the top of the chimney, but I think it'll still work."

When he lighted the wick and put the broken chimney back in place, the lamp cast a circle of illumination. Kitt fought flinching at Mel's cuts and bruises. But then she looked beyond him, and what she saw made her gasp.

"My God," she said. The natural spring and basin were gone. They were covered with ragged slabs and chunks of limestone. Fully a third of the cave was buried in the mountain's own rock. Half its mouth was blocked with a dark and jagged wall of fallen stones.

He turned and looked. "Yeah," he said grimly.

She knew he was thinking the same thing she was: *If we'd been on that side, we'd be dead now.* Kitt was not a person who cried, but tears smarted in her eyes and her chin trembled.

"I'm going to push back some of those vines to get the air circulating," Mel said, moving toward the cave's mouth. "I'd rather be wet than smothered."

The lamp in his left hand, he began to tear at the vines with his right. He gritted his teeth, and his movements were almost savage in intensity. Fresh air, damp with rain, wafted in. It was cold, but she breathed it deeply and gratefully.

He said, "I'm going to step out and—"

He stopped as suddenly as if a wizard's spell had turned him to stone. Holding up the lamp, he stared downward, outside the cave. His mouth had dropped open, and horror etched his face.

"The ledge is gone," he said. He said it with a deathly finality.

Kit had pulled the blanket around her again. "What?" she said.

"The ledge. It's gone. We can't get out of here."

She swallowed hard. She remembered the ear-splitting crashing, the shaking of the cave. She imagined boulders tumbling down the mountain's side, smashing against the ledge, tearing it away.

"It's sheared off like somebody took a stone cutter to it," Mel said, still staring, transfixed. "There's no way to get back to the path. If there still *is* a path."

The enormity of his words sank into her consciousness. She looked at him staring out at the rainy blackness. She looked at the fall of rock that had destroyed so much of the cave's space. Then she looked at him again.

"We're trapped," she said. A frightening numbness crept through her.

"Yes," he said. He held the rag of his shirt out to wet it in the downpour.

Fear began to mount in her. "And it's still raining...."

"Yes."

"We could have another—another slide, another cave-in," she said.

"Yes."

She had an idiotic desire to descend into hysteria, to start crying and screaming "We're going to die here!" and other futile nonsense. Even as she fought back the urge, she could imagine the rock layers above them shifting, slipping, sliding. Even a minute movement of those layers could be deadly.

Mel didn't look at her. Almost mechanically, he held the wetted cloth to his face and kept watching the lantern light glint on the falling rain. She took a deep breath and tried to make her voice sound calm. "Come here and sit by me," she said levelly. "Let me clean those cuts."

How MUCH TIME HAD PASSED?

Mel didn't know. His watch face had been smashed in another lifetime. And in another lifetime, he'd been vowing to keep this woman safe from harm forever. Now, he realized how helpless he was to keep her alive until even morning.

He sat beside her, his good arm draped around her shoulders. She leaned her head against his bare chest. In her lap, she still clutched the bloody fragment of shirt she'd used to clean his wounds.

"Get rid of that thing," he said, gently prying it from her fingers. She'd been hanging onto it as if it was a talisman or charm. He took it and flung it toward the mouth of the cave.

As he did, he heard the stone ceiling above them groan, as if it were in too much pain to bear. She heard it, too. She tensed and looked up. A pebble dislodged from it and dropped to the floor with an ominous rattle.

Don't make it worse for her, he lectured himself. "You hungry?" He made the question as casual as if they were sitting at a nice, warm bar somewhere. "I could open a can of something."

"I'm not hungry." He could tell she struggled to keep her voice steady.

For a moment they were both silent. She put her forefinger to his cut lip. "How did you get cut on your face? Did you look up?"

"Hell, no," he said with feeling. He didn't know how. "I guess something bounced. A shard of rock. Something."

"It cut that handsome mouth of yours," she said.

The dark irony made him give a small, bitter laugh. "How fitting."

"Why is it fitting?" she asked. "That's one of the first things I noticed about you. You've got an almost perfect mouth."

She was trying to flirt with him, distract him, God love her. He remembered the rumbling moan the ceiling had made, and he decided life was too short for lies, too short for anything but truth.

"Yeah," he said, touching the cut. "It's a nice mouth. The best money could buy. If we get out of here, I'll tell Fabian you admired it. He'll be gratified."

She frowned. "What do you mean?"

He shrugged almost negligently. "This wasn't the mouth I was born with. Or the nose. Fabian paid to have it all—fixed."

Her frown grew more perplexed. Her hand against his lip went still. "What are you saying?"

He made a sound of self-disgust. "My older brother's a good-looking guy. So's my younger brother. Handsome, both of them."

She said nothing. She waited.

He wanted to tell her, for her to know who he was, and why. "I wasn't like them. I didn't imagine I'd ever be like them. I was born with a cleft lip, a misshapen nose. My mother cried when she saw me. She thought it was *her* fault. Somehow."

Kitt's hand moved to his chin, turned his face more fully toward hers. Her eyes were disbelieving. "You mean you had a cleft palate?"

He shook his head. Odd, but now that he'd finally said it to someone, it didn't seem as shameful, as important to keep secret. "No. That's more serious still. I had a cleft lip. A harelip, they call it."

His classmates over the years had come up with some other, more imaginative descriptions of his appearance. He'd hated his classmates, hated his life, hated himself. How stupid that all seemed—now.

He said, "What I had is called a unilateral cleft, just on one side, but it went clear up to my nose. My nose was flattened. My mother couldn't afford to pay a doctor, so she—so she—"

He made an angry, helpless gesture. "So she took me to this sort of—charity clinic. I can't remember it. I was— what?—a year old. The lip got sewed up—but not well. Left a bad scar. The nose they didn't bother with. But at least I could learn to talk okay. Just didn't have much to say."

She stroked his cheek softly. "You were unhappy?"

His smile was rueful. "That's an understatement." He paused, remembering. "I wouldn't let my picture be taken. If my mother sneaked one, and I found it, I'd tear it up. I wouldn't make friends. I joined nothing. Except for track. I liked running. I was good at it."

"The loneliness of the long-distance runner," she said studying his face.

"Exactly," he said. "To run until it hurt. Then to run more until it *didn't* hurt. Till you feel the high of just— escaping."

"Yes. Things are bad. So you run."

He touched his cut lip. "My mother, of course, was over-protective. Nicky—Nick was another matter. He wouldn't baby me. Just the reverse. I guess he thought it was his job to make a man out of me. God, I hated him sometimes."

He shook his head at the memory. "He'd needle me. And

I'd hate his pretty face and take a swing at him. But the damn thing about Nick was that he would never hit back. He'd say anything. But hit? Never.''

He took a deep breath, wrapped his arm more tightly around her. ''Once he was ragging me for sulking about something, and I hauled off and smashed him good. Split his lip clear open. He just spit blood, then smiled. He said, 'Well. Now I guess I look like you.' And he walked away. I wanted to kill him.''

He sank into silence. Nick had meant well, he supposed. And he supposed Nick might have been jealous himself. It was Mel who was their mother's biggest concern. Nicky was supposed to be ''the man of the family.'' A loner himself, Nick had never seemed to doubt his ability—or his charm when he wanted to use it. Or, of course, his looks.

Mel raised one eyebrow. ''Then my aunt sent us money to come to New York. My mother got a job with Fabian. He took an interest in her. In us.''

She cradled his chin in her hand. ''But why? Everybody talks as if he's a monster, a raging egotist. Why was he different to you?''

He pressed his lips together, then grimaced because it hurt. ''How can I explain? First, my mother. She's a dynamo. She reminded him of his own mother. And we—we boys—reminded him of—him.''

''How?''

''We were poor. But smart. We did well in school. We were Italian. Catholic. There were three of us. He'd been a middle son, too.''

''Been?'' Kitt asked, narrowing her eyes.

''His mother, both his brothers died,'' Mel said. ''In a car crash. Left him alone in the world. With nothing. Except a very big settlement. And ambition. And he was like me.''

''You?'' she asked, leaning closer.

''He's kind of—freakish, too. A little guy. Twisted up from bone disease. He's got a nervous syndrome. It gives him facial tics, makes his hands flap. It also gives him enormous powers of concentration. But narrow interest. He's not good at social things.''

Mel leaned back against the damp stone. ''But my mother—she saw past that. She saw somebody lonely. She'd invite him over. Over to our *dump*. For spaghetti. Pizza. Meatloaf. And he *came*. By God, he came.''

Mel watched another pebble fall, bounce. ''So he made my mother this offer. He'd help all three of us with our schooling and fix my face—if we'd agree to work for him. My mother thought he was our guardian angel. My face? Presto chango. There's some magic that money *can* buy.''

''Surgery?'' Kitt said.

''Many surgeries,'' he corrected. ''Many.''

''When did this happen to you?'' she asked.

''When I was sixteen. That spring I'd been a miserable kid in public school. That fall, I was in private school, and I wasn't a freak any longer.''

She shook her head, her face full of sympathy. He'd always despised sympathy, but hers was different. He didn't know how, only that it was.

''There were other surgeries after that. To make it better still. Fabian said, 'Let's make it as perfect as possible.' And finally, I was even better-looking than Nicky. I, the ugly duckling…''

''Became a swan,'' she said softly.

''No. Became a son of a bitch. Became a complete arrogant, cynical bastard. Girls who wouldn't have looked at me before? Hell, I could have them like that.'' He snapped his fingers.

''But I knew it wasn't me they wanted. All they wanted was the facade. So that's what I gave them. That's what I took from them. I didn't want anything deeper.''

''And Nick?'' she asked.

''Nick was never crazy about the idea of selling his future to Fabian. He did it partly for me. But he needled me. Like always. I was superficial. I was cold. I was overcompensating. Nick can be very good at psychobabble when he wants. But he had a point."

She kissed him softly beside his wounded lip. "Everything I thought about you at first was wrong."

"No," he said. "It was right. I'd kiss you back, but I'd bleed on you."

"Bleed away," she said.

He didn't kiss her, but he pulled her closer, wanting her again. Above them the ceiling creaked. It moaned. It dropped another pebble.

KITT NESTLED AGAIN in the crook of his arm. "I tasted your blood," she said pensively. "I should feel like a vampire."

"No," he said, nuzzling his nose against her hair. "Vampires take life. You give it."

Another pebble fell from above, and then another. Kitt should have been frightened, but she felt strangely at peace.

Outside the wind keened. The rain dropped more slowly now, but steadily, and blew inside in moist gusts. The points of the fire rose and fell.

"If we don't get out of here," Mel said, "I want you to know that I—well—love you. You're the only one I ever have. Loved, I mean."

She burrowed closer, pulling the blankets tighter. "I love you, too."

He put his hand on her upper arm, squeezed affectionately. "So are you going to tell me about why you went to Stobbart?"

"Sure," she said, almost airily. "Why keep a few little secrets when a mountain might fall on you any minute?"

"An excellent question," he said. "So what happened?"

She exhaled, suddenly wearied by how long she'd kept her own past hidden. "You can probably guess," she said.

"My guess is abuse," he said. "Your stepfather. Or one of your stepbrothers."

She nodded, her head against his shoulder. "My stepfather. My mother wouldn't believe me. I see now that she was *afraid* to believe me. She had my little brothers to bring up. What would she *do* if I was telling the truth?''

''If she wouldn't listen, how did you get to Stobbart?''

Kitt's teeth clenched as she remembered. ''One day the bastard came after me in the stable. In broad daylight. Cal McKinney caught him. Punched him almost halfway across the stable.''

She smiled wanly at the memory. ''And I was glad. Glad to see *him* be hurt for a change.''

''So,'' Mel said, ''your stepfather. Did he actually do anything to you? Or just try?''

She turned her face against his bare chest. ''Up till then, he'd just tried. That day he almost succeeded. He had his hand over my mouth, had me pinned, was unzipping his jeans with the other hand—ugh.''

She shuddered. Mel whispered, ''It's over, love. It's in the past.''

She tapped her temple. ''Not up here it isn't. Not completely. Cal took me to Miss Pauline. That was J.T.'s first wife. She called Reverend and Mrs. Blake.''

''And they got you to Stobbart?''

''The Blakes had a friend there. The family took in kids from time to time. I begged them to keep it quiet. I *pleaded.* And they did. They concocted a story that Stobbart wanted me for the track team.''

She paused. ''Miss Pauline had my stepfather fired. I don't think even J.T. knew the whole truth. My mother had to be told, of course. But she still wouldn't believe it. It took me a long time to forgive her for that.''

Mel wiped a smudge from her cheekbone. ''But you did?''

''Yes. Finally.'' Kitt made a regretful face. ''Myself, I didn't forgive so fast.''

He wrapped both arms around her again. ''I know what people say. *Some* people. If that's what you mean.''

She looked down at the stones. ''That I went away to

have somebody's baby? Cal McKinney's? And that the McKinneys paid my way to Stobbart?''

He nodded. ''Yes. That's what I heard.''

She raised her gaze to his again, defiance burning in their eyes. ''Well, it's a lie. I didn't have anybody's baby. Miss Pauline helped me—that's true. Cal? He never touched me.''

''But you had a crush on him?''

Her mouth quirked ruefully. ''I thought I was in love. I was barely sixteen. He'd saved me. He was handsome and kind and—dashing. To me, he was a knight on a white horse.''

She shrugged, angry with herself. ''I was terrible. I wrote him letters. Embarrassing letters. *Highly* embarrassing letters. He never answered them. I came back to Crystal Creek a few times. I pretended it was to see Nora. In truth, all I wanted to do was throw myself at Cal. I'd dress up, very feminine, very flirty. I was shameless. He finally told me to leave him alone. He was nice about it. But he made it clear. To him, I was a child.''

Mel leaned his forehead against hers. ''And your heart was broken.''

''Into a zillion pieces,'' she admitted. ''Split into atoms. I swore I'd never chase anybody again. Or even care for them very much.''

''He was always on your mind?''

''In different ways as I got older. Yes.''

''Will he be there forever?''

She put her hands on either side of his face. ''No. From now on, it'll be you. Always on my mind.''

A flurry of pebbles rattled down, and some hit the fire, making it sizzle and hiss. Outside, she heard a boulder roll thunderously down the slope, and the clatter of smaller rocks tumbling in its wake.

She tensed, and so did he.

It should seem foolish to talk of always at such a time. But it seemed right. She lifted her lips to press them against his cheek. He held her tight.

SHORTLY AFTER DAWN, Kitt dozed uneasily, her head on Mel's shoulder. From time to time she made small, apprehensive murmurs in her sleep.

Mel was glad she could sleep at all. He'd close his eyes, but sinister noises kept him awake: the inexorable driving of the rain, the scattershot sound of pebbles dropping from the ceiling like warnings.

Worst were the strange, dim moans of the cave itself. He'd sworn to protect Kitt, but he realized there were forces too strong for him to fight. It was humbling. Too damn humbling.

But then, as the sky grew faintly gray, the rain slowed. It became almost gentle. And then it stopped.

He wanted to breathe easier, but he knew the great cliff was a riddle of life and death. If its primeval layers and slabs of rock stayed still, Kitt and he might escape. If they shifted…

Mel held her, and as he watched the sky lighten, he did something he hadn't done since childhood: he tried to make bargains with God. He bargained with all his heart and soul.

Then, he heard the distant thut-thut-thut of a helicopter. He was certain of it. And it seemed to grow closer.

Mel shook Kitt awake. "'Copter," he said, gripping her shoulders. Her eyelids fluttered in confusion. "'Copter," he repeated with urgency.

He sprang to his feet, snatched up the blue blanket, and sprang to the entrance of the cave. He yanked more foliage out of the way and began to wave the blanket with all his might.

If he looked down, he saw only desolation. Everything Fabian had built had vanished or turned to wreckage. The wet ground looked as if a thousand bulldozers had scraped it into an utter wasteland.

So he didn't look down. He looked up. And far away, he

saw it, the helicopter, only a speck in the sky, but flying closer. Then Kitt was beside him, laughing and crying and waving the red blanket like a flag.

NICK BELYLE DESCENDED out of the sky like a delivering angel. Except that angels don't swear.

"How in bloody hell did you get here?" he yelled. He had to bellow like an elk to be heard over the roar of the chopper's motor. Its noise was as deafening as the landslide's.

Nick dangled from a flexible ladder lowered from the helicopter. His position looked more dangerous to Mel than his own and Kitt's. If J. T. McKinney made a wrong move, Nick would be smashed against the cliff like a bug against a windshield.

"Take the girl! Take the girl!" Mel screamed at him. "Her ankle's hurt. She can't climb that thing!"

"What?" Nick screamed back.

Mel cried out even louder for Nick to take Kitt. He shouted until his throat felt raw as meat.

Nick swung back and forth before Mel's eyes, a surreal figure, doing an airy dance with death. The wind from the helicopter's blades blew the leaves at the cave's entrance until they bent backward. It whipped through Kitt's long red hair so it streamed like a flame behind her. It slapped Mel's bare chest, made him squint his eyes.

Back and forth went Nick, the air current flapping his shirt and tangling his black hair. He pointed to his belt with one gloved hand. Mel saw Nick wore a safety harness of some kind. He was pointing to a second harness clipped to his belt, then to Kitt.

Mel could no longer make out what Nick was yelling. He could only understand that Nick would throw the second harness, that Kitt should get into it, and somehow the men would get her into the 'copter. But in the meantime, Nick went to and fro, an erratic and fragile pendulum.

He flies through the air with the greatest of ease, Mel

thought with wondrous illogic. *The daring young man on the flying trapeze.*

Nick mouthed words that Mel could not hear but could read. "I'm going to throw this. Don't miss it, asshole."

The insult galvanized Mel. He caught the harness on the first throw. Anything less, and Nick would have mocked him through eternity.

Kitt objected and gestured that she didn't want to go without him. The cacophony from the chopper ripped away the sound of her voice. He ignored her protests and strapped her into the harness. He gestured to Nick that she was ready, and Nick gestured to someone above him.

The helicopter tipped so that Nick practically swung into the cave's mouth. He shortened his hold on the rope and gestured for Kitt to come to him.

Mel screamed, "Jump!" He screamed it so loudly that something seemed to tear in his throat. He didn't want to push her, and he didn't have to.

As if she had no fear, Kitt leaped into space toward Nick. And missed him.

She plunged down, three—four feet until the rope jerked tight. Nick, his own harness snapped to the ladder, leaned out and pulled her up toward him, inch by inch. Nick's jaw was tight, the tendons in his neck stood out, and Mel could see the agonized strain in his body.

The helicopter had tipped away from the cliff's face again. Mel stood as if frozen. He watched as the woman he loved hung in that harness like a parachutist in trouble. But her head was thrown back in determination, and damned if she wasn't hanging onto that rope for all she was worth.

She was being carried farther and farther away from Mel. He watched, helpless, as his brother hauled her up and at last had her in his arms. He saw Nick clip Kitt's harness to the ladder and give another signal to the unseen person above.

The ladder began to ascend up into the belly of the helicopter. Kitt clung to Nick, and Nick held her with all his might. When she disappeared, Mel knew she was safe. He fell to his knees on the wet rocks, and his eyes stung with tears of relief.

He wanted them to take her away, to get her somewhere out of harm's way, far from the mountain. But the helicopter kept hovering, making feints back and forth.

Then for the second time, the ladder began to descend. Nick was on it, swaying in space again. They were coming back for Mel.

He yelled for them to go away, to get him later, but the ladder lengthened, the chopper and its ear-splitting noise drew nearer.

In a few moments, Mel was strapped into the harness that had held Kitt.

Then he was in space, falling toward oblivion.

And then he was in his brother's arms, being drawn skyward.

CHAPTER EIGHTEEN

KITT, SHOWERED, her hair freshly washed and dried, sat at the McKinneys' kitchen table while Cal rebandaged her ankle. She wore a green terry-cloth robe of Cynthia's that was too big for her.

Her body ached everywhere, but she hardly noticed. She was too dazed with happiness at being alive and in a wonderful, ordinary place like a kitchen. And Mel was near. Sam Russell, Lynn's husband, was patching him up in a back bedroom while Lynn searched for clothes to fit him.

Now Kitt greedily downed her third helping of pancakes and bacon, and drank her third cup of cocoa. She was ravenous for butter, syrup, chocolate and sugar. The taste of it all was blissful.

The kitchen was crowded, and at Kitt's feet, Cal was in high spirits, recounting the rescue. "Oh, hell, it was *great*," he said. "Daddy's tryin' like hell to hold that chopper steady, and Nick is hangin' from the ladder like Jackie Chan."

J.T. gave his son a narrow look. "And you—hanging out the door and trying to coordinate us. Most of the time all I could see was your butt. Your best angle."

"It is mighty cute," Cal said, unfazed. "And Ol' Nick's swingin' back and forth. Could have smashed right into that cliff just like Wile E. Coyote in a Roadrunner cartoon. Kersplat!"

Shelby winced, and Nick put his arm around her. "Please," he said to Cal. "Don't put it like that. That's the same image I kept having. Smacking into that rock like a wrecking ball.''

"An Acme wreckin' ball," Cal said cheerfully.

"You could have been killed," Shelby Belyle said, her face pale.

"Naw, honey," Cal said, adjusting the bandage. "Not with Cool Hand Daddy at the controls."

J.T. looked pleased in spite of himself. Cynthia stared at him accusingly. "I've begged you to sell that helicopter. You could have crashed into that cliff yourself. I don't ever want you in that thing again—ever."

But J.T.'s face went stern. "They may need me to go up again before the day is out. If they do, I will."

Cynthia clearly didn't approve, but she didn't argue. It was just as well, for a few minutes later, Sheriff Jackson phoned and asked J.T. to fly over the Comanche Hills area. There were rumors of marooned hikers on the other side of the creek's lower branch.

Cal, of course, would not miss the action. This time Ken joined them, but Nick stayed behind with Shelby. Nora, Cynthia and Serena went to the helipad to see their husbands off.

Kitt was left alone in the kitchen with Shelby and Nick. Shelby had her arm around Nick's waist, as if afraid to let him go. She stared up adoringly at him, and he returned her look. Kitt suddenly felt like an intruder.

"I—I think I'd like to lie down," she said to Shelby. "If you'd just help me to the sofa or somewhere…"

"Of course," Shelby said. She came, slipped her arm about Kitt's shoulders and helped her to stand. "Nora said to take you to her house. You can have the guest room."

Kitt didn't object. She rose and discovered her knees were unpleasantly shaky. She leaned on Shelby, took a small step, but staggered.

"Let me help," Nick said, taking a step toward her. But at that moment a figure appeared in the doorway—Mel.

Kitt's mind seemed to grow clear and turn fuzzy at the same moment, and her heart vaulted with emotion.

He was dressed in jeans, cowboy boots and an unbuttoned yellow Western-cut shirt over a white T-shirt. He had a bruise on his forehead, and white tape held gauze in place over the cut on his face.

The bandage ran from his upper lip to the outer edge of his cheekbone. It made him hold his mouth in a rigid line, but she could read the depths of his blue eyes.

I love you, he said to her in silence.

I love you, she replied in silence.

Between them stood Nick, his body taut. He looked his brother up and down. "Where are Sam and Lynn?" he asked, voice brusque.

"Outside," Mel said stiffly. "Sam's going with the others."

The two men eyed each other almost warily. Kitt sensed the complex bonds and tensions that ran between them.

Mel said, "You're not going this time?"

Nick didn't answer immediately. The silence grew awkward.

Shelby spoke. "I didn't want him to." Her tone was both apologetic and defiant.

Mel lifted one dark brow as if to say *so what do I care?*

Nick said, "I need a rest break. Hauling your ass out of trouble nearly gave me a hernia."

Mel's expression went scornful. He looked as if he were going to say something edged. But he didn't. Instead his eyes glittered with unshed tears. He stepped toward Nick, and Nick stepped toward him.

The two men almost fell together. They embraced.

"Thanks," Mel muttered in a choked voice. "Thanks."

"Oh, shut up," Nick said. But he held him fast.

THE PHONE RANG. The men jerked apart like two fighters coming out of a clench. The four people in the kitchen looked uneasily at one another as the phone shrilled again.

Shelby left Kitt's side and picked up the receiver. Kitt, her ankle still wobbly, clung to the back of the kitchen chair. Mel came to her, put his arm around her with an air of rightful possession. He tried to smile, but the bandage wouldn't let him.

Kitt rose on her tiptoes and kissed him on the chin, just under his mouth.

"It's for you," Shelby said to Nick, but Mel barely heard. He looked at Kitt in her dark green bathrobe, with her cloud of fiery hair. Her face was pallid. She wore no makeup, she had a Band-Aid on her forehead, and he'd never seen anyone as beautiful.

"You all right?" he asked. His throat still felt choked, and the tape slightly distorted his words; his voice sounded strange in his ears. But, Lord, how her blue eyes did shine with love, and he knew that look was for nobody else in the world. It was for *him*.

"I'm fine," she said, but her voice was unsteady. She raised her hand and touched the bandage. "And you?"

"If you're fine, I'm fine," he said, taking her hand in his. He bent and touched his forehead to hers. He sighed, closed his eyes, and just savored that she was here, she was safe, she was safe, and, oh, God, yes, she was here and he was touching her.

He didn't know how long they stood like that. His brother's voice jarred him back to reality. "Hey, Caveman. You—Fred Flintstone. You've got a phone call."

Mel opened his eyes and drew back reluctantly from Kitt. He frowned in puzzlement at Nick, but Nick's face gave away nothing. He simply held the receiver out to Mel.

Mel crossed the kitchen, took the phone. He realized that his back hurt, his legs hurt, and his shoulder hurt. He leaned against the door frame, ran his hand over his eyes and said, rather rudely, "What?"

"What do you mean 'What'?" demanded an irascible voice. "Whatever happened to 'Hello'?"

Fabian. Mel straightened up as if an electric bolt had shot through him.

"'Hello' got drowned," he said. "Your lousy lake overflowed. You own two and a half thousand acres of frigging disaster."

"So I heard," Fabian said in a snide voice. "And please don't say you told me so."

"I told you so."

"I also heard you disappeared for a while. Inconsiderate of you."

"Thanks to you," Mel retorted, from between set teeth. "I've nearly been killed by lightning, flood, cave-in, rockslide and falling from a helicopter."

"Have you left out anything?" Fabian asked acidly. "Vampire bats? Cannibals? Killer bees?"

"My life, however, is nothing," Mel shot back. "You almost got a journalist killed. I imagine you'll be reading about it soon in *Exclusive* magazine. Unless, of course, she becomes part of the enormous class-action suit that's certain to be filed against you."

"Who reads *Exclusive* magazine?" sneered Fabian. "Nobody but the ladies who lunch and their pansy friends. Let her write away. Let her sue away. It doesn't concern me. And it doesn't concern you."

Mel's scorn turned to an ominous puzzlement. "It doesn't concern me?"

"You are off this case, off this project. Permanently. Destroy your files and get back to New York."

Mel took a deep breath. "I see. Because you're sending the *real* bully boys down here. Let me tell you something, Brian. These people will fight. They'll fight to the end. They'll—"

Fabian interrupted him. "They've got nobody to fight. I'm declaring bankruptcy on Bluebonnet Meadows. I'm dumping the place. It's unlucky. It's brought me nothing but grief."

Mel felt as if he'd been hit on the head with a large oak

plank. His ears rang, and the kitchen went out of focus. ''What?'' he said in disbelief. ''Where did *this* idea come from?''

''Your mother,'' Fabian said bitterly.

''My *mother?*''

''Is there an echo in this phone? Yes, your mother. I had to fly to Atlanta, hold her hand all night long. Me, in all my suffering. She was hysterical. Over you. And where were you? Camped out in some cave with your new girlfriend. While your poor old mother thought you were drowned. Floating dead in the wild water. And it was all *her* fault. Ergo, it was all *my* fault. I'm a monster. I've set her sons against each other and drowned you like a puppy. Blah, blah, blah. She'd sold her soul to the devil, i.e., me. Good Lord, it was like an opera. She did *arias*. Hours of them.''

''What's this got to do with Bluebonnet Meadows?'' Mel frowned.

''Along about two or three in the morning,'' Fabian snarled, ''when the guilt trip was like *Star Trek*, making me go where no man has ever gone before, your mother says, 'Promise me if he's alive, you'll sell that place. Pledge that to me. Make that a sacred oath to the Virgin.'''

Mel shook his head to clear it. ''What? But what if I'd *died?* Were you supposed to keep it in penance?''

''How do I know? She asked me to promise, I promised. You do not reason with a person in that state. Now that she knows you're alive, she's told me to get you and your brother to make peace.''

Fabian paused. ''You and Nicky—just—make it up. Nicky says it's not impossible. This is right? You could be friends again?''

Mel stole a glance at his brother. Nick, his arm around Shelby, watching him, his face stiff and unreadable. Mel tried a tentative smile in spite of the tape. It must have worked. Nick smiled back, almost in the old way.

Mel looked away, embarrassed by another show of affection, even one that small. "Yeah," he told Fabian, "It's not impossible."

"Fine. Excellent. Jim Dandy. Go bond with him. Build some model airplanes or something. Collect Pokémon cards. Play pirates. Whatever."

"We've played pirates for years—for you," Mel countered. "And don't be flippant. You're in trouble down here. You're going to be sued to hell and back. I don't know what the property damage comes to, but—"

"Screw it," Fabian said, weariness in his voice. "I'll settle out of court."

"But all that land—who'll give you what you've got in it?"

"I don't care. If the Three Amigos corporation still wants it, they can damn well have it. Tell Cal McKinney to call me in an hour. Before I change my mind."

"He's out rescuing people from your flood."

"So make it two hours. I don't feel like being patient with this guy. As for you, rest up and be back in New York in two days. I have widows and orphans for you to evict."

Mel managed another crooked smile. That was Fabianese for a tricky, top-dollar deal.

"As for your dear old gray-haired mother," Fabian said with mock despair, "she says I have to change my ways. She's had a divine revelation. Bah, humbug, and so forth. Fat chance, as you know."

Mel wasn't so sure. "Can I talk to her?"

"For just a minute. She's still—how shall I say it?— volatile. She didn't sleep at all last night. I'll take the phone to her."

Mel listened to the other man swear and grumble as he moved through Minnie's apartment. Then he heard Fabian say, "Here he is. Minnie, it's your boy."

"Hi, Ma," Mel said, trying to sound healthy and unscathed.

"Melburn," his mother said. "I'm so happy you're alive that I could just *kill* you." Then she began to cry.

"I'm fine, Ma. Everything's fine." Mel must have told her this a dozen times. It didn't help. At last Fabian took the phone from her. "Jack's going to give her a pill and put her to bed. Do me a huge favor. Get back here and *prove* to her that you're alive. You are coming back—aren't you? Or are you going to jump ship like your brother, whom I, of course, have been forced to forgive completely."

Mel thought. He thought of Fabian's many failings. He thought also of his loneliness and strange kindness. He thought of himself and Nick and Jack and especially Minnie. He thought of Kitt. And her story. That story could end things between him and Fabian. Maybe it should. And yet…

"Coming back? I don't know yet," he said.

As Mel hung up, he didn't know what his relationship to Fabian might become. He was a different man than he was yesterday.

He looked from Nick to Shelby to Kitt. "Fabian's selling the land. Even if it's at a loss. He'll let Three Amigos buy it if they still want it. Bluebonnet Meadows is over. It's history."

Nick gave a cynical shrug. "That doesn't mean things around here go back to normal. Far from it."

"I know," Mel said, looking at Kitt.

Nick eyed his brother suspiciously. "Are you going to stay with Fabian? He wants you to."

Mel saw the question repeated in Kitt's blue gaze. "I can't say yet," he answered. "It depends."

Nick nodded toward Kitt. "What about her story?"

Mel said to her, "That's partly what it depends on."

He realized that in the cave, he had told her everything. Including too many truths about Fabian. She stared at him as if for the first time, she realized it, too. Her eyes were wide and wary. If she wrote what she knew, he would never work for Fabian again. It had been Mel's job to keep secrets. But hers was to discover and reveal them.

He moved to her, touched the bandage on her forehead.

"Let's not talk about that now. It's too soon. Get some rest."

He heard the women coming back to the house. He bent and kissed Kitt lightly on the mouth. It made his lip sting. He didn't mind.

"Oh," Cynthia cried delightedly when she saw him, "you're here. Let's get some breakfast into you. It's Lettie Mae's day off, but—"

"—that's all right, because I know how to cook," laughed Nora.

"—and I know how to wash dishes," Serena said.

"I'll make a fresh pot of coffee," offered Lynn.

Shelby squared her shoulders and addressed the other women. "Brian Fabian just phoned. He's pulling out of Bluebonnet Meadows. He'll sell to Three Amigos."

"Good Lord," Serena breathed. "They won't have to go through a legal battle. They just might pull this off…"

Cynthia looked stunned, but Lynn grinned happily. "Then it's over, isn't it? Everything will go back like it was. All the troubles are solved."

Cynthia nodded uncertainly, and Serena gave a relieved smile. Nick had gone stone-faced again. And Kitt, still clutching the back of the chair, seemed torn.

Things *wouldn't* go back like they were, Mel knew. All the troubles weren't solved. There were choices to be made. Hundreds.

Of all of those decisions, Kitt's would be one of the hardest. Hardest because it involved far more than money. It involved honor, ambition, loyalty—and love.

NORA MOVED KITT into her tiny guest room. She propped her up in bed and made her drink a hot toddy. It was fragrant with lemon and spices, and potent with Ken's best whiskey.

The toddy made Kitt's muscles feel warm and liquid; it quieted the ache in her bones. It also loosened her tongue. She told Nora about Hometown Restaurants and Mel Belyle.

She said, "It's something he wanted to do, Nora. Let him do it."

"The Longhorn was Dottie's," Nora said stubbornly. "She wanted me to have it."

Kitt said, "She'd want you to be happy. You know that. To go back and follow your dream."

"What on earth would Mel Belyle do with a small-town restaurant?" Nora demanded.

"To him it's an investment, that's all. This Hometown Restaurant—thing—will run it for him. He doesn't want to change it, if that's what bothers you."

Nora put one hand on her hip. "Look, don't worry about me—all right? Worry about yourself. Something's happened between you and Mel. I can tell. What are you going to do about it?"

"Don't change the subject. What are *you* going to do with the Longhorn? Keep it until you die? Then leave it to Rory and tell him that he has to keep it until *he* dies? It's a legacy, a destiny—and an albatross around your neck?"

For the first time, Nora looked uncomfortable. "Of course, I don't expect Rory to take it over. He's got other things to do with his life."

"So do you," Kitt said, pressing on. "Face it, Nora. That restaurant has pulled you through some tough times, but you don't have to keep it forever. Let go of it while you've got the chance."

"I'm not listening to you, so just be quiet," Nora ordered. "You're half out of your head with exhaustion. Drink that toddy down. Get some sleep."

Kitt sighed and took another drink. Her eyelids were growing deliciously heavy. So she yawned, which wasn't difficult and wasn't faked.

Nora shook her head and took the mug away. She pulled the soft blanket up to Kitt's chin. "Sweet dreams, toughie," she said.

KITT SLEPT for eight hours straight. Nightmares crowded in on her. She dreamt of flood waters lunging after her to drown her, of landslides thundering down to crush her. The cave groaned and rumbled, growing smaller and darker and pressing in on her.

Then, magically in these dreams Mel suddenly would be there. When he was, she felt euphoric—and almost safe. Yet not *quite* safe. To her dismay, Mel would vanish as inexplicably as he appeared, leaving her alone in the shadows and showers of falling stone.

She dreamed that the cave sighed monstrously. A wall shuddered and cracked. From deep inside this fissure, she heard a strange voice calling her name. She looked about in fear, praying for Mel to return.

He did not. The stones whined, inching closer to her. The crack in the rock wall widened. It became a jagged black door. From deep beyond it, she again heard her name being called, as if she was being beckoned into the dark center of the mountain.

Come, said the voice. *There's treasure here. For you. For you alone. You alone. Alone.*

Somehow she knew if she went through that door, the blackness would claim her, and she would never return. Yet she took a step toward it. And then she took another.

Kitt cried out, waking herself. She shot bolt-upright in bed. Her heart thudding, she stared wildly about Nora's guest room. She didn't need a psychiatrist to tell her what the dream meant. She pushed a hand through her tumbled hair and thought, "I need to talk to Cronin. Right now."

THE MCKINNEYS' RANCH HOUSE had an immense stone patio. It was surrounded by autumnal flowers, mums and Jerusalem cherries, asters and tuberoses. At the far end was a pool, its blue shimmering iridescently from its underwater lights. Artificial torches sent bright flames flaring up against the night sky.

The sky was cloudy, but a few stars peeped out like faint promises. It was almost midnight, but Mel had left word with Nora for Kitt to phone him at any hour. He would meet her at the patio if she felt well enough. He was staying at the McKinneys' guest house for the night.

Now Kitt waited on an ornamental stone bench beneath the torches. She was self-conscious in Nora's lavender peignoir set. They were the only clothes Nora would loan her.

"You're not going out there in Cynthia's bathrobe," Nora had lectured her. "You have to roll up the sleeves three times, and it drags on the ground. You look like a cartoon character."

Nora was not as petite as Kitt, and she said the set was a gift, years ago, from Dottie right before she died. Though it was too small, Nora had never had the heart to exchange it; this was the first time it would ever be worn.

The negligee was simply cut, a layer of something sheer over a layer of something silky. The peignoir matched, but was more flowing, with three-quarter length sleeves. It was open and ornamented only by a lace border up each side and around the low-cut neckline.

Kitt had taken one look in the mirror and swallowed. This was not her style. She heartily wished she could put on her vest over it.

"Oh, wear it," Nora had teased. "Dottie always liked you. She'd want you to."

"It's too—too seductive," Kitt had objected.

Nora had only laughed. "At this point? I don't think so."

Does it really show that much? Kitt wondered. *That he and I made love? It must. It must show like crazy.*

Now a breeze played with the gossamer fabric of her sleeves and addled her with the intoxicating scent of tuberoses. Along the gravel path that led to the outer gate of the patio, she heard a man's sure step.

Mel entered the gate between the pillars with their rearing stone mustangs. Light from the torches flickered on his tall figure. He still wore the boots, jeans, and yellow shirt. The narrow bandage that curved across half his face was tinted gold in the fire's glow.

He came to the bench and stared down at her. "I—never saw you look like this," he said, his voice tight.

She shrugged sheepishly. "I don't usually go around looking like this. It doesn't feel natural."

"You look beautiful," he said. "Can I join you?"

She gave a laughing sigh. "You shouldn't have to ask permission after all we went through."

"I'm struggling to be a gentleman."

"I guess I'm struggling to be a lady," she said. "It's new to me. And *not* easy."

"You look the part," he said. He put one booted foot on the stone bench, crossed his arms over his knee and smiled down at her.

She couldn't bring herself to smile back. She stared off at the gem-blue of the pool. "I talked to Heywood Cronin," she said. "Just before I called you. I had to talk to him. About the story."

She didn't have to see him to know that his body tensed. "So soon?" His tone was careful. "I thought you might want to think it over for a while."

She shook her head. "You want to stay with Fabian, don't you?"

The breeze fluttered her sleeves, stirred the perfumed air, made the flames dance in the torches. He said, "If it's over, it's over. I told you things about Fabian, things I'd sworn never to tell. I told you of my free will. What you do with that information is your choice."

She kept staring at the glittering blue. "That doesn't answer the question. Do you want to keep working for him?"

He was silent a moment. "I'd like to try it for a while. If he wants me. If he doesn't, that's that. But my family owes him. *I* owe him. He needs my mother. In a strange way, he needs me."

"Nick quit," she said, still not looking at him.

"I'm not Nick," he said quietly. "I know Fabian can be a bastard. But I also know, better than most, where he's coming from."

She let her gaze drift to her hands, which were scratched and bruised, the nails broken. How she had struggled last night to survive. And so had Mel—to save them both. He'd carried her when she'd fallen. During the cave-in, he'd shielded her body with his.

He said, "Fabian's not always a good human, but he's human. Even arrogant bastards need friends. I ought to know."

She swallowed. The truth about Fabian's past was a good story. It would make her career. It would destroy Mel's—at least with Fabian.

He leaned nearer to her, but he didn't try to touch her. "I mean it," he said. "I told the facts to you willingly. I knew you're a reporter. Use what I said as you like. It's your choice."

She took a deep breath and looked him in the eyes. "My choice is not to write it. I don't want to write the article at all."

"It's the chance of a lifetime for you," he said.

"There'll be other chances," she said. "What you told me last night was—personal. You weren't being a lawyer. And I wasn't being a reporter. We were being…" *Ourselves,* she thought, but didn't say. *For once we were being ourselves.* She only made a helpless gesture.

"Kitt, if you're doing this for me, know I can get another job. A good one. Easily."

"I'm doing it for me," she said with feeling. "I can't write this story. I'm in the middle of it. I can't be objective. I don't want to tell truths that can hurt people. Even people like Brian Fabian. But especially not you. No. Especially you."

Mel bent nearer. "Is that what you told Cronin?"

"I told him the truth. I never should have accepted the assignment. This place has too much of a hold on me. I just didn't know it. I wouldn't admit it. Maybe I couldn't."

She had confessed to Cronin the truth about her stepfather. She'd told him that the McKinney family had helped her escape the danger, to pursue her dreams. She'd even told him that she'd had an intense and embarrassing crush on Cal McKinney, and if this was known it would be an embarrassment to both her and the magazine. She'd come to Crystal Creek filled with bad memories, unresolved conflicts, secrets she'd wanted kept at all costs.

How could she, of all people, write about this place?

"At first," she said, bitter at her own foolishness, "I was almost glad to see this town in trouble—because I'd been hurt here. I was wrong to feel that way. And then..."

"And then?" he asked.

"And then I fell in love with you," she said. "And I don't want to write a story that hurts the town and people that I love."

Tears rose in her eyes, and she blinked them back fiercely. "I don't want to hate this town any longer. And I don't want to write about it. Its story is already written on my heart. On my mind. And it's being rewritten even now, here with you."

"Kitt," he said, taking her hand, "I mean it. Don't do it for me—"

"No," she said. "I told Mr. Cronin I don't want to try to explain Crystal Creek to the world. I'm just starting to explain it to myself."

"Was he angry?"

"No. He said it was good I told him. And now—now the story's changed so much, he's not sure it's right for *Exclusive*."

"You're not fired?"

"No. He thanked me for my frankness. I'll be fine."

"And if I go back to work for Fabian? For a while?"

"I hope you can at least reform him," she said. "A *little* bit."

She said it with so much of her old spirit that he laughed. He took her face between his hands. "One thing at a time, babe. I'm still reforming myself. How about some motivation?"

He kissed her.

It was a rather sideways kiss because of the bandage, but Kitt didn't mind. She put her arms around his neck and drew him down beside her. She lost herself in the balmy night, the bewitching perfume of the roses, and most of all, in loving him.

J.T. AWOKE to the night's silence. He thought about this long day. He'd taken the 'copter up—for the last time probably. But he and Cal and Nick Belyle had saved two people. It was a good day's work, and the way to walk away from the chopper—triumphant.

The flood wasn't as bad as it might have been, and it seemed his prodigal son would be coming home at last. Not immediately, and by taking some hellacious gambles, but he was coming home. Maybe the Double C was going to stay in the McKinney family another generation or two, after all.

Cynthia had scolded him for taking chances with the helicopter—and he'd taken far more than she'd realized. But she'd also looked at him with unfeigned admiration and even called him a hero.

He'd been thinking over something all evening, but he hadn't been ready to speak out about it yet. Now, suddenly, he wanted to talk. He rose on his elbow and shook Cynthia's shoulder gently.

"Mmm?" she said sleepily. "What is it? Is it raining again?"

"No," he said in her ear. "You know what Cal said about coming back?"

Cynthia stirred and nuzzled his shoulder. This excited J.T. She smelled like the roses in her garden, and her hair was like silk against his bare skin.

She said, "Darling, he thinks he can't get everything ironed out to get here for at least a year. But I know you'll be glad to have him back."

J.T. kissed her throat, a light but lingering kiss. "So for

that year, how would you like to take a trip? Like you used to talk about. Paris? Rome? Athens? London?''

Cynthia sat upright. ''J.T., is that you? Has somebody else crept into this bed?''

''I mean it,'' he said. ''I could hire my cousin to come manage the ranch for a year. He's tired of Idaho. He wants to come back to Texas. I think he'd do it. I'm going to offer it to him.''

''But, honey,'' she said, ''what about Jennifer? We'd have to take her out of school—''

''Hell,'' J.T. said, ''she can do her lessons by correspondence. Cal's kids do. And travel's an education in itself. Let's take her to see all this stuff while I've still got a hike or two left in me. How about it? Want to leave Crystal Creek for a while, and see the world?''

''Oh, J.T.,'' she said. Her voice was trembling with disbelieving happiness. ''A whole *year?*''

''A whole year,'' he said. ''Like a long second honeymoon. We need to be together more. We need—to talk more.''

He kissed her. She pressed close to him, opening her lips. And with hunger and confidence, J.T. began to make love to his wife.

EPILOGUE

LETTIE MAE REESE'S retirement party at the Double C was going to be the social event of the year. Nora, arm in arm with Ken, couldn't stop smiling. It was the biggest spread J.T. had ever thrown.

He had flown in every member of Lettie Mae's far-flung family—her cousins, her brother, her sister, her two half sisters, even an elderly aunt. Tyler and Ruth came back from California. Cal and Serena came back from Mexico, where Cal was arranging to sell his share of a brewery.

Even Kitt and Mel made it back from New York.

Kitt, still limping slightly, even wore a gray silk pantsuit and had her hair upswept. "Who are you?" Ken demanded with mock sternness when he saw her. "What have you done with Kitt Mitchell?"

She only laughed and nestled closer to Mel. His bandages were off, but the cut across his lip was clearly going to leave a scar.

"What's Fabian got you working on now?" Nick asked his brother.

"I'm supposed to be forming a charitable trust," Mel said wryly. "The general consensus is that he needs to start paying more attention to PR. A *helluva* lot more."

"That's been clear for years," Nick said skeptically. "Who convinced him?"

"Ma," Mel said with a rueful laugh. "She didn't like what people said about him after the flood fiasco. Before she ignored his reputation. Now she's on his case."

"He's going to pay a fortune in damages," Nick observed.

"But he'll do it like a pussycat," Mel said. "Or Ma will get him."

"And so will you," Kitt said, hugging his arm. "I think your official position now is the corporation's conscience."

Nick raised a dark brow satirically. "We'll have to get you a nice Jiminy Cricket suit. Spats. Top hat. The umbrella. Whole shebang."

One guest who surprised Nora was J.T.'s cousin, Bret McKinney, from Idaho. Nora hadn't seen him for so many years that she'd almost forgotten his existence.

Serena took her aside and told her his story. For the past nineteen years, Bret McKinney had been foreman of a large ranch in Portola Valley, Idaho. Now the ranch's owner was embroiled in a battle with the Bureau of Land Management. Bret was sick of being in the middle of the mess.

Bret was a handsome man, tall with a burly chest and surprisingly slim hips. In his early fifties, he had thick dark hair without a trace of gray. His eyes were black, his nose was roman, but imperfectly so, his mouth was thin, and his jaw was stubborn.

Serena said he was a widower with three grown sons. Several unmarried women, like Kasey and Sandra Thurman, were eyeing this new, single man with considerable interest. Nora didn't blame them.

And, Serena confided, J.T. had reached a decision and would be making an important public statement tonight.

Nora's throat tightened. She and Ken had made a choice themselves. But they would tell J.T. before anyone else. In private and after he announced his own news.

And announce it he did. He asked for quiet and put his arm around Cynthia. He raised his wineglass and said, "Friends, neighbors, to my cousin Bret McKinney. Bret's coming back to Texas in two weeks. He's going to manage the Double C. While I take my beautiful wife and daughter on a long trip—to celebrate my retirement. We'll be back.

This will always be our home. But I'm turning the business end over to Bret.''

Some people gasped, some smiled knowingly. Cal applauded and hooted. Tyler grinned and nodded with approval. Lynn blinked back sentimental tears and clapped as hard as she could.

The crowd drank a toast to Bret, who looked uncomfortable at the attention. Then Cal toasted J.T. and Cynthia and their trip, and Tyler toasted Cal, and wished the Three Amigos success. The other two ''Amigos'' hadn't been able to come, and Cal said it was just as well. It would have turned into a different sort of shindig. Those boys partied *hard.*

Then there were countless toasts to Lettie Mae, until Nora's head was starting to spin from so many salutations and sips of champagne. But then the toasts and well-wishing were over, and the party went back to normal. People gathered around Lettie Mae's niece, LaTasha, who could play piano and sing the most soulful blues north of New Orleans.

Ken seized Nora by the hand and led her through the crowd. Nora's breath caught in her chest as Ken tapped J.T. on the shoulder. ''We need to have a word with you in private,'' Ken said.

THEY WERE IN J.T.'s private study. J.T. stared at Nora with something akin to horror. ''Sell the Longhorn?'' he said in disbelief.

Nora lifted her chin. ''Yes. I got the offer almost two weeks ago. It hasn't been an easy decision, but I'm going to take it. I—I have a teaching job lined up in Fredericksburg next spring.''

Suddenly J.T. had a piercing headache. He wanted to put his hand to his forehead and groan, possibly even whine. But he loved Nora, and he knew he had to spare her his disappointment. It would be a selfish display.

But good Lord, hadn't he made enough concessions to change? Lettie Mae was leaving—that alone would alter his life profoundly.

Brian Fabian hadn't won the land war, but neither had J.T., not completely. Crystal Creek would change. Not as radically as Fabian had threatened. But change it would, and he could not stop it.

The helicopter was gone, sold to a Dallas millionaire the first day J.T. put it up for sale. He was uprooting himself from his beloved ranch for a whole year. Face it, hell, he really *was* retiring.

Couldn't *something* stay the same? The Longhorn was the very heart of the town. He couldn't count the breakfasts and lunches he'd eaten there with his cronies. He couldn't number the cups of coffee he'd drunk there over years too many to count.

Yet he could see from the protective look on Ken's face and the almost pleading one on Nora's: this was what she wanted.

"J.T.," she said, "the Longhorn won't change. I get to pick the new manager. I'm asking Kasey to do it for me. It'll stay just the way it is."

It won't be the same without you, he wanted to say. He did not say it. Instead he put his hands on Nora's shoulders and kissed her cheek. "May all your dreams come true," he said.

"Thank you, J.T.," she said. "We'll tell other people later. This is Lettie Mae's party. But we sign the papers tomorrow, and we wanted you to be the first to know."

J.T. gave Ken a look of mock sternness. "You're not going to quit on me, are you?"

"Nope," Ken said. "I plan to stay on until I'm old as Grandpa Hank was."

"Good," J.T. said gruffly. "Good to know. Now, get back to the party, you two."

They left. For a moment J.T. heard the sounds of the party, and LaTasha Reece belting out "Middle Aged Blues Boogie." The door shut and he stood alone in relative silence for a moment.

Then Cynthia came with a worried expression on her

face. "J.T.," she said, "why are you all by yourself in here? Is something wrong?"

He sighed and told her about Nora selling the Longhorn.

Cynthia's eyes shone with sympathy. "Oh, you'll miss her, won't you, darling? But I'm so glad she'll finally get to do what she really loves."

"I'm glad, too," J.T. said, embracing his wife. "I'm glad for all of us. We're lucky people, Cynthia."

"Yes, we are," she whispered.

HAND IN HAND, Kitt and Mel had drifted to the patio. Only a few people had gathered there. Mel intended to get Kitt in a secluded corner of the garden and kiss her enough to show her he had fine plans for later in the evening.

But Dr. Purdy detached himself from a small group and made his way toward them. He looked Kitt up and down. "How's that ankle?"

"It's going to be fine," she assured him. "A little tender still, that's all."

"That's normal," muttered Nate, "normal." Then he took a step closer to Mel and scrutinized his lip. "Humph," he said. "That's going to leave a scar, I'm afraid. Well, with what plastic surgery is today—"

"No," Mel said firmly. He shook his head. "I don't want it removed."

"No?" Nate repeated in surprise. "Think about it, son. The operation wouldn't be that serious. And once over, no scar at all."

Mel touched his upper lip. "No," he said again. "I'll keep it. It's part of who I am."

He smiled and nodded goodbye to Nate. He led Kitt deeper into the shadows of the garden. He'd been rehearsing a speech all night. He had the ring in his pocket.

But when they stopped beside the gate, the speech stuck in his throat. He, usually so glib, could not get out a word. He could only take the blue velvet box from his pocket, open it so she could see the glitter of the diamond, and hold it toward her. He could not put in words what he wanted to say. He could only look into her eyes.

She seemed struck almost as mute as he was. "Oh," she managed to whisper. "Yes. Yes."

She held out her hand. He slipped the ring on her finger. He put his arms around her, bent and kissed her in a way that told her much more than any speech, no matter how eloquent.

From the house came LaTasha's strong, young, beautiful voice. Overhead, stars sparkled in a cloudless sky.

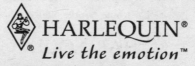

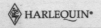

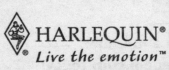

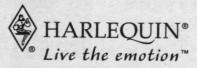

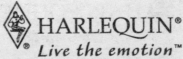